William Faulkner's

The Sound and the Fury

MODERN CRITICAL INTERPRETATIONS

William Faulkner's

The Sound and the Fury

Edited and with an Introduction by

Harold Bloom

Viva Books

New Delhi | Mumbai | Chennai | Kolkata | Bengaluru | Hyderabad | Kochi | Guwahati

First Indian Edition 2010
Reprinted 2013

VIVA BOOKS PRIVATE LIMITED

- 4737/23 Ansari Road, Daryaganj, New Delhi 110 002
  E-mail: vivadelhi@vivagroupindia.net, Tel. 42242200
- 76, Service Industries, Shirvane, Sector 1, Nerul, Navi Mumbai 400 706
  E-mail: vivamumbai@vivagroupindia.net, Tel. 27721273, 27721274
- Jamals Fazal Chambers, 26 Greams Road, Chennai 600 006
  E-mail: vivachennai@vivagroupindia.net, Tel. 28290304, 28294241
- B-103, Jindal Towers, 21/1A/3 Darga Road, Kolkata 700 017
  E-mail: vivakolkata@vivagroupindia.net, Tel. 22836381, 22816713
- 7, Sovereign Park Apartments, 56-58, K. R. Road, Basavanagudi, Bangalore 560 004
  E-mail: vivabangalore@vivagroupindia.net, Tel. 26607409, 26607410
- 101-102 Mughal Marc Apartments, 3-4-637 to 641, Narayanguda, Hyderabad 500 029
  E-mail: vivahyderabad@vivagroupindia.net, Tel. 27564481, 27564482
- Beevi Towers, First Floor, SRM Road, Kaloor, Kochi 682 018, Kerala
  E-mail: vivakochi@vivagroupindia.net, Tel: 0484-2403055, 2403056
- 232, GNB Road, Beside UCO Bank, Silpukhuri, Guwahati 781 003
  E-mail: vivaguwahati@vivagroupindia.net, Tel: 0361-2666386

www.vivagroupindia.com

Published by arrangement with
Facts on File, Inc.
132 West 31st Street
New York 10001
USA

ISBN : 978-81-309-2375-8

All links and web addresses were checked and verified to be correct at the time of publications. Because of the dynamic nature of the web, some addresses and links may have changed since publication and may no longer be valid.

Every effort has been made to trace the owners of copyrighted materialand secure copyright permission. Articles appearing in this volume generally appear much as they did in their original publication with little to no editorial changes. Those interested in locating the original source will find bibliographic information on the first page of each article as well as in the bibliography and acknowledgments sections of this volume.

Published by Vinod Vasishtha for Viva Books Private Limited, 4737/23, Ansari Road, Daryaganj, New Delhi-110 002. Printed and bound by Anand Sons, Delhi - 110092.

L0000

Contents

Editor's Note

My introduction suggests some of the limitations of *The Sound and the Fury,* though I would not deny its near-greatness. And yet the narrative mode of Joseph Conrad, and the intricate medley of voices in the style of James Joyce, both are influences not wholly transcended by Faulkner.

Gail M. Morrison tells the intricate tale of the composition of *The Sound and the Fury,* while Stephen M. Ross examines the voicing of Reverend Shegog's Easter sermon, and André Bleikasten argues for the reader's share in holding the novel together.

Mrs. Compson, in Philip Weinstein's view, is punished by her representation and yet rhetorically quested after by Faulkner and his protagonists.

Citing Joyce, T. S. Eliot, and Freud as formative influences, Daniel Joseph Singal studies the genius of *The Sound and the Fury.*

Alcoholism, about which Faulkner knew all too much, is investigated in relation to Caddy by Gary Storhoff.

Margaret D. Bauer argues that Quentin's suicide is due to his realization that Caddy has been permanently convinced by him that she has been damned, while Thomas L. McHaney gives a very full account of the interlocking themes of *The Sound and the Fury.*

By interpreting the man with the red tie as a homosexual emblem, Michelle Ann Abate sees Miss Quentin's Easter escape as a liberation to a better life.

In this volume's final essay, Jeffrey J. Folks reads *The Sound and the Fury* as a dramatization of Faulkner's own sense of defeat, from which the book comes to rescue him.

HAROLD BLOOM

Introduction

WILLIAM FAULKNER (1897–1962)

The Sound and the Fury always moved Faulkner to tenderness, far more than his other novels. It was for him a kind of Keatsian artifact, vase or urn invested with a permanent aesthetic dignity. His judgment has prevailed with his critics, though some doubts and reservations have been voiced. Like *Absalom, Absalom!, The Sound and the Fury* seems to me a lesser work than *Light in August,* or than *As I Lay Dying,* which is Faulkner's masterwork. The mark of Joyce's *Ulysses* is a little too immediate on *The Sound and the Fury*, which does not always sustain its intense rhetoricity, its anguished word-consciousness. There is something repressed almost throughout *The Sound and the Fury*, some autobiographical link between Quentin's passion for his sister Caddy and a nameless passion of Faulkner's, perhaps (as David Minter surmises) for the sister he never had, perhaps his desire for Estelle Oldham, later to be his wife, but only after being married to another. Jealousy, intimately allied to the fear of mortality, is a central element in *The Sound and the Fury.*

Hugh Kenner, comparing Faulkner's novel to its precursors by Conrad and Joyce, dismisses the Compson family saga as excessively arty. The judgment is cruel, yet cogent if Joyce and Conrad are brought too close, and Faulkner does not distance himself enough from them. This makes for an unhappy paradox; *The Sound and the Fury* is a little too elaborately wrought to sustain its rather homely substance, its plot of family disasters. But that substance, those familial disorders, are entirely too available to Freudian and allied reductions; such repetitions and doublings are prevalent patterns, vicissitudes of drives too dismally universal truly to serve novelistic ends. Only Jason, of all the Compsons, is individual enough to abide as an image in the reader's memory. His Dickensian nastiness makes Jason an admirable caricature, while Quentin, Caddy, and Benjy blend into the continuum, figures of thought for whom Faulkner has failed to find the inevitable figures of speech.

Faulkner's Appendix for *The Sound and the Fury,* written for Malcolm Cowley's *The Portable Faulkner,* not only has become part of the novel, but famously constitutes the definitive interpretation of the novel, or Faulkner's will-to-power over his own text. The Appendix is very much Faulkner the yarn-spinner of 1946, soon to write such feebler works as *Intruder in the Dust, Knight's Gambit,* and *Requiem for a Nun,* before collapsing into the disaster of *A Fable.* It is not the Faulkner of 1928, commencing his major phase, and yet the Appendix does have a curious rhetorical authority, culminating in Faulkner's tribute to the blacks (after simply listing Dilsey's name, since she is beyond praise): "They endured." Sadly, this is an authority mostly lacking in the actual text of *The Sound and the Fury.* Quentin's voice makes me start when it is too clearly the voice of Stephen Daedalus, and Joyce's medley of narrative voices fades in and out of Faulkner's story with no clear relation to Faulkner's purposes. Only Poldy, fortunately, is kept away, for his sublime presence would be sublimely irrelevant and so would sink the book.

I emphasize the limitations of *The Sound and the Fury* only because we are in danger of overlooking them, now that Faulkner has become, rightly, our canonical novelist in this century, clearly our strongest author of prose fiction since the death of Henry James. *As I Lay Dying* was a radical experiment that worked magnificently; its forms and voices are apposite metaphors for the fierce and terrifying individualities of the Bundrens. *The Sound and the Fury* was also a remarkable experiment, but too derivative from Joyce's *Ulysses,* and perhaps too dark for Faulkner's own comfort.

What saves the Compson saga is that it is a saga; and finds a redeeming context in the reader's sense of larger significances that always seem to pervade Faulkner's major writings. We read *The Sound and the Fury* and we hear a tale signifying a great deal, because Faulkner constitutes for us a literary cosmos of continual reverberations. Like Dilsey, we too are persuaded that we have seen the first and the last, the beginning and the ending of a story that transcends the four Compson children, and the squalors of their family romance.

GAIL M. MORRISON

The Composition of The Sound and the Fury

Faulkner's early—and succinct—judgment on *The Sound and the Fury* was that his fourth novel was "a real sonofabitch."[1] Although its sales would turn out to be as disappointing as those of his first three novels and do little to alleviate his financial distress, the reviews were generally favorable and more than justified Faulkner's remark. Since that time this brilliant, difficult work has continued to attract more critical attention than any other single Faulkner work, and its popularity seems unlikely to fade. Faulkner's initial sense of exhilaration would become tempered in his maturity by his sense of having attempted something other than what he had achieved—of having written a book that was "the most gallant, the most magnificent failure."[2] But that reservation notwithstanding, Faulkner's moving and frequently quoted remarks about the novel uniformly testify to the very special place, to the highly personal significance, he accorded the work that was a long awaited and, from the artist's point of view, a timely critical if not financial breakthrough.

His first two novels, *Soldier's Pay* and *Mosquitoes,* had failed to sell. When his publisher, Horace Liveright, rejected *Flags in the Dust,* Faulkner wrote him in wry dismay in February 1928:

> I want to submit the mss. which you refused, to another publisher.

The Sound and the Fury: A Critical Casebook, edited by André Bleikasten (New York: Garland, 1982): pp. 33–64.

> Will you agree to this with the understanding that I either pay you the what-ever-it-is I owe you, or that I submit to you the next mss. I complete? I do not know just when I'll have another ready, but if I can place the one I have on hand and get an advance, I can pay you the money. I have just sent some short stories to an agent; perhaps I shall derive something from them with which to pay you. Otherwise I dont know what we'll do about it, as I have a belly full of writing, now, since you folks in the publishing business claim that a book like that last one I sent you is blah. I think now that I'll sell my typewriter and go to work—though God knows, it's sacrilege to waste that talent for idleness which I possess.[3]

Although for Faulkner *Flags in the Dust* was "THE book, of which those other things were but foals" and "the damdest best book you'll look at this year,"[4] Liveright remained unencouraging. Even after considerable revision the novel spent almost a year making the rounds at various publishers under the auspices of Faulkner's friend and literary agent Ben Wasson.[5] Ultimately, Wasson's friend Harrison Smith at Harcourt, Brace agreed to publish an abbreviated form of the novel as *Sartoris*. Faulkner was in New York when the contract was issued on September 20, 1928. There he finished the typescript of *The Sound and the Fury,* inscribing the date "October 1928" on its last page.

A remarkable thing had occurred during the interval between the rejection of *Flags* in February 1928 and the completion of the *Sound and the Fury* typescript that October. As Faulkner expressed it a few years afterwards, "one day it suddenly seemed as if a door had clapped silently and forever to between me and all publishers' addresses and booklists and I said to myself, Now I can write. Now I can just write."[6] That door closed, apparently, because, as Faulkner commented in 1932, "I believed then that I would never be published again. I had stopped thinking of myself in publishing terms."[7] *The Sound and the Fury* would be written "for fun"[8] and would evoke, Faulkner recalled in 1933, an "emotion definite and physical and yet nebulous to describe . . . that ecstasy, that eager and joyous faith and anticipation of surprise which the yet unmarred sheets beneath my hand held inviolate and unfailing. . . ."[9] The rejection of *The Sound and the Fury* by Harcourt, Brace would not elicit the despair produced by Liveright's refusal of *Flags,* in part, Faulkner wrote, because "I did not believe that anyone would publish it; I had no definite plan to submit it to anyone. I told Hal [Harrison Smith] about it once and he dared me to bring it to him. And so it really was to him that I submitted it, more as a curiosity than aught else."[10]

When Faulkner closed the door between himself and his publishers after his initial failure to place *Flags in the Dust,* the conjunction was evidently a happy one of his sense of freedom from the strictures imposed on an author attempting to write a marketable book and whatever compelling personal problems he referred to years later as besetting him at that time.[11] Certainly the technical virtuosity of *The Sound and the Fury* is the most striking manifestation of this freedom. Another is the display of what he called in later years the responsibility of the artist to be "completely amoral" and "completely ruthless" in his need to "rob, borrow, beg or steal from anybody and everybody to get the work done."[12] And "rob, borrow, beg, or steal" he did, consciously or unconsciously—and not just from Shakespeare and Milton, Keats and Shelley, Flaubert and Dostoevski, Lawrence and Joyce, Conrad and Hardy, Swinburne, Eliot, Housman, Wilde, Yeats, Hemingway, Anderson, and Fitzgerald, but from Freud and Jung, Frazer, Nietzsche, Kierkegaard, Bergson, and others—drawing not only on specific literary masters but on the rich social and cultural milieu of the 1920s and indeed of all Western civilization, to make clear that what he called his carpenter's workshop was not centered in a cultural vacuum in those bleak and barren Mississippi hills.[13] Or, as he wrote in the summer of 1933 in an introduction for a projected new edition of the novel by Random House:

> I wrote this book and learned to read. I had learned a little about writing from Soldiers' Pay—how to approach language, words: not with seriousness so much, as an essayist does, but with a kind of alert respect, as you approach dynamite; even with joy, as you approach women: perhaps with the same secretly unscrupulous intentions. But when I finished The Sound and The Fury I discovered that there is actually something to which the shabby term Art not only can, but must, be applied. I discovered then that I had gone through all that I had ever read, from Henry James through Henty to newspaper murders, without making any distinction or digesting any of it, as a moth or a goat might. After The Sound and The Fury and without heeding to open another book and in a series of delayed repercussions like summer thunder, I discovered the Flauberts and Dostoievskys and Conrads whose books I had read ten years ago. With The Sound and The Fury I learned to read and quit reading, since I have read nothing since.[14]

This is not to imply in the least that *The Sound and the Fury* is a derivative book, although its literary borrowings are perhaps not as assimilated in this early work as they are in the later fiction. If, in some ways, it seems to grow logically out of the three novels which preceded it, it is nevertheless safe to say that *Soldiers' Pay, Mosquitoes,* and *Flags in the Dust* simply do not prepare us for the achievement of *The Sound and the Fury.* Its complexity of character and theme, its emotional intensity, and its technical virtuosity far surpass those of the earlier works.[15] However, neither our own sense of the uniqueness of Faulkner's fourth novel nor Faulkner's comments about it should delude us into believing that the novel sprang into being, like the mythical phoenix, full grown in all its resplendent plumage. While the published and unpublished earlier works cannot entirely explain the flowering of genius, the sudden achievement of tremendous artistic control, they do show that Faulkner's phoenix did not step totally unassisted out of the flames. A rich and fertile ten-year apprenticeship as a writer lay behind Faulkner, and if in closing the publishers' doors he learned to read, he also drew again on materials, both published and unpublished, prose and poetry, that lay strewn around his carpenter's workshop.[16]

Adumbrations of *The Sound and the Fury*, for instance, have frequently been pointed out in the prose sketches written in the twenties, especially those written for the New Orleans *Times-Picayune* and the *Double Dealer*:[17] the idiot who grasps a narcissus, bellows inarticulately, and has eyes that are intensely blue in "The Kingdom of God;" the appearance of a Little Sister Death figure in "The Kid Learns;" a Mr. Compson-like philosophy that "living is not only not passionate or joyous, but is not even especially sorrowful" in "Out of Nazareth;"[18] the use in "The Priest" of twilight, lilacs, hyacinths, and the famous passage from *Macbeth* that gave Faulkner's novel its title.[19] To these might be added the experimentation with Negro dialect in "The Longshoreman" and other pre-Jason vernacular expressions in sketches such as "Frankie and Johnny."

Perhaps even more interesting are several prose sketches that Faulkner did not publish, which display close affinities with *The Sound and the Fury*. Juliet Bunden, the protagonist of "Adolescence," for example, reminds us particularly of Caddy Compson: Juliet is a tomboy, climbs better than a boy, possesses a "fierce sensitive pride"[20] and spends long hours in the creek. Like Caddy's family, Juliet's is composed of three brothers, the youngest of whom is her favorite. Juliet's attitude toward the male members of her family, including her weak, ineffectual father, mirrors something of Caddy's affection for Mr. Compson, Quentin, and Benjy. Even some of the imagery of the sketch looks forward to that of the novel, not only in its several references to twilight, but also in Juliet's feeling that she is "like one who has cast the dice and must wait an eternity for them to stop" and that "the attainment of happiness was thwarted by blind circumstance."[21] These recall Jason's sense of helpless entrapment as he chases his niece about the countryside "where the rear guards of Circumstance peeped fleetingly back at him" and "the opposed forces of his destiny and his will [drew] swiftly together."[22]

To turn from this awkward yet curiously moving sketch of a lost and almost tragic young girl to "The Devil Beats His Wife" is to come to what amounts to a fragment—three unnumbered manuscript pages without much merit—rather than a fully developed sketch.[23] One of the unnumbered pages begins with a description of the black maid Della returning to her cabin. Here in embryonic form is the opening of the fourth section of the novel, although Dilsey will not "waddle" across the yard like Della. Nevertheless, Della's dominant characteristic, her "placid implacability" as reflected on her "placid inscrutable face," foreshadows Dilsey's more fully realized character. Both women wear a "stiff black straw hat" (p. 330) over a turban, and this phrase occurs in both opening paragraphs.

Equally noteworthy is Della's interaction with a young white girl named Doris, who is unhappily married, and who in her briefly delineated, whining immaturity somewhat foreshadows the young girl Quentin. In one scene, Della and Harry, Doris's husband, knock at the door of her bedroom in much the same way that Jason, Mrs. Compson, and Dilsey knock at Quentin's on the morning they discover her theft and flight. The description of Doris's room anticipates the fine passage in the novel in which Quentin's empty room is described.

A much more ambitious prose sketch, and one with considerably more artistic merit, is "Nympholepsy," probably written early in 1925 shortly after Faulkner's arrival in New Orleans.[24] An expansion of an earlier sketch, "The Hill," published in the *Mississippian,* "Nympholepsy" displays close affinities to the imagery of the novel. Even more striking, however, is the use of the quest as a controlling structural device. Carefully complicated as it is by flashbacks, Quentin's monologue depicts his spending the last day of his life wandering through the countryside evoking the past and his memory of Caddy. In the earlier sketch, the laborer pursues an equally unattainable woman across hill and field and eventually falls into a pool of water, at which point the woman is revealed as yet another of the early associations of a beautiful woman with death, an image which culminates in the association of Caddy with Little Sister Death.

Another early, unpublished work that has tangential relationship to *The Sound and the Fury* is an unfinished novel entitled "Elmer," which was begun in Paris in 1925. The characters and ideas apparently retained some degree of fascination for Faulkner since he returned to the material in the early 1930s and attempted to salvage portions of it in the short story "Portrait of Elmer."[25] Despite Faulkner's unsuccessful treatment of an artist as a comic figure in this work, he returns to the problem of the artist in *The Sound and the Fury* with Quentin's monologue, which has often been viewed as Faulkner's version of *A Portrait of the Artist as a Young Man.*[26] Most striking is Faulkner's depiction of another pre-Caddy figure who looks backward not only to Juliet Bunden but also forward to Addie Bundren and the young protagonist of "Barn Burning."

While much of the Elmer material is clearly related to the Snopes material which Faulkner would explore in the unfinished novel "Father Abraham" (out of which at least tangentially grew *As I Lay Dying* [1930]), Elmer's sister, Jo-Addie, foreshadows several crucial details of the portrait of Caddy as conveyed particularly in Benjy's monologue. In the corrected 123-page typescript of "Elmer," while the early description of Elmer's family sounds more like Snopeses than Compsons, Elmer's relationship with his sister shares something of both Benjy's and Quentin's obsessive concern with Caddy. Elmer, like Benjy, is identified as the baby in his family; and like Benjy, Elmer sleeps in the same bed with his sister. However, that he quite unabashedly sleeps naked with her suggests something more of Quentin's sexual preoccupations than of Benjy's fulfilling in Caddy his need for maternal affection. In one scene, Elmer asks Jo-Addie to sleep with him after the family has moved again. In the later novel this scene is paralleled by Caddy's lying down beside Benjy to comfort him when he is thirteen and has trouble falling asleep by himself. Despite their physical differences, Caddy and Jo-Addie are both associated with the masculine virtues of daring and strength which Quentin so admires in his sister. Further, both girls are associated with fire, Jo-Addie as her home burns, Caddy through Benjy's associations of love and tenderness with the flames in the fireplace and the reflection of light in the mirror. In the eyes of the young Elmer, Jo-Addie "stood fiercely erect as ever, watching the fire in a dark proud defiance, ridiculing her sorrowing brothers by her very sharp and arrogant ugliness"; Elmer sees her as "a young ugly tree" and as "a fierce young mare."[27] Jo-Addie, too, disappears from her family forever, although, as McHaney notes, we are given a brief glimpse of her as a New Orleans prostitute. This is perhaps echoed in the later novel, which clearly implies that such is Caddy's fate; the later Compson Appendix seems to confirm those suspicions.

In contrast to these awkward and unfinished pieces are two more ambitious, polished accomplishments: *Marionettes,* written in 1920 and prepared by its author in several hand-lettered and hand-illustrated copies, and *Mayday,* another hand-lettered, illustrated booklet dated January 27, 1926, which Faulkner gave to Helen Baird. Like *Mayday,*[28] *Marionettes* reveals a number of Faulkner's early literary sources as well as his experiments with crucial structural devices, including the frame, shifting point of view, and counterpointed plot, that recur in the later novel. And, as the character of Galwyn in *Mayday* anticipates Quentin in so many respects, so the figure of Marietta adumbrates Caddy as well as her brother Quentin. Through Marietta's seduction and abandonment by Pierrot, the themes of change, time, sexuality, and death are explored, issues which lie at the very heart of *The Sound and the Fury* and are mirrored in Caddy's seduction and abandonment by Dalton Ames. However, although Marietta is associated with trees, like Caddy Compson and so many of the young women in Faulkner's early prose and poetry, including Cecily Saunders and Patricia Robyn, she reminds us rather more of the elder Quentin than of Caddy. Like Marietta, who is troubled by "strange desires" so that her "garden is like a dark room when the candles are extinguished," Quentin refuses, or at least lacks the capacity, to acknowledge that both his and Caddy's entries into the world of sexuality are part of the natural order of things, part of the natural flux of time.[29] Caddy has nothing in her of Marietta's cold reluctance to acknowledge that change, symbolized specifically in both works through sexual initiation, is as necessary as the inevitable passage of the seasons. And while Caddy, like Marietta, immerses herself in water, Caddy's stream signifies her fertility, her capacity for love, rather than her narcissism. The scene at the pool, where Marietta admires her reflection is more accurately a precursor of Quentin's staring down into the Charles River, bent on stasis and self-destruction, insisting on a denial of life rather than acceptance of change.

A final piece of Faulkner's apprenticeship must be mentioned as a significant precursor to *The Sound and the Fury.* Originally composed for Margaret Brown, Faulkner later made a copy of a little fable he entitled *The Wishing Tree* for his future wife's daughter by her first marriage.[30] Several commentators have cited a number of details emphasized in *The Wishing Tree,* including the wisteria-scented breezes, grey mists, the use of a flat-iron, a clock, a rolling pin, and a shoe, as parallels to *The Sound and the Fury.*[31] But it is with Dulcie's descent down a ladder from her bedroom window that we move closer to the double image at the heart of the later novel. In the novel, Caddy climbs up a tree to peer into Damuddy's window and thus begins metaphorically her journey toward knowledge and experience. Her ascent is later reflected in the descent of her daughter Quentin down a pear tree. The image of Caddy climbing up the tree was frequently cited by Faulkner as the inception of the short story which grew into the novel.

Caddy's three brothers peer up at her from the ground below and are soon joined by Dilsey; in *The Wishing Tree* Dulcie climbs down the ladder assisted by the boy magician Maurice while her neighbor, George, and her little brother, Dicky, accompanied by their black nurse, Alice, watch from below. In the fable, Faulkner not only explores the possibilities of perception from a child's point of view but plays variations on a theme by differentiating among the children as to their levels of sensitivity and awareness. Maurice, the leader of Dulcie's expedition, appears to be the most knowledgeable; it is he, after all, who controls their magical adventures. Like Maurice, who shares with Quentin a name with romantic, chivalric connotations, Quentin is clearly differentiated from the other children by virtue of his more sophisticated understanding of the situations in which they are involved, in both the novel and the closely related short story "That Evening Sun." Like George, Jason remains oblivious to everything but the gratification of his own desires. His gluttony as a child is mirrored in George's wish for a bowl of strawberries and a chocolate cake, which he eats until he feels sick. George's stubborn contrariness may also remind us of the young Jason's bratty behavior. Both wish themselves home, and in *The Wishing Tree,* at least, Maurice's magical powers are obliging and whisk George directly out of the tale. Dulcie's little brother, Dicky, is a baby like Benjy. His limited vocabulary, pronunciation, and syntactical difficulties suggest that he is around three, approximately the same age as Benjy.

Still other characters in *The Wishing Tree* foreshadow their more masterful and extended counterparts in *The Sound and the Fury.* Alice, for instance, has something in her of Dilsey without Dilsey's complexity and maturity. Despite her child-like amazement and strained relationship with her husband, which ally her with Nancy in "That Evening Sun," Alice is as protective of the children, particularly of Dicky, as Dilsey is of Benjy. Dilsey will, as a matter of fact, echo two of Alice's lines: "'You hush yo mouf'" (p. 355)/ "'Hush your mouf'" (TS 33) and "'You vilyun'" (p. 395)/ "'You triflin' vilyun'" (TS 35). The jaybirds of the fourth section of the novel that "came up from nowhere, whirled up on the blast like gaudy scraps of cloth or paper" (p. 331) cannot but recall that huge jaybird which "whirled about them" (TS 53) in *The Wishing Tree,* although the image also appears in Faulkner's poetry. Alice even protests Maurice's giving a whip to Dicky to use on the pony that pulls their cart. Dilsey's response to Luster's whip, as he prepares to take Benjy for a ride in the carriage in the closing pages of the novel, is similar, although, unlike Alice, she does not relent.

Other details suggest the close relationship of the two works, including the importance of ponies and the birthday motif which look forward to the Benjy section of the novel where both come to figure so prominently by the typescript stage.[32] Suffice it to say that *The Wishing Tree* seems very close indeed to what Faulkner described as the kernel of *The Sound and the Fury,* minus that one ingredient which perhaps gave Faulkner the tremendous creative spurt with which to begin it:

> [*The Sound and the Fury*] began as a short story, it was a story without plot, of some children being sent away from the house during the grandmother's funeral. They were too young to be told what was going on and they saw things only incidentally to the childish games they were playing . . . then the idea struck me to see how much more I could have got out of the idea of the blind, self-centeredness of innocence, typified by children, if one of those children had been truly innocent, that is, an idiot. So the idiot was born. . . .[33]

The carpenter would find other scraps of material scattered around his workshop. The poetry would contribute many images, even specific lines, such as "Nazarene and Roman and Virginian" from Poem XLII of *A Green Bough,* although this line would be deleted from the typescript of the novel. Faulkner would turn to "Father Abraham" and reuse passages describing the pain from Armstid's broken leg to depict Quentin's in similar circumstances as well as to characterize Louis Hatcher's voice.[34] For the opening description of Quentin's room at Harvard Faulkner would turn to a three-page untitled manuscript fragment about two characters named Brad and Jack, which is now located with the *Soldiers' Pay* typescript and other related materials pertaining to that novel.[35] But whatever materials from his apprenticeship he may have drawn on, Faulkner's later remarks about the novel make clear—in retrospect, at least—that the novel's creative impetus began with "perhaps the only thing in literature which would ever move me very much: Caddy climbing the pear tree to look in the window at her grandmother's funeral while Quentin and Jason and Benjy and the negroes looked up at the muddy seat of her drawers."[36] Echoing Heathcliff's reference to Catherine Earnshaw in *Wuthering Heights,* Caddy was for Faulkner "the beautiful one, she was my heart's darling. That" "what I wrote the book about and I used the tools which seemed to me the proper tools to try to tell, try to draw the picture of Caddy."[37] Thus, *The Sound and the Fury* is the bringing to life of an image that had, in various forms—from the young tree-like girls of the poetry to Marietta to Juliet Bunden, to Jo-Addie to Doris to Dulcie—intrigued Faulkner almost from the beginning of his career as a writer.

This is not to say that the path to *The Sound and the Fury* is an orderly, logical sequence of development, for such is clearly not the case. Nothing by Faulkner, published or unpublished, before this novel equals it in sheer creative brilliance nor foretells the arrival of this work. Rather, the ten years preceding its writing saw tentative explorations made by the maturing writer—explorations of character, imagery, structure, theme, and tone—striking out in different directions with varying degrees of success but with no lesson lost on the struggling craftsman. Then, finally, when he was ready, Faulkner closed that door between himself and the world and wrote the first of his great novels.

II

Given the frequency and consistency of statements made later in his career, it seems virtually certain that the novel did originate as a short story: it "began as a short story, it was a story without plot, of some children being sent away from the house during the grandmother's funeral,"[38] Possibly that story was originally conceived in connection with "a collection of short stories of my townspeople" about which Faulkner wrote Horace Liveright on February 18, 1927.[39] However, Carvel Collins has argued for an even earlier composition date on the strength of testimony from a "friend" of Faulkner's who in Paris in 1925 read a work in progress that dealt with a girl and her brothers. Although he vigorously defends the accuracy and reliability of this friend's memory, Collins does not identify him. While it is possible that what Collins alludes to is "Elmer," or a fragment, or a short story later incorporated into the novel, or even an early version of "That Evening Sun," Faulkner's own comments do not seem to support such an early date for the beginning composition of the novel proper.[40]

For example, in the 1932 introduction for the Modern Library reissue of *Sanctuary,* Faulkner wrote that "with one novel completed *[Flags in the Dust]* and consistently refused for two years, I had just written my guts into *The Sound and the Fury* though I was not aware until the book was published that I had done so, because I had done it for pleasure."[41] In interviews Faulkner's statements regarding the time it took him to write the novel, though they vary somewhat, most frequently cite six months: "I wrote *As I Lay Dying* in six weeks, *The Sound and the Fury* in six months. . . ."[42] In a letter to Horace Liveright written in mid- or late February 1928, Faulkner states that he had "gotten no further forward with another novel as yet, having put aside the one I had in mind to do some short stories."[43] He is presumably referring to the "Father Abraham" novel about the Snopes family which he worked on sporadically beginning in late 1926 or early 1927. But by early March 1928, Faulkner was able to write Liveright that he had "got going on a novel, which, if I continue as I am going now, I will finish within eight weeks."[44] While he was in New York City in the fall of 1928, Faulkner wrote Alabama McLean that Harcourt, Brace was bringing out a book (*Sartoris,* the cut version of *Flags in the Dust*) in February and "Also another one, the damndest book I ever read. I dons believe anyone will publish it for 10 years."[45]

Commentators have occasionally suggested that the manuscript of the novel's first section, entitled "Twilight," may have been the seminal short story to which Faulkner referred. However, given its complexity and length, this claim seems highly unlikely; but an earlier version of it may well have been completed as a story, and may even have been intended for the collection of stories about Faulkner's townspeople projected in 1927. Another possible precursor to the novel is the closely related story "Never Done No Weeping When You Wanted to Laugh," an unpublished manuscript that later became "That Evening Sun Go Down" and finally "That Evening Sun."[46] Although this story focuses on the Compson children, it does not contain the image of the little girl climbing up a tree to peer into the window of her grandmother's funeral which Faulkner originally envisioned as requiring a ten-page treatment and which he cited as constituting the starting point of the novel—an image which does figure prominently in "Twilight."[47] We can only speculate which story, "Twilight" or "Never Done No Weeping When You Wanted to Laugh," came first.

The general point, then, is that we must be extremely cautious in assuming that "Twilight" and "Never Done No Weeping" were composed sequentially or that the latter story necessarily precedes the novel, for available evidence is simply not conclusive as to order or date of composition. However, an examination of the paper used for both works is suggestive. The handwriting in both is similar, and the onionskin paper on which "Never Done No Weeping" is written is similar to the paper used—*not* in the Benjy section of the manuscript of the novel which is entitled "Twilight" and in the rejected and repositioned manuscript opening of Quentin's monologue, which are on heavier paper—in the new opening and the remainder of Quentin's section, excluding the repositioned pages.

In light of both Faulkner's later, well-established method of building novels out of short stories (*The Hamlet* [1940] and *Go Down, Moses* [1942], for instance) and his ability to extract a story out of a novel in progress for the more lucrative short story market ("The Bear" out of *Go Down, Moses,* for example), it is certainly possible that Faulkner turned to characters brought to life in "Twilight," perhaps after recognizing the novelistic potential of that material, and used them in a far less ambitious, more narrowly circumscribed work in hopes of alleviating increasing financial burdens and buying time in which to write the novel. Further, the revision of "Never Done No Weeping" into "That Evening Sun Go Down" is intriguing in suggesting that it may have played a crucial role in leading Faulkner to the novel's second narrator, particularly if the story was composed after "Twilight" and before Faulkner began over again on the novel's second section after rejecting its original opening.

The rejected opening (ultimately positioned as pages 70–76 in the manuscript; Vintage text 185.20–200.18) consists of the dramatic confrontation of Quentin and Caddy at the branch after Caddy loses her virginity to Dalton Ames. It is dramatic in form, whereas the final opening of the novel's second section is characterized by an immediate sense of the presence of the first-person narrator, Quentin. In "Never Done No Weeping" the events involving Nancy and Jesus are recounted by Quentin as first-person narrator, but as in the rejected opening for the novel's second section, his personality is entirely submerged in the events of the narrative. In "That Evening Sun Go Down," however, the addition of a narrative frame, which introduces Quentin as a narrator recounting from a point in time fifteen years later when he is twenty-four years old events that took place when he was nine, places the story in an entirely different context and shifts the focus of events from Nancy and Jesus to Quentin's perceptions and reminiscences in which, like the narrator of Sherwood Anderson's "Death in the Woods," he is attempting to come to terms with an important childhood incident by assessing his father's handling of Mrs. Compson and his behavior in regard to Nancy. It is, then, an intriguing possibility that the revisions of the short story moved

Faulkner away from the neutral, dramatic presentation of events with which Quentin's monologue began originally and closer to the shift in focus to the sensitive, reflective, brooding personality of Quentin which is so striking in the opening pages of the final version of the manuscript. But this must remain only speculative unless further external evidence turns up to assist in dating these writings more precisely.

In any event, by early March 1928 Faulkner's new novel was well under way. He completed typing the manuscript in New York in October and submitted it to Harrison Smith at Harcourt, Brace, the publisher that accepted *Flags in the Dust* in its condensed form, *Sartoris.* In a letter dated February 15, 1929, Harcourt rejected it, and when Harrison Smith left Harcourt to form a partnership with Jonathan Cape, he took the typescript with him.[48] Faulkner made some extensive revisions in the novel's second section, withdrawing forty-one pages of the typescript and substituting forty-one rewritten pages in their place, presumably before copy editing was begun on the typescript. A contract was executed on February 18, 1929. Ben Wasson copy edited the typescript, perhaps with the assistance of another editor at Cape & Smith.[49] Robert Ballou designed the book, and it was set in type.[50] When Faulkner read galley proofs in Pascagoula, Mississippi, in July 1929, he rejected a number of changes made by Wasson and made a number of additional changes himself. Published on October 7, 1929, a small printing of only 1,789 copies was sufficient until the notoriety of *Sanctuary* led to a second printing of 518 copies in February 1931; a third printing of 1,000 copies from a copy of the second impression was made by offset lithography the following November.[51]

On completion of the novel, the "belly full of writing" that Faulkner had experienced as a result of his failure to place *Flags in the Dust* yielded to quite different emotions. He would variously refer to the process of writing *The Sound and the Fury* with such favorable nouns as "pleasure," "joy," "anticipation," "ecstasy," "surprise." Such exuberance would be displayed for no other novel. Yet, paradoxically, Faulkner would affirm later that this novel "was the one that I anguished the most over, that I worked the hardest at, that even when I knew I couldn't bring it off, I still worked at it."[52] Perhaps because he began the novel with no "plan"[53] other than the image of a tragic little girl climbing a tree, the first and second sections of the manuscript especially show the author hard at work. As James B. Meriwether has noted, "[o]ne or more complete drafts, or none; extensive working notes or none, may have preceded the extant manuscript but have not been preserved. For this particular novel, we might well suppose such measures a necessity; for this particular novelist, we may well assume that they were not."[54] Given the complexity of the novel, the manuscript is remarkably close to the published novel. However, its first two sections display considerable revision, above and beyond the expected verbal polishing that occurs between manuscript and typescript and again between typescript and the first edition, including frequent cancellations and marginal additions.

Of the considerable number of manuscript revisions, certainly the most interesting involves the rejected opening of Quentin's monologue. In fact, how to open Quentin's monologue presented Faulkner with perhaps the most difficult organizational task wrestled with in the course of this enormously complex novel. In the original manuscript, the second section opened with a six-page confrontation between Quentin and Caddy at the branch concerning Dalton Ames, Caddy's first lover. At the top of the first of these pages, this episode bears the heading "June 2, 1910." According to deleted page numbers this episode occupied three different positions (MS 34–40; 43–49; 44–50) before coming to rest toward the end of the monologue (MS 70–76; Vintage text 185.20–200.18) where it was placed with drastic alterations in punctuation but very little substantive revision. However, almost three additional pages (Vintage text 200.19–203.11) were added to the original version.

That these pages originally opened Quentin's monologue is evinced not only by their heading but because the paper matches that of Benjy's section and is far heavier than the rest of the paper used for Quentin's monologue. This suggests that the particular scene was probably composed about the same time as the novel's first section, or very soon after, with Faulkner moving forward at high creative speed to reveal the actual events of the evening that upset Benjy so dreadfully in the closing pages of his monologue. After completing the Dalton Ames-Caddy-Quentin confrontation scene, Faulkner may have set aside the novel and then returned to it, perhaps after rereading the first section. Resuming work on the novel's second section on different paper, Faulkner evidently revised his plan as to how to proceed since the scene was relocated several times before coming to rest toward the end of the monologue.

The rejected opening grew directly out of Benjy's monologue and suggests that it was composed in the same burst of creative energy, with the same emotional fervor, that led to the composition of the novel's first section. Toward the end of his monologue, in two separate flashbacks, Benjy remembers Caddy's coming in to supper from outside (pp. 84, H5). When he sees her, Benjy pulls at her dress, remembering that "we went to the bathroom" (p. 85). With these events Quentin's monologue originally opened:

> one minute she was standing there the next he was yelling and pulling at her dress they went into the hall and up the stairs yelling and shoving at her up the stairs to the bathroom door and stopped her back against the door and her arm across her face yelling and trying to shove her into the bathroom when she came in to supper (p. 185)

Within the context of Benjy's monologue alone, the two flashbacks Benjy makes to these events are, at best, cryptic. Yet they are placed strategically toward the end of the novel's first section, unexplained, mysterious, provocative, and the monologue winds down with an intermingling from past and present of the activities of eating supper and being put to bed. Thus it seems clear that Faulkner originally intended to begin Quentin's monologue by clarifying those two incomplete, brief fragments by Benjy which provoke such an outburst from him, thereby expanding our understanding of events by elucidating immediately Caddy's behavior on that evening through Quentin and his more detailed knowledge and more sophisticated inferences about his sister's activities.

However, the events in this scene gave Faulkner pause. In this episode Quentin attempts to kill Caddy and then himself. Unsuccessful, he goes so far as to hold a knife to her throat before—pitifully, helplessly—dropping the knife. This desperate effort and Quentin's anguished failure have great dramatic impact, but by opening his monologue with these tortured and tormented actions, Faulkner must actually backtrack to offer much more detailed explanation for such extraordinary behavior. Only Quentin's two references to the evening of Damuddy's funeral during his confrontation with Caddy ("do you remember the day damuddy died when you sat down in the water in your drawers" [p. 188] and "Caddy do you remember how Dilsey fussed at you because your drawers were muddy" [p. 189]) seem to provide some meager insight into Quentin's state of mind by recalling his childhood slapping of his sister when she attempted to remove her dress as well as the image of her muddied undergarments. That Caddy has violated Quentin's early-developed sense of maidenly virtue and modesty seems clear, but this oversimplification of Quentin's complex character undoubtedly was one of the reasons that Faulkner postponed the scene until considerably more amplification of Quentin's character could occur. Thus Faulkner could also preserve the climactic drama of the confrontation by revealing it late in the monologue; by positioning it early he might have been aware that the rest of the monologue could not help seeming anticlimactic.

Structurally, additional elements seem likely to have prompted the postponement of this key scene. Along the lines of Joyce's *Ulysses,* Benjy's monologue had traced a character's behavior and thought from morning to evening during the course of one apparently but not in actuality typical day in his life. The repetition of a similar pattern could not only greatly expand characterization possibilities for Quentin but could also provide a series of reflections and refractions of the events narrated by Benjy, thereby enhancing the work's novelistic unity in spite of its apparently so disparate narrators and narrative voices. Further, by withholding information about Quentin's first, unsuccessful suicide attempt until the reader can learn that June 2, 1910, is Quentin's last day and that the activities he pursues on that day are linked to the suicide which he commits later that evening, Faulkner creates a dramatic convergence of the past and present which Quentin finds increasingly difficult to separate.

Thus Faulkner recreated the structural pattern observed in Benjy's monologue. That is, Quentin's narrative no longer begins *in medias res,* but, like Benjy's and Jason's, it begins at the beginning, in the morning of a special day whose particular events will be presented in chronological sequence. Appropriately, Quentin will recall in flashback the twilight confrontation with Caddy and Ames on the evening of his last day on earth. Possibly after he wrestled with organizational strategy and decided finally to imitate the morning-afternoon-evening pattern of the novel's first section, the novel's last two sections presented Faulkner with fewer structural problems as well as with already established characters, themes, and conflict. With their increasingly lucid styles, in manuscript these two sections are even closer to the published text than are Benjy's and Quentin's monologues and display no major recasting or repositioning of material.

Nevertheless, after the completion of Jason's monologue, work on the novel may have been interrupted for approximately a month before Faulkner began the final section:

> So I wrote Quentin's and Jason's sections, trying to clarify Benjy's. But I saw that I was merely temporising; That I should have to get completely out of the book. I realised that there would be compensations, that in a sense I could then give a final turn to the screw and extract some ultimate distillation. Yet it took me better than a month to take pen and write *The day dawned bleak and chill* before I did so.[55]

Ironically, this distancing produces an emotional decrescendo, and while the novel's fourth section contains some of the most effective, most mature, and most tightly controlled writing in the entire novel, it has received far less than its critical due.

Similar accounts of the novel's having taken shape in "quarters" were often repeated in interviews late in Faulkner's career:

> When I'd finished [with Benjy's monologue] I had a quarter of the book written, but it still wasn't all. It still wasn't enough. So then Quentin told the story as he saw it and it still wasn't enough. Then Jason told the story and it still wasn't enough. Then I tried to tell the story and it still was not enough.[56]

There is considerable charm to Faulkner's description of his wish to tell the same story four different times and his sense of having failed each time to achieve the desired end. But this litany must be regarded with a certain amount of skepticism. For one thing, none of the "quarters" is an exact recapitulation of the same story, although that may have been what Faulkner originally intended. (Might this have been the source of his sense of having failed to tell "enough"?) While there are a number of intersecting events that link each of the various "quarters" with the others, the narrative thrust forward is a strong one that moves through Caddy's childhood, depicted largely in Benjy's monologue; her adolescence, emphasized in Quentin's section; and various events of her adulthood, especially as they concern her daughter, as depicted in the novel's third and fourth sections, which simultaneously increase their focus on Jason and his reenactment with his niece of his brother Quentin's conflict with Caddy. But as Michael Millgate has pointed out, Faulkner's account is extremely important in that it suggests that the novel was "evolved under creative pressure, not conceived beforehand."[57] Nowhere is it more evident than in the novel's final section that Faulkner did *not* attempt to tell the *same* "story" four times albeit from four different vantage points. The brilliant technical achievements in the first three sections of the novel, as well as their very diversity, help to obscure the very traditional, chronologically based, horizontal plot line which emerges with greatest clarity in the fourth section.

III

Faulkner surely must have realized well before completing what came to be the novel's first section that the restrictions of Benjy's idiocy and his resultant limited knowledge of events would ultimately render him inadequate to tell this particular tale of sound and fury. Nevertheless, when confronted with the difficulties of Quentin's monologue, those of Benjy's seem at second glance far less rigorous. Ultimately, the unconventionality of narrative technique in Benjy's monologue is neither chaotic nor absurd. Quite the contrary, it is governed by rigid, although terribly literal, rules of logic. Often beyond his control and understanding, a word, a phrase, or an object triggers Benjy's memory, but these associational devices are always readily visible. For the unwary, there are a few quagmires along the way: confusion of names (two Quentins, two Jasons, two Maurys), or the inadvertent omission of italics to signal a time transference to a different scene, for example. Yet despite the apparent fragmentation of Benjy's consciousness, he persistently returns to three major episodes: Damuddy's funeral when he is around three; the evening his name is changed from "Maury" to "Benjy" when he is five; the traumatic evening of Caddy's wedding. Although his memory returns to each of these scenes at different times throughout his monologue, it is important that the events involved in each of these major episodes are nevertheless presented sequentially, albeit in fragmented form.

Because of his literalness, his very inability to understand and therefore reason and draw conclusions, Benjy is a remarkably reliable narrator. He reports only what he sees, not what he thinks: action, not abstraction; fact, not probability; dialogue itself rather than the meaning behind it. The amount of detail and word-for-word dialogue that Benjy remembers is astounding, although narrowly restricted to episodes in which Caddy plays a particularly important role or in which there is some heightened emotional content. If any conclusions are to be drawn from Benjy's reports, the reader must infer them, and although a number of significant gaps are not filled in until later in the novel, the reader can predict accurately a remarkable number of occurrences.

In actuality, however, Quentin's monologue is far more complex than Benjy's. In style it differs markedly from Benjy's faithful journalistic recording of every detail. Instead, Quentin's narrative is more properly a stream-of-consciousness monologue, much like Eliot's "The Love Song of J. Alfred Prufrock," in which factual details of the present are mingled with memories of the past and speculations about events and their significance by a protagonist who is torn and divided against himself.

Those very attributes lacking in Benjy which ideally ought to make Quentin superior as narrator—including his articulateness, his sensitivity, and his intelligence—compound the complexity of his tautly strung, frenzied stream of consciousness. Despite Quentin's facility with words, his narrative is as fragmented between past and present as Benjy's, but unlike Benjy's monologue, the associational devices in Quentin's are not always clear. Because his intelligence is far more sophisticated than his retarded brother's, Quentin's transitions and leaps are frequently more subtle and far-ranging than Benjy's, and hence considerably more difficult to follow. Unlike Benjy, Quentin is obsessed with emotion rather than action; he is a subjective interpreter rather than an objective, detached reporter. He draws conclusions freely and as freely draws on his extensive reading for phrase and allusion in which to couch these conclusions. The style of his monologue, unlike Benjy's, varies extensively from tightly controlled, dispassionate narrative and descriptive passages which focus on events in the present to unpunctuated, uncapitalized fragments of inner consciousness.

Given the unusual demands of Benjy and Quentin as the novel's first two narrators, then, it is not surprising to find that Faulkner revised the manuscript rather extensively as he typed it, particularly its first two sections. Although it is not possible within the confines of this essay to do more than cast a cursory glance at the major revisions, Faulkner was working toward what Michael Millgate has so aptly termed "an elaboration and a simplification of his technique in the opening section of the book."[58] Millgate was among the first commentators who pointed out the major substantive changes made in Benjy's monologue: the addition of the material concerning Benjy's birthday, the cake Dilsey has made for him, Luster's search for his lost quarter, and his obsession with visiting the show.[59] All of this material occurs in the narrative present of the novel and thereby serves, Millgate notes, "as a kind of motif or signal of present time in the section and [can] thus assist the reader in keeping his bearings among the shifting and merging time-planes."[60] The only other passage of some length added in typescript in the novel's first section is the discussion between Mrs. Compson and T.P. about turning the carriage around (Vintage text 11.06–11.25). This dialogue is evidently intended to expand the portrait of Mrs. Compson's exaggerated fearfulness and her pitiable indecisiveness, which are such potent eroding forces of affection, warmth, and stability in the family. She is afraid to continue forward; she is afraid to turn around; she is afraid to hurry.

Millgate has also noted that among the even more extensive revisions in Quentin's monologue are those which emphasize the importance of time as a thematic motif and heighten our sense of Mr. Compson's presence and the weight of his voice throughout the monologue.[61] This is achieved through the frequent addition of the phrase "Father said." There are substantially more expansions and additions in Quentin's monologue as well as more shifting of material and extensive rewriting than in Benjy's. Particularly noteworthy are the stream-of-consciousness passages that are added in typescript and retained in substantially the same form in the published text.[62] For instance:

> *Roses. Roses. Mr and Mrs Jason Richmond Compson announce the marriage of.* Roses. Not virgins like dogwood, milkweed. I said I have committed incest, Father I said. Roses. Cunning and serene. If you attend Harvard one year, but dont see the boat-race, there should be a refund. Let Jason have it. Give Jason a year at Harvard. (p. 95)

> Like all the bells that ever rang still ringing in the long dying light-rays and Jesus and Saint Francis talking about his sister. Because if it were just to hell; if that were all of it. Finished. If things just finished themselves. Nobody else there but her and me. If we could just have done something so dreadful that they would have fled hell except us. *I have committed incest I said Father it was I it was not Dalton Ames* And when he put Dalton Ames. Dalton Ames. Dalton Ames. When he put the pistol in my hand I didn't. That's why I didn't. He would be there and she would and I would. Dalton Ames. Dalton Ames. Dalton Ames. If we could have just done something so dreadful and Father said That's sad too, people cannot do anything that dreadful they cannot do anything very dreadful at all. . . . (pp. 97–98)

> Dalton Ames. Dalton Ames. Dalton Shirts. I thought all the time they were khaki, army issue khaki, until I saw they were of heavy Chinese silk or finest flannel because they made his face so brown his eyes so blue. (p. 113)

A number of such passages were evidently added in light of Faulkner's decision to reject his original opening for Quentin's monologue, which focused on the Ames-Caddy-Quentin confrontation. With their disjointed, fragmented styles, many of these passages heighten our sense of Quentin's inner torments and the conflicts that will result in his decision to commit suicide.

Another group of passages added after the manuscript was completed pertain to Quentin's purchase of and subsequent thoughts about the two flat-irons. Faulkner apparently decided that stronger signals concerning Quentin's intention to kill himself at the end of his monologue were necessary to intensify the dramatic tension between the past and present throughout Quentin's stream of consciousness. Typical of such passages are:

> I saw the hardware store from across the street. I didn't know you bought flat-irons by the pound.
>
> The clerk said, "These weigh ten pounds." Only they were bigger than I thought. So I got two six-pound little ones, because they would look like a pair of shoes wrapped up. They felt heavy enough together, but I thought again how Father had said about the reducto absurdum of human experience, thinking how the only opportunity I seemed to have for the application of Harvard. Maybe by next year; thinking maybe it takes two years in school to learn to do that properly. (p. 105)

> . . . the shadow of the package like two shoes wrapped up lying on the water. Niggers say a drowned man's shadow was watching for him in the water all the time. It twinkled and glinted, like breathing, the float slow like breathing too, and debris half submerged, healing out to the sea and the caverns and the grottoes of the sea. The displacement of water is equal to the something of something. Reducto absurdum of all human experience, and two six-pound flat-irons weigh more than one tailor's goose. What a sinful waste Dilsey would say. . . . (p. 111)

> In three years I can not wear a hat. I could not. Was. Will there be hats then since I was not and not Harvard then. Where the best of thought Father said clings like dead ivy vines upon old dead brick. Not Harvard then. Not to me, anyway. Again. Sadder than was. Again. Saddest of all. Again. (pp. 117–118)

Yet another group of passages is added to intensify the portrait of Quentin's paradoxical fascination with and abhorrence of sexuality, which clarifies not only his conflict with Ames and Caddy but elucidates the reasons for his suicide:

> Ah let him alone, Shreve said, if he's got better sense than to chase after the little dirty sluts, whose business. In the South you are ashamed of being a virgin. Boys. Men. They lie about it. Because it means less to women, Father said. He said it was men invented virginity not women. Father said it's like death: only a state in which the others are left and I said, But to believe it doesn't matter and he said, That's what's so sad about anything: not only virginity, and I said, Why couldn't it have been me and not her who is unvirgin and he said, That's why that's sad too; nothing is even worth the changing of it, and Shreve said if he's got better sense than to chase after the little dirty sluts and I said Did you ever have a sister? Did you? Did you? (p. 96)

> It's not not having them. It's never to have had them then I could say O That That's Chinese I dont know Chinese. And Father said it's because you are a virgin: dont you see? Women are never virgins. Purity is a negative state and therefore contrary to nature. It's nature is hurting you not Caddy and I said That's just words and he said So is virginity and I said you dont know. You cant know and he said Yes. On the instant when we come to realise that tragedy is second-hand. (p. 143)

Other changes exist, including the drastically rewritten closing paragraphs of the monologue. However, the preponderance of the major alterations occurs in the first half of Quentin's section.

By contrast, and not surprisingly, given its less rigorous narrative structure, Jason's monologue exhibits comparatively little revision from manuscript to typescript to published text. Only two major additions exist. The first is the scene with Jason and Mrs. Compson where she burns the phony support check she believes is from Caddy (Vintage text 272.10–273.26). The second is the marvelous little exchange between Jason and Mac (Vintage text 314.01–314.27) where Jason stubbornly disparages the great Yankees team of 1928 and its star, Babe Ruth. The novel's fourth and closing section is even closer to the manuscript.

Paradoxically, the typescript is striking in two different ways. On one hand, this extremely complex novel is remarkably close to the manuscript, i.e., the bulk of the novel is present in the manuscript and, collectively, revisions made in the typescript and in later stages of the production of the novel are remarkably few given the complicated design of the novel. On the other hand, there is sufficient rewriting, reorganizing, and adding of material to support Faulkner's claim that he worked carefully with the novel—anguished over it—as he sorted out various problems in designating time, revealing character, clarifying plot, heightening image and theme.

Important as such concerns are, they were not the only points that absorbed Faulkner's attention. Perhaps more than any other of his novels, *The Sound and the Fury* shows Faulkner grappling with the crucial minutiae of spacing, punctuation, paragraph indentation, and italicization as he worked toward the unconventionality of Benjy's and Quentin's monologues. Again, however, as with the substantive revisions, the third and fourth sections presented virtually no problems in comparison to the novel's first two monologues. Despite his efforts, despite his tinkering with these details virtually until the actual printing of the book, considerable inconsistency and a minor number of demonstrable errors are displayed. Hence, again, we can speculate that Faulkner's comments about anguishing over the novel and his sense of having failed to achieve a desired end—"the most gallant, the most magnificent failure"[63]—reflect in part his dissatisfaction with the details of its presentation. Meriwether notes that Faulkner's concern about printing the novel was expressed in a proposal to Ben Wasson and Harrison Smith that parts of the sections be printed in inks of different colors.[64] In the absence of such a possibility, Faulkner used other tools more readily at his disposal and experimented with them.

For instance, Faulkner experimented with punctuation almost to the actual printing of the book.[65] Although the manuscript is consistent in its use of traditional punctuation except in Quentin's section, where some experimentation occurs, the typescript is inconsistent in its use of nontraditional punctuation and contains many passages that are punctuated conventionally. However, a number of unusual changes appear (although again not with complete consistency) in the published book, thus suggesting that perhaps as late as galleys or page proofs Faulkner was still experimenting, especially with the intricacies of Benjy's section and the complexities of utilizing such a character as first-person narrator, with the end punctuation of direct address and the punctuation of speaker identification tags when they interrupt direct address. Faulkner eventually evolved a system of punctuating all spoken discourse in Benjy's monologue with periods, rather than other kinds of end punctuation, including commas, exclamation points, or question marks, as a technique for establishing the limits of Benjy's comprehension. Benjy records all spoken discourse literally, without understanding its meaning or differentiating among vocal inflections and interrogatory, declarative, and imperative sentences. However, since Faulkner evolved this method of punctuating unconventionally with periods terminating all spoken discourse only after completing the typescript, it seems likely that implementation would have been left to editorial hands, and thus we may perhaps account for its considerable inconsistency in the published text.[66] In addition, the typesetter(s), already challenged by a difficult text, and confronted with others of Faulkner's unusual but generally consistent practices (omitting apostrophes in words like "dont" and "cant" or periods after "Mr" and "Mrs") may have followed setting copy inconsistently and further complicated matters.

Ben Wasson's tampering with the text (presumably copy editing Faulkner's ribbon typescript before it went to the printer) has been well established.[67] Wasson questioned Faulkner's use of italics, and although Faulkner vigorously defended it, a comparison of the manuscript, typescript, and published book makes clear that he changed italicized passages extensively and added italics heavily when he read proof. Italics were used initially to signal what Faulkner called a "transference" from one point in time to another.[68] They may signal the beginning of a flashback, or they may signal a return from the past to a different time level, which is frequently but not always the novel's narrative present (April 1928). On other occasions, italics are used to indicate "a speech by one person within a speech by another," which led Faulkner to speculate that his "use of italics has been too without definite plan" but was adopted to perform this last function to avoid clumsy paragraphs.[69] Wasson suggested that Faulkner use new breaks—extra spaces—between paragraphs instead of italics, a suggestion which Faulkner emphatically rejected, although a printer's sample octavo gathering, including the first fourteen pages of *The Sound and the Fury,* was printed adopting Wasson's rather than Faulkner's method.[70] The romanization of italicized passages, the italicization of roman passages, and the general addition of new italicized passages are extensive. Therefore, it is not surprising that in Benjy's monologue in four instances italics were inadvertently omitted.[71]

Critics have long been aware that additional revision occurred between the extant carbon typescript and the published book. The ribbon typescript, which presumably served as setting copy, the galleys, and the page proofs have apparently not survived. However, some new light is shed on those revisions by a forty-one-page ribbon typescript and two leaves of Faulkner's requests for revisions on pages not contained within the first forty-one. This typescript of irregularly numbered pages from Quentin's monologue has only recently surfaced, purchased in November 1975 from J. Periam Danton by the University of Virginia Library.[72]

We can only speculate as to the timetable of Faulkner's revision of the forty-one pages. The typescript contains no printer's marks; thus Faulkner must have decided to make the revisions after copy editing but before type was set for the novel's second section. Arriving in New York in late September 1928, Faulkner completed typing the manuscript in Greenwich Village in October 1928 according to the date on the final page of the typescript. He returned to Mississippi in December without having had a definite acceptance from Harcourt, Brace. In a letter dated February 15, 1929, however, Alfred Harcourt rejected the novel, which Harrison Smith subsequently took with him when he entered into partnership with Jonathan Cape. Copies of the contract for publication were executed on February 18, 1929, and it is unlikely although not impossible that the typescript was copy-edited much before this date. Galley proofs were sent to Faulkner in early July 1929, in Pascagoula, Mississippi, where he was honeymooning. Thus it is probable that sometime in that four-and-a-half-month period Faulkner must have revised the Quentin section and substituted forty-one retyped pages for the pages already at Cape & Smith. These revisions were probably made before Faulkner's wedding on June 20, 1929, but it is possible that they were made as early as December 1928 or January 1929, when Faulkner would presumably have had a good idea that Cape & Smith was going to publish *The Sound and the Fury* but before February 1929, by which time he was writing *Sanctuary*.[73] However, whether Faulkner wrote Cape & Smith from Mississippi requesting that the pages be substituted or whether he made the revisions while he was in New York in November and December 1928 (although in light of the above chronology the former seems far more likely)[74] as well as *when* he made these revisions is impossible to say with absolute certainty in the absence of further evidence.

Apparently, Faulkner remained dissatisfied with Quentin's monologue and decided at a relatively late date that it required additional revision. The underlying motivation for these revisions seems to have been Faulkner's determination that his use of double or triple spaces to designate shifts in the narrative time level was not sufficient to guide his readers through the complexities of Quentin's monologue. Most, although not all, of the rejected pages employ this spacing device. In the rewritten pages (whose ribbon copies evidently were reunited with the original ribbon typescript that served as setting copy and whose carbons were included in the bound carbon typescript Faulkner preserved for himself), Faulkner substituted paragraph indentations and added more italicized phrases as the vehicle by which greater clarity in designating the time shifts could be achieved. Considerable stylistic polishing occurs: tightening for clarity and precision; expanding passages slightly for accuracy; deleting overblown, overwritten phrases or passages; revising punctuation to make it more traditional, especially insofar as designating word groups to facilitate the reader's following Quentin's stream of consciousness; and intensifying Mr. Compson's presence. The two pages of additional corrections contain requests for changes that occur largely at beginnings of pages immediately following rewritten ones where changes became necessary in light of the revisions. By far the second largest area of concern in these two sheets is the request to italicize twelve passages and to delete italics in two others.

IV

The novel was published October 7, 1929. The generally favorable reviews[75] must have been some compensation for the anguish of Faulkner's labors as well as confirmation of his exuberant sense that he had not only learned to read but to write. If Faulkner would emerge from behind his closed door as master rather than as apprentice, however, the Compson story was not yet exhausted. Throughout the remainder of Faulkner's long career it would remain firmly linked with demanding, innovative works in which Faulkner continued to experiment with point of view, from *Absalom, Absalom!* (1936) to *Go Down, Moses* (1942), where in a typescript of "The Old People" Quentin Compson is the character who later becomes Ike McCaslin.

Perhaps the most experimental work of all is the 1946 Compson Appendix which reveals the imaginative fascination the Compson material continued to hold for Faulkner. In retelling the Compson story, he cast it in yet another narrative form, provided the family with a rich, sweeping historical context, and amplified, modified, reassessed, and reinterpreted the characters, recreating them in the process. The Appendix became a separate work of fiction rather than the simple recapitulation of a work written seventeen years earlier which Faulkner had intended to provide for Malcolm Cowley's 1946 Viking *Portable Faulkner.*

Thus, it is little wonder that in later years Faulkner looked backward to *The Sound and the Fury* and called it his "heart's darling."

Notes

1. James B. Meriwether, "The Textual History of *The Sound and the Fury*" in *The Merrill Studies in The Sound and the Fury,* comp. James B. Meriwether (Columbus, Ohio: Charles E. Merrill, 1970), p. 5. This important article first brought together much of the information about the publication of the novel and I have drawn on it throughout this essay.

2. *Faulkner in the University: Class Conferences at the University of Virginia 1957–1958,* ed. Frederick L. Gwynn and Joseph L. Blotner (New York: Vintage, 1965), p. 61.

3. *Selected Letters of William Faulkner,* ed. Joseph Blotner (New York: Random House, 1977), p. 39.

4. *Selected Letters,* p. 38. For additional information pertaining to the publication of *Flags in the Dust* see George F. Hayhoe, "William Faulkner's *Flags in the Dust,*" *Mississippi Quarterly,* 28 (Summer 1975), 370–386.

5. Hayhoe, "William Faulkner's *Flags in the Dust,*" pp. 370–374.

6. James B. Meriwether, ed., "An Introduction to *The Sound and the Fury,*" *Mississippi Quarterly,* 26 (Summer 1973), 412–413.

7. "Introduction" to the Modern Library issue of *Sanctuary* (1932), in *Essays, Speeches and Public Letters,* ed. James B. Meriwether (New York: Random House, 1965), p. 177.

8. *Selected Letters,* p. 236.

9. "An Introduction to *The Sound and the Fury,*" p. 414.

10. *Selected Letters,* p. 43.

11. See "The Preface to *The Sound and the Fury*" by Maurice Coindreau in *The Time of William Faulkner: A French view of Modern American Fiction,* ed. and trans. George M. Reeves (Columbia: University of South Carolina Press, 1971), p. 49.

12. Interview with Jean Stein Vanden Heuvel in 1956 in *Lion in the Garden: Interviews with William Faulkner, 1926–1962,* ed. James B. Meriwether and Michael Millgate (New York: Random House, 1968), p. 239.

13. In *Faulkner in the University,* p. 103, Faulkner commented that "the writer has three sources, imagination, observation, and experience . . . , he uses his material from the three sources as the carpenter reaches into his lumber room and finds a board that fits that particular corner he's building."

14. James B. Meriwether, ed., "An Introduction for *The Sound and the Fury,*" *Southern Review,* N.S. 8 (Autumn 1972), 708. For a fuller discussion of the significance of this statement see André Bleikasten, *The Most Splendid Failure: Faulkner's The Sound and the Fury* (Bloomington: Indiana University Press, 1976), pp. 44–47.

15. The best treatment to date of the relationships of Faulkner's first three novels to his fourth is in Bleikasten, *The Most Splendid Failure,* pp. 3–42.

16. For an expanded discussion of the significance of key works from Faulkner's apprenticeship to the novel, see Gail M. Morrison, "William Faulkner's *The Sound and the Fury:* A Critical and Textual Study," Diss. University of South Carolina, 1980, pp. 1–64.

17. These sketches have until recently been most readily available in Carvel Collins, *New Orleans Sketches* (New York: Random House, 1968). However, a soon-to-be-published University of South Carolina dissertation by Leland H. Cox, Jr., "Sinbad in New Orleans: Early Short Fiction by William Faulkner—An Annotated Edition" (1976), should be consulted for its detailed introduction as well as for its annotations. Both Collins and Cox point out similarities among the works under discussion here.

18. Collins, *New Orleans Sketches,* p. 47.

19. "The Priest," ed. James B. Meriwether, *Mississippi Quarterly,* 30 (Summer 1976), 445–450.

20. William Faulkner, "Adolescence" in *Uncollected Stories,* ed. Joseph Blotner (New York: Random House, 1979), p. 460. In his biography, *Faulkner: A Biography, 2 vols.* (New York: Random House, 1974), Joseph Blotner provides a plot summary of this sketch and states that it "may have been written" around 1922 (pp. 333–334). Michael Millgate in *The Achievement of William Faulkner* (New York: Vintage, 1971) discusses briefly the relationship of "Adolescence" to "Elmer" and *As I Lay Dying* (pp. 11 and 12).

21. "Adolescence," p. 472.

22. William Faulkner, *The Sound and the Fury* (New York: Vintage, 1963), pp. 382, 384. Subsequent quotations from the novel will be indicated parenthetically in the text.

23. Blotner states that Faulkner remembered writing "The Devil Beats His Wife" shortly after his return from Europe In December 1925 (I, 491). Although Faulkner's memory for dates was not entirely accurate, he did remember sequences of events accurately. It is interesting to note that the first page is in the form of dialogue in a play and thus indicates Faulkner's early interest in a form later used in

Requiem for a Nun (New York: Random House, 1951). This fragment is located in the William Faulkner Foundation Collection of the University of Virginia Library.

24. "Nympholepsy," ed. James B. Meriwether, *Mississippi Quarterly,* 26 (Summer 1973), 403–409.

25. This story was submitted for publication to Bennett Cerf at Random House. For a thorough discussion of the Elmer materials, see Thomas McHaney, "The Elmer Papers: Faulkner's Comic Portraits of the Artist," *Mississippi Quarterly,* 26 (Summer 1973), 281–311.

26. See, for instance, Lewis P. Simpson, "Faulkner and the Legend of the Artist" in *Faulkner: Fifty Years After the Marble Faun,* ed. George H. Wolfe (University: University of Alabama Press, 1976), and Jackson J. Benson, "Quentin Compson: Self Portrait of a Young Artist's Emotions," *Twentieth Century Literature,* 17 (July 1971), 143–159.

27. "Elmer," p. 5. This typescript is in the William Faulkner Foundation Collection of the Alderman Library of the University of Virginia.

28. For a more detailed discussion of the relationship of *Mayday* to *The Sound and the Fury,* see Gail M. Morrison, "'Time, Tide, and Twilight': *Mayday* and Faulkner's Quest Toward *The Sound and the Fury,*" *Mississippi Quarterly,* 31 (Summer 1978), 337–357.

29. William Faulkner, *The Marionettes: A Play in One Act* ([Charlottesville:] The Bibliographical Society of the University of Virginia and the University Press of Virginia, 1975), pp. 11 and 12. See also Noel Polk, "Introduction" to *The Marionettes.* Charlottesville: The Bibliographical Society of the University of Virginia and The University Press of Virginia, 1977, for discussion of the structural devices experimented with in this work.

30. Although this work has been published (New York: Random House, 1967), I have quoted from the seventy-one-page bound manuscript in the Alderman Library at the University of Virginia since the published text contains a number of silent emendations. These will be indicated parenthetically in the text. Blotner incorrectly states that Faulkner initially composed *The Wishing Tree* for Victoria (I, 1718–1719); however, he cites a letter from Faulkner to Harold Ober (February 4. 1959) in which Faulkner stated that he "invented this story for Mrs Brown's daughter, about ten at the time, who was dying of cancer" (II, 1718–1719; *Selected Letters,* p. 421). Although actual dates of the gift giving may have been such that Victoria received her copy before Margaret did, references in the typescript inscribed to Margaret to Sir Galwyn and *Mayday* (which do not appear in Victoria's copy) suggest that Margaret's is the earlier of the two typescripts.

31. See Boyd Davis, "Caddy Compson's Eden," *Mississippi Quarterly,* 30 (Summer 1977), 381–394.

32. See Morrison, "William Faulkner's *The Sound and the Fury:* A Critical and Textual Study," pp. 47–56, for a more extended discussion of the parallels between the novel and the fable.

33. *Lion in the Garden,* p. 146.

34. The "Father Abraham" manuscript is in the Arents Collection of the New York Public Library.

35. This fragment is in the Berg Collection of the New York Public Library.

36. "An Introduction for *The Sound and the Fury,*" p. 710.

37. *Faulkner in the University,* p. 6. Heathcliff calls Cathy his "heart's darling" in Brontë, *Wuthering Heights* (1847; rpt. New York: Modern Library, 1926), p. 33.

38. *Lion in the Garden,* p. 146.

39. *Selected Letters,* p. 34.

40. The claims for a 1925 date are advanced in Carvel Collins, "Faulkner's *Mayday*" in *Mayday* ([South Bend, Ind.:] University of Notre Dame Press, 1977), p. 19. This afterword has become the "Introduction" (and is slightly expanded) in the trade edition (South Bend, Ind.: University of Notre Dame Press, 1980), pp. 23–26.

41. "Introduction" to the Modern Library issue of *Sanctuary* (1932), in *Essays, Speeches and Public Letters,* pp. 176–177.

42. *Lion in the Garden,* p. 55.

43. *Selected Letters, p.* 39.

44. *Selected Letters,* p. 40.

45. *Selected Letters,* p. 41.

46. The manuscript is located in the Beinecke Library at Yale University. "That Evening Sun Go Down" was published in *American Mercury,* 22 (March 1931), and revised for inclusion in *Collected Stories* (New York: Random House, 1950) as "That Evening Sun."

47. Blotner, I, 566–567. Blotner equates this image with the funeral of Faulkner's grandmother, also called Damuddy, on June 2, 1907.

48. *Selected Letters,* p. 43; Blotner, I, 602–603; Meriwether, "The Textual History of *The Sound and the Fury,*" pp. 8–9.

49. See Meriwether, "The Textual History of *The Sound and the Fury,*" pp. 9–15, for details pertaining to Wasson's copy editing.

50. *The Making of William Faulkner's Books 1929–1937: An Interview with Evelyn Harter Glick,* ed. James B. Meriwether (Columbia: Southern Studies Program, University of South Carolina, 1979), p. 4. Mrs. Glick was in charge of production and design at Cape & Smith and notes that "I came in when *The Sound and the Fury* was already in the works. Bob Ballou had planned it, and I carried through on it. Then I went on to the others. *As I Lay Dying* was my first. But Bob had done the whole job on *The Sound and the Fury.*"

51. Meriwether, "The Textual History of *The Sound and the Fury,*" p. 13.

52. *Faulkner in the University,* p. 61.

53. "An Introduction for *The Sound and the Fury,*" p. 710.

54. Meriwether, "The Textual History of *The Sound and the Fury,*" p. 6. The only "notes" that have been preserved are a sheet entitled "Twilight" which lists birth, death, and marriage dates for many of the novel's characters, some of which do not conform to internal evidence provided within the novel. Blotner (I, 572) has reproduced these notes.

55. "An Introduction to *The Sound and the Fury,*" p. 415.

56. *Lion in the Garden,* p. 222. See also pp. 147 and 245.

57. Millgate, *The Achievement of William Faulkner,* p. 90.

58. Millgate, *The Achievement of William Faulkner,* p. 92.

59. Passages from the published text such as 17.19–17.24; 18.27–19.15; 23.12–23.13; 60.02–61.08; 73.08–73.13 are among the many added in typescript.

60. Millgate, *The Achievement of William Faulkner,* p. 93.

61. Millgate, *The Achievement of William Faulkner,* p. 95.

62. I am quoting from the published text here, but obviously these passages do not occur verbatim in the typescript, although they are very close indeed.

63. *Faulkner in the University,* p. 61.

64. Meriwether, "The Textual History of *The Sound and the Fury,*" pp. 9–10.

65. See Morrison, "William Faulkner's *The Sound and the Fury:* A Critical and Textual Study" for more detailed discussion of the textual collation between typescript and first edition.

66. See Morrison, "William Faulkner's *The Sound and the Fury:* A Critical and Textual Study," pp. 706–743, for my recommendations to emend the first edition.

67. See Meriwether, "The Textual History of *The Sound and the Fury,*" pp. 8-9; Blotner, I, 626–667; *Selected Letters,* pp. 44–46.

68. *Selected Letters,* p. 44.

69. *Selected Letters,* p. 45.

70. See Meriwether, "The Textual History of *The Sound and the Fury,*" p. 14, for a reprinting of one of these sample pages.

71. See *The Sound and the Fury,* published text, 40.13–40.15; 46.14–46.15; 52.03–52.05; 53.16–53.17, and Morrison, "William Faulkner's *The Sound and the Fury:* A Critical and Textual Study," pp. 736–737.

72. I am grateful to Joan St. C. Crane, Curator of American Literature Collections at the University of Virginia Library, for first drawing it to my attention. Mr. Danton began collecting Faulkner materials in 1930–1933 and believes that it was during this time that he acquired the typescript pages from a book dealer. In a telephone interview on June 23, 1980, Ben Wasson expressed considerable surprise at my explanation of these pages, and was quite emphatic that he had not been involved. He suggested that Faulkner may have worked with Lenore Marshall, and stated that he had not known Mr. Danton.

73. Blotner, I, 598, 602–604, 626.

74. Also, Faulkner was evidently going through the carbon typescript in his possession and making corrections.

75. For a summary of the reviews, see O. B. Emerson, "William Faulkner's Literary Reputation," Diss. Vanderbilt University, 1962, pp. 15–38, and Blotner, I, 632–633.

STEPHEN M. ROSS

Rev. Shegog's Powerful Voice

Nowhere in Faulkner's oeuvre is the presence and power of voice more beautifully conceived than in the fourth section of *The Sound and the Fury,* when Dilsey takes Benjy to her church's Easter service to hear Rev. Shegog's sermon. Contained within this one episode are all the strategies for creating phenomenal voice that Faulkner used throughout his fiction: contrasting figuration of vision and voice, attention to voice in itself, and separation of voice from speaker. Here, too, we find the full significance of voice as a phenomenon directly articulated.

However despairing or nihilistic a given reader may find *The Sound and the Fury,* the momentary ameliorative affirmation engendered by the Easter sermon is almost universally acknowledged. The sermon's power has been registered on a number of scales. Thematically, its depiction of Christ's resurrection envisions a salvation that will transcend the world's and the Compsons' degeneration: "the eloquent sermon [is] a vision of eternity which gives meaning to time and will wipe away all tears in a final vindication of goodness and in a full consolation of those who mourn" (C. Brooks, *Yoknapatawpha Country,* 345). Structurally, the sermon provides closure for the "tragic-Christian" strands running through the novel (Hagopian 46–47). The sermon marks Dilsey as the novel's "ethical center" (Vickery 47–49). In social terms the church scene depicts a congregation of listeners sharing a

Fiction's Inexhaustible Voice: Speech and Writing in Faulkner (Athens: University of Georgia Press, 1989): pp. 36–45.

communal moment in which their hearts speak each to each, an impossibility for the Compson family. The very content of the sermon ironically echoes and comments upon the variations of "Compson devilment" we have seen throughout the story (Matthews 108–110). Rhetorically, the sermon testifies to Faulkner's mimetic skills in its faithful rendering of Southern black preaching (Rosenberg). André Bleikasten best expresses the overall significance of Shegog's performance: "The voice that takes hold of the preacher induces a vision, and this moment of vision, fully shared in by the congregation, is in fact the only experience of spiritual enlightenment recorded in the whole book. To Dilsey, in particular, the preacher's words bring the encompassing revelation of eternity, the mystical and prophetic vision of 'the beginning and the ending'" (*Most Splendid Failure,* 201).

The movement from part 3 into part 4 of *The Sound and the Fury* has been described as an emergence from confining voice into clear sight. We escape from the novel's solopsistic monologues into highly visual description where objects and, most important, people can now be seen—if not objectively at least with striking clarity (Blanchard passim; Bleikasten, *Most Splendid Failure,* 176–180). No longer buttonholed by Jason, we can watch Dilsey step out of her cabin door without feeling claustrophobic dependence upon what an obsessed or idiotic talker is telling us. Yet for all its visual clarity, the opening portion of section 4 mingles voice with vision in an orchestration of imagery that will culminate in Rev. Shegog's Easter sermon. Implanted within the visual imagery at the opening are sounds, voices, and moments of listening. Some sounds are described abstractly or even visually, dropped into the silent envisioned scene like pebbles dropped into water. The jaybirds' "harsh cries" are whipped away by the wind like "scraps of paper or of cloth" (*SF* 307; 331–332); Mrs. Compson calls Dilsey's name "into the quiet stairwell that descended into complete darkness . . . with machinelike regularity" (308, 312; 333, 337); Dilsey sings "something without particular tune or words, repetitive, mournful and plaintive, austere" (312; 336); the clock tick-tocks in "enigmatic profundity" (316; 341); and Luster plays a soundless tune with his fingers as he feeds Benjy (319–320; 345). The opening pages also contain a number of acts of listening, of one person listening not *to* others but *for* them. Dilsey listens for Luster and for Mrs. Compson: "She ceased and tilted her head upward, listening. But there was no sound save the clock and the fire" (317; 342). We *see* Jason and his mother, in a description that emphasizes their eyes, as they *listen* to Dilsey "mount the final stair" to call Quentin:

> When she called the first time Jason laid his knife and fork down and he and his mother appeared to wait across the table from one another in identical attitudes; the one cold and shrewd, with close-thatched brown hair curled into two stubborn hooks, one on either

> side of his forehead like a bartender in caricature, and hazel eyes with black-ringed irises like marbles, the other cold and querulous, with perfectly white hair and eyes pouched and baffled and so dark as to appear to be all pupil or all iris. (323; 348)

When Quentin does not answer, Jason stands at her door "as if he were listening to something much further away than the dimensioned room beyond the door, and which he already heard. His attitude was that of one who goes through the motions of listening in order to deceive himself as to what he already hears. Behind him Mrs Compson mounted the stairs, calling his name" (324; 349–350).

The intrusion of sound into the Sunday morning silence, recorded both in images of sound and in acts of listening, predicts the more stately orchestration of vision and voice that begins when the Easter service episode itself gets under way. In this episode the three discursive gestures that engender voice's power—the contrast of vision and voice, the treatment of voice as a phenomenon separate from its function as a vehicle for speech, and the breaking of voice away from speaker and speech—come to fruition.

As Dilsey, Benjy, and Luster prepare to leave for the church, Faulkner describes Benjy's voice twice. Benjy's bellow has served, in the novel's earlier sections, as a palpable index of Caddy's loss. Now Faulkner renders Benjy's wailing as "hopeless and prolonged. It was nothing. Just sound. It might have been all time and injustice and sorrow become vocal for an instant by a conjunction of planets" (332–333; 359). The figurative meaning of the sound as "time and injustice and sorrow become vocal" is offered tentatively ("it *might* have been") as confirmation of the symbolic role Benjy's bellow has played earlier in the novel; yet the description emphasizes the voice's emptiness. It is voice as a hollow sound from which meaning has been extracted, now lacking its earlier significance as moral index. The second description, a few paragraphs later, even more explicitly empties Benjy's wailing of meaning as a "slow hoarse sound that ships make, that seems to begin before the sound itself has started, seems to cease before the sound itself has stopped" (333; 359). The voice is objectified as something present and hearable, and nothing more, separated from Benjy as a human source. A gap opens between the voice and its sound, for the one begins and ends before the other starts and stops. A visual counterpart to this aural image of Benjy's voice comes a few short paragraphs later. Luster has "a stiff new straw hat with a colored band" to wear to church. A comically ill-fitting hat, it seems "to isolate Luster's skull in the beholder's eye as a spotlight would, in all its individual planes and angles . . . the hat appeared to be on the head of someone standing immediately behind Luster" (334; 360).

The descriptions of Benjy's bellowing and of Luster's appearance begin a narrative pattern in which aural and visual images alternate with one another as contrasting strands in the texture of the discourse. The highly descriptive narration maintains a rhythm of representation between moments dominated by voice and by images of objects seen. Under the sky *seen* "broken now into scudding patches that dragged their swift shadows up out of the shabby garden" we *hear* Benjy wailing and Dilsey soothing him, "'Hush,' Dilsey said. 'Hush, now. We be gone in a minute. Hush, now'" (333; 360).

The alternation between vision and speech continues throughout the stately procession to church. First comes talk. Luster and Dilsey fuss at each other about Luster's hat and the umbrella, Benjy stops wailing as they leave the drive, and Dilsey nags Frony about her dress getting wet ("'Mammy always talkin bout hit gwine rain,' Luster said" [335; 361]). Then comes vision. We see the street's "quiet length" with "white people in bright clumps mov[ing] churchward, under the windy bells, walking now and then in the random and tentative sun" (335; 362). Talk returns in Frony's complaint about Benjy because "folks talkin" (335; 362), a complaint Dilsey dismisses as coming from "trash white folks." Vision returns as the street passes between small cabins "set in small grassless plots littered with broken things . . . [and] rank weeds [and] trees that partook also of the foul desiccation which surrounded the houses" (336; 362–363). Out of this visualized clutter voices emerge once again, as "from the doors negroes spoke to them as they passed, to Dilsey usually:

> "Sis' Gibson! How you dis mawnin'?"
> "I'm well. Is you well?"
> "I'm right well, I thank you." (336; 363)

Another visual description of the churchgoers follows, delineating their dress and accoutrements. Then more voices, disembodied, written in speakerless stychomythia as the children talk about Benjy:

> "I bet you wont go up en tech him."
> "How come I wont?"
> "I bet you wont. I bet you skeered to."
> "He wont hurt folks. He des a loony." (337; 364)

The discourse reverts to vision again in a striking picture of the church "like a painted church" instead of a real one: "the whole scene was as flat and without perspective as a painted cardboard set upon the ultimate edge of the flat earth, against the windy sunlight of space and April and a midmorning filled with bells" (337; 364). The men converse against the backdrop of the church as the women and children enter, also to talk: "the women were gathered on one side of the room. They were talking" (338; 365). Sound and sight continue to alternate in the two paragraphs introducing Rev. Shegog from "Saint Looey," who has come to preach the Easter service. Between the choir's singing and the children's singing in "frightened, tuneless whispers," the congregation watches Rev. Shegog with disappointment. He is "undersized," with "a wizened black face like a small, aged monkey." Faulkner often depicts the sound of a voice as physically affecting sight (or vice versa), an oxymoron that highlights the palpable solidity of sound's presence. Here the regular minister, himself a man of "imposing bulk," introduces Rev. Shegog "in rich, rolling tones whose very unction served to increase the visitor's insignificance" (339; 366). The journey to the Easter service ends as Dilsey again hushes Benjy, and Shegog's preaching begins.

Commentators on *The Sound and the Fury* have normally seen Shegog's sermon as divided into two parts, his "white" and his "black" rhetoric (see, for example, Davis 113–117). Important as the racial-phonetic distinction is, the sermon is not bifurcated simply along these lines. Faulkner actually renders Shegog's sermon in *three* stages. The first is purely descriptive. The diegetic discourse informs about, but does not show, the qualities of Shegog's voice: "He sounded like a white man. His voice was level and cold. It sounded too big to have come from him" (339; 366). We find this vocal tag, "level and cold," employed frequently in Faulkner as a mark upon the discourse of any speaker not participating in a shared or sharable voice. To speak in a level and cold voice is to speak only for oneself, *at* but not *with* others. The congregation responds properly to this level and cold voice—that is, they respond visually, watching him and his voice as they would watch circus performers: "They listened at first through curiosity, as they would have to a monkey talking. They began to watch him as they would a man on a tight rope" (339; 366). The performance is a tour de force as Shegog "ran and poised and swooped upon the cold inflectionless wire of his voice." His performance depletes him and he stands "reft of all motion as a mummy or an emptied vessel"—visual images of voiceless things. This first stage ends with the congregation unmoved (except to sigh and "move a little in its seats"). Dilsey comforts Ben, who apparently has moaned, by promising him that soothing voices will follow—"Dey fixin to sing in a minute" (340; 367).

Stage two of Shegog's sermon opens with a voice separate from its source, but a voice that can now *speak* instead of merely stretch like a wire to demonstrate a performer's verbal footwork: "Then a voice said, 'Brethren.'" For the first time the narrative depicts the voice distinctly as sound: "The voice died in sonorous echoes between the walls. It was as different as day and dark from his former tone, with a sad, timbrous quality like an alto horn" (340; 367). To this voice the congregation *listens,* as the sermon now sinks "into their hearts and speak[s] there again when it had ceased in fading and cumulate echoes." We "hear" Rev. Shegog in an oral performance: "I got the recollection and the blood of the Lamb!" The imagery reaches a crescendo of evocation here, as Shegog tramps back and forth behind the pulpit: "He was like a worn small rock whelmed by the successive waves of his voice. With his body he seemed to feed the voice that, succubus like, had fleshed its teeth in him. And the congregation seemed to watch with its own eyes while the voice consumed him, until he was nothing and they were nothing and there was not even a voice but instead their hearts were speaking to one another in chanting measures beyond the need for words" (340; 367). Now the congregation listens. Yet it still watches, too, as the voice "consumes" Shegog until he becomes "a serene, tortured crucifix that transcended its shabbiness and insignificance" (340–341; 368). The second stage of Shegog's sermon has transformed the visualized voice of the first stage into a voice powerful and sonorous—but a voice still "white," still that of a stranger. The congregation is caught, letting out a "long moaning expulsion of breath," and a "woman's single soprano" responds; but the total immersion in voice is yet to come.

A brief return to Dilsey again indicates a break between stages, as we see her sitting "bolt upright, her hand on Ben's knee." Ben, apparently, is no longer moaning. The third stage begins with Rev. Shegog shifting from white speech to black:

> "Brethren," the minister said in a harsh whisper, without moving.
>
> "Yes, Jesus!" the woman's voice said, hushed yet.
>
> "Breddren en sistuhn!" His voice rang again, with the horns. He removed his arm and stood erect and raised his hands. "I got de ricklickshun en de blood of de Lamb!" They did not mark just when his intonation, his pronunciation, became negroid, they just sat swaying a little in their seats as the voice took them into itself. (341; 368)

The third stage *imitates* voice, re-creating the rhythms and sounds of Southern black preaching: "When de long, cold—Oh, I tells you breddren, when de long, cold. . . . I sees de light en I sees de word, po sinner!" (341; 368). Shegog's sermon is one of Faulkner's most sustained examples of black speech fully rendered and maintained in dialect writing. But now we see that the voice has more than imitated speech; it has been transformed into phenomenal voice, emerging as palpable and significant discourse out of a carefully modulated narrative episode in which vision and voice alternate to evoke the presence of annealing voice in the world and human presence caught up in that voice.

The three stages have carried us from description to imitation, from visualized voice to heard voice recorded so that the reader, like the congregation, can be taken into its communal "chanting measures beyond the need for words." Bleikasten's insight that Shegog's voice "induces a vision" aptly describes the paradoxical result of the sermon. Shegog hammers into the congregation what he has *seen:* "I sees de light en I sees de word, po sinner!" "I sees" punctuates his evocation of Christ's suffering. Thus within the represented world the power of voice is appropriately gauged by Dilsey's reaction to Shegog: "I seed de beginnin, en now I sees de endin" (344; 371). Furthermore, the dialect spelling produces powerfully "voiced" writing that marks the alteration from white to black intonation. Faulkner makes us literally see so that we may hear: "breddren en sistuhn"; "ricklickshun"; "Ma'y settin in de do' wid Jesus on her lap." The dialect is, as usual in Faulkner, deftly controlled. Some of the dialect spellings mark phonetic differences between black and white speech, though others exaggerate those distinctions. (Many white Southerners would probably say "po" for "poor" just as black speakers would, but, as is necessarily true in dialect writing, the "standard" speech has virtually no unconventional phonetic markers [Ives, "Theory of Literary Dialect," 158–163].) Some of the spellings, too, are pure eye dialect, signifying differences they do not really render: "wus" for "was," or "whut" for "what." While the dialect is heavy, Faulkner carefully resists misspelling every word: we have "ricklick*shun*" but also "lamenta*tion*" and "resurrec*tion.*" Only a visual analog this skillfully modulated can render voice's supreme triumph here.

The role of vision in Shegog's dialect is not a trivial matter of technique but an essential ingredient in that process by which Faulkner empowers written, visually accessible discourse to emerge as meaningful voice. Perhaps Faulkner gives us in this Easter service episode what Roland Barthes would have called an *erotics* of voice in narrative. Amidst a scene evoking divine love, this episode is a text of pleasure in which the discourse creates suspense through blockage and release of voice, through the alternating presence and absence of voice. We are led toward a climactic union with voice that, in promise at least, answers all questions and dispels all disappointments. Suspense results from the episode's steady movement toward something (a something that will turn out to be voice) that promises to overcome the disappointment of sight. What we see disappoints us, just as the sight of Rev. Shegog disappoints the congregation. What we seek at the narrative's end, then, is fulfillment and release from disappointment, or at the very least an explanation of our disappointment. We are disappointed by the weather, by the clutter of the Negro families' yards, by the church, which is "crazy," flat, perched on the precipice. Rev. Shegog disappoints by his small, wizened features that seem an insufficient vessel for the word of God—the word that is all encompassing, the word that is the world. The three stages of the sermon create tremendous suspense because we are led to believe that something crucial is imminent, as indeed it is. And the suspense maintains its rhythm, as it must, by forward movements blocked by delay. The metaphors themselves delay our hearing of Shegog: the authorial narrative *hides* Shegog's voice even as it describes it, offering instead verbal figures that reify the voice we want to hear. The image of the high-wire walker may delight with its inventiveness, but the reader does not want scenic ingenuity here; the reader wants to *hear* that voice. The pauses between stages delay our progress also, and may be the kind of passage that Barthes tells us is often skipped or read quickly (in the classic narrative) in the drive toward fulfillment of the story's promise, as we are "impel[led] to skim or to skip certain passages . . . in order to get more quickly to the warmer parts of the anecdote (which are always its articulations: whatever furthers the solution of the riddle, the revelation of fate)" (*Pleasure of the Text,* 11).

The suspense ends when the denouement is reached in Shegog's actual words as quoted and thus as heard both by the reader and by the congregation. The immersion into voice, and the lull and peace such immersion provides, turn out to have been the narrative's goal all along. When we enter the dialect passage we cannot read blindly or even too quickly. Shegog's heavy eye dialect is surely a "warmer part of the anecdote" that releases visionary voice by, in part, slowing our reading—even our literally measurable reading speed. And so the disappointment ends when the climactic union of heart and person has been achieved.

I would emphasize here that it is not the content of Shegog's sermon that provides this fulfillment, any more than the particular solution to a mystery provides pleasure. As long as a solution has been provided, the narrative has reached its goal. Critics who deduce a Christian "message" from Dilsey's tears or Shegog's retelling of the Easter story misconstrue the function of voice in this scene (and in much of Faulkner) as a function of communication, when voice truly functions to satisfy and fulfill. The sermon's power is not transferable to the world outside the church or, as an experience of reading, to the rest of the novel's text. Thadious Davis is right that "the church service occurs in isolation," and that we are not told "how the Negro's experience might have meaning or bearing on the white-centered world that is [Faulkner's] subject" (110). But I disagree with her assumption that the service's isolation constitutes a *failure* of "Faulkner's vision," for his "vision" is discoverable in the energetics of voice. Eric Sundquist, in the strongest denigration of the sermon's thematic value, cautions against being "taken in by [the sermon's] pose of cathartic naturalism." This pose leads only to "the eschatological sublime of *Uncle Tom's Cabin,*" which in effect "declar[es] that, Negroes and idiots aside, it is of no real value whatsoever" (12–13). But even if thematically unsatisfying, the rendering of Shegog's voice still exerts "cathartic" force that is not fraudulent. John Matthews sees this force as authorial (if not necessarily authoritative) in that Shegog "complexly figures the role of the author in his work as he strives to deliver the word that will interpret experience truly and establish the communion of speaker and hearer" (108). But, ironically, for this communion to emerge, voice must be turned loose and separated from the author in order to enter the visual discourse of our reading. Whether such a turning loose is as Sundquist calls it "a pose of cathartic naturalism" may matter less to this novel than how the power of voice exerts itself.

Shegog embodies the role that phenomenal voice plays in this process. A soundful world in which voice moves like a presence, like God's voice upon the water, is a world in which the power of communion is efficacious. Although elsewhere Faulkner renders that power less positively, here, in the voice that for Dilsey affirms the tragic beauty of mourning, Faulkner perhaps sought to transcend the limiting dependence of fiction's voices upon vision and to release voice to engender a communion not only beyond the need for words but beyond the site of fiction's written language.

Works Cited

Barthes, Roland. *The Pleasure of the Text.* Trans. Richard Miller. New York: Hill and Wang, 1975.

———. *S/Z.* Trans. Richard Miller. New York: Hill and Wang, 1974.

Blanchard, Margaret. "The Rhetoric of Communion: Voice in *The Sound and the Fury.*" *American Literature* 41 (1970): 555–565.

Bleikasten, André. *The Most Splendid Failure: Faulkner's* The Sound and the Fury. Bloomington: Indiana University Press, 1976.

Brooks, Cleanth. *William Faulkner: The Yoknapatawpha Country.* New Haven: Yale University Press, 1963.

Davis, Thadious M. *Faulkner's "Negro": Art and the Southern Context.* Baton Rouge: Louisiana State University Press, 1983.

Hagopian, John V. "Nihilism in Faulkner's *The Sound and the Fury.*" *Modern Fiction Studies* 13 (1967): 45–55.

Ives, Sumner. "A Theory of Literary Dialect." *Tulane Studies in English* 2 (1950): 137–182.

Matthews, John T. *The Play of Faulkner's Language.* Ithaca: Cornell University Press, 1982.

Rosenberg, Bruce A. "The Oral Quality of Reverend Shegog's Sermon in William Faulkner's *The Sound and the Fury.*" *Literatur in Wissenschaft und Unterricht* 2 (1969): 73–88.

Vickery, Olga W. *The Novels of William Faulkner: A Critical Interpretation.* Baton Rouge: Louisiana University Press, 1959.

ANDRÉ BLEIKASTEN

An Easter Without Resurrection?

Nous sonimes nés pour porter le temps, non pour nous y soustraire.
—Jean-Paul de Dadelsen

The fourth trial

Having, on his own admission, failed to tell his story through the three Compson brothers, Faulkner resolved "to write another section from the outside with an outsider, which was the writer, to tell what had happened on that particular day."[1] But this new extraterritorial voice is neither that of an omniscient narrator nor that of a detached observer.[2] The narrative approach here is one found in many of Faulkner's novels: free and flexible, keenly attentive to what is happening, while engaging at the same time in the process of interpretation. But if what is reported is not left totally unexplained, there is no full elucidation either. Meanings are suggested but never asserted. Faulkner's method is throughout conjectural, and its tentativeness is evidenced by the recurrence of comparative-conditional clauses (introduced by *as if* or *as though*) and words or phrases denoting uncertainty *(seemed, appeared, it might have been).* In this, section 4 differs notably from the preceding ones: in the first section, we were given raw facts and raw emotions without discernible meaning; in the second and even in the third, meanings were so rigidly self-centered constructs as to

The Ink of Melancholy: Faulkner's Novels from The Sound and the Fury *to* Light in August (Bloomington: Indiana University Press, 1990): pp. 125–145.

distort facts altogether; only the last section avoids the extremes of blank factualness and blind fantasizing. The monologue from which it differs least is perhaps Quentin's, insofar as the latter is also quest for meaning, albeit a doomed one; on the other hand, it is the very antithesis of Jason's: the paranoid Jason has ready explanations for everything, and, as we have seen, his explanations all narrow down to murderous prejudice. He is a model of interpretative terrorism, a telling exemplification of massive ignorance and irrational bias parading as truth, and serves therefore as a foil to the outside narrator of the fourth section. Reporting what he sees and hears, and trying to find plausible explanations without twisting the evidence, this narrator seems more trustworthy than any of the Compsons, but Faulkner carefully refrains from establishing him as a source of undisputable authority. His position is in fact very close to the reader's: sharing in the reader's perplexities rather than answering his questions, he enjoys no other privileges than those of his intellectual and imaginative alertness.

A gray dawn

Distance is the reader's major gain. No longer constrained to adopt the narrowly limited viewpoint of an idiot or the distorted vision of a neurotic, we can at last stand back and take in the whole scene. And yet the opening of the fourth section hardly mitigates the oppressive atmosphere of the previous ones. For being broader, the vision seems just as bleak as before:

> The day dawned bleak and chill, a moving wall of gray light out of the northeast which, instead of dissolving into moisture, seemed to disintegrate into minute and venomous particles, like dust that, when Dilsey opened the door of the cabin and emerged, needled laterally into her flesh, precipitating not so much a moisture as a substance partaking of the quality of thin, not quite congealed oil. (306)

Suggesting the close of day rather than its beginning, the grim grayness of this limbo landscape reminds one of the twilight associated with the Quentin section. Nothing here points to the promise of a world born afresh. Space is enclosed and constricted by "a moving wall of gray light"; humidity, hanging ominously in the air, threatens to crumble into an infinity of "minute and venomous particles, like dust," or assumes the repulsive quality of "congealed oil." Disquieting and desolate, and seemingly fraught with evil intent, the landscape here described would indeed not have been out of place in the second section. And not only does it lack the breadth and depth of living space; with no principle of order and cohesion to sustain it, it looks as though its disintegration were close at hand. It might almost stand as an emblem for the novel, materializing the mental and moral falling asunder of the Compsons, and its metaphorical significance is all the more plausible as the same suggestions of noncohesion occur in the portrait one finds a few pages later:

> Luster entered, followed by a big man who appeared to have been shaped of some substance whose particles would not or did not cohere to one another or to the frame which supported it. His skin was dead looking and hairless; dropsical too, he moved with a shambling gait like a trained bear. His hair was pale and fine. It had been brushed smoothly down upon his brow like that of children in daguerrotypes. His eyes were clear, of the pale sweet blue of cornflowers, his thick mouth hung open, drooling a little. (317)

Here comes Benjy, the Idiot, and no reader will fail to recognize him in this lumpish, slobbering giant. His lack of motor coordination recalls his mental debility, his hairless skin and fat body indicate his castrated condition, and his cornflower-blue eyes are reminders of the childish innocence buried within this ungainly mass of adult flesh.

In much the same way the almost caricatural sketches of Jason and Mrs. Compson seem to be just what one would have expected. The physical resemblance between mother and son comes so to speak as a natural extension of their moral affinities:

> When she called for the first time Jason laid his knife and fork down and he and his mother appeared to wait across the table from one another, in identical attitudes; the one cold and shrewd, with close-thatched brown hair curled into two stubborn hooks, one on either side of his forehead like a bartender in caricature, and hazel eyes with black-ringed irises like marbles, the other cold and querulous, with perfectly white hair and eyes pouched and baffled and so dark as to appear to be all pupil or all iris. (323)

The characters so portrayed make for a new sense of reality. Emerging from the claustrophobic ambience of the three brothers' monologues into the common space of the visible, it is as if after *listening* to the voices in the dark, we were suddenly allowed to *see* their owners in broad daylight and to relate each voice to a face and body, and the spectacle is the more startling as what we see strikes us as oddly familiar: the shock which the reader experiences in discovering Benjy or Jason is a shock of recognition.

Of the many changes taking place in the fourth section, this shift from *within* to *without* is the most readily perceptible. But what we have learned through living in the minds of the three brothers comes at once to inform our new mode of perception and to condition our reading. Building on all that precedes it, the reading of the last section is necessarily the "richest," and everything in the text becomes instantly pregnant with significance. All readings of fiction may be said to move from the literal to the symbolic, for as a narrative develops, it is bound to produce meanings which cross-refer and interrelate and combine into complex semantic clusters. In *The Sound and the Fury,* however, this process is deliberately emphasized through Faulkner's fictional strategy: in the first section he maintains the narrative at the most literal level by having the story told by an idiot; in the last, he achieves a maximum of symbolic reverberation by multiplying "objective correlatives" of the distress, disorder, and decay which he had so far been intent on revealing from within.

Easter Sunday begins ironically with a gray dawn, and this gloomy grayness continues almost unabated to the end. When Dilsey appears at her cabin door, she looks at the sky "with an expression at once fatalistic and of a child's astonished disappointment" (307). As a further sinister omen, the air is soon filled with the shrill cries of jaybirds, which southern folklore associates with hell:

> A pair of Jaybirds came up from nowhere, whirled up on the blast like gaudy scraps of cloth or paper and lodged in the mulberries, where they swung in raucous tilt and recover, screaming into the wind that ripped their harsh cries onward and away like scraps of paper or of cloth in turn. Then three more joined them and they swung and tilted in the wrung branches for a time, screaming. (307)[3]

When Dilsey and her family start off for church, the rain has stopped, but the sun is "random and tentative" (335), and when it does manage to shine through, it is so weak that it looks like "a pale scrap of cloth" (332). The countryside around them is desolate as far the eye can see:

> A street turned off at right angles, descending, and became a dirt road. On either hand the land dropped more sharply: a broad flat dotted with small cabins whose weathered roofs were on a level with the crown of the road. They were set in small grassless plots littered with broken things, bricks, planks, crockery, things of a once utilitarian value. What growth there was consisted of rank weeds and the trees were mulberries and locusts and sycamores—trees that partook also of the foul desiccation which surrounded the houses; trees whose very burgeoning seemed to be the sad and stubborn remnant of September, as if even spring had passed them by. . . . (336)

It is indeed a dismal landscape, a "waste land" forgotten by spring, and its barrenness, brokenness, and shabbiness are curiously reminiscent of the squalid suburb of New England where Quentin walked with the little Italian girl on the day of his suicide. And just as in Quentin's monologue, the suspicion arises that this world has been drained of its substance, that it is no more than a mirage poised on the edge of the abyss or a flimsy, deceptive décor masking nothingness:

> The road rose again, to a scene like a painted backdrop. Notched into a cut of red clay crowned with oaks the road appeared to stop short off, like a cut ribbon. Beside it a weathered church lifted its crazy steeple like a painted church, and the whole scene was as flat and without perspective as a painted cardboard set upon the ultimate edge of the flat earth. . . . (337)

In the center of this unreal scenery stands the Compsons' house. As in other Faulkner novels, its fate is closely bound up with that of the family. The splitting up of the land and the gradual shrinking of the estate betoken economic and social decline, and point as well to the breakup of the family group itself, whose sole male survivor is a bachelor without progeny. As to the dilapidation of "the square, paintless house with its rotting portico" (344), it is yet another sign of the destructive work of time, and so even more specifically is the endless ticking of the clock, "the dry pulse of the decaying house itself" (329). Like Sutpen's mansion in *Absalom, Absalom!*, the Compsons' house, once the stately seat of the genos and the emblem of dynastic pride, has become a monument to decay and death. The destinies of the house and its inmates are neatly summed up in the Appendix, where Faulkner refers to "the rotting family in the rotting house."[4]

All these suggestions of disorder and decay should warn us against a hasty "positive" reading of the final section. The traditional symbols of rebirth are ironically reversed: dawn and spring are described in terms of desolation, and the irony is the more pointed as the action takes place on an Easter Sunday. At first glance, then, the tonality of the section is largely consonant with that of the preceding ones, especially with that of Quentin's monologue. The narrator's eye is certainly less distraught than Quentin's; it is the more remarkable that we are confronted again with the same imagery of destruction and exhaustion.

Counterpoint

Are we to infer that Quentin's vision of despair possesses more general validity than we originally assumed? The conclusion seems warranted by the general "atmosphere" of the fourth section. There is one notable exception, however: the Easter service episode, whose function and significance we have not yet examined. On the other hand, the reader's spontaneous response to imagery and atmosphere is certainly no reliable starting point for a full critical assessment. Yet, if one turns to structure, one apparently reaches very similar conclusions. Thus one critic contends that "a structural analysis of the closing chapter of *The Sound and the Fury* does, in fact, reveal nihilism as the meaning of the whole."[5] Section 4 consists of four distinct narrative units. It begins with a prologue, going from dawn to about 9:30 A.M. and focusing successively on Dilsey (306–320), Jason (320–329), Benjy and Luster (329–332). The three scenes of the prologue foreshadow in order the three more extended narrative sequences on which the novel ends. The first of these sequences (from 9:30 A.M. to 1:30 P.M. deals with Dilsey's departure for church, the Easter service, and her return home (332–348); the second sequence (chronologically parallel to the first) links up with section 3 and relates Jason's pursuit of Miss Quentin and the carnival man (348–363); the third and last sequence is centered upon Benjy's and Luster's trip to the cemetery, and ends with the incident near the monument to the Confederate Soldier (363–371). However brief, this outline of the section's narrative structure allows one to dispel one or two misconceptions: it establishes irrefutably that Dilsey is not the focal figure throughout and that the narrative of the Easter service does not occupy the whole section. With a writer so deeply concerned with the architectonics of fiction, meaning cannot lie dissociated from form, and in a novel like *The Sound and the Fury* the internal patterning of each section is surely as significant as the ordering of the four sections within the book.

Thus the counterpointing of the Easter service and of Jason's futile pursuit of his niece is obviously deliberate. As elsewhere, the montage of parallel actions allows Faulkner to weave a network of identities and differences. Their simultaneity, indicated at the outset by the morning bells tolling at Dilsey's departure (332) as well as at Jason's (348), is repeatedly recalled by references back and forth from one sequence to the other.[6] Through this temporal parallelism the contrasts are made the more conspicuous: the black people walk to the church in almost ritual procession, "with slow sabbath deliberation" (337), while Jason is driving to the carnival (a profane travesty of a religious festival) with increasingly frantic haste. The first sequence is marked by a sense of peaceful social communication (illustrated by the exchange of greetings between Dilsey and her friends, 336), and, at church, by religious communion (340); the second emphasizes Jason's extreme isolation: alone in pursuit, alone in defeat. Similarly, Dilsey's humble piety, shared by the black community, is set over against Jason's sacrilegious pride as he defies divine power itself in his Satanic rage (354). Lastly, while the celebration of the Resurrection of Christ brings the promise of eternal life to the faithful, Jason's "passion" ends appropriately in a grotesque parody of death ("So this is how it'll end, and he believed he was about to die," 359).

The Easter service follows a slowly ascending curve culminating in Reverend Shegog's visionary sermon; Jason's tribulations, on the other hand, evoke a furious and farcical dive to disaster. The antithesis is worked out in the smallest details, and from a Christian point of view it is indeed tempting to read it as the opposition between Satan's wretched fall and the glorious Resurrection of Christ. Yet at this point it is important to remember that the Jason sequence comes *after* the paschal episode. True, in the last section Jason no longer appears as formidable as before, and the failure of his chase gives us for once the satisfaction of seeing the forces of evil beating a retreat. Everything suggests, however, that the rout is only temporary and that Jason has lost nothing of his power to harm. And the very order of the episodes tips the balance in Jason's favor: the chase sequence reestablishes Jason in the leading role, even though it ends in his punishment, and so throws us back into the sordid, hate-filled atmosphere of the third section.

Returns

This regressive movement is pursued to the novel's close. From Jason the focus shifts to Benjy; coming full circle, the final pages carry us back to the beginning. Here again, as in the opening section, is Benjy with his guardian Luster. Once more, moaning and whimpering, he squats before his private "graveyard," the small mound of earth with its empty blue bottle and its withered stalk of jimsonweed (364); once more, clinging to the fence, he watches the movements of the golfers (365). Even Caddy's ghost reappears, summoned by Luster's perverse whispering of her name to Benjy (365), and the latter immediately starts bellowing, only to be assuaged by Caddy's satin slipper, "yellow now, and cracked, and soiled" (366).

As for the very last scene, Benjy and Luster's trip by horse and surrey to the town cemetery, it was likewise anticipated in the first section. Yet this time the funeral excursion does not follow its customary route. We first get a glimpse of Benjy almost restored to tranquility, "his eyes serene and ineffable" (369), clutching his broken narcissus stalk.[7] Yet when, after reaching the Confederate statue in the town square, Luster turns the horse to the left instead of the accustomed right, Benjy once again begins to roar in agony. But then Jason looms up, back from Mottson and seemingly resurrected in all his avenging fury, to reestablish the order violated by Luster's swerve:

> With a backhanded blow he hurled Luster aside and caught the reins and sawed Queenie about and doubled the reins back and slashed her across the hips. He cut her again and again, into

> a plunging gallop, while Benjy's hoarse agony roared about them, and swung her about to the right of the monument. Then he struck Luster over the head with his fist. (371)

Finding at last an opportunity to vent his anger and frustration, Jason brutalizes the old mare and lashes out at Luster. He even strikes Benjy, whose flower stalk is broken again. Yet order is indeed reestablished, and in the last sentence of the novel, Benjy's world seems to have recovered its balance:

> The broken flower drooped over Ben's fist and his eyes were empty and blue and serene again as cornice and façade flowed smoothly once more from left to right; post and tree, window and doorway, and signboard, each in its ordered place. (371)

Order is restored, but it is as empty as Benjy's idiotic stare or the petrified gaze of the Confederate Soldier (370). It brings to mind the endings of all the earlier sections: the smooth flow of things recalls the "smooth, bright shapes" signaling Benjy's falling asleep, and in its utter meaninglessness the close of the novel also recalls the ultimate absurdity of Quentin's fussy funeral toilette in section 2 and the demented dream closing Jason's monologue in section 3. And what makes the scene so memorable is not so much the final glimpse of peace regained as the ironic effect of contrast resulting from its juxtaposition with Jason's outburst of violence. The title of the book is given here a further illustration, the most startling perhaps in its harsh stridence, and also the most literally accurate: with Benjy's wild howling—"Just sound"—and Jason's unleashed rage, there is indeed nothing left of the Compson world but "sound and fury."

In terms of plot, this ending is no ending at all. The final scene with Jason and Benjy puts an arbitrary stop to the action; it does not bring the expected dénouement. No dramatic resolution, whether tragic or comic, is provided; the tensions built up in the course of the narration are left undiminished, and the novel's complexities and ambiguities are as baffling as ever. Thematically, however, the scene is a powerful and poignant echo of the violence and disorder we have been witnessing all along, a condensed representation of all that has been presented before.[8]

The cry and the rhetoric

As in so much of modern fiction, the knots are not untied, the threads not unraveled. Our bafflement at the novel's close is not unlike Benjy's sense of outrage and disorder. All we can do is to return to the beginning and attempt another reading of the book—with little hope ever to find out its supposed secret. Yet the impossibility—for author and reader alike—of reaching a safe conclusion does not imply the absence of all closure. *The Sound and the Fury* is open-ended as far as plot is concerned, and it is inconclusive in its meaning. But this does not prevent it from achieving an aesthetic integrity of its own.

Formal closure should not be confused with semantic closure, and in the present case the former even seems to have been achieved in some measure at the cost of the latter. In traditional fiction endings are pointers to a fixed rationale, outside the text, in the light of which its contradictions are eventually resolved; in *The Sound and the Fury* the ending refers us back to the text itself, that is, to a tissue, a web of words, in which meanings are held in abeyance.

It is therefore wrong to assume that the closure of the final episode with Benjy "shapes the ultimate meaning of the novel"[9] and that this meaning is an authorial corroboration of Mr. Compson's nihilistic pronouncements in the second section. If structure *is* meaning, meaning does not arise from structure alone. The examination of the last section must therefore be taken further: it is not enough to isolate the broad units of the narrative and to see how their ordering inflects significance; it is indispensable as well to scrutinize the finer mesh of the section's texture.

The shift in style is certainly one of the most arresting features of section 4. Free of the restrictions of the interior monologue, Faulkner now seems to speak in his own person, and a richer, denser, more ceremonious style comes to unfold. Previously held in check or fraught with ironic intent, Faulkner's rhetoric now bursts into full flower. Not that it dominates the whole section, but it infuses the prose of the narrative with new energies, and projects a very different light upon the various actors of the drama. Consider, for example, the portrait of Dilsey in the two opening pages:

> The gown fell gauntly from her shoulders, across her fallen breasts, then tightened upon her paunch and fell again, ballooning a little above the nether garments which she would remove layer by layer as the spring accomplished and the warm days, in colour regal and moribund. She had been a big woman once but now her skeleton rose, draped loosely in unpadded skin that tightened again upon a paunch almost dropsical, as though muscle and tissue had been courage or fortitude which the days or the years had consumed until only the indomitable skeleton was left rising like a ruin or a landmark above the somnolent and impervious guts, and above that the collapsed face that gave the impression of the bones themselves being outside the flesh, lifted into the driving day with an expression at once fatalistic and of a child's astonished disappointment, until she turned and entered the house again and closed the door. (306–307)

The portrait cruelly emphasizes Dilsey's deformity and decrepitude, and multiplies the signs of impending death: with her fallen breasts and her dropsical paunch, the old black woman—a mere skeleton wrapped in a skin-bag—appears here as a grim *memento mori*. Yet, solemnized by the abstract magnificence of the epithets (most of which are ponderous polysyllabic Latinisms) and expanded by the suggestive power of the similes, the description goes well beyond the demands of realism, and far from degrading Dilsey to a macabre scarecrow, it raises her to tragic dignity. Dressed in "regal" color—a "dress of purple silk" and a "maroon velvet cape" (306)[10]—she is lent from the outset an aura of majesty which belies the wretchedness of her ravaged, age-worn body. The servant, the descendant of slaves is turned into a sovereign figure. A queen of no visible kingdom, a queen dispossessed and "moribund" but whose "indomitable" skeleton rises in the gray light of an inauspicious dawn as a challenge to death—a paradoxical symbol of that which transcends mortal flesh and triumphs over time, of that which "endures."[11] And similarly ennobled and embellished by the baroque "coruscations" of Faulkner's eloquence, Dilsey's tears become the essence of universal grief: "Two tears slid down her fallen cheeks, in and out of the myriad coruscations of immolation and abnegation and time" (341).

Benjy likewise appears in a different light. The figure of the idiot had gradually faded from the scene; now he comes right to the forefront again, not only in the closing scene but also at the beginning of the section and in the episode in the Negro church. What is perhaps most remarkable about Benjy in the final section is that his presence there is predominantly vocal: apart from the startling visual description we are given at his first appearance, he is more often heard than seen. His cries and whining—made haunting through the repetition of "crying," "wailing," "whimpering," "slobbering," "bellowing"—supply what might be called the basic soundtrack of the section. Never articulated as speech, scarcely human, Benjy's cries are the abject and pathetic expression of his nameless and unnameable suffering:

> Then Ben wailed again, hopeless and prolonged. It was nothing. Just sound. It might have been all time and injustice and sorrow become vocal for an instant by a conjunction of planets. (333)

> But he bellowed slowly, abjectly, without tears; the grave hopeless sound of all voiceless misery under the sun. (366)

> There was more than astonishment in it, it was horror; shock; agony eyeless, tongueless; just sound. . . . (370)

These passages are reminders of Benjy's intense and inarticulate suffering, but in a sense they also suggest the writer's paradoxical gamble in the very act of creation. Indicative of a double deprivation—the absence of happiness and the absence of speech—Benjy's helpless cries convey lack by lack, and in the text this state of extreme dispossession is forcibly emphasized by the recurrence of privative suffixes. Benjy's cries fail to say what he failed to preserve; they are the burning language of absence and the blind eloquence of the absurd. They are nothing: "just sound." This nothing, though, encompasses "all time and injustice and sorrow," "all voiceless misery under the sun." But is this conjunction of nothing and everything not to be found too in what seems to be at the very antipodes of the cry, that is, literature? And is not the voicing of the voiceless, the naming of the nameless also the deepest desire of the writer? Language at its most ambitious refers dialectically back to the inarticulateness of the cry: it is its negation in that it relies on the signifying powers of the word, while being also its completion insofar as it manages to recapture the immediate pathos of the cry. Not that all literature nurses this ambition, but *The Sound and the Fury* is surely a case in point, and may be considered Faulkner's most daring attempt to come as close as possible to that which is both revealed and silenced in the "eyeless" and "tongueless" agony of the cry. It was of course an impossible wager: to keep it was to lose it. For in the pregnant silence of the printed page the cry is no longer a cry; Benjy's whimperings and bellowings, by being named, are absorbed into the mute eloquence of written discourse and appropriated by literature, which turns them into symbols of its own impotence, of its own vanity.

The cry and the rhetoric. From one the novel moves to the other, and the very ordonnance of the book may be said to reflect this movement of reappropriation. The first section is in its extreme confusion the closest approximation to the "voiceless misery" of the cry; the last, where literature reasserts its claims and the writer reestablishes his authority, is seemingly the furthest from it. Yet Faulkner's rhetoric in the final section attempts to preserve something of the primal urgency of the cry, and in a way reverts to it, making it "vocal for an instant" by a conjunction of words. Moreover, this rhetoric obviously gains strength and persuasiveness from coming after Benjy's "sound," Quentin's *cri du coeur,* and Jason's "fury." Far from describing arabesques in the void, it traces them on soil already prepared. When Dilsey and Benjy reappear in the fourth section, they have already gathered so much weight and substance that their metamorphosis into archetypes of endurance and suffering does not strike us as arbitrary allegorizing.

A simple heart

From the particulars of limited individual experience the last section moves toward the universality of the mythic. Without ceasing to be a slobbering idiot, Benjy comes to stand for crucified innocence in the context of the Easter service at the Negro church; the man-child becomes an analogon of Christ. But the character in which the fusion of realism and symbolism is most successfully achieved is without any doubt Dilsey. Even though her function has often been misunderstood or overemphasized, there can be no question that she is the most memorable character in the last section. Technically, the point of view is not hers, and in dramatic terms her role is a limited one. Yet critics should not be blamed too roundly for attributing the last section to her; even Faulkner called it "the Dilsey section."[12] The one truly admirable character in the novel, she had a special place in the writer's affections: "Dilsey is one of my favorite characters, because she is brave, courageous, generous, gentle, honest. She is much more brave and honest and generous than me."[13] She is no less admirable as a literary creation. Her portrait is so sharply individualized and her figure so warm and earthy that the charge of excessive idealization is hardly relevant. As Cleanth Brooks has rightly noted, Dilsey is "no noble savage and no *schöne Seele.*"[14] Nor should she be reduced to a racial stereotype. True, she seems to fit rather nicely in the tradition of the black mammy, and her literary lineage is readily traced back to Thomas Nelson Page.[15] However, the point is that her virtues, as they are presented in the novel, owe nothing to race.[16]

That she was meant to counterbalance the Compsons is obvious enough. Her words and actions offer throughout an eloquent contrast to the behavior of her masters. In her role of faithful—though not submissive—servant, Dilsey represents the sole force for order and stability in the Compson household.[17] Not only does she see with tireless diligence and devotion to the family's material needs; she also tries, albeit with little success, to stave off the day of its disintegration. Taking on the responsibilities traditionally assumed by the mother, she comes to replace the lamentable Mrs. Compson as keeper of the house. In the later sections, she appears as Benjy's last resort,[18] and she also defends Caddy and her daughter against Jason, the usurper of paternal authority.

In the face of the whining or heinous egoism of the Compsons, Dilsey embodies the generosity of total selflessness; in contrast to Quentin's tortured idealism and Jason's sordid pragmatism, she also represents the active wisdom of simple hearts. Without fostering the slightest illusion about her exploiters, expecting no gratitude for her devotion, Dilsey accepts the world as it is, while striving as best she can to make it somewhat more habitable. Unlike the Compsons, she does not abdicate before reality nor does she refuse time, which she alone is capable of gauging and interpreting correctly:

> On the wall above a cupboard, invisible save at night, by lamp light and even then evincing an enigmatic profundity because it had but

> one hand, a cabinet clock ticked, then with a preliminary sound as if it cleared its throat, struck five times.
>
> "Eight oclock," Dilsey said.... (316–317)

In his rage against time, Quentin tore off the hands of his watch. The Compsons' old kitchen clock has but one hand left and its chime is out of order. Yet Dilsey does not take offense at its "lying" and automatically corrects its errors. To her, time is no matter of obsession. Not that she adjusts to it out of mere habit. Her time is not simply a "natural" phenomenon, any more than her moral qualities are "natural" virtues. Faulkner describes her as a Christian, and no analysis of the character can afford to discount the deep religious convictions attributed to her. Hers is a seemingly naive piety, a simple faith unencumbered by theological subtleties, but it gives her the courage to be and persevere which her masters lack, and provides her existence with a definite meaning and purpose. Dilsey envisions everything in the light of the threefold mystery of the Incarnation, Passion, and Resurrection of Christ. In Benjy she sees "de Lawd's chile" (367), one of the poor in spirit promised the Kingdom of God, and for her all human suffering is justified and redeemed in the divine sacrifice commemorated during Holy Week.

Dilsey's attitude toward time proceeds quite logically from the tenets of her Christian faith. Whereas for Quentin, the incurable idealist, time is the hell of immanence, it is transfused with eternity for Dilsey. Not "a tale full of sound and fury signifying nothing," but the history of God's people. The Christ of her belief has not been "worn away by the minute clicking of little wheels" (87); his crucifixion was not a victory by time but a victory over time. Guaranteed in the past by the death and resurrection of the Son of God and in the future by the promise of His return, bounded by the Passion and the Second Coming, time regains a meaning and a direction, and each man's existence becomes again the free and responsible adventure of an individual destiny. Dilsey's Christ-centered faith allows her to adhere fully to all of time's dimensions: her answer to the past is fidelity; the present she endures with patience and humility, and armed with the theological virtue of hope, she is also able to face the future without alarm. While for Quentin there is an unbridgeable gap between the temporal and the timeless, Dilsey's eternity, instead of being an immobile splendor *above* the flux of time, is already present and at work *in* time, embodied in it just as the word was made flesh. Time, then, is no longer felt as endless and senseless repetition; nor is it experienced as an inexorable process of decay. It does have a pattern, since history has been informed from its beginnings by God's design. And it can be redeemed and vanquished, but, as T. S. Eliot puts it in the *Four Quartets,* "Only through time time is conquered."[19] Which is to say that the hour of its final defeat will be the hour of its fulfillment and reabsorption into eternity.

Firmly rooted in the eschatological doctrine of Christianity, Dilsey's concept of time is theo-logical and teleo-logical, not chrono-logical. The assumptions on which it rests remain of course implicit, but it is in this orthodoxly Christian perspective that we are asked to interpret Dilsey's comment after Reverend Shegog's sermon: "I've seed de first en de last. . . . I seed de beginnin, en now I sees de endin" (344; see also 348). Given the context of Easter in which they occur, her words obviously refer to the beginning and end of time, to the Alpha and Omega of Christ. But it goes without saying that they apply as well to the downfall of the Compsons which Dilsey has been witnessing all along. The implication is certainly not that after all the Compsons may be saved, but what the oblique connection between the Passion Week and the family tragedy suggests is that for Dilsey the drama of the Compsons is above all one of redemption denied.

Black Easter

Yet what the Compson story means to Dilsey is not necessarily what it means to us, nor what it was meant to mean. At this point the impossibility of any final interpretation becomes obvious again. For how are we to take the many references to Christianity included in the novel? And how do they relate to this story of decline and death? One may argue that Faulkner's use of them is ironical, that they point—derisively or nostalgically—to a vanishing myth and expose its total irrelevance as far as the Compsons are concerned. Or one may interpret them in terms of paradox, the more legitimately so, it seems, as paradox has been a major mode of Judeo-Christian thought and is indeed central to Christian faith itself. According to whether irony or paradox is taken to be the clue to Faulkner's intentions, diametrically opposed interpretations of the novel will suggest themselves to the reader. But the question is one of effects rather than intentions, and it is extremely difficult to settle, since paradox and irony alike work by way of inversion.

Inversion is one of Faulkner's favorite techniques. In *The Sound and the Fury* its procedures can be traced in many places, but nowhere perhaps are they as consistently and as intriguingly used as in the episode of the Easter service.[20] With regard to the rest of the novel (and more directly to the juxtaposed Jason sequence), the episode fulfills a contrasting function homologous to that of Dilsey in relation to the other characters. And the contrast is so sharp and so unexpected that the reader is jolted into a radically different mood. It is as if a spring of pure water suddenly welled up in an arid desert, or as if the dismal clamor of the accursed family were momentarily suspended to let us listen to a gospel song. But the episode is no less surprising in the detail of its composition and the movement of its development, both of which owe a good deal of their impact to Faulkner's handling of inversion. The sequence opens rather inauspiciously with the description of the desolate setting of Dilsey's walk to the church (335–336): nothing yet heralds the upsurge of Easter joy. A sense of expectancy is soon created, however, by the gathered congregation impatiently awaiting "dat big preacher" (335) from St. Louis. But when he at last arrives, he turns out to be a shabby, monkey-faced gnome:

> when they saw the man who had preceded their minister enter the pulpit still ahead of him an indescribable sound went up, a sigh, a sound of astonishment and disappointment.
>
> The visitor was undersized, in a shabby alpaca coat. He had a wizened black face like a small, aged monkey. And all the while that the choir sang again and while the six children rose and sang in thin, frightened, tuneless whispers, they watched the insignificant looking man sitting dwarfed and countrified by the minister's imposing bulk, with something like consternation. (338–339)

The frustration, though, is turned into starry-eyed wonderment when the preacher begins his sermon:

> His voice was level and cold. It sounded too big to have come from him and they listened at first through curiosity, as they would have to a monkey talking. They began to watch him as they would a man on a tight rope. They even forgot his insignificant appearance in the virtuosity with which he ran and poised and swooped upon the cold inflectionless wire of his voice, so that at last, when with a sort of swooping glide he came to rest again beside the reading desk with one arm resting upon it at shoulder height and his monkey body as reft of all motion as a mummy or an emptied vessel, the congregation sighed as if it waked from a collective dream and moved a little in its seats. (339)

Belying the shabbiness and grotesqueness of his physical appearance, Reverend Shegog displays the mesmerizing talents of a brilliant orator. But there is more to come: a second, even more stunning metamorphosis occurs when the cold virtuosity of the "white" sermon suddenly bursts into the incantatory vehemence of "black" eloquence:

> Then a voice said, "Brethren."
>
> The preacher had not moved. His arm lay yet across the desk, and he still held that pose while the voice died in sonorous echoes between the walls. It was as different as day and dark from his former tone, with a sad, timbrous quality like an alto horn, sinking

> into their hearts and speaking there again when it had ceased in fading and cumulate echoes. (340)

This is the moment of the decisive reversal: the preacher is no longer master of his rhetoric, nor is he anymore master of his voice. Instead of being the flexible instrument of his eloquence, the voice, "a voice"—having seemingly acquired a will of its own—now seizes his body and uses it as its tool. The tightrope artist has vanished; Shegog has become the docile servant of the Word:

> He was like a worn small rock whelmed by the successive waves of his voice. With his body he seemed to feed the voice that, succubus like, had fleshed its teeth in him. And the congregation seemed to watch with its own eyes while the voice consumed him, until he was nothing and they were nothing and there was not even a voice but instead their hearts were speaking to one another in chanting measures beyond the need for words. . . . (340)

The consuming voice not only reduces the preacher to a mere medium of the Easter message; it reaches out toward the congregation and, delving into the innermost recesses of souls, unites them in a wordless chant of communion. The orderly discourse of cold reason, significantly associated with the facile tricks of "a white man" (339), has given way to the spontaneous language of the heart, a language moving paradoxically toward its own extinction as it resolves itself into "chanting measures beyond the need for words." All that "white" rhetoric could achieve was "a collective dream" (339); what is accomplished now is a truly collective experience, a welding of many into one. For the first time in the novel, separation and fragmentation are at least temporarily transcended; consciousness, instead of narrowing down to private fantasy and obsession, is expanded through the ritual reenactment of myth. In this unique instant of grace and ecstasy, all human misery is miraculously transfigured, all infirmities are forgotten, and the preacher's puny silhouette rises before the faithful like a living replica of the crucified God: "his monkey face lifted and his whole attitude that of a serene, tortured crucifix that transcended its shabbiness and insignificance and made it of no moment" (340–341).

The sermon

The reader is now prepared to *listen* to the sermon itself, to its sounds and rhythms, as the congregation listens. Again there will be surprises, ruptures, reversals, but the dominant mood is at present one of trust and exaltation, any remaining doubts being swept away by the intimate certainty of redemption: "I got de ricklickshun en de blood of de Lamb" (341). Yet the sermon begins on a plaintive note, faintly recalling Quentin's obsessions with time and death: "Dey passed away in Egypt, de swinging chariots; de generations passed oway. Wus a rich man: whar he now, O breddren? Wus a po man: whar he now, O sistuhn?" (341). There follows a breathless evocation of the persecuted childhood of Christ: "Breddren! Look at dem little chillen setting dar. Jesus wus like dat once. He mammy suffered de glory en de pangs. Sometime maybe she helt him at de nightfall, whilst de angels singin him to sleep; maybe she look out de do en see de Roman po-lice passin" (342). Jesus here becomes the paradigm for martyred innocence, and the relevance of this paradigm to present circumstances is poignantly emphasized by the implicit reference to Benjy, the innocent idiot, sitting amid the black community, "rapt in his sweet blue gaze" (343).

The legendary and the actual, the past and the present are thus not only contrasted, but significantly linked. Myth infuses reality: projected into an immemorial past, Benjy and Dilsey are transformed into archetypal figures through their identification with Christ and the Madonna. Conversely, the remote events of the Passion are brought back to life again and quiver pathetic immediacy in the compelling vision of the preacher:

> "I sees hit, breddren! I sees hit! Sees de blastin, blindin sight! I sees Calvary, wid de sacred trees, sees de thief en de murderer en de least of dese; I hears de boasting en de braggin: Ef you be Jesus, lif up yo tree en walk! I hears de wailing of women en de evenin lamentations; I hear de weepin en de cryin en de turnt-away face of God: dey done kilt Jesus; dey done kilt my Son!" (342–343)

With the death of Christ, the sermon reaches its nadir. The preacher now witnesses the seemingly absolute triumph of Evil, and his vision becomes one of utter chaos and destruction: "I sees de whelmin flood roll between; I sees de darkness en de death everlastin upon de generations" (343). Yet this note of despair (again reminiscent of the Quentin section) is not sustained, and immediately after everything is reversed by the miracle of the Resurrection. Shadows disperse, death is forever conquered in the glory of the Second Coming:

> "I sees de resurrection en de light; sees de meek Jesus sayin Dey kilt Me dat ye shall live again; I died dat dem whut sees en believes shall never die. Breddren, O breddren! I sees de doom crack en hears de golden horns shoutin down de glory, en de arisen dead whut got de blood en de ricklickshun of de Lamb!" (343)

Although Reverend Shegog's Easter sermon only occupies a few pages in the novel, it looms very large. And while it is true that it would carry even greater weight if Faulkner had chosen to place it at the novel's close, its impact is greater than a purely structural analysis of the fourth section would lead one to expect. Literary meanings and effects are differential, to be sure, but to assess them correctly is not enough to see how they are "placed" within the text; it is also important to measure the amplitude of the differences. For the singularity here is not only one of subject and theme, nor does it merely arise from a tonal switch. A radical reversal occurs, operating on all possible levels and altering the very fiber of the novel's texture. As the narrator's own preliminary comments suggest, another *voice* takes over, which is not that of any speaker in the novel, nor that of the narrator/author—a voice enigmatically self-generated and mysteriously compelling, *the subjectless voice of myth.*

Another language is heard, unprecedented in the novel, signaled at once by the cultural-ethnic shift from "white" to "black," the emotional shift from rational coldness to spiritual fervor, and lastly by the stylistic shift from the mechanical cadences of shallow rhetoric to the entrancing rhythms of inspired speech. Not that this new language dispenses with formal devices: Shegog's sermon, so far from being an uncontrolled outpouring of emotion, is very firmly patterned and makes extensive use of rhetorical emphasis (questions and exclamations) as well as of such classical procedures as parallelism and incremental repetition (most conspicuous in the abundance of anaphoric constructions). The sermon is the ritual retelling of a mythic story fully known by all the members of the congregation: its narrative contents form a fixed sequence, and the mode of its transmission conforms likewise to a stable code. What needs to be stressed, too, is that the specific tradition to which this speech belongs is the folk tradition—well-established, particularly, in African-American culture of the *oral* sermon.[21] Ritualized as it is, the preacher's eloquence is the eloquence of the spoken word, and Shegog's sermon reads indeed like the transcript of an oral performance. The effect is partly achieved through the faithful phonetic rendering of the black dialect. Yet Faulkner's greatest success is that he has also managed to capture the musical quality of the sermon: the "sad, timbrous quality like an alto horn, sinking into their hearts and speaking there again when it had ceased in fading and cumulate echoes" (340). More than anything else it is this musicality (i.e., that which, in his speech, belongs to another, nonverbal language) that ensures true communication between the speaker and the listeners, and among the audience itself. Myth and music cooperate in this Easter celebration to free all participants from "the need for words" as well as from the tyranny of time. Is it not precisely in their relation to time that music and myth are alike? As Claude Lévi-Strauss has noted, "it is as if music and mythology needed time only to deny it. Both, indeed, are instruments for the obliteration of time."[22]

What matters here is not so much the message conveyed as the collective ceremony of its utterance and its sharing, a ceremony allowing at once personal identity to be transcended and cultural identity to be confirmed. In contrast to the painful and derisory remembrances of the Compsons, the *commemoration* of the mythic event by the black community appears to be a victory over solitude.

The mythic word

Shegog's Easter sermon may be called a triumph of Faulkner's verbal virtuosity. It is noteworthy, however, that this *tour de force* was achieved through a gesture of humility. For the novelist refrained from improving on the tradition of the oral sermon as he found it. There is no literary embellishment, and there is hardly a personal touch one might attribute to the author. Silegog's sermon has been compared with records of sermons actually delivered: the difference between the latter and Faulkner's creation is barely noticeable.[23] Which is to say that, strictly speaking, it is no creation at all, but only evidence of Faulkner's extraordinary mimetic abilities. The writer here lays no claim to artistic originality, and his self-effacement is carried to such lengths that his own voice is no longer heard. Instead we are *truly* listening to the anonymous voice of an unwritten tradition, grown out of ancient roots and periodically revivified by the rites of popular piety—a voice, that is, whose authority owes nothing to the talents of an author. From *auctor* the writer has become *scriptor,* a modest scrivener scrupulously transcribing a prior text.

This is what makes the sermon a unique moment in the novel: it marks the intrusion of the spoken into the written, of the nonliterary into the literary, of the mythic into the fictional, and by the same token it also signals the writer's willing renunciation of his authorial pride and of his prerogatives as a fiction-maker (or, to put it in Heideggerian terms, his capacity to *be spoken* rather than to speak). It becomes tempting, then, to see the preacher-figure as a double of the novelist himself: do not both surrender their identity as speakers/writers to become the vehicles of an impersonal mythic voice?

Given the importance accorded to the biblical text and to the living word in the Christian—and especially in the Puritan—tradition, it is of course hardly surprising that a writer with Faulkner's background should have been fascinated with the voice of myth. In the register of the imaginary, myth is in the novel's last section what fantasy is to the prior ones. Much like fantasy, myth is a creation of human desire negating time and death. However, as long as myth remains an object of collective belief periodically reactivated by ritual, it also fulfills a gathering function and testifies to the permanence of a shared culture. Hence the novel invokes as a last resort traditional mythic values and ritual practices, and finds them in a community in which their sacred aura has been, to all appearances, fully preserved.

Religion is *religio,* what binds man to man, man to God. The novel's last section is clearly haunted by nostalgia for religion as a binding power, but also as a way of seeing if not of knowing. The voice that takes hold of the preacher induces a vision, and this moment of vision, fully shared by the congregation, is in fact the only experience of spiritual enlightenment recorded in the whole book. Illumination or illusion? In Faulkner's text, at any rate, this capacity for vision is set against the chronic blindness of the Compsons.[24] Both Dilsey and Shegog *see,* and their vision is apparently one that goes beyond the confines of time and flesh; it brings order and significance to their lives and gives them the strength to endure pain and loss. To Dilsey, in particular, the preacher's words bring the encompassing revelation of eternity, the mystical and prophetic vision of "the beginning and the ending."

Is this to say that they embody Faulkner's novelistic "vision," and that the Easter service at the Negro church provides the key to the novel's interpretation? For those who read *The Sound and the Fury* from theological premises, there is no doubt about the answer. Comparing the sermon in Faulkner's novel to the legend of the Grand Inquisitor in *The Brothers Karamazov* or to Father Mapple's sermon in *Moby-Dick,* they do not hesitate to invest it with the same central hermeneutic function: "it tells us the meaning of the various signs and symbols as on a geographical map; it tells us how to read the drama, how to interpret the characters of the plot that has been unfolding before us."[25] From there to calling *The Sound and the Fury* a Christian novel is a short step. It is one step too many, however, for although there is much to suggest such an interpretation, there is little, in the last resort, to validate it. Faulkner's work is misread as soon as it is *arrested,* and critics go astray whenever they seek to reduce its intricate web of ambiguities to a single pattern of meaning. *The Sound and the Fury* stubbornly resists any attempt to dissolve its opaqueness into the reassuring clarity of an ideological statement.

That Faulkner's fiction is heavily indebted to the Christian tradition is beyond question, and the writer himself, in his interviews, freely acknowledged the debt.[26] But it is essential to relate it to the specific context of the novelist's creation: to Faulkner, Christianity was first of all an inexhaustible fund of cultural references, a treasure of images and symbols or, to borrow one of his own favorite words, an extremely useful collection of "tools." This, of course, does not settle the question of his relationship to Christianity. There is surely more than a mere craftsman's debt: myth is both the bad conscience and the utopia of Western fiction, and for Faulkner as for many other modern novelists, the Christian myth remains an ever-present paradigm, an ordering scheme, a pattern of intelligibility toward which his fiction never ceases to move as toward a lost horizon of truth, or rather *through* which it is moving to produce its own myths. Faulkner's quest and questioning remain to a very large extent caught up in Christian modes of thought and expression, as can be even more plainly seen in later works such as *Go Down, Moses, Requiem for a Nun,* and *A Fable.* Yet Faulkner's life-long involvement with Christianity entailed no personal commitment to Christian faith, and none of his public pronouncements substantiates the claim that he considered himself a Christian writer. Besides, even if Faulkner had been an avowed believer, the relationship of his work to Christianity would still be problematical, for insofar as it is literature, it displaces the myths on which it feeds. Aspiring to turn fictions into myths, it is fated to turn myths into fictions.

The success of failure

"A work of literature," says Roland Barthes, "or at least of the kind that is normally considered by the critics (and this itself may be a possible definition of 'good' literature) is neither ever quite meaningless (mysterious or 'inspired') nor ever quite clear; it is, so to speak, *suspended* meaning; it offers itself to the reader as a declared system of significances, but as a signified object it eludes his grasp. This kind of *dis-appointment* or *deception* . . . inherent in the meaning explains how it is that a work of literature has such power to ask questions of the world . . . without, however, supplying any answer."[27] Faulkner's fiction fully bears out Barthes's assumptions. The wealth of Christian allusions we find in *The Sound and the Fury* adds immeasurably to its semantic pregnancy, but in the last analysis Christian values are neither affirmed nor denied. Episodes such as the Easter service and figures such as Dilsey are impressive evidence of Faulkner's deep understanding of Christianity, and they seem to hint at possibilities of experience which the ego-bound Compsons have irremediably lost. Yet, as Cleanth Brooks rightly notes, "Faulkner makes no claim for Dilsey's version of Christianity one way or the other. His presentation of it is moving and credible, but moving and credible only as an aspect of Dilsey's own mental and emotional life."[28] The reader's "disappointment" in this respect is all the greater as Faulkner's novel often *seems* to imply the existence of sizable significances: his ironies do suggest a radically negative vision, and his paradoxes bring us very close indeed to the spirit of Christianity. However, the point about Faulkner's ironies and paradoxes is that they are irreducibly *his.* Etymologically, irony implies dissembling, or feigned ignorance, and paradox refers likewise to a hidden truth. If these classical definitions are retained, Faulkner's inversions are neither ironies nor paradoxes: they are not disguised affirmations but statements of uncertainty and modes of questioning.

So the final leap is never made, nor should it be attempted by the reader. Shall we then agree with those critics to whom *The Sound and the Fury* is simply an ingenious montage of contrasting perspectives, a brilliant exercise in ambiguity? To pose the question in these terms is again to miss the point. Those who think that the novel should have a determinable sense and deplore its inconclusiveness are just as mistaken as those who assume that it has one and therefore refuse to acknowledge its indeterminacies. Both approaches fail to acknowledge the specificity of literary discourse and disregard the very impetus of Faulkner's writing. For far from being inert antinomies, its contradictions generate a field of dynamic tension and are in fact what sets his books in motion. The tension is not solved, nor can it be, but this irresolution is to be imputed neither to an incapacity to make up one's mind nor to a masochistic pursuit of failure. No more than to a Christian or a nihilistic statement should *The Sound and the Fury* be reduced to a neutral balancing of contrary views.

To Faulkner the choice was not between affirmation and denial, sense or nonsense, so much as between writing and silence. As soon as words get written, meanings are produced, that is, are both brought forth and exhibited, and the elaborately deceptive uses of language characteristic of literary discourse, far from canceling significance, open up its infinite possibilities. It is true that in their different ways modern and postmodern novelists such as Beckett, Blanchot, and Robbe-Grillet (not to mention the posterity of Rimbaud among poets) have done their utmost to rarefy meaning, to bring literature as close as possible to the condition of silence, and in one sense to do so is every writer's hope. Faulkner, however, was in no way a minimalist. His literary ancestors are to be sought among the more robust of the great nineteenth-century masters, and if we relate him to his contemporaries or quasi-contemporaries, he is clearly closer to the omnivorous Joyce than to the almost anorexic Beckett. His drive was toward more and more, not less and less. And like Joyce, Faulkner pursued his quest in the teeth of absurdity. "Prendre sens dans l'insensé,"[29]—to make sense of and in the senseless, to take up one's quarters where absurdity is at its thickest, is how Paul Eluard defined the function of modern literature. The definition also applies to Faulkner's design, and nowhere perhaps is this design more in evidence than in the final section of *The Sound and the Fury.* While the novel's tensions are there raised to an almost unbearable pitch, the shrill irony of its ending leaves them forever unresolved

Yet simultaneously a countermovement develops, away from absurdity toward some tentative ordering. Faulkner's rhetoric here is both at its most ambitious and at its most humble: at its most ambitious when it gathers its energies to reassert the powers of language and the authority of the writer; at its most humble when it effaces itself behind the sacred eloquence of an Easter sermon and yields to the anonymous authority of the myth. It is most significant, too, that in this section Faulkner's inversions so often take on the colors of paradox. Given their cultural context, these paradoxes seem to call for a Christian interpretation, but one may wonder whether they do not all refer back to the central paradox of the writer's own endeavor. For the writing process also tends to operate a radical inversion of signs; it too draws strength from its weakness and glories in its want. As we have seen, Shegog, the frail vessel of the sovereign Word, may be taken for an analogon of the novelist himself, reaching the point of inspired dispossession where his individuality gives way to the "voice." And the mystical vision granted to the preacher may likewise be said to metaphorize the unmediated vision sought after by the writer. What these analogies seem to point to is the mirage of an ultimate reversal: that which would restore the absolute presence of language to itself and convert its emptiness into plenitude, its fragmentation into wholeness—fiction raised to mythos, speech raised to logos.

It is of course an impossible dream: the quest is never completed, the reversal forever postponed. There is no denouement, no final unknotting. The last section does not provide the hoped-for perspective from which the dissonant earlier sections could be seen as parts of a coherent and understandable whole. It only introduces us to another, less solipsistic "world," juxtaposed to the worlds of Benjy, Quentin, and Jason but incapable of holding them together. Yet even though the gap between language and meaning is always there, as readers we insist—cannot but insist, as we do with all works of art we wish to understand and make our own—that what falls apart only seems to do so and actually falls together. The illusion cannot be dispelled that the writing process has managed to create an order of its own, assigning each word and sentence to "its ordered place." And it is not just an illusion; there is indeed an order, or rather an ordering, generated out of the very vacuum of language and the very emptiness of desire. The text of *The Sound and Fury,* does hold together, and achieves admirable integrity as an aesthetic design. And while the furious and helpless voices of the Compson brothers exhaust themselves in utter solitude, the patterned incompleteness of *The Sound and the Fury* waits for readers and requires their active participation. Not that they can succeed where the author failed. But if their reading of the novel is not mindless consumption (which it can hardly be), they, too, will take part in the unending process of its production. Reading and rereading the book, they will write it again.

Notes

1. *LG,* p. 147. See also p. 245 and *FU,* p. 32.

2. See Margaret Blanchard, "The Rhetoric of Communion: Voice in *The Sound and the Fury,*" *American Literature,* 41 (January 1970), 555–565.

3. That Faulkner knew about the meaning of jaybirds in folklore is attested a few pages later, when Luster throws a rock at the birds, shouting "Git on back to hell, whar you belong at" (311). See Charles D. Peavy, "Faulkner's Use of Folklore in *The Sound and the Fury,*" 442–443.

4. "Appendix," p. 421. In *The Mansion* we are told that a few years later Benjy set fire to the house and burned to death in it. These facts are not consistent with the information provided in the "Appendix." Benjy's death and the destruction of the house by fire are obviously afterthoughts, probably suggested to Faulkner by the similarities between the Compson story and that of the Sutpens.

5. John V. Hagopian, "Nihilism in Faulkner's *The Sound and the Fury*," *Modern Fiction Studies*, 13 (Spring 1967), 46.

6. On leaving Jefferson, Jason thinks that "every damn one of them will be at church" (353); Dilsey, back in the house, "[enters] a pervading reek of camphor" in Mrs. Compson's room (345), while Jason misses the camphor that would relieve his headache (363). Lastly, at one o'clock, Dilsey tells Luster and Benjy that Jason will not be home for dinner (348); the latter, at the same moment, is leaving Mottson, where people are "turning peacefully into houses and Sunday dinners" (363).

7. According to Faulkner, "The narcissus was given to Benjy to distract his attention. It was simply a flower which happened to be handy that 5th of April. It was not deliberate" (*LG*, p. 246). Whether deliberate or not, this flower is an apt emblem for the self-centered Compsons. Lawrence E. Bowling, on the other hand, reminds us that beyond its roots in Greek mythology "the narcissus has also a Christian tradition, for it is the flower which in the Bible is called 'the rose' and is identified with Jesus (Isaiah 35:1, Song of Songs 2:1). Thus the narcissus, like Benjy himself, symbolizes not only the world's selfishness but also its need for love. The association of Benjy's narcissus with the Savior is made more specific and significant by the fact that the flower has been broken twice, the two breaks symbolizing the two crucifixions: the first by the ancient world and the second by the modern world," "Faulkner and the Theme of Innocence," *Kenyon Review*, 20 (Summer 1958), 485–486.

Given the novel's thematics, it seems equally relevant to call attention to the etymological link between *narcissus* and *narcotic*. The ancients knew about the soporific deathlike effect of the flower and used it for the adornment of tombs. The association of the narcissus with death is also evident in the story of Demeter and Persephone. The Homeric Hymn to Demeter establishes a close connection between the narcissus and the rape of Persephone by having Hades use the beauty and fragrance of the flower to lure her into the underworld. In Quentin's allusion to Euboelus (170), there was already in implicit reference to the rape of Persephone, the mythical equivalent of the abduction of Caddy by Dalton Ames.

Lastly, the flowers associated with Benjy could be read as images of his mutilated manhood. Like jimson weed, the narcissus may be another inverted phallic symbol, the more plausibly so as it belongs in the category of *broken* things, references to which are particularly numerous in sections 1 and 2, that is, where castration is at stake. It appears, moreover, that all of Benjy's objects and playthings represent and compensate losses, whether they are phallic substitutes like the flowers or, in D. W. Winnicot's phrase, "transitional objects" (i.e., substitutes for the mother's breast) like the cushion. The most obviously symbolic of these objects is the soiled satin slipper, a reminder of Caddy and her wedding but also a classic sexual fetish—which sends us back again to the pervasive issue of castration.

8. As Beverly Gross notes, "the ending of *The Sound and the Fury* is a significant and suggestive reflection on the novel as a whole. It concludes not an action, but the enactment of a process; the novel ends not with an ending, but with

an unforgettable epitome of itself." See "Form and Fulfillment in *The Sound and the Fury*," *Modern Language Quarterly*, 29 (December 1968), 449.

9. Hagopian, "Nihilism in *The Sound and the Fury*," 47.

10. Purple and maroon are royal colors, but in the Christian tradition purple is also a liturgic color (associated with Advent, Lent, and Good Friday) and the color of martyrdom. The terrestrial symbolism of purple, with its suggestions of sacrificial suffering, mourning, and penitence, is contrasted with the celestial symbolism of blue. When Dilsey later reemerges from her cabin, she is dressed in blue gingham. In medieval color codification blue was the color of chastity and therefore of the Virgin; in the novel, it also stands for Benjy's innocence. In the episode of the Easter service the symbolic equation of Dilsey with the Virgin and of Benjy with Christ is repeatedly suggested (342–344).

11. In this the portrait of Dilsey announces the tribute that Faulkner was later to pay to her and to her kin: "They endured" ("Appendix," p. 427).

12. See letter to Malcolm Cowley, *SL*, p. 202.

13. *LG*, pp. 244–245. An early casting of Dilsey is to be found in "The Devil Beats His Wife," a story Faulkner began after his return from Europe in December 1925 but never completed. A number of critics assume that Dilsey was modeled on Caroline Barr, the "mammy" of the Faulkner family to whose memory *Go Down, Moses* was dedicated thirteen years later. The resemblances, however, are rather tenuous. Molly, Lucas Beauchamp's wife in *Go Down, Moses*, comes much closer to being a portrait of Caroline Barr.

14. Brooks, *The Yoknapatawpha Country*, p. 343.

15. See George E. Kent's sharply critical assessment of Faulkner's "mammies" "The Black Woman in Faulkner's Works, with the Exclusion of Dilsey," part II, *Phylon*, 36 (March 1975), 55–67.

16. This is not to say that there is no significant contrast between whites and blacks. Some of Quentin's observations aptly summarize the function of blacks in the novel: "a nigger is not a person so much as a form of behaviour; a sort of obverse reflection of the white people he lives among" (98); "They come into white people's lives like that in sudden sharp black trickles that isolate white facts for an instant in unarguable truth like under a microscope" (195). Dilsey and, to a lesser degree, her husband, her children, and grandchildren testify to the virtues which Ike McCaslin attributes to blacks in *Go Down, Moses:* endurance, pity, tolerance, fidelity, love of children (see *GDM*, p. 295). In the younger generation of the Gibsons, however, these virtues seem to be less developed than among their elders, as can be seen, for example, from Luster's occasional cruelty toward Benjy. And there is nothing to suggest that the Negroes are morally superior to the whites because they belong to a different race. Dilsey, with her customary clear-sightedness, tells her grandson Luster that he is just as fallible as his white masters: "Lemme tell you somethin, nigger boy, you got jes es much Compson devilment in you es any of em" (319). Faulkner's treatment of blacks in *The Sound and the Fury*, albeit not free of stereotypes, is never tritely sentimental, testifying to a tact and intelligence seldom found among white southern novelists. But, though the contrast between the white family and the black community provides an oblique comment upon the downfall of the Compsons, racial relationships are not central in *The Sound and the Fury* as they are in *Light in August, Absalom, Absalom!, Go Down, Moses,* and *Intruder in the Dust.*

17. In his interviews Faulkner stressed the principle of cohesion represented by Dilsey in the Compson household. See *FU*, p. 5, and *LG*, p. 126.

18. Dilsey's solicitude for Benjy is already emphasized in the first section. She is the only one to remember his thirty-third birthday and to celebrate it with a cake she buys with her own money. The manuscript of the novel includes no reference to Benjy's birthday—an indication that in revising the section Faulkner felt the need to provide further illustration of Dilsey's kindness and so to prepare the reader for the full revelation of her personality in section 4. See Emily K. Izsak, "The Manuscript of *The Sound and the Fury:* The Revisions in the First Section," *Studies in Bibliography,* Bibliographical Society, University of Virginia, 20 (1967), 189–202.

19. T. S. Eliot, *Collected Poems, 1909–1962* (New York: Harcourt, 1963), p. 178.

20. See Victor Strandberg, "Faulkner's Poor Parson and the Technique of Inversion," *Sewanee Review,* 73 (Spring 1965), 181–190.

21. On Faulkner's indebtedness to the tradition of the oral sermon, see Bruce A. Rosenberg, "The Oral Quality of Reverend Shegog's Sermon in William Faulkner's *The Sound and the Fury,*" *Literatur in Wissenschaft und Unterricht,* 2 (1969), 73–88.

22. Claude Lévi-Strauss, *The Raw and the Cooked,* trans. John and Doreen Weightman (New York: Harper & Row, 1969), pp. 15–16.

23. See Rosenberg, "The Oral Quality of Reverend Shegog's Sermon."

24. References to empty eyes or troubled vision abound: the "blurred" eye of the jeweler (95), Caddy's eyes "like the eyes in the statues blank and unseeing and serene" (187), Benjy's vacant gaze (369, 370), not to mention the empty eyes of the Confederate soldier (370). The picture of the eye on page 360 also points to the importance of the motif of seeing/not seeing.

25. Gabriel Vahanian, *Wait without Idols* (New York: George Braziller, 1964), p. 111. See also Amos N. Wilder, "Faulkner and Vestigial Moralities," *Theology and Modern Literature* (Cambridge, Mass.: Harvard University Press, 1958), pp. 113–131.

26. See *FU,* pp. 86, 117; *LG,* pp. 246–247.

27. Roland Barthes, "Criticism as Language," *Times Literary Supplement* (September 27, 1963), 739–740; translated from "Qu'est-ce que la critique?" *Essais critiques* (Paris: Editions du Seuil, 1964), pp. 256–257.

28. Brooks, *The Yoknapatawpha Country,* p. 348.

29. Paul Eluard, *Poési Ininterrompue* (Paris: Gallimard, 1946), p. 32.

Works Cited

Faulkner in the University, Frederick L. Gwynn and Joseph L. Blotner, editors, Charlottesville: University Press of Virginia, 1959.

Go Down, Moses. New York: Random House, 1942.

Lion in the Garden: Interviews with William Faulkner 1926–1962, James B. Meriwether and Michael Millgate, editors. New York: Random House, 1968.

Faulkner, William. *The Mansion.* New York: Random House, 1959.

———. *The Sound and the Fury.* New York: Jonathan Cape and Harrison Smith, 1929; Vintage, 1987.

———. *Selected Letters of William Faulkner.* Edited by Joseph Blotner. New York: Random House, 1977.

PHILIP WEINSTEIN

"If I Could Say Mother": Construing the Unsayable About Faulknerian Maternity

My title sounds insistently psychoanalytic, promising to uncover the covered-up, to find the key that will unlock the mystery and reveal its hitherto concealed treasure. This game of penetrating/mastering is itself distinctly phallic: there must be a better way to pursue the mother. I concede at the outset that I cannot say the Unsayable about Faulknerian maternity, that my argument bears most directly on the brilliantly disturbed novels between *Flags in the Dust* and *Light in August,* and that the text I shall examine at length—the source of the quotation in the title—is *The Sound and the Fury.* Faulkner's rendering of Mrs. Compson is, within the representational economy of that novel, uniquely punitive. I intend to identify the discursive model that underlies that rendering, then to reconceive the model, drawing on some contemporary feminist criticism, and finally return to Mrs. Compson. At the end I shall suggest ways in which Faulkner's texts of this troubled period are trying to say Mother and how they are succeeding.[1]

"If I could say Mother" recurs twice in Quentin's section of *The Sound and the Fury,* and in each case the phrase arises out of the memory of an April 1910 conversation between Herbert Head and Mrs. Compson:

> What a pity you had no brother or sister *No sister no sister had no sister.* Dont ask Quentin he and Mr Compson both feel a little

---

Faulkner's Subject: A Cosmos No One Owns (Cambridge: Cambridge University Press, 1992): pp. 29–39.

> insulted when I am strong enough to come down to the table I am going on nerve now I'll pay for it after it's all over and you have taken my little daughter away from me *My little sister had no. If I could say Mother. Mother*
>
> Unless I do what I am tempted to and take you instead I dont think Mr Compson could overtake the car.
>
> Ah Herbert Candace do you hear that *She wouldn't look at me soft stubborn jaw-angle not back-looking* You needn't be jealous though it's just an old woman he's flattering a grown married daughter I cant believe it.
>
> Nonsense you look like a girl you are lots younger than Candace color in your cheeks like a girl A *face reproachful tearful an odor of camphor and of tears a voice weeping steadily and softly beyond the twilit door the twilight-colored smell of honeysuckle.* (108)

In the second passage, near the end of Quentin's section, the smell of gasoline on his shirt reevokes this same scene of Herbert and the car, and it concludes with *"if I'd just had a mother so I could say Mother Mother"* (197).

Quentin's arresting phrase of abandonment is embedded, both times, in the context of Mrs. Compson's own fantasy return of adolescence. As she flirts with Herbert, drawing on the social model she used to know, that of the Southern belle, her son registers her maternal absence from his life. "Color in your cheeks like a girl A *face reproachful tearful an odor of camphor and of tears*": these are the only roles Mrs. Compson can play—premarital coquetry or postmaternal grief. Her abandonment of her children emerges here as saturated in the rituals and assumptions of her own virginal past. Between her childless adolescence and her child-complicated middle age no other viable script has become available to her. Between virginal flirtation and postmaternal complaint Mrs. Compson literally has nothing else to say.

As though to emphasize the alienation of her married state, the text rarely pairs her with her husband. Faulkner often has Benjy's first memories of Mrs. Compson join her instead with Uncle Maury. The novel signals recurrently that the man most on her mind, the man she uses as a shield between herself and her husband, is Uncle Maury. In this textual sense he vies with Mr. Compson for the position of husband. (One might argue that her textual husband is her son Jason, with whom she maintains a peculiarly intense relationship. In this regard they echo Gerald Bland and his mother, also an oddly incestuous pairing in which the titular husband has been conveniently removed.)[2] In either case Mr. Compson himself is arguably the third male in his wife's life. Appearing most saliently in Quentin's chapter, he registers textually more as his son's father than as his wife's husband.

Her brother Maury seems to serve as her way of remaining a Bascomb, of refusing to consummate her entry into Compsonhood. (My discovery at the Faulkner and Yoknapatawpha Conference in 1986 that Faulkner's family pronounces Maury as Murry, the name of Faulkner's father, may strengthen this fantasy conflation of the mother's brother with the mother's husband.)[3] Incestuous pairings thus suggest themselves at the parental level as well, and Mrs. Compson's preference for her brother leads with compelling logic to Quentin's preference for his sister. Refusing to be a wife, Caroline Bascomb refuses to be a mother, and Caddy must therefore—and fatally—play that role for her brothers.

The picture of Mrs. Compson that emerges is of a woman whose life ceased to be narratable after her entry into marriage and its sexual consequences. She has no stories to tell that can accommodate in a positive way even a grain of her postconsummation experience. Her entry into mature sexuality is swiftly followed by her exit. Having delivered her children, she takes to her bed—the childbed, not the marriage bed—acting like a child, exacting from her children the sustenance she should be offering them.[4]

She speaks obsessively of the rules she learned before marriage, and of her refusal to learn anything different since:

> "Yes," Mother says. "I suppose women who stay shut up like I do have no idea what goes on in this town."
>
> "Yes," I [Jason] says, "They don't."
>
> "My life has been so different from that." Mother says. "Thank God I dont know about such wickedness. I dont even want to know about it. I'm not like most people." (299)

I am still a virgin, her camphor and tears keep saying: I don't know anything about checks, about report cards, about business deals, about what girls do on the street or within their own bedrooms. Weeping and mourning, ritually heading for the cemetery throughout the novel, she registers her marital and maternal experience as a curse that makes a mockery of all her training: "when I was a girl I was unfortunate I was only a Bascomb I was taught that there is no halfway ground that a woman is either a lady or not" (118).

This rigid either-or posture indicates that it is Mrs. Compson, not her husband, who is possessed by the binarisms of the Symbolic order—but possessed by them as only someone locked into Imaginary identifications and repudiations can be. Despite John Irwin and other critics who fault Mr. Compson for not upholding paternal authority, his considerable appeal resides in his shrewd perception that a Symbolic order based upon traditional notions of morality and virginity is bankrupt, that it is an invented script.[5] He relates to this order as a produced structure, not an inalterable essence, whereas his wife would live it as the Real itself. She thus incarnates what Roland Barthes terms the cultural code, the already known: "If we collect all such knowledge, all such vulgarisms, we create a monster, and this monster is ideology," Barthes writes (*SIZ* 97). Mrs. Compson is such an ideological monster.

We touch here upon the source of her failure as a mother. Deformed by her social training—a training shaped by class and race to the requirements of virginity—she abandons her own flesh and blood upon the loss of that virginity. She has outlived her image of herself. Simultaneously rushing forward to death and backward to childhood, she repeats herself and takes to black. The novel's attack upon her seems to be this: mothers are meant to nourish their young; their trucking with (male-authored) ideological scripts can only lead to overlectured and undernurtured offspring.[6]

This paradigm of ideological insistences perverting maternal function may shed light on that strange scene in which Jason wrestles with his mother over the key to Quentin's room. Noel Polk has pointed to the repression wrought into this image of the key-laden woman ("Dungeon" 61–93), but there is a sexual dimension to the assault as well. Faulkner takes a full page to show us Jason all over his mother, "pawing" at her skirt, while she resists the attack. Finally, "'Give me the key, you old fool!' Jason cried suddenly. From her pocket he tugged a huge bunch of rusted keys on an iron ring like a mediaeval Jailer's" (325). Pawed at, pressed, her invaded pocket reveals its cache of hideous keys like a grotesque parody of the children who should instead have come forth from her womb. And indeed her womb is terrifying—a space imaged here as rusted, iron, a jailor's fortress, as was also earlier implied by Quentin's image of the dark place in which he was imprisoned: "The dungeon was Mother herself" (198).

No child escapes from this dungeon, and insofar as the dungeon is a womb, no child gets fully born. In place of nourishment she feeds her children repressive ideology, and they sicken on it. From Mrs. Compson's failure to mother we move through her daughter Caddy's failure to mother and finally, reductively, into *her* daughter Quentin's refusal to conceive. "Agnes Mabel Becky," the phrase spoken by the man in the red tie upon seeing that shiny container connected with Quentin, is the term used half a century ago in the South for a three-pack of condoms.[7] Mrs. Compson's inability to nourish here literalizes into her granddaughter's well-earned decision to seal off the reproductive functions of her womb.

Noel Polk helps us to generalize the model that Mrs. Compson fails abysmally to uphold. He writes of Faulkner's mothers of this period as "almost invariably, horrible people," failing to meet "even minimal standards of human decency, much less . . . the ideal of mother love as the epitome of selfless, unwavering care and concern" ("Dungeon" 66). "Selfless, unwavering care and concern": this is exactly what these mothers lack. It is also what they are posited by the culture as *supposed to possess,* and what they are excoriated for not possessing. Freud writes in his study of Leonardo: "A mother's love for the infant she suckles and cares for is something far more profound than her later affection for the growing child. It is in the nature of a completely satisfying love-relation" (*Standard* 11:117). Freud assumes, as does Faulkner, that, unlike fathers (unlike all other human beings), mothers enjoy "a completely satisfying love-relation." They *naturally* fulfill their identity in this bond with the infant. Mothers are defined as just those creatures whose subjective needs are supremely realized through the act of nurturing their own offspring.

Freed from ideology themselves, reservoirs of milk and loving kindness, mothers are meant to be sacred servants. *The Sound and the Fury* hammers this point home in the fourth chapter through the massive comparison, move for move, of Mrs. Compson with Dilsey, the latter a perfect instance of how mothers should care for offspring. And what is Dilsey's model if not the Virgin Mary herself, celebrated in the Reverend Shegog's sermon as Jesus' inexhaustibly loving "mammy [who] suffered de glory en de pangs," who "helt him at de nightfall, whilst de angels singin him to sleep," and who filled heaven with "de weepin en de lamentation" (342) at his death? This model of what a mother is supposed to do resonates throughout not just *The Sound and the Fury* but countless narratives in Western culture.

Such a model assumes that the Word—the realm of spirit, of the Symbolic—is articulated through a male voice, announcing the Kingdom of Heaven. Mary serves as the bodily carrier of the spirit. Her function is to nurse her infant son and to bemoan his tragic death. She emerges thus—in her role as the suffering mother, the ubiquitous Pieta of Western art—as a register for the emotional loss suffered through Christ's crucifixion. She herself has no new word to utter, but her natural care for her child is the precondition for his divine utterance in which he reveals his kinship with his father.

If we secularize this text, we arrive at something like the following. The domain of the father is the domain of the Spirit, of all Symbolic activities that make up culture and that achieve articulation in the medium of language. This domain takes the inherently binary form of language, an endless series of constructed oppositions that constitute the (male) paradigm of meaning itself. The domain of the mother, on the other hand, is the domain of the unfissured, prelinguistic body. Her function is to nourish the child that he (the model for the child is implicitly male) becomes somatically prepared for the vertigo and alienation that accompany entry into the Symbolic order of the father. In other words, the time of bonding exists as a prelinguistic, prelogical plenitude in which mother and child are each other, in which self and world, self and other, interpenetrate. If successful, this quasi-magical bonding bequeaths to the child somatic sufficiency—bodily grounding—that enables him to sustain his later and lifelong encounter with the world outside himself, and eventually to deliver his word within that world.

The gender distinctions essential to this paradigm are common to the discourses of both Christianity and psychoanalysis. The mother is simultaneously sacred and subservient, the enabler but not the speaker of the word. If we return to Faulkner with this script in mind, we can better place the anger toward the mother that suffuses the early novels. In those novels the mother fails at her sacred bodily task. Charged with pre-oedipal responsibilities, she not only neglects these but barges into the terrain of the law, often in its most outdated and repressive forms. The unnourished child therefore emerges into the world too soon. He has no somatic grounding that might hold the imprint of the culture's proliferating codes, consequently no basis for stabilizing the *"maelstrom of unbearable reality"* (*AA* 186). Thus we get Benjy, Quentin, Darl, Vardaman, and Joe Christmas: boy children unsure of the integrity of their own bodies, dizzyingly vulnerable to sensory overload, unable to maintain their identity within boundaries that might stabilize the relations between past and present, there and here, self and other, male and female, child and parent, brother and sister, white and black.

French and American feminists seem to agree that this male-scripted model of the nonspeaking mother is disabling rather than empowering. In "Stabat Mater" Julia Kristeva critically explores the myth of the Virgin Mary. Focusing on the iconography of breast, ears, and tears, Kristeva reads the Virgin as a figure of speechless succor. One of Kristeva's commentators, Mary Jacobus, writes:

> The function of the Virgin Mother in Western symbolic economy (according to Kristeva) is to provide an anchor for the nonverbal and for modes of signification closer to primary processes. In the face of the fascinated fear of the powerlessness of language which sustains all belief, the Mother is a necessary pendant to the Word in Christian theology—just as the fantasized preverbal mother is a means of attempting to heal the split in language, providing an image of individual signs, plenitude, and imaginary fulness. (169)

This subtext of the ideal mother as sanctuary, as preverbal plenitude, as pendant to the word and yet also a preserve against its possible emptiness, exerts a powerful punitive influence upon the representation of women in secular texts, including (as we have seen) Faulkner's texts. Kristeva, for her part, is in the difficult position of seeking to maintain the centrality of the pre-oedipal bonding without fictishizing it or making it immune to stress. Jacobus goes on to say that "for Kristeva, division is the condition of all signifying processes. No pre-oedipal language, no maternal discourse, can be free of this split." Kristeva enacts this split in her essay by inserting another discourse (this one fragmented, impulsive, lyrically focused on childbirth, breastfeeding, and body parts—what she calls the "semiotic") within the surrounding "Symbolic" portion of her text.[8]

The entry of the "semiotic" into the discourse of maternity would both restore the place of the maternal body within language itself and announce that the mother's desire is, like all desire, conflicted and tension-filled, rather than speechlessly satisfied through the suckling of her son. Thus Kristeva would revise the male-coded scripting of maternal desire—what she punningly calls "pèreversion." These feminist revisions (in their insistence that women's desire exceeds male scripts for maternity, that women's desire must find a way into language, that maternity must be demythologized and approached from the perspective of the mother herself) allow us to see how gender biases in that previous script polarize Faulkner's representational strategies.

• • •

Let us now return to Mrs. Compson. What we see is a portrait of maternity crazily arrested in the "virginal" phase of the Virgin Mary model. Of the three divine components—succor, silence, and virginity—she has betrayed the two that Faulkner values and retained the one that he deconstructs. The ideal silent nourisher has degenerated into a non-nourishing nonstop talker. More, the language that pours out of her is wholly male-scripted; she speaks the defective Symbolic order at its most repressive.

Her white middle-class culture insists not merely that her desire be contained within mothering purposes. Rather, given the American South of the early twentieth century with its array of racial phobias and its constraining model of white womanhood, her desire is virtually taboo.[9] Enjoined to marry and procreate, Mrs. Compson is also enjoined to abhor her status as an incarnate creature replete with sexual organs. She may now appear to us more clearly what she is—a socially constructed figure— taught by her culture in such a way as to be unable to survive her own sexual initiation. The only story she has learned is a virginal one, and on this she dwells, within this she hides from the unbearable facts of her own parturition: a son whose idiocy indicts the very fertilization of egg by sperm; a daughter whose burgeoning sexuality promises, at best, the same disaster she has undergone; another son whose needs she did not (could not) assuage, and who punished her for it by committing suicide; and a third son whose fantasy name of Bascomb assures her that he is hers alone: no Compson seed in him, she is still a virgin.

Why has her adoption of the virginal script kept her from also participating in the nurturance script? Why does the tension (always latent) between these two "stories" become so inflamed in Faulkner's narratives? To answer this, we might look at Faulkner's representation of the female body in *The Sound and the Fury*. In so doing we discover that the other story for Mrs. Compson, the nurturance story, is simply intolerable in its fetishistic focus on the body and its linkage of fecundity with filth. The polarization of these two narratives reveals the suffocating binarism of the culture's texts of female maturation:

> Because women so delicate so mysterious Father said. Delicate equilibrium of periodical filth between two moons balanced. Moons he said full and yellow as harvest moons her hips thighs. Outside outside of them always but. Yellow. Feet soles with walking like. Then know that some man that all those mysterious and imperious concealed. With all that inside of them shapes an outward suavity waiting for a touch to. Liquid putrefaction like drowned things floating like pale rubber flabbily filled getting the odor of honeysuckle all mixed up. (*SF* 147)

If the virginal story presupposes a blank body (a body, as Luce Irigaray puts it, that is "pure exchange value . . . nothing but the possibility, the place, the sign of relations between men" [181, translation mine]), the body that Quentin fantasizes here is unbearably full, though no less constructed through a male lens. (How telling that Mr. rather than Mrs. Compson speaks to Quentin of menstruation.) This "delicate" body is more urgently imagined as huge, moonlike (moons that sway the blood tides, moons that are her hips and thighs), filled with liquid rot, spaces that you desire to enter and in which you drown. This is a disaster site. It is also a female womb. A place of periodical filth, this womb is obsessively scripted within an economy of decay: what could grow here? The mother's threat seems most to inhere in her leaky and fluctuating wetness, a female wetness that menaces all projects of male enclosure and mastery.

Luce Irigaray has written suggestively of the male hostility to fluidity: "La mecanique des fluides," in Ce *Sexe qui n'en pas* un), and Jane Gallop discusses her argument as follows: "Fluidity has its own properties. It is not an inadequacy in relation to solidity. In phallic fantasy, the solid-closed-virginal body is opened with violence; and blood flows. The fluid here signifies defloration, wound as proof of penetration, breaking and entering, property damage. . . . [But] menstrual blood is not a wound in the closure of the body; the menstrual flow ignores the distinction virgin/deflowered" (*Daughter* 83). Most of Faulkner's males recoil in horror from this female economy of the blood. *Sanctuary* and *Light in August* are concerned with male-induced penetrations of the body. The blood their male protagonists focus on is the blood they can make flow, the blood whose flowing signals male mastery of the object. Or it is the symbolic "blood" of patriarchal lineage or racial difference, not the material blood that simultaneously— and so troublingly to the male mind—carries growth and decay.[10]

A "dry" virginal script that denies desire and repudiates intercourse, a "wet" adulterate script that concedes desire and equates the fertile womb with rot and drowning: there are no other alternatives in *The Sound and the Fury*'s lexicon for constructing maternity. "I was taught that there was no halfway ground that a woman is either a lady or not" (118). In Mrs. Compson's desiccated Symbolic world, ladies and sex organs are incompatible notions. This polarization means that, here and elsewhere, Faulkner's narrative treatment of white maternity takes a schizoid form.

On one side there is the "wet" drama— always illicit, always for not-ladies—of a sexed and rebellious younger woman heading toward unsanctioned labor (Caddy, Dewey Dell, Lena, to a certain extent Temple, Charlotte, and Eula). This drama, suffused with narrative empathy, focuses intimately upon the scandal of the penetrated and/or swelling body itself. Faulkner seems mesmerized by the image of the female body escaping the propriety of its male proprietor, usually the husband/father/brother who would confine its activity within the scripts of the Symbolic order. Because that order is (and needs to be shown as) without grounding, this drama is usually narrated with understanding. But the mothers-to-be in this drama are mute; they are mainly subsumed within their own bodies. When, later (as with Temple and Eula), Faulkner does endow them with speech, they have become defenders—often tragic defenders—of the Symbolic. It seems that they cannot simultaneously break the law and speak.

On the other side, there is the "dry" retrospective drama within which are imprisoned the proper wives, the repressed older women heading toward menopause or death. Mrs. Compson, Joanna Burden in her final phase, and of course Addie Bundren— a case unto herself— come to mind.[11] In general Faulkner cannot keep his narrative eye on the same woman moving through all the stages of the female life cycle. (Addie and Joanna cross into and out of sexual activity at the expense, so to speak, of their lives.) Maternity is thus a sort of narrative Waterloo: an incoherent zone his fiction can lead up to and away from but which none of his women can traverse and still remain themselves. Is it too much to say that once his pregnant women *deliver,* they cease to be figures of empathy or desire, for he has then entered the fantasy role of their infant needing succor? In any case, the representation of maternity ruptures on this incoherence.

With these constricting representational scripts in mind, I conclude by returning to Mrs. Compson's plight. As the quotation in my title indicates, we see her—Faulkner sees her—only through the freighted and damaged lenses of her offspring. (Indeed, psychoanalytic discourse itself, and a fortiori its commentary on the mother, has centered until recently upon the [male] child in need. What treatment the mother has received has tended to come very sharply angled.) This narrative deprivation of sympathy is decisive. Yet Mrs. Compson's gestures, when attended to against the grain of the text itself, have their pathos. Her refusal to accede to the name of Compson, for example, is heavily marked as vanity or regression, though we might also see it as a desperate attempt to preserve a shred of her own identity from the marital exchange that alters her name from that of one male to that of another. (If she were a male being exchanged, if she were Joe Christmas or Charles Etienne de St. Valery Bon, we would be invited so to read her.) Behind her tyranny within the house—she who changes others' names as though in revenge for the unwanted alteration of her own—we can espy a woman with no other moves to make.

"It is our duty to shield her [your lady mother] from the crass material world as much as possible" (258), Uncle Maury writes Jason: shield her while we men invest her money in the real world of business affairs. Jason, for his part, plays the check-burning ritual upon her once a month. Men know better, they are permitted to discard when necessary the unreal rhetoric of honor (the no longer valid terms of the Symbolic). Mrs. Compson may also, at rare moments, know better—"If you want me to, I will smother my pride and accept them [the checks from Caddy]" (252)—but she remains imprisoned within her learned rhetoric, forced to believe she is repudiating her daughter's money. Born and brought up within defective male Symbolic scripts, she spends each day dying within those same scripts. "The dungeon was Mother herself," Quentin thinks; his mother is the jailor. Yes, she is the jailor, but she is also the jail and the inmate. Alienated from the powers of her own body, deprived by male scripts of any language of access to her bodily desires, she is the prisoner of her own womb. The dungeon is not mother but motherhood.[12]

• • •

I have sought to indicate the ways in which Faulkner's representational strategies cannot say mother. Let me finish by suggesting that the fiction of this troubled period is nevertheless engaged, paradoxically, in "trying to say" Mother. "I was trying to say," Benjy tells us, and Faulkner invents an extraordinary rhetoric to convey to us the tangled torment of Benjy's "say." What American writer has refused more forcefully the blandishments of the "already said"? Although Faulkner never spoke of it as the Symbolic order, although he never thought of language as decisively marked by gender, although he would certainly have cringed at neologisms like phallogocentrism, in a certain sense he knew. He knew that language is the Symbolic, that it comes to us alienated from our speechless feeling, and that if words are to do more than be a shape to fill a lack, they must be tortuously reinvented, recombined, such that the "self" they articulate may appear in its incarnate, de-centered, and insecurely gendered pathos. And he would have agreed with poststructuralists that, even in his most ambitious undertakings, he failed to make the words (which "go straight up in a thin line," *AILD* 160) ever cling to the earth.

What he created in his most experimental early work seems to me analogous to Kristeva's "semiotic": a use of language that gets behind the crisp and repressed male structures of the Symbolic, and that is seeking (in its gaps and incoherencies) to make its way back to the mother. Radically nonjudgmental, open to the confusions of past and present, self and other, Faulkner's experimental rhetoric enacts so often (within the character, within the reader) an experience of immediate, un-demarcated identification. "The process of coming unalone is terrible" (*AILD* 56), thinks Dewey Dell. Faulkner in his early masterpieces frees language from its conventional forms of thinking and feeling in just such a way as to articulate this terrifying collapse of ego boundaries that is common to psychosis, to discovery, and to motherhood. The regressive urge of Faulkner's work of this period—its focus on assault, on overwhelming, on the unchosen—testifies to his desire to find words for the subject's inexpressible vulnerability, its boundary-riddled plight.[13]

Identification is itself primordially rooted in the infantile relation with the mother; perhaps this is why Freud was so wary of its capacity to erode ego boundaries.[14] One of his recent critics writes that for Freud, "Maturity (that is, *masculine* maturity) means being well-defended against one's past, which amounts to the same thing as having a strong capacity for resisting identification. . . . In effect, Freud's picture of maturity is of a man driven to outrun . . . identification with the body of his mother, the original unity of mother and infant" (Swan 9–10).

This description sounds as much like Thomas Sutpen as it sounds unlike William Faulkner. Penetrated through and through by the history of his region and his family, Faulkner outran none of it, and he invented a rhetoric unequaled in its capacity to express penetrability, the phenomenon of being wounded. The biography and the representations in the fiction give us reason to construe him as damaged by his own mother, expelled too soon, not nourished enough.[15] But if this is so, the hunger it generated was for "chanting measures beyond the need for words" (*SF* 340), and the activity it inspired was an attempt to use words to get past the Symbolic itself, "to retrieve the plenitude of the origins," as Bleikasten puts it, "by remembering the . . . body of the lost, forgotten, and unforgettable mother" ("Praise" 140).

"There is at least one spot in every dream at which it is unplumbable," Freud writes in *The Interpretation of Dreams,* "a navel, as it were, that is its point of contact with the unknown" (*Standard* 4:iii). Freud's project of male autonomy makes him insist upon mystery here, but it is possible to know what that navel connects us with. In his early dream novels, where the experiments with language are greatest and the psychic wounds least concealed, where the mother is punished representationally and yet sought after rhetorically, Faulkner made that unsettling connection.

Notes

1. I want to express here a general indebtedness to my colleague Abbe Blum, who made my path through contemporary feminist criticism more manageable.

2. Andre Bleikasten's *The Most Splendid Failure* briefly notes this point. See 225, n. 24, for commentary on the Blands.

3. I am indebted to conversations with James Hinkle for this information.

4. Vincent and Cixous's portrait of the hysteric captures succinctly the economy of desire transformed into suffering that characterizes Mrs. Compson's behavior: "The hysteric . . . tries to signify eros through all the possible forms of anesthesia. . . . A witch in reverse, turned back within herself, she has put all her eroticizing into internal pain" (39).

5. Irwin develops this reading of Mr. Compson throughout his *Doubling and Incest;* see especially 67, 75, 110–13, and 120–122. Bleikasten reads the father also in terms of his failure "as lawgiver" (*Splendid* 113). See also Bleikastcn's "Fathers in Faulkner."

6. This is one of the reasons that Lena Grove (not to mention Dewey Dell or Eula Varner) can be rendered with such affection: she does not meddle in the Symbolic order. Her unflappable comments about a family needing to be together "when a chap comes" (*Light in August* 18) are tonally the reverse of Mrs. Compson's outraged protestations of the flouted system.

7. Paul Gaston, professor of history at the University of Virginia, supplied me with this enlightening bit of information.

8. Kristeva describes the mother's extraordinary experience of one-in-two/two-in-one in terms that illuminate Faulkner's fear of and fascination with this figure: "For a mother . . . the arbitrariness that is the other (the child) goes without saying. For her the impossible is like this: it becomes one with the implacable. The other is inevitable, she seems to say, make a God of him if you like; he won't be any less natural if you do, for this other still comes from me, which is in any case not me but an endless flux of germinations. . . . This maternal quietude, more stubborn even than philosophical doubt . . . cats away at the omnipotence of the symbolic. . . . Such an attitude can be frightening if one stops to think that it may destroy everything that is specific and irreducible in the other, the child; this form of maternal love can become a straitjacket, stifling any deviant individuality. But it can also serve the speaking subject as a refuge when his symbolic carapace shatters to reveal that jagged crest where biology transpierces speech: I am thinking of moments of illness, of sexual-intellectual-physical passion, death" ("Mater" 117–118).

9. Joel Kovel's *White Racism* attempts to chart psychoanalytically this intersection of latent racial phobias and overt gender models, as these operate within American black-white relations, Winthrop Jordan's authoritative *White Over Black* attends as well to the fantasy structures subtending American racism, while James Snead's *Figures of Division* usefully places the issue of racial polarization within the larger problematic Western philosophy's falsely polarizing yet inescapable binariams.

10. Adequate consideration of this point would take more space than I can allow here. In Chapter 2, I return to the fixation with blood letting in *Light in August* and the investment in patriarchal lineage in *Go Down, Moses.* In Chapter 4, I examine at length the social mapping of male and female bodies in all four of the novels under scrutiny. More broadly, the male penchant to treat errant liquids as containable solids is a strategy of colonization that surfaces in the well-constructed plots—built upon oppositions encountered and satisfyingly overcome—of male narrative itself. Gallop writes, "This problem of dealing with difference without constituting an opposition may just be what feminism is all about" (*Daughter* 93). Roland Barthes sees the work of the critic as an attempt to keep difference from degenerating into opposition: "[D]ifference dispenses with or triumphs over conflict. Conflict is sexual, semantic; difference is plural, sensual and textual; meaning and sex are principles of construction, of constitution; difference is the very movement of dispersion, of friability, a shimmer, what matters is not the discovery, in a reading of the world and of the self, of certain oppositions but of encroachments, overflows, leads, skids, shifts, slips" (*Roland Barthes by Roland Barthes* 69). Teresa De Lauretis explores the gendered bias of (male) plots throughout *Alice Doesn't.*

11. Addie Bundren is the exception to my schema, the closest Faulkner ever comes to narrating an unco-opted female's move from virginity through intercourse and maternity and child nurturing into adulthood. This move in *As I Lay Dying,* however, is rendered as anything but continuous. Addie's remarkable awareness of body and presence of mind are premised upon the spatially and temporally unplaccable scene of her protracted dying.

12. Mrs. Compson's body that is not her own illustrates with uncanny aptness Foucault's claim that the body, rather than being one's private sanctuary, "is the inscribed surface of events (traced by language and dissolved by ideas), the locus of a dissociated Self (adopting the illusion of a substantial unity), and a volume in perpetual disintegration ("Nietzsche" 148). I return in Chapter 4 to a sustained commentary on the social annexation of "private" resources.

13. In the second half of Chapter 3 and throughout Chapter 4, I pursue the implications of this claim as they illuminate the trajectory of Faulkner's career. Put too summarily, I want to argue the following: as Faulkner freed himself from his fascination with the "semiotic," as his narratorial voice took on coherence and cultural alignment, his rhetoric became increasingly predictable and his work began to lose its capacity for outrage.

14. Bleikasten has written of the relevance of Freud's "Mourning and Melancholia" to Quentin's inability to sever his "narcissistic identification with the lost object" (*Splendid* 116). In both of these accounts such identification is seen as a regressive and self-damaging move.

15. For biographical information/speculation, see Minter (1–23) and Martin.

Works Cited

Barthes, Roland. *Roland Barthes by Roland Barthes.* New York: Farrar, Straus, & Giroux, 1977.

———. *S/Z.* Translated by Richard Miller. New York: Farrar, Straus, & Giroux, 1974.

Bleikasten, André. "Fathers in Faulkner." In *The Fictional Father: Lacanian Readings of the Text,* edited by Robert Con Davis, 115–145. Amherst: University of Massachusetts Press, 1981.

———. "In Praise of Helen." In *Faulkner and Women: Faulkner and Yoknapatawpha 1985,* edited by Doreen Fowler and Ann J. Abadie, 128–143. Jackson: University Press of Mississippi, 1986.

———. *The Most Splendid Failure: Faulkner's "The Sound and the Fury."* Bloomington: University of Indiana Press, 1976.

Faulkner, William. *Absalom, Absalom!: The Corrected Text.* New York: Random House, 1986.

———. *As I Lay Dying: The Corrected Text.* New York: Random House, 1987.

———. *Go Down, Moses.* New York: Random House, 1942.

———. *Light in August: The Corrected Text.* New York: Random House, 1987.

———. *The Sound and the Fury: the Corrected Text.* New York: Random House, 1987.

The Standard Edition of the Complete Psychological Works of Sigmund Freud, edited and translated by James Strachey. London: Hogarth Press, 1953–1974.

Gallop, Jane. *The Daughter's Seduction.* Ithica: Cornell University Press, 1982.

Irigaray, Luce. *Ce Sexe qui n'en est pas un.* Paris: Editions de Minuit, 1977.

Irwin, John. *Doubling and Incest, Repetition and Revenge: A Speculative Reading of Faulkner.* Baltimore: Johns Hopkins University Press, 1975.

Kovel, Joel. *White Racism: A Psychohistory.* New York: Random House, 1970.

Kristeva, Julia. Stabat Mater." In *The Female Body in Western Culture: Contemporary Perspectives,* edited by Susan R. Suleiman, 99–118. Cambridge: Harvard University Press, 1986.

Polk, Noel. "The Dungeon Was Mother Herself: William Faulkner: 1927–1931." In *New Directions in Faulkner Studies: Faulkner and Yoknapatawpha 1983,* edited by Doreen Fowler and Ann J. Abadie, 61–93. Jackson: University Press of Mississippi, 1984.

Snead, James. *Figures of Division: William Faulkner's Major Novels.* New York: Methuen, 1986.

Swan, Jim. "Mater and Nannies: Freud's Two Mothers and the Discovery of the Oedipus Complex." *American Imago* 31 (1974).

DANIEL JOSEPH SINGAL

All Things Become Shadowy Paradoxical

Outwardly the William Faulkner who sent off the manuscript of *Flags in the Dust* to his publisher in the fall of 1927 did not seem much different from the one the town of Oxford had long known. Having just passed his thirtieth birthday, with no apparent employment prospects and a growing reputation for producing scurrilous literature (a reputation *Mosquitoes* served to augment), he was still the eccentric and floundering offspring of one of the county's more illustrious families. Jack Cofield, arriving in Oxford about this time to open his photographic studio, heard stories of a local character known as "Count No'Count" whose only skills in life were those of a mediocre handyman. As Cofield remembers it, Faulkner's uncle, Judge John W. T. Falkner, was so embarrassed by his nephew that he was barely willing to acknowledge their relationship, while a preacher, at the mere mention of Faulkner's name, launched into a tirade about how "that reprobate should be driven out of town."[1]

Within William Faulkner, however, a crucial transformation was nearing completion. The changes were at once personal, cultural, and artistic, and they were closely interrelated. For one thing, the trial identities on which Faulkner had been relying, such as the persona of the wounded war hero or footloose bohemian, were appearing less frequently and were fast becoming incorporated into a more consistent and permanent identity slattern. Marriage, fatherhood,

William Faulkner. The Making of a Modernist (Chapel Hill: University of North Carolina Press, 1997): pp. 113–143.

and homeownership—all about to befall him in the next few years—would cement that new identity and establish a basic style of existence that would continue throughout his career. And in his writing a giant leap into mastery was about to occur that would separate his mature work from the juvenilia that preceded it. To borrow Andre Bleikasten's phrasing, Faulkner was at last becoming Faulkner.

What is most significant is the way Faulkner effected this final step in creating his mature identity. In essence, he was able to move beyond the post-Victorian stage, dampen the battle between two cultures going on inside him, and establish a workable sense of self precisely by arriving at the realization that he would never achieve—and did not want to achieve—a fixed and sure identity in the nineteenth-century sense. Instead, he would define himself henceforth in Modernist terms, relying on a set of interrelated partial identities that would change and develop over time but that, taken as a whole, nonetheless retained a certain degree of continuity and coherence. The solution to his search for identity, in short, was to be found in the process of Modernist integration itself, with its emphasis on fashioning a provisional unity out of continuously shifting fragments. In describing T. S. Eliot's Modernist masterpiece, *The Waste Land,* Michael H. Levenson writes of how the poem "does not achieve a resolved coherence, but neither does it remain in a chaos of fragmentation. Rather it displays a series of more or less stable patterns, regions of coherence, temporary principles of order . . . engaged in what Eliot calls the 'painful task of unifying.'" It is striking how easily one can apply the same model principle to Faulkner's emerging sense of selfhood. Indeed, that principle applies equally well to Faulkner's work taken as a whole. Again and again critics have remarked on how diverse in style and content his novels are, yet how in different ways they can all be placed within the same matrix—a matrix whose shape nonetheless kept changing throughout his career.[2]

Although Faulkner's mature identity pattern remained fluid, it is also possible to discern a pronounced bipolarity within it corresponding to the two major cultures that had taken root in his psyche, as he more or less compartmentalized the two in separate personae and alternated between them as his artistic and existential needs dictated. As we shall see, this required a continuous balancing act that he was not always able to sustain but could on most occasions keep up sufficiently to achieve his purposes (often using his heavy drinking, it might be noted, as a means of relieving the strain that these conflicting selves inevitably generated). "A divided man," Panthea Reid Broughton writes of him, "he cultivated both sides of his personality at once." The result would be it marked division between his personal and authorial selves. Though from this time onward the Modernist Faulkner was generally dominant when he was at work, it was often by a thin margin and as the result of considerable effort. The Victorian Faulkner remained very much alive in his psyche, acting as a kind of internal censor to block the full realization of his literary intentions when they became too bold or subversive. Whatever distress this must have caused him, he seems to have made his accommodation to it, for, as he must at some level have sensed, it was to be the continuing tension between these two selves that would give such depth and resonance to the great novels he now started to produce.[3]

What precipitated this identity shift was the severe crisis Faulkner found himself in from late 1927 through the early months of 1928. As several biographers have observed, it was a time in his life when everything seemed bleak. Still living with his parents, he was finding it nearly impossible to place his short stories and gain a decent income from his profession. In the past he had been able to shrug off such matters, but his financial responsibilities would soon increase dramatically once Estelle Oldham Franklin obtained her divorce and became available for marriage. Adding to his troubles was a two-hundred-dollar debt, incurred as a result of foolish gambling losses in Memphis, that he owed to his publisher Horace Liveright. But most of all there was Liveright's emphatic decision to reject *Flags in the Dust,* the book on which Faulkner had pinned his hopes for establishing his reputation. On shipping the manuscript Faulkner had boasted that it was "the damdest best book you'll look at this year, and any other publisher"; now he was told that the work was so lacking in coherent characterization and plot structure that it could not possibly he salvaged. According to Faulkner's own account, his reaction was first rage, then intense despair. "I think now that I'll sell my typewriter and go to work," he wrote Liveright, "though God knows, it's sacrilege to waste the talent for idleness which I possess."[4]

In fact, he did just the opposite. Convinced by Liveright's letter and the poor sales of *Mosquitoes* that nothing he wrote would ever be published again, he decided to indulge himself in his craft solely for his own pleasure. He would pour his private visions onto paper, satisfying his personal aesthetic standards, exploring questions about his self, art, and region that preoccupied him without any concern for communicating to a wider audience. Just before making this decision he had drafted a pair of short stories about three children from a once prominent southern family named Compson brushing against the realities of adult life, but the pieces had been written with an eye to magazine sales and so had not really plumbed the family's full literary potential. Now he started a new story tentatively entitled "Twilight," narrated by a fourth Compson child who even when grown would retain the mental status of a five-year-old. This radical device, forcing him to view his subject through a disjointed consciousness, seemed to provide the impetus to liberation Faulkner had been searching for. As the story turned into a novel, in time renamed *The Sound and the Fury*, its composition became an exercise in self-analysis and self-construction in which the medium of literature became his means for gaining control of the conflicting perceptions and experiences that roiled within his psyche, thus enabling him to piece together at last the puzzle of his own identity.[5]

The foremost vehicle for that self-analysis is the book's central character, Quentin Compson, who resembles Faulkner in many ways. The oldest of four children, Quentin possesses a sensitive disposition, has a keen sense of his family's illustrious past, and does not adjust readily to modernity. But he is not by any means a straightforward autobiographical character. Rather, he can most accurately be seen as an extrapolated version of the post-Victorian self Faulkner was then in the final throes of shedding. That William Faulkner, one recalls, had been most evident in the early 1920s, infatuated with Swinburne and writing poetry about a realm of pure transcendent beauty that the artist was destined endlessly to pursue. In similar fashion Quentin, as many critics have remarked, evinces many of the standard characteristics of the late romantic poet and is intent on achieving, in Eric Sundquist's words, a state of "Pateresque purity." To be more precise, Quentin is Faulkner during his fin de siècle stage shorn of all elements of Modernist influence; his tragic trajectory is the one Faulkner sensed might have been his own had he not encountered Eliot, Joyce, Freud, and the other Modernist masters. In turn, the act of externalizing this post-Victorian self in Quentin and thus gaining a measure of control over it proved to be the essential final step in Faulkner's effort to fashion his mature identity.[6]

Quentin, by contrast, finds it impossible to determine who he is. More precisely, he is unable to establish a coherent identity that will allow him to adapt to the historical circumstances in which he has been placed. Burdened with personal roles and values that are no longer viable in the early years of the twentieth century, he can discover no new ones to replace them. Accordingly, his monologue becomes, as Bleikasten so aptly puts it, the record of "a process of derealization" during which "the entire fabric of a self is unraveled and comes apart." There is simply no center around which his various identity fragments can begin to coalesce, no means of fusing together the cultural ideals he has inherited. Instead of exercising the leadership role, whether political or intellectual, that his talents and lineage would indicate for him, he is doomed to an existence fraught with absurdity in a society he can neither relate to nor understand.[7]

The Compsons, with a governor and three generals to their credit, clearly fall within the Cavalier tradition, but it is also apparent that that tradition has become threadbare, with the sad fate of Quentin's father providing a measure of its decline. Far from being able to transmit an aristocratic ethos intact to his children, Jason Lycurgus Compson III has turned into a gloomy advocate of fin de siècle stoicism, a southern A. E. Housman who believes that a person's lot is to bear without complaint the aimless vicissitudes of fate. A scion of the old planter elite whose misfortune it was to come of age amid the desolation of the post-Reconstruction era, he has lost all hope of finding a purpose to life. "Because no battle is ever won," he tells his son, "they are not even fought. The field only reveals to man his own folly and despair, and victory is an illusion of philosophers and fools." The losses suffered by his society and family have shattered his faith in any "higher" or "spiritual" capacity of human nature, leaving him to wallow in sheer materialistic reductionism: "Man the sum of what you have. A problem in impure properties carried tediously to an unvarying nil: stalemate of dust and desire." Consequently his advice to his son runs directly counter to the old Cavalier pursuit of noble ideals: "we must just stay awake and see evil done for a while its not always." In this fashion the trauma of the Civil War defeat has descended to Quentin's—and Faulkner's—generation.[8]

Nor does Quentin receive a usable worldview from his mother. As a Bascomb, her origins lie in a different part of the southern social landscape, the lower middle class, which had long lived under the shadow of planter families like the Compsons. Desperate for status in a culture weighted against them, members of this class in the period after the war often became models of probity, populating the evangelical churches and grasping Victorian morality as their ticket to respectability. Caroline Compson clearly follows this pattern, compensating for her sense of social inferiority to her husband by imposing a repressive moral standard on her children to the point where, as Noel Polk remarks, she virtually turns their home into a prison. Though she has almost totally abdicated her maternal responsibilities, Quentin nonetheless imbibes much of her value system, with its concern for formality and ritual. When she, in her quest for propriety, insists that the youngest child "Benjy" be called "Benjamin," Quentin dutifully complies. And his preoccupation with his sister Caddy's virginity is clearly an extension of his mother's.[9]

The question has frequently been raised as to whether Faulkner was drawing on his own parents in creating Quentin's. There are certainly some resemblances. Like Mrs. Compson, Maud Falkner came from a family well below her husband's on the social scale and was also very much a Victorian stalwart, determined to drum morality and culture into her four sons. Yet there are also important differences: Mrs. Falkner was closely involved with the upbringing of her children, unlike the withdrawn and hypochondriacal Mrs. Compson, who in this regard seems much closer in character to Phil Stone's mother. And although Murry Falkner and Quentin's father were both descended from proud families, the former was plainly far less genteel, learned, and articulate than his fictional counterpart.[10]

In short, although Faulkner may have used his parents as starting points, he went considerably beyond them in creating the Compsons in order to craft literary incarnations of the two most powerful cultural forces in the

South at the time—the intertwined Cavalier and Victorian legacies. It was that nineteenth-century heritage, he was in effect saying, that had become so stifling to young southerners of his generation, cutting them off from the world of experience where they could begin to construct a new set of identities for their region.* Faulkner himself had been able to avoid this historical cul-de-sac thanks primarily to his involvement with contemporary literature, which had provided him with a vital arena for exploring new cultural possibilities. That, in fact, was probably the most important factor attracting him to Modernism in the first place. But Quentin has no such escape; through the agency of his parents history bears down on him relentlessly, leaving him no room to maneuver, no space to achieve authenticity as a person.

Foremost among the instruments of that entrapment stands the Victorian moral dichotomy. All of Quentin's thoughts and perceptions are shaped by his underlying belief that a chasm exists between the finite and the eternal. On one side of that gap is a purely spiritual plane of existence, the repository of beauty, virtue, and honor where everything is endowed with lasting meaning; on the other side is the natural world filled with animality, corruption, and transience. To a large extent Quentin's life becomes dedicated to keeping himself and his family on the right side of that dichotomy, fulfilling what he conceives of as an ancestral obligation to make certain that the Compsons remain above the steamy animal passions that characterize mere mortals. He is accordingly devastated when his sister Caddy, whose virginity has become in his eyes the emblem of the family's moral purity, gives herself over to promiscuity. His father wisely counsels against this, warning him that one should never attempt to create "all apotheosis in which a temporary state of mind will become symmetrical above the flesh." But the advice is lost on Quentin, for whom Compson honor is inherently timeless rather than "temporary" and who can envision no greater imperative than to keep it safely "above the flesh."[11]

What makes Quentin's quandary so unbearable, and what stamps him as a post-Victorian instead of a Victorian proper, is his secret realization that his father is right. A keen observer of the world around him, he knows all too well that his values have become outmoded and his defense of them quixotic, but he can envision no alternative standard of meaning. Caught in a cultural no-man's-land and unable to adopt his father's self-protective tactic of stoicism, he is overwhelmed by a profound ambivalence in all realms of life. That paralyzing ambivalence is especially painful for Quentin in light of the Cavalier identity he aspires to, with its traits of firm resolve and courageous leadership. His will never be the sort of personality that gives rise to governors and generals. Rather, beset by forces that constantly pull him in opposite directions, he has become emotionally hamstrung, a psychological cripple cut off from any possibility of decisive action, someone for whom only suicide can finally provide relief.

We can see this powerful sense of division pervading Quentin's life quite clearly in his troubled relationship to time. As a Victorian, he views time as a natural force over which he must establish rational control, leading him to become preoccupied with knowing what time it is and with ordering his life by the clock. But, simultaneously sensing that time, with its rigid order, has imprisoned him, he is equally determined to liberate himself from his fixation on chronology. Thus in the opening scene of his monologue, his first deed on waking is to pull the hands off his heirloom watch so that it continues to run but can no longer tell him what time it is—allowing him, in other words, to remain within time but not be captive to it. That expedient, however, works no better than all the others he has tried to break the spell of time over his imagination. Passing a jeweler's shop a few hours later, he congratulates himself on how he "looked away in time," only to be drawn back to the window as if by a magnet. Staring at the clocks and watches on display, he is struck by how they show "a dozen different hours and each with the same assertive and contradictory assurance that mine had, without any hands at all"—leaving him free (at least within his own mind) to choose whichever time he wants.[12]

Part of Quentin yearns to synchronize with the natural flow of time. Those able to do so earn his envy, particularly his college classmate Gerald Bland, whom Quentin pictures rowing "in a steady and measured pull" up the Charles River "like an apotheosis, mounting into a drowsing infinity." Quentin is likewise fascinated by the large trout he spots in the river that, seemingly without exertion, can swiftly snap up a mayfly and resume its previous position, "nose into the current, wavering delicately to the motion of the water above." Spending its days in the midst of onrushing water—an obvious symbol for the Bergsonian flow of time—the trout possesses perfect control over the terms of its existence, to the point where it can "hang" in the water as if flying. Quentin, by contrast, moves fitfully and aimlessly, getting on and off streetcars without knowing where they are headed, dependent on mechanical devices for his locomotion. When he finally enters the river's current, it will not be as an effortless rower or swimmer but with two flatirons attached to his body, causing him to sink to the bottom like a stone.[13]

For the reigning, Victorian part of Quentin's sensibility fears the flux of time and seeks desperately to stop it. Though he knows that it is impossible for humans ever to overcome time and achieve the absolute, he nonetheless makes every effort, as Sanford Pinsker puts it, "to replace an existential flux with an artificial permanence," relying on rituals and abstractions to isolate and rigidify experience. His ultimate aim, much like that of Faulkner himself in the early 1920s, is not only to stop time but somehow to soar above his earthly environment into the "drowsing infinity" of the ether, that realm of spiritual splendor fit only for a Sartoris or Compson—or a Falkner. What is most notable, however, is the shift in Faulkner's own allegiance to that ideal. Where once he had shared his protagonists' urge toward transcendence, he was now clearly detached from it, portraying it in Quentin's case not as romantic and noble but as dangerously self-destructive.[14]

The same framework of beliefs, leading to the same disastrous results, appears in Quentin's relationship to sexuality. At the deepest stratum of his thought, writes James C. Cowan, "love is linked with the saintly ideal and sex with destructive animality." Sexual intercourse becomes the ultimate degradation for him, conjuring up in his mind the sordid images of "the beast with two backs" and *"the swine of Euboeleus running coupled."* The result is his ironclad commitment to virginity: he will be entirely pure, right down to the neurotic compulsion he develops concerning personal cleanliness. But in an environment where sexual mores are changing, and where his own sister is openly conducting liaisons, the natural human instincts that Quentin seeks to repress will not go away. Sexual desire pervades his consciousness to the point of obsession, just as its symbol, the smell of honeysuckle, becomes so thick for him that he cannot breathe. This crossfire of emotion is visible in his response when Caddy finds him in the barn one rainy afternoon engaged in typical early adolescent sexual play with a young neighboring girl named Natalie. Reminded of his breach of Compson honor by Caddy's interruption, Quentin, who had been thoroughly enjoying himself, feels compelled to jump at once into the hog wallow. In Quentin's contorted thinking, nothing less than a bath in physical filth can atone for his dalliance with moral filth; only a full-scale immersion in animal muck will make him clean again.[15]

As was so often the case during the nineteenth century, this allegiance to the moral dichotomy leads Quentin to a highly warped view of gender relations, in which women typically appear as either delicate and chaste, or oversexed and "filthy." Masculinity becomes indelibly associated for him with control, logic, and order, especially the chronological order of time. Femininity, by contrast, comes to suggest the uncontrollable flow of nature—that river of force that Quentin feels helplessly caught up in, whether it takes the form of the rush of events, the surging stream of his consciousness, or the wild current of sexual energies inside him that he can barely dam up. Given this symbolism, women in his eyes become at once beautiful and terrifying, enticing and repellent:

> Because women so delicate so mysterious Father said. Delicate equilibrium of periodical filth between two moons balanced. Moons lie said full and yellow as harvest moons her hip thighs. Outside outside of them always but. With all that inside of them shapes an outward suavity waiting for a touch to. Liquid putrefaction like

> drowned things floating like pale rubber flabbily filled getting the odor of honeysuckle all mixed up.

Romantic full moons and used contraceptives, suavity and "periodical filth"— Quentin desperately juxtaposes these divergent images but cannot integrate them into a workable perception of reality. Though he may admire men like Bland and Ames whose ability to cope with the natural flow of time allows them to deal successfully with women, he cannot shake his belief, in James Cowan's words, that they "achieve their masculine virility at the expense of the finer qualities that would make them fully human." To Quentin, nothing is more important than retaining those "finer qualities" that keep him on the "human" side of the dichotomy.[16]

It is precisely his desire to escape this dilemma, to resolve the terrible ambivalence that is tearing him apart, that leads Quentin to his fatal fixation on his sister. Caddy is highly alluring to him; in his fantasies he excitedly imagines himself replacing her lovers:

> *you thought it was them but it was me listen I fooled you all the time it was me you thought I was in the house where that damn honeysuckle trying not to think the swing the cedars the secret surges the breathing locked drinking the wild breath the yes Yes Yes yes*

Yet because she is his sister, she is also unattainable and therefore "safe." Though their relationship is so intimate on the Platonic level that they virtually cohabit the same ego, Quentin can rest assured that she will never surrender to him physically. Given his perverse needs, it is a "perfect" arrangement.[17]

The dynamics of this strange union become manifest in the scene by the branch after Caddy has lost her virginity to Dalton Ames. As they lie beside the stream in the moonlight like twc lovers, Quentin first offers to run off with her, then takes out his knife in an attempted double suicide that is filled with erotic overtones. The language is patently sexual throughout, especially when Quentin tries to block her from keeping a late-night rendezvous with Ames:

> Im stronger than you
> she was motionless hard unyielding but still
> I wont fight stop youd better stop
> Caddy dont Caddy
> it wont do any good dont you know it wont let me go

Ostensibly Quentin is engaged in the brotherly task of protecting his sister, yet at the same time their interaction mimics a sexual assault. Their respective roles are just sufficiently blurred to sustain in his mind the possibility of sexual intimacy. But, though he savors his arousal, he is also terrified by it. Breathing hard, he returns to the branch, lying down on the bank "with my face close to the ground so I could not smell the honeysuckle" until he finally recovers self-control.[18]

With Caddy's virginity irretrievably lost, Quentin tries one final ploy: a resort to pure fantasy in which he confesses to his father that he and his sister have committed incest. It is a complicated strategy, serving many important psychological functions for him and allowing the reader the deepest possible insight into the workings of his tormented mind. Its most obvious function involves the creation of a comforting alternative reality that can help blot out the hopeless situation he faces—a reality in which he has displaced Caddy's lovers and enjoys uncontested possession of her. At the same time, since he and Caddy have never consummated their love, his admission of incest serves to reverse the fact of her illegitimate pregnancy and restore her virginity. *"Do you want me to say it do you think that if I say it it wont be,"* she asks somewhat incredulously. But that is exactly what Quentin has momentarily succeeded in making himself think. Nor is the fantasy all that implausible, at least from his standpoint, given the intense spiritual incest in which he and Caddy have long been engaged. Even as young children, Mrs. Compson recalls, they were "together too much," and Caddy's possessiveness toward him almost matches his toward her, as is evident from the incident with Natalie. Indeed, if Quentin's account can be believed, Caddy herself is unsure whether or not they have actually committed incest: *"We didnt we didnt do that did we do that."*[19]

Another key advantage of this fantasy from Quentin's standpoint is the opportunity it provides for realizing his dream of transcendence. Only this time, as Olga Vickery observes, it is a curious sort of reverse transcendence, taking the form of a private purgatory into which he and Caddy are cast to pay for their terrible sin. *"If it could just be a hell beyond that," he reflects to himself, "the clean flame the two of us more than dead. Then you will have only me then only me then only the two of us amid the pointing and the horror beyond the clean flame."* Here are all of the essential attributes of his spiritual "apotheosis" Quentin has yearned for, including the cauterizing "clean flame" to safeguard innocence. Above all, he and Caddy will be alone together, inviolably isolated from the flow of time and the corruption of human existence. To Quentin even eternal imprisonment in hell is better than mortality—so long as it is the transcendent hell that he has devised in his imagination. That is why he does not really wish to commit incest but only to confess to it; actualizing his fantasy, notes Vickery, would ruin everything "by involving him in the terrible reality of experience." Or, as Quentin puts it to his father, had Caddy in fact consented, "it wouldnt have done any good but if i could tell you we did it would have been so and then the others wouldnt be so and then the world would roar away."[20]

But perhaps the most valuable of the many symbolic comforts that Quentin's incest strategy supplies is the way it permits him to heal his deep-seated psychic division between body and spirit by returning to the oceanic feelings of wholeness associated with earliest childhood. It is clear that Caddy, in addition to being a sister and lover, also represents a mother substitute for Quentin, providing him with the primal maternal love that his real mother is incapable of—a love at once powerful and asexual, all-enveloping yet non-threatening. To be able to immerse himself in such a safe wellspring of emotion without fear or reservation is the ultimate aspiration of his post-Victorian sensibility. "What Quentin yearns for," writes Constance Hall, "is angelic love—pure, unbounded, unimpeded," which is why incest becomes "the near-perfect vehicle for [his] effort to possess absolutely and to achieve complete oneness." Beyond this, confessing publicly to so terrible a sin offers him the chance to act decisively, to take control of his seemingly purposeless existence and escape from his father's nihilistic philosophy that denies the possibility of meaningful human action. But again, such resolution is possible for Quentin only within his imagination; in the real world events remain intolerably fluid and moral choices uncertain. "If things just finished themselves," he keeps complaining, but, as Faulkner with his Modernist perspective is now at pains to tell us, that is simply not how the universe works.[21]

•••

Equally telling is the degree of detachment Faulkner was able to muster in handling such emotion-laden material. There can be no doubt that he viewed the tragedy of the Compsons from the inside, sharing every stab of Quentin's pain. It was his own story, his own subjective experience, that he was writing from. And yet it is also clear that he had finally managed to surmount that experience, gaining sufficient mastery over it so that he could at last make it serve his artistic purposes as a Modernist writer. In *Mayday* one can not really tell his ultimate verdict on Sir Galwyn's quest for romantic illusion, but in *The Sound and the Fury* there can be no doubt of how he regards the sad plight of Quentin.

His progress is especially evident in his treatment of that "fierce proud Dianalike girl" who served to express his continuing attachment to his mother. With her slender body and dark hair, Caddy Compson surely represents another in this long line of characters, which helps to explain why Faulkner, as he once put it in an interview, always considered her his "heart's darling." Nonetheless, Caddy ends up disgraced and exiled from home as a result of her own moral failings (in the appendix to the novel written in 1945 we are told that she has become the mistress of a Nazi general, a perfectly plausible outcome given what we know of her earlier life). The "Dianalike girl," previously an avatar of innocence who could do no wrong, is now depicted as a creature mired in pathology. At the same time, *The Sound and the Fury* marks the first Faulkner novel providing a full-scale portrait of a mother figure (we see Elmer Hodge's mother only briefly, and those of Donald Mahon, Joe Gilligan, Bayard Sartoris, and Horace Benbow are either dead or absent). Nor is it a flattering picture; on the contrary, in Caroline Compson one finds gathered the worst aspects of late Victorian culture as it had taken hold in the South. What these developments signify is that Faulkner was at last succeeding in disengaging himself from his mother—and from the tradition she symbolized for him. It was a step that Quentin, by contrast, was entirely incapable of taking.[22]

Simultaneously, Faulkner was managing to distance himself further from the Cavalier tradition. In *Flags in the Dust* he had lost no opportunity to cover Colonel John Sartoris with glory, but the Compsons' distinguished ancestors are mentioned only rarely and obliquely, amid hints (later confirmed in the appendix) that their record was characterized more by quixotic failure than legendary exploits. At one point Quentin even drops the astounding suggestion that his grandfather may have somehow been responsible for the Confederacy losing the Civil War. To be sure, there is no real exploration of the ways in which men like General Compson had set the South on the path to ruin; that subversive topic would await the writing of *Absalom, Absalom!* five years later. What we are left with for the moment is the legacy of fatality—the question, as John Irwin put it, "of whether any male descendant of the Compson family can avoid repeating the General's failure and defeatism and avoid passing it on to the next generation."[23]

The source of that fatality, we discover, lies within the Cavalier identity itself. Whatever virtues it might once have embodied, by Quentin's time it has become a mythic construct almost completely abstracted from the flow of experience. That is why it is so dangerous. A rigid stereotype no longer subject to the influence of history, it chains Quentin to the past, dooming him to a life of endless repetition. His very name, handed down in cyclic fashion through his family, epitomizes this process of imposed identification, as does his grandfather's watch, which, his father warns him, "can fit your individual needs no better than it fitted his or his father's." Again, his response is one of hopeless ambivalence—he is both narcissistically enamored of his Cavalier identity and aware that it is the source of his entrapment. Thus on the day of his suicide we find him desperately attempting to break free of the Compson past by prying the hands off his watch but unable to take the decisive action of smashing it completely. Faulkner's symbolism becomes exquisite: the watch keeps running relentlessly, its constant ticking from Quentin's inside pocket a virtual echo of his heartbeat, reflecting the way the family ethos continues to rule over the innermost core of his being.[24]

As his interactions with other people keep revealing, however, that ethos passed down from the Old South has become virtually emptied of meaning under the conditions of modern life. Faulkner underscores this point through the character of Quentin's Harvard classmate Gerald Bland, a rank pretender from Virginia who manages to set himself up as a gentleman overnight by mastering the required external behavior and acquiring a few basic props, such as Oxford flannels and an English motoring cap. While Bland is employing his store-bought identity to captivate a pair of attractive young women, Quentin, for whom the status of gentleman is bound up with the values of honor and obligation, is doing his best to rescue a maiden in distress—a filthy little girl from an immigrant family who he believes has lost her way home. The final ironic indignity comes when the girl's brother repays Quentin for his noble efforts by pressing charges of child molesting, leaving Quentin to howl with uncontrollable laughter at the absurdity of it all. Clearly, everything he holds sacred has become outmoded; the universe has been turned upside down. *"Father said it used to be a gentleman was known by his books,"* he recalls ruefully; *"nowadays he is known by the ones he has not returned."*[25]

Ironically, the only southerners in the novel capable of achieving the solid sense of self that Quentin desperately seeks are black. In contrast to his plight, they seem able at will to slide in and out of the roles that white society imposes on them, meeting each situation on its own terms thanks to the firm identities with which they are blessed. The various masks they put on are no more than masks—useful for dealing with whites but not their real selves. As Faulkner has Quentin observe, "A nigger is not a person so much as a form of [external] behavior; a sort of obverse reflection of the white people he lives among." No one illustrates this better than Deacon, the obsequious black factotum who befriends southern students at Harvard. As Quentin comes to realize, Deacon is capable anytime he wishes of shedding "that self he had long since taught himself to wear in the world's eye" to reveal his authentic self below. And there are other blacks, like Dilsey Gibson or Louis Hatcher, who wear no masks at all. With his primitive, resolute faith that he can ward off catastrophe simply by keeping his lantern clean, Hatcher, as Thadious Davis remarks, is "a man prepared for living" who continuously "displays a personal integration of self and harmony with the world." He represents, in short, an alternative identity, firmly rooted in physical reality and human community, that white southerners of good family like Quentin covertly crave—which is why Quentin's thoughts keep coming back to him, trying without success to penetrate the barrier of race in order to divine his secret.[26]

Whenever he ruminates on blacks, Quentin's stream-of-consciousness narrative turns almost invariably to his shadow, implying an important link between it and black identity. Clearly, this is no ordinary shadow; in his mind it is nothing less than an autonomous creature that controls its own motions:

"I stopped inside the door, watching the shadow move. It moved almost imperceptibly, creeping back inside the door, driving the shadow back into the door." Though never expressing actual hostility toward it, Quentin is forever "tricking" the shadow, as if he could somehow rid himself of it through sheer cleverness, or actively trying to harm it, as when he walks along the sidewalk "trampling my shadow's bones into the concrete with hard heels." Watching it dance on the surface of the river, he wishes he could "blot it into the water, holding it until it was drowned." Dark, lithe, fluid, and "impervious," the shadow simultaneously fascinates and threatens Quentin. He both relishes its presence and seeks intently to destroy it.[27]

This is because Quentin projects onto the shadow a major component of his ego—in Bleikasten's phrase, his "mortal bodily self." This "bodily self" is the part of him that lives in the finite, material world; it possesses the attributes of corporeality and vitality that he admires in men like Louis Hatcher and needs so badly for his survival. But Quentin, following the dictates of his moral dichotomy, also cannot help but consider that physical self dangerous and forbidden—something he must dissociate himself from at all costs. He views it as in the deepest sense representative of "blackness," containing powerful forces and passions that, while enticing, also threaten to undermine his efforts to remain "white" and "civilized." The shadow, in other words, embodies in concentrated form all the traits that southern whites have traditionally projected onto blacks in order to shore up the supposed "purity" of white identity. Hence Quentin's obsession with controlling and punishing his shadow, which becomes for him a kind of psychological punching bag, safely external and containing (since his mind has transferred them to it) all the impulses that he believes might imperil his status as a gentleman. Again, this is a "perfect" arrangement: by tricking and trampling the shadow, he repeatedly demonstrates his moral rejection of his dark self without the risk of either injuring or losing it.[28]

This perverse relationship with his shadow makes clear the extent to which Quentin's post-Victorian culture has served to debilitate him. His mind and body have become foes, functioning as if they were warring entities. One's corporal self can never be trusted, he informs us: "When you don't want to do a thing, your body will try to trick you into doing it, sort of unawares." His body is so detached from his consciousness that he doesn't even realize it when he cuts himself breaking the crystal on his grandfather's watch. Not until he finally notices the blood he has shed, allowing him to conceptualize what has happened, does he experience pain: "There was a red smear on the dial. When I saw it my thumb began to smart." The division between mind and body is that complete. As in other respects, Quentin has taken the Victorian dichotomy to its logical extreme, emancipating his "higher" faculties from his physical being. But, while he may have managed to retain his "purity," the results are hardly enobling. Such, Faulkner was saying, are the wages of transcendence in the modern era.[29]

In the end, Quentin's sense of self has become so weakened, so detached from reality, that everything seems out of kilter for him. His attempts to preserve his Cavalier heritage by defending the chivalric code of honor have not so much failed as collapsed into fiasco. Each such venture—confronting Gerald Bland or Caddy's seducer, Dalton Ames, or protecting the little Italian girl—results not in a clear-cut triumph or defeat but in a muddle of misunderstanding. "Bud," his friend Spoade comments after the fight with Bland, "you excite not only admiration but horror." And in an age when women themselves are overthrowing the old moral standards, the identity of a virgin has become meaningless: "if it was that simple to do it wouldn't be anything and if it wasn't anything, what was I . . ."[30]

The problem, Faulkner is at pains to tell us, resides not in the world itself but within Quentin. The final afternoon of his agony takes place against the backdrop of a peaceful rural setting where a group of carefree boys are enjoying themselves fishing, sunning, and swimming. Those around him go about their activities in a world that they find reasonably solid and hospitable, while for Quentin not even his bed offers a respite from vertigo:

> I seemed to be lying neither asleep nor awake looking down a long corridor of gray halflight where all stable things had become shadowy paradoxical all I had done shadows all I had felt suffered taking visible form antic and perverse mocking without relevance inherent themselves with the denial of the significance they should have affirmed thinking I was I was not who was not was not who.

The passage captures vividly the plight of a person impaled by cultural change, trapped within a major historical value system that he knows is now hopelessly obsolete.[31]

It is precisely to escape this state of psychic limbo that Quentin plans his suicide. With a decisive blow, he will at last set his affairs right; for once things will finish themselves. Thus a slew of conflicting but intricately balanced motives lie behind his leap from the bridge—in Freudian terms, his behavior is "overdetermined." As Sundquist points out, one can see the suicide as a sexual act, consummating Quentin's incestuous love for Caddy in her guise as a water nymph; yet Quentin is simultaneously engaging in a rite of purification by water similar to his earlier jump into the hog wallow. Drowning also represents a return to the maternal womb, with his body "healing" to "the caverns and the grottoes of the sea" to find the uterine peace that has eluded him. *"I will sleep fast,"* he promises himself. At the same time, this plunge into the depths will paradoxically permit him to realize at last his quest for transcendence. On Judgment Day, he tells us, the flatirons weighting down his body will rise to the surface by themselves, while his eyes "will come floating up too, out of the deep quiet and the sleep, to look on glory"—suggesting that his spiritual self (symbolized by the eyes) will be rid permanently of the burden of his flesh. His battle against time will be over, and he will be transported to a sort of post-Victorian paradise—it celestial refuge where all his dearest values and desires can be perpetually affirmed, no matter how much they may have contradicted each other here on earth.[32]

Perhaps nothing conveys the dynamics of his mind better than the two extraordinary dream images that appear at the end of his soliloquy. The first centers on a picture of a dungeon he recalls from a children's book—"a dark place into which a single weak ray of light came slanting upon two faces lifted out of the shadow." The two faces, he realizes, are those of his parents, with himself and his siblings "lost below even them without even a ray of light." This nightmare of an existence devoid of identity or hope contrasts diametrically with another childhood vision deeply etched in his memory:

> It used to be I thought of death as a man something like Grandfather a friend of his a kind of private and particular friend . . . I always thought of them as being together somewhere all the time waiting for old Colonel Sartoris to come down and sit with them waiting on a high place beyond cedar trees . . . Grandfather wore his uniform and we could hear the murmur of their voices from beyond the cedars they were always talking and Grandfather was always right.

To Quentin's dualistic mind, the alternatives are stark and simple: the dark and degraded place below, or the "high place" just beyond the cedar where the southern Cavaliers dwell and where firm moral judgment can be had for the asking from a man who "was always right." It is a choice that must be made, for, unlike Faulkner himself, Quentin is incapable of abiding "gray halflight." Dressed in his finest clothes and meticulously groomed, he will be well prepared to meet his grandfather's special friend.[33]

Quentin is not the only victim of the deadly pull of the South's cultural past to be found in *The Sound and the Fury;* in their own ways his sister Caddy and brother Jason are also destroyed by inherited tradition. Unlike Quentin, both rebel against that tradition, but in each case the rebellion exacts a terrible price, maiming them psychically and depriving them of the vital thread of cultural continuity they need to advance into the future. By the novel's end they have each arrived at a sort of living death, having lost all hope of generativity (to borrow Erikson's term for the quality that marks a healthy and creative adulthood). As bereft of viable identity as Quentin, and as thoroughly trapped by compulsive behavior, the two supply further evidence of Faulkner's bleak prognosis for his region in the late 1920s. The planter class, to which southern society had always turned for direction, had now reached a historical dead end, a cultural morass from which it would likely never extricate itself. That is the ultimate meaning of the story of the Compson children.

One sees this in Caddy Compson's dramatic flight from the stereotyped identity of the southern lady, an act of rejection that shapes her whole life. Sensing how the Victorian ethos has disfigured her mother's personality, she adamantly refuses to suppress her emotions for the sake of propriety. Against her mother's orders she continues to lavish affection on her younger brother Benjy and does not hesitate to seek out sexual relationships on reaching adolescence. Her ingrained instinct for rebellion is apparent even at age seven, when she disobeys her parents by getting her dress wet playing in the branch. "I dont care whether they see or not," she tells Quentin defiantly. "I'm going to tell, myself" Likewise she thinks nothing of ignoring her father's injunction against climbing the pear tree to spy on what is taking place at her grandmother's funeral. Faulkner highlights her insurgency by comparing her to Eve in the Garden and to Satan—two figures diametrically opposed to the ideal of the southern lady.[34]

Caddy's tragedy, however, is that she can discover no suitable identity to replace the one she rejects. The only thing she can find in the family storehouse, so to speak, is the legacy of military valor handed down by her Compson forebears—an identity hardly considered appropriate for a female in the social context in which she lives. In their childhood play, Quentin remembers, "she never was a queen or a fairy she was always a king or a giant or a general." Likewise it is Caddy who always insists on being in control, demanding, for example, that her siblings mind her the night of Damuddy's death. While Quentin safeguards his purity as if he were a southern lady, Caddy carries on like an aggressive young man displaying sexual prowess. *"I didn't let him I made him,"* she informs Quentin after kissing a boy for the first time. The two also unmistakably exchange sexual roles when Quentin walks to his "duel" with Dalton Ames while Caddy rides up later on Quentin's own horse, that perennial symbol of planter authority. Galloping to the scene like a Cavalier, she finds her brother lying on the ground, having "passed out like a girl." For these descendants of the antebellum elite, Faulkner is suggesting, the entire process of gender identification has irretrievably broken down.[35]

Here lies the root cause of Caddy's nymphomania. Having repudiated the model of womanhood represented by her mother, she can maintain her fragile hold on femininity only by yielding herself sexually to men as often as possible. Not all men will do. Rather, Caddy is drawn to lovers who act and appear hypermasculine, such as the former soldier Dalton Ames, who can hold her "in one arm like she was no bigger than a child," or the Nazi general whose mistress she in time becomes. They alone are strong enough to overpower her Compson self and force her to submit as a woman. Because her feminine identity is so weak, she must repeat this behavior pattern over and over. Sexuality in this way becomes as compulsive for her as virginity is for Quentin; she has no control over her actions and, in keeping with the clinical syndrome of nymphomania, derives no pleasure or satisfaction from them. On the contrary, she increasingly comes to associate sexual encounters with death. There have been "too many," she confides to Quentin, and "when they touched me I died."[36]

As Faulkner makes clear, Caddy's sexuality has become truly perverted for her. It has turned into an obsession, a kind of specter perpetually haunting her: *"There was something terrible in me sometimes at night I could see it grinning at me I could see it through them grinning at me through their faces."* At each step of her self-degradation she is filled with shame and attempts, in a manner reminiscent of Quentin, to restore her innocence with water. Prompted by Benjy, who senses her corruption, she washes off her perfume after her first date, cleans her mouth out with soap after her first romantic kiss, and, most dramatically of all, bathes herself in the branch the night she loses her virginity. She is obviously in immense pain: Quentin recalls her, accosted by Benjy's bellowing, *"shrinking against the wall getting smaller and smaller with her white face her eyes like thumbs dug into it."* She knows the consequences that will flow from her promiscuity—how it will drive her father to drink himself to death, destroy Quentin, and leave Benjy without anyone to protect him. "I wont anymore, ever," she fervently promises Benjy while holding him and sobbing. But for all her Compson will to dominate, to make the world "mind" her, she is in the grip of forces she cannot master.[37]

Various writers on *The Sound and the Fury* have seen Caddy as a fertility goddess symbolizing the southern land itself, with a bountiful capacity to nurture an entire society. If so, then the dark implication embedded in this novel is that that source of nurturance has now dried up. As Caddy tells Quentin the night before her marriage, she is so emotionally desiccated that she cannot generate a tear: *"I cant cry I wont even cry one minute."* Far from being able to provide the maternal qualities of caring and sustenance that would prevent the Compson household—and, by extension, the region—from succumbing to the wasteland, she has entered a state equivalent to death (when Jason suggests after their father's funeral that she would be better off dead, she instantly agrees). In this sense the "Dianalike girl" had now evolved in Faulkner's imagination well beyond its origins in his own mother to encompass the female ethos itself. At least within the white South, Faulkner appears to have been saying, that feminine spirit had become corrupted, condemning the society to perpetual barrenness.[38]

The glimpse supplied of Caddy's daughter seems to confirm this reading of Faulkner's intent. Though named for her deceased uncle in a last, desperate attempt on Caddy's part to perpetuate the family line, Miss Quentin is endowed with no identity whatsoever. Never told who her parents are, she does not become a Compson, a Bascomb, or even fully a human being, as the description of her room discloses: "It was not a girl's room. It was not anybody's room, and the faint scent of cheap cosmetics and the few feminine objects and the other evidences of crude and hopeless efforts to feminise it but added to its anonymity, giving it that dead and stereotyped transience of rooms in assignation houses." Significantly, it is the same room that once belonged to Damuddy, the family matriarch. Deprived of any sense of self, Miss Quentin is forever "gobbing paint on her face" and dressing like a whore, for that is the only identity left to her. In contrast to her mother, however, her hypersexuality arises not out of deep psychological compulsion but from the simple fact that there is nothing else in her life. If Caddy's eyes show guilt and terror, Quentin's are "hard as a fice dog's." Above all, her vicious treatment of Benjy serves to indicate how the maternal instinct, once so powerful in Caddy, has entirely withered in Quentin. "I'm bad and I'm going to hell, and I don't care", she screams at Jason in an ironic echo of the uncle for whom she is named. Appropriately enough, she runs off with a circus worker, cutting all ties to her family and immersing herself in a tawdry and transient existence where identities can be had through masks and greasepaint.[39]

Just as steeped in pathology is her chief antagonist within the household, Jason. As numerous critics have pointed out, Faulkner's description of Jason in the appendix as "logical rational contained" and "the first sane Compson since Colloden" is true only in the most sarcastic sense. In fact, there are striking resemblances between Jason and Quentin that become apparent as soon as one looks beneath the surface. Both are reacting to the volatility of being a Compson in the modern world—Quentin by clinging to his inherited identity, Jason by violently repudiating his. Like Quentin, Jason is completely unable to master time, forever racing about behind schedule with no hope of catching up, and has thoroughly repressed his sexuality. Though he does not actually kill himself, his behavior during the period we observe him can only be called self-destructive, culminating in his fight with the hatchet-wielding old man at the circus camp ("What were you trying to do? commit suicide?" the circus owner asks him).[40]

In clinical terms, Jason suffers from paranoia, a psychotic disorder in which a person comes to believe himself the victim of an immense conspiracy whose sole purpose is to persecute him. The paranoiac, we are told, "feels that he is being controlled, observed, influenced, criticized," and often hears voices telling him "'he is crazy, he is insane!'" Such delusions pervade Jason's monologue, centered on his persistent fear that the rest of the community will think him mentally unbalanced: "All the time I could see them watching me like a hawk, waiting for a chance to say Well I'm not surprised I expected it all the time the whole family's crazy." Everyone, it seems, is responsible for what has befallen him—his ancestors, Caddy, his niece, his servants, his employer, and the "dam eastern jews" on Wall Street who are trying to steal his money. Even the telegraph company shares the blame for his losses on the cotton market: "They're hand in glove with that New York crowd. Anybody could see that."[41]

Indeed, Jason believes that the universe itself takes special delight in harassing him. Like Quentin, he refuses to accept his father's teaching that the natural world operates according to blind chance, with human beings no more than helpless pawns in an indifferent cosmos. To counter that prospect, he ascribes magical powers to nature, convincing himself that rain pours down from the heavens just to drench him and that the brambles and poison oak he encounters while spying on his niece were put there primarily for his torment. "The only thing I couldn't understand," he tells us, "was why it was just poison oak and not a snake or something." The conspiracy extends all the way to the malicious sparrows that victimize him in the courthouse square: "First thing you know, bing. Right on your hat." Of course, in reality it is Jason who is forever placing himself in the path of misfortune, creating his own disasters and then taking inordinate delight in his suffering. He is the one who orders his New York broker to buy after receiving urgent advice to sell and who, in the apt words of Donald Kartiganer, "spends his Good Friday crucifying himself."[42]

Such self-victimization is an integral part of the mechanism of paranoia. As Freud explains, the paranoiac seeks to relieve himself of the burden of his superego by projecting it onto the outside world. What in the normal individual takes the form of a personal conscience, with its incessant promptings and attendant feelings of guilt, in the paranoiac turns into a conspiracy of voices that are forever criticizing him and of sinister forces deliberately out to harm him. Like all neurotic arrangements, paranoia provides certain "advantages." In Jason's case it allows him to escape the enormous weight of moral responsibility from his family's past that fatally crushes his older brother. Jason does not feel obliged to live up to the tradition of Compson honor; on the contrary, he has no apparent scruples and is capable of committing one outrageous act after the next, seemingly without remorse. At the same time he has the psychologically necessary satisfaction of being continuously punished for his sins by a long string of misfortunes (most of which he has brought upon himself). Since he views those punishments as arising from hostile agencies beyond his control, he is spared any sense of self-reproach. "They" are always to blame. Through his self-deception, Jason, in contrast to Quentin, can at least go on living in his home community. In effect, he escapes the paralysis of inner division by externalizing his problem into a relatively straightforward conflict between his own ego and everything lying outside it—thus heightening his chances of survival.[43]

In *The Sound and the Fury,* Faulkner began using Freudian concepts not only to get access to his characters at the unconscious level of their minds but also as tropes symbolizing larger trends within the culture. That is again the case here. If Quentin's neurosis serves as a metaphor for the cultural crisis that thoughtful young southerners faced in the early twentieth century (with the symptoms heightened to make the dynamics of the crisis more visible), Jason's derangement illustrates the plight of many ordinary folk within the region swept up in the social and economic turmoil of that era. As Bleikasten puts it, Faulkner was engaged in a "radioscopy of the Southern mind," using Jason to capture latent tendencies that could he found in "all the malcontents of the new South of the twenties: decayed aristocrats, grubbing small businessmen, hard-pressed dirt-farming rednecks, all those whom the hazards of the economic system had condemned to grovel in mediocrity and to boil with chronic frustration." Reality had in large extent become unbearable for these denizens of a society where military defeat was still a fresh memory and who now sensed that they were being left behind, perhaps irrevocably, as the rest of the country surged forward toward prosperity and modernization. The result was an intensification of the South's long-standing "siege mentality," with its inclination to see other regions as endemically hostile and to blame them for southern backwardness. In this way Jason's paranoia works as a Modernist literary device bringing starkly into view this darker side of the New South mentality in which the South's internal troubles were so often recast into an ongoing battle between "us" and "them."[44]

Faulkner not only depicts that mentality but goes on to unmask it, pinpointing the real forces at work beneath its proffered self-image. For example, Jason, in keeping with the archetypal New South persona, conceives of himself as a man of firm resolve, rational and businesslike, who, as Olga Vickery notes, "alone has a firm grasp on reality." He is likewise at pains to assert his independence. "I guess I dont need any man's help to get along," he boasts; "I can stand on my own feet like I always have." His constant point of reference is his alcoholic father, whose failed stewardship let the family slip into its present state of genteel poverty. Utterly rejecting his father's model—Jason won't touch a drop of whiskey—he sees his mission in life as stopping that slippage: "Somebody's got to hold on to what little we have left, I reckon." "Man enough" to keep the flour barrel full, as he puts it, he will be a strong head of household, restoring some of the family's lost property and status if the world will just give him a fair chance, much as the leaders of the New South movement sought to recoup the supposed failures of their predecessors.[45]

Again and again, however, Faulkner undercuts this posture of autonomy, revealing Jason's claims as mere swagger. Far from being a strong father figure, Jason, we discover, is more like a helpless child. Unable to work steadily at his job, he behaves like a schoolboy playing hooky, dodging up and down alleyways so that Earl, his boss, won't see him. Utterly self-centered, he displays the sort of petty spite one might associate with a five-year-old, as when he destroys a set of carnival tickets rather than give one free to his black retainer, Luster. "A big growed man like you," Dilsey appropriately scolds him. Nor does he truly earn his paycheck; rather, the money is a gift from Earl, who generously supports the family out of an abiding affection for Mrs. Compson—that is what keeps the flour barrel full. Moreover, beyond doubt it is the servants who actually run the household, not Jason.[46]

Most telling of all, Jason has inordinate difficulty handling money—one of the key indicators of a mature sense of autonomy in modern society and an obvious prerequisite for any aspiring capitalist. The basic modalities of autonomy, Erikson explains, are "holding-on" and "letting-go"—which in the realm of finance means that a person has mastered the skills of saving and investing money and also knows how to spend it wisely or give it away when appropriate. But Jason is completely irrational in his attitude toward money. In his mind, it exists not to meet various practical needs but mainly to gratify his ego by giving him a sense of power. He tends to hoard his wealth, locking it away in a strongbox in his closet, and can be tyrannical about small sums, allowing his niece only ten dollars out of the fifty-dollar money order her mother has sent her in order to show who is in charge. "You've got to learn one thing, and this is that when I tell you to do something, you've got it to do," he insists. At the same time, he will impulsively lavish a forty-dollar tip on his mistress, again primarily to establish his control: "Gave it to her. I never promise a woman anything nor let her know what I'm going to give her. That's the only way to manage them." His disastrous ventures in the cotton market are likewise guided not by actual market conditions but by his unquenchable desire to assert himself. He will buy or sell—hold or let go—with no regard to financial consequences, so long as he can maintain the illusion that he is in command: "After all, like I say, money has no value; it's just the way you spend it. It dont belong to anybody, so why try to hoard it. It just belongs to the man that can get it and keep it."[47]

However, the central problem for Jason and the others who share his plight is precisely that their loss of status has left them feeling that they no longer have control over their lives. A member of a family that once ranked among the most powerful in the community, Jason has been relegated to the role of clerk in a hardware store, where he must respond patiently to the trivial demands of hayseed customers, like the "dam redneck" who "spent fifteen minutes deciding whether he wanted a twenty cent hame string or a thirty-five cent one." Nothing galls him more than to hear Earl tell a simple farm woman: "Yes ma'am, Mr. Compson will wait on you." Compsons are not supposed to wait on anyone, but for Jason there is no other choice. As often as he may deny that he cares about his family's former standing, it is clear that the experience of decline has been exceedingly painful for him. When he overhears people talking about the family's dire straits, he assures his mother, "You can jest bet I shut them up by telling them how my people owned slaves here when you all were running little shirt tail country stores and farming land no nigger would look at on shares." But, as Jason well knows, virtually all of the Compsons' landed domain has now been sold.[48]

Jason's attempted solution to his predicament takes the shape of what Erikson calls "distantiation," In one bold stroke he seeks to repudiate his Compson heritage altogether: "I haven't got much pride, I can't afford it with a kitchen full of niggers to feed and robbing the state asylum of its star freshman. Blood, I says, governors and generals. It's a dam good thing we never had any kings or presidents; we'd all be down there at Jackson [the state insane asylum] chasing butterflies." Encouraged by his mother, who informs him he is "a Bascomb, despite your name," he attempts to cut all ties between himself and Compsonhood. It will be Jason, we learn from the appendix, who will finally sell the family home, allowing the once gracious mansion to be turned into a boardinghouse. But while such distantiation, like his paranoia, may permit his short-term survival, Faulkner leaves no doubt that Jason's fate is not to be admired. A "childless bachelor," he represents as much of a historical dead end as his ill-fated siblings. Jason has "no human ties with anyone," observes Isadore Traschen, "his family, servants, whore, or employer; he is divorced from the South and its traditions, from nature and God, and finally from himself, as his headaches suggest." By the close of his section he has become not only detestable but utterly pathetic, "sitting quietly behind the wheel of a small car, with his invisible life ravelled out about him like a worn sock." His sad saga becomes a cautionary tale, a reminder to contemporary readers that no shortcuts existed for resolving the crisis of southern identity so poignantly symbolized in the fall of the house of Compson.[49]

•••

Perhaps the most indisputable sign that Faulkner's Modernist authorial self was firmly in charge of writing *The Sound and the Fury* lies in the character of Benjy Compson. Again and again, Benjy stands the Victorian value system on its head: a creature of undiluted moral purity, by far the noblest of the Compsons and the only one capable of genuine religious feeling, he is also a drooling idiot, with skin that is "dead looking" and "dropsical," who walks "with a shambling gait like a trained bear." Unable to care for himself or even to speak, Benjy appears at first sight barely human; in a later interview Faulkner explicitly referred to him as "an animal." Yet Arthur Geffen is surely not alone in describing Benjy as "a holy idiot . . . capable of intuitive acts and knowledge denied to far more 'intelligent' people." Benjy reflects the paradoxical Modernist beliefs that virtue is especially likely to be found among those conventionally dismissed as "savage" or "primitive" and that the kind of knowledge that really matters comes through extensive suffering rather than formal learning. Benjy's function, then, is not to illustrate southern degeneracy, as so many of the book's initial readers believed, but to supply it Modernist standard of judgment. Unimpeachably authentic, he is a device for ensuring that the reader grasps the full moral meaning, the existential truth, of what is happening to the Compsons—which is why the novel begins and ends with him.[50]

He performs that task so well because of the unique way his mind operates. "Benjy," writes Kartiganer, "is perception prior to consciousness, prior to the human need to abstract from events an intelligible order." His soliloquy is made up of a continuous flow of experiential fragments, both immediate and remembered, unimpeded by any effort at rational interpretation. Those fragments are presented in a sequence determined not by logic or chronology but by the emotional associations that the events carry for him. In other words, Benjy's thinking takes place at the level of the mind that Modernist writers on epistemology from William James onward have tended to privilege. Raw sensory perceptions, they have claimed, provide human beings with their most direct access to reality. As those perceptions continue through subsequent stages of the thought process, rising into consciousness and ultimately becoming transformed into abstract concepts, they are increasingly distorted. Each application of the intellect, however valuable it might be for practical purposes, takes us further from the "truth." Benjy, however, avoids such distortion by never engaging in cerebration. In addition, he relies heavily on his sense of smell, which for him is akin to a moral sense. He can, we are told, actually "smell" impending death and Caddy's loss of innocence. Again, this metaphoric device is in keeping with his role as a vehicle for Modernist perspective. As Geffen points out, smell is "the sense least associated with intellectual perception" and is often regarded in folk belief "as the mysterious means which gifted people use to pierce through appearances to truth."[51]

Paradoxically, Benjy can function as such an accurate reporter of events precisely because he has no ego to interfere with or bias his perceptions. Repeatedly he leaves himself out of his own narrative; we often learn he is crying, for example, when others tell him to hush. He is a man totally lacking in self-integration, "shaped of some substance whose particles would not or did not cohere to one another or to the frame which supported it." Castrated after a supposed attack on a schoolgirl and, although an adult white male, subservient to his black servant Luster, Benjy cannot even identify himself in terms of the basic categories of gender and race. Indeed, he has no real name—"Benjamin" was given him to replace "Maury" after his mother, realizing he was abnormal, decided she did not want him to carry the same name as her brother. She cannot imagine a more dramatic rendering of the crisis Faulkner discerned in modern southern identity.[52]

His fractured and incomplete persona, in turn, makes Benjy acutely sensitive to the lack of identity and integrity surrounding him. In contrast to Quentin, Compson honor and social status as such mean nothing to Benjy; they are abstractions far beyond his grasp. But he can and does register his horror whenever he senses decay, fragmentation, and loss. He does so by the simple expedient of weeping, a direct form of emotional response that in his case serves as a remarkably effective tool of communication. Always exactly calibrated to the moral circumstances at hand, it can range from a subtle whimper to a full-throated bellow that "might have been all time and injustice and sorrow become vocal for an instant." A vivid example comes on Easter Sunday morning when he senses that Miss Quentin has run away, marking the final step in the family's disintegration. Dilsey, realizing that Ben is "smellin hit," correctly predicts that he will stop crying once they "git off de place." But just as predictably he starts again on their return from church as soon as "the square, paintless house with its rotting portico" comes into view. Such scenes of decay are measured in Benjy's mind against remembered occasions when the family was intact and all was peaceful. Of these memories none is treasured more than the one that closes his narrative, when all four Compson children are in bed in the same room: "Caddy held me and I could hear us all. . . . Then the dark began to go in smooth, bright shapes, like it always does, even when Caddy says that I have been asleep."[53]

To accentuate this portrait of the disintegration of white southern society, Faulkner toward the novel's end, just as in *Soldiers' Pay,* offers the counterposed image of a black church service. Again, he relies on the Modernist premise that true insight is most often grounded in intense experience and cannot be accurately transmitted through mere words or logic. The church may be dilapidated and the visiting Reverend Shegog so "undersized" and "insignificant looking" that the congregation does not even notice when he enters, but nonetheless, once he has left behind the "level and cold" voice of white intellect for the "sad, timbrous quality" born of his people's tragic lives, his sermon becomes a message of hope and rebirth that moves Dilsey to tears of ecstasy. There is no real narrative or argument to what he says and little order or cohesion—just a montage of phrases and images conveying the sufferings of Jesus, "de resurrection and de light," and the promise of eternal glory to those "whut got de blood en de ricklickshun of de Lamb." As he speaks, his body, with its "shabbiness and insignificance," virtually disappears for his listeners, achieving that transcendence of physical self of which Quentin could only dream. His voice, we are told, utterly envelops them, "until he was nothing and they were nothing . . . but instead their hearts were speaking to one another in chanting measures beyond the need for words." "Yes suh. He seed hit," Dilsey remarks afterward of Shegog's immediate sensory apprehension of religious faith. "Face to face he seed it."[54]

This "oneness of emotion and purpose" that the black churchgoers possess, in Davis's phrase, could not contrast more sharply with the alienation exemplified by the Compsons. It is the sort of all-encompassing integrative experience they and other twentieth-century white southerners desperately need but from which their hopelessly divisive culture has completely shut them off. If the congregation can envision "de power and de glory," there is nothing left for descendants of the old planter class save for Benjy's lamenting sound and Jason's impotent fury. "I seed de beginnin, en now I sees de endin," Dilsey tells her daughter, referring at once to the alpha and omega she has glimpsed in her moment of passion and to the family whose sad saga she is witnessing.[55]

The summary image, encapsulating all that Faulkner had been seeking to express in the book, comes in the final pages when Luster is driving Benjy on his weekly pilgrimage to the cemetery to visit the family graves. The route takes them northward through the town square, at the center of which stands the commemorative statue of a Confederate soldier found in virtually all southern towns. By dint of ritual, the carriage always goes around the square counterclockwise; that way, keeping his head locked to the right, Benjy can entirely avoid seeing the soldier. But this time, on impulse, Luster turns left at the entrance to the square. Suddenly, the heroic past looms directly before Benjy, staring down to remind him of how far the white South has fallen: "For an instant Ben sat in an utter hiatus. Then he bellowed. Bellow on bellow, his voice mounted, with scarce interval for breath. There was more than astonishment in it, it was horror, shock; agony eyeless, tongueless; just sound." It is indeed "just sound,"[†] echoing through the reader's ears, forming a sensory bond between author and reader at the most profound level of understanding, capturing in a reverberating instant the anguish that welled up inside Faulkner whenever he contemplated the history of his region and that would now supply the motor force for the balance of his career.[56]

Notes

* At the risk of redundancy, it should again be emphasized that Faulkner was not proceeding consciously here. He assuredly did not pick up his pen with the express intent of engaging in cultural analysis. Rather, as the materials gathered from personal experience, observation, and wide reading circulated in his mind, he instinctively brought them together in a narrative that reflected his intuitive

understanding of the cultural dilemmas he and his southern contemporaries faced—exactly as a literary artist is supposed to (14).

† John V. Hagopian, among others, has badly misinterpreted the novel's closing scene by arguing that Benjy's outburst is set off by it violation of "his purely meaningless sense of order." In other words, Benjy is used to going around the monument on the right, and when he finds that Luster has instead gone to the left, he begins screaming until the familiar route is restored.

This interpretation ignores several things, including the intensity of Benjy's protest. Throughout the novel his cries have always been finely tuned to the moral outrage of the stimulus that has set them off. He whimpers when Luster mildly mistreats him, but screams in agony when Caddy loses her virginity. Clearly, the bellowing in the town square, with its "unbelievable crescendo," must have a cause greater than a simple flouting of arbitrary ritual. Moreover, in Faulkner's work the appearance of Confederate imagery is never without significance. A clue to its importance in this particular scene can be found in the spiritual kinship that Faulkner carefully establishes between Benjy and the soldier. After telling its how the latter "gazed with empty eyes beneath his marble hand in wind and weather," Faulkner just a few sentences later describes Benjy as sitting with "His gaze empty and untroubled," Throughout the fourth section, in fact. Benjy's eyes are repeatedly described as "empty" and set in a "sweet vague gaze." Finally, when Benjy and Luster turn around and head toward home, they are again violating their accustomed ritual. Presumably, if Benjy was the fanatical stickler for order that Hagopian suggests, nothing less than a resumption of the trip to the cemetery (this time going around the square the "correct" way) would finally quiet him.

The crucial phrase for understanding this incident comes in the book's last sentence, when we are told how, as Benjy looks out from the carriage, "cornice and façade [i.e., the houses they are passing] flowed smoothly once more *from left to right*" (italics added). That is the clue that informs us that his head is always turned to the right, avoiding the monument. Further confirmation appears in the map of Yoknapatawpha County* that Faulkner prepared a few years later for the first edition of *Absalom, Absalom!*. It includes a notation for the "Confederate monument which Benjy had to pass on his *left* side." The italics this time are Faulkner's own, employed, one suspects, to ensure that readers would not continue to misread the climactic scene of his Modernist masterpiece.

See Hagopian, "Nihilism in Faulkner's *The Sound and the Fury*," in Kinney, *Critical Essays: The Compson Family*, 203. I am grateful to Carolyn Jerose, my student at William Smith College, for bringing the notation on the map to my attention.

1. Cofield, "Many Faces, Many Moods," 108.

2. Levenson, *Genealogy of Modernism*, 190–193

3. Panthea Reid Broughton, "Faulkner's Cubist Novels," 87–88. On Faulkner's use of drinking to relieve internal tensions, see the excellent discussion in Karl, *William Faulkner*, 131–132.

4. Blower, *Faulkner*, 1:559–562; Wittenberg, *Faulkner*, 76; Kreiswirth, *William Faulkner*, 128; Faulkner to Horace Liveright, n.d. [October 16, 1927], November 30, [1927], and n.d. [mid- or late February 1928], in Faulkner, *Selected Letters*, 38–39.

5. Faulkner to Alfred Harcourt, February 18, 1929, in Faulkner, *Selected Letters*, 43; Blotner, *Faulkner*, 1:570, 565–567; Minter, *William Faulkner*, 93; Faulkner, "An Introduction for *The Sound and the Fury*," *Southern Review*, 710.

6. Rubin, "Dixie Special," 73; Jackson J. Benson, "Quentin Compson: Self-Portrait of the Young Artist's Emotions," in Kinney, *Critical Essays: The Compson Family,* 222, 214–217, 220; Donald Kartiganer, "Quentin Compson and Faulkner's Drama of the Generations," in Kinney, *Critical Essays: The Compson Family,* 400 n; Sundquist, *Faulkner,* 22; Irwin, *Doubling and Incest,* 158; Putzel, *Genius of Place,* 143–144.

7. Bleikasten, *Most Splendid Failure,* 133, 95.

8. Faulkner, *Sound and the Fury,* 76, 124, 176; all references will be to the "corrected edition" of *The Sound and the Fury* published in 1984 unless otherwise indicated.

9. Ibid., 66, 102; Noel Polk, "'The Dungeon Was Mother Herself': William Faulkner, 1927–1931," in Fowler and Abadie, *New Directions,* 62.

10. Davis, *Faulkner's "Negro,"* 98; Benson, "Quentin Compson," 215–216; Snell, *Phil Stone of Oxford,* 8, 15, 32.

11. Bleikasten, *Most Splendid Failure,* 193; Stonum, *Faulkner's Career,* 81; Faulkner, *Sound and the Fury,* 116, 177.

12. Faulkner, *Sound and the Fury,* 76, 80, 88, 83–85; Pilkington, *Heart of Yoknapatawpha,* 70; Slater, "Quentin's Tunnel Vision," 7.

13. Faulkner, *Sound and the Fury,* 86, 89, 105, 120–121, 116–117; Broughton, *William Faulkner,* 114; Slater, "Quentin's Tunnel Vision," 10–11.

14. Stonum, *Faulkner's Career,* 82; Olga Vickery, "Worlds in Counterpoint," in Cox, *William Faulkner,* 189; Sanford Pinsker, "Squaring the Circle in *The Sound and The Fury,*" in Corey, *Faulkner,* 119; Slater, "Quentin's Tunnel Vision," 7–8; Bleikasten, *Most Splendid Failure,* 139, 140.

15. Cowan, "Dream-Work in the Quentin Section," 98, 101; Faulkner, *Sound and the Fury,* 78, 148, 134–136; Bleikasten, *Most Splendid Failure,* 98–99.

16. Slater, "Quentin's Tunnel Vision," 6, 8–11; Faulkner, *Sound and the Fury,* 128; Cowan, "Dream-Work in the Quentin Section," 94–95.

17. Bleikasten, *Most Splendid Failure,* 108, 224; Faulkner, *Sound and the Fury,* 149; Faber, "Faulkner's *The Sound and the Fury,*" 331, 335.

18. Faulkner, *Sound and the Fury,* 150–156.

19. Ibid., 148–149, 122.

20. Ibid., 116, 148, 177; Olga Vickery, "Worlds in Counterpoint," 188–189.

21. Irwin, *Doubling and Incest,* 43; Hall, *Incest in Faulkner,* 42–43, 45, 49; John Earl Bassett, "Family Conflict in *The Sound and the Fury,*" in Kinney, *Critical Essays: The Compson Family,* 421; Faulkner, *Sound and the Fury,* 79.

22. Gwynn and Blotner, *Faulkner in the University,* 6.

23. Faulkner, *Sound and the Fury,* 101, 82; Irwin, *Doubling and Incest,* 69; Sundquist, *Faulkner,* 17.

24. Kartiganer, *Fragile Thread,* 185; Bleikasten, *Most Splendid Failure,* 94, 129–131; 217 n; Faulkner, *Sound and the Fury,* 76.

25. Faulkner, *Sound and the Fury,* 90–91, 146, 130, 81.

26. Ibid, 86, 97–100, 114; Davis, *Faulkner's "Negro,"* 94–96, 98. I would take issue with Davis's superb analysis of Quentin's attitude toward blacks on one minor point. She suggests that the "model for living" provided by Louis Hatcher, Deacon, and the Gibson family is "incomprehensible" to Quentin. My reading of the text (particularly his remarks on Hatcher) leads me to believe that he does at some level understand that model but realizes that it will always remain inaccessible to him.

27. Faulkner, *Sound and the Fury,* 81–82, 90, 92, 95–96, 112.

28. Bleikasten, *Most Splendid Failure,* 124–125; Faber, "Faulkner's *The Sound and the Fury,*" 338.

29. Faulkner, *Sound and the Fury,* 83, 80.

30. Ibid., 167, 147.

31. Ibid., 170.

32. Irwin, *Doubling and Incest,* 22–23, 90–91, 151; Sundquist, *Faulkner,* 17–18; Brown, "Language of Chaos," 549; Faulkner, *Sound and the Fury,* 90, 112, 173, 116, 80; Bleikasten, *Most Splendid Failure,* 119, 140–142.

33. Faulkner, *Sound and the Fury,* 173, 176, 81, 178–179; Slater, "Quentin's Tunnel Vision," 5.

34. Faulkner, *Sound and the Fury,* 9, 63, 19–20, 39, 45; Hall, *Incest in Faulkner,* 39.

35. Faulkner, *Sound and the Fury,* 24–27, 46, 74, 173, 133, 159, 162.

36. Gwynn and Blotner, *Faulkner in the University,* 263; Faulkner, *Sound and the Fury,* 15–55, 115, 149, 123–124; Faulkner, *The Sound and the Fury* (1946), 12–13; Brooks, *William Faulkner: The Yoknapataupba Country,* 334; Fenichel, *Psychoanalytic Theory of Neurosis,* 244. In recent years the Freudian concept of nymphomania has come under attack from feminists who regard it as yet another example of the alleged misogyny to be found at the heart of psychoanalytic theory. The fact remains, though, that Faulkner in the late 1920s was very much aware of Freud's work on sexuality and appears to have drawn heavily on nymphomania, as it was understood in his day, in fashioning the character of Caddy. To date, moreover, we do not have an equivalent gender-neutral term to describe the hypersexual behavior that can become compulsive for some women (as it can for some men)—hence the employment of "nymphomania" here in an effort to stay close to Faulkner's universe of meaning.

37. Faulkner, *Sound and the Fury,* 112, 148–150, 40–43, 47–48, 124.

38. Bleikasten, *Most Splendid Failure,* 60; Adams, *Faulkner,* 218; Pilkington, *Heart of Yoknapatawpha,* 37; Faulkner, *Sound and the Fury,* 124, 203.

39. Faulkner, *Sound and the Fury,* 282, 180, 48, 187, 70, 189.

40. Faulkner, *Sound and the Fury* (1946), 16; Kartiganer, *Fragile Thread,* 15–16; Millgate, *Achievement of William Faulkner,* 101; Bleikasten, *Most Splendid Failure,* 173–174, 151–152, 158–160, 167; Brooks, *William Faulkner: The Yoknapataupha Country,* 328; Hall, *Incest in Faulkner,* 51; Faulkner, *Sound and the Fury,* p. 313.

41. Fenichel, *Psychoanalytic Theory of Neurosis,* 430; Sigmund Freud, "Certain Neurotic Mechanisms in Jealousy, Paranoia, and Homosexuality," in *Sexuality and the Psychology of Love,* 163; Longley, *Tragic Mask,* 222; Faulkner, *Sound and the Fury,* 233, 191, 227.

42. Faulkner, *Sound and the Fury,* 305, 240–242, 248; Bleikasten, *Most Splendid Failure,* 235 n; Kartiganer, *Fragile Thread,* 15–16.

43. Fenichel, *Psychoanalytic Theory of Neurosis,* 431–434; Sigmund Freud, "On the Mechanism of Paranoia," in *General Psychological Theory,* 41.

44. Bleikasten, *Most Splendid Failure,* 169–170. On the southern siege mentality, see F. Sheldon Hackney, "Southern Violence," in Graham and Gurr, *Violence in America,* 496–497.

45. Vickery, "Worlds in Counterpoint," 192–193; Faulkner, *Sound and the Fury,* 206–208, 214 257; Stonum, *Faulkner's Career,* 87.

46. Faulkner, *Sound and the Fury,* 216,235, 196, 254–255; Davis, *Faulkner's "Negro,"* 84.

47. Erikson, *Identity and the Life Cycle,* 69–70, 107–108; Faulkner, *Sound and the Fury,* 277, 211–215,193–194, 244, 264.

48. Faulkner, *Sound and the Fury,* 194–195, 239; Davis, *Faulkner's "Negro,"* 89–91.

49. Erikson, *Identity and the Life Cycle,* 96; Faulkner, *Sound and the Fury,* 230, 233, 181, 313; Faulkner, *Sound and the Fury* (1946), 17; Traschen, "Tragic Form of *The Sound and the Fury,*" 807; Hall, *Incest in Faulkner,* 54.

50. Faulkner, *Sound and the Fury,* 274; Jean Stein, "William Faulkner: An Interview," in Hoffman and Vickery, *William Faulkner,* 74; Arthur Geffen, "Profane Time, Sacred Time, and Confederate Time in *The Sound and the Fury,*" in Kinney, *Critical Essays: The Compson Family,* 234; Waggoner, *William Faulkner,* 44.

51. Kartiganer, *Fragile Thread,* 8; Traschen, "Tragic Form of *The Sound and the Fury,*" 800–801; Schwartz, *Matrix of Modernism,* 12–21; Miligate, *Achievement of William Faulkner,* 91; Gail M. Morrison, "The Composition of *The Sound and the Fury*", in Bleikasten, Faulkner's "*The Sound and the Fury,*" 50; 11. R Absalom, "Order and Disorder in *The Sound and the Fury,*" in Kinney, *Critical Essays: The Compson Family,* 144; Geffen, "Profane Time, Sacred Time, and Confederate Time," 235.

52. Bleikasten, *Most Splendid Failure,* 71; Absalom, "Order and Disorder in *The Sound and the Fury,*" 147; Faulkner, *Sound and the Fury,* 10, 274.

53. Faulkner, *Sound and the Fury,* 288, 281, 298, 71.

54. Ibid., 293–297; Davis, *Faulkner's "Negro,"* 119–121.

55. Davis, *Faulkner's "Negro,"* 108, 116, 112, 126; Faulkner, *Sound and the Fury,* 297, Geffen, "Profane Time, Sacred Time, and Confederate Time," 240.

56. Faulkner, *Sound and the Fury,* 319–321.

GARY STORHOFF

Caddy and the Infinite Loop: The Dynamics of Alcoholism in The Sound and the Fury

The fathers have eaten sour grapes, and the children's teeth are set on edge.

Ezekiel 18:2

Arthur F. Kinney points out that William Faulkner's entire career is "family-centered" (83). Seeing this truth within the dimensions of family systems theory provides another framework with which to understand Faulkner's work, especially his first masterpiece, *The Sound and the Fury*. Family systems theorists, like Faulkner, investigate how the family shapes, patterns, and partially determines an individual's life choices. Faulkner's novel reveals the interactive bond that develops among family members as they negotiate conflicts through codes of stability they tacitly, and always covertly, create. By highlighting the occluded structures the Compsons live by, Faulkner shows us how completely the Compson family has failed to fulfill its presumed function as a site of moral guidance and emotional intimacy.

This dimension of the Compson's family life, the disguised creation of systems and subsystems to maintain stability in support of an alcoholic father, offers an explanation for Caddy's motivations, especially the disastrous choices Caddy makes in her adulthood.[1] Criticism of *The Sound and the Fury* has often identified Caddy as the noble Compson since she "retains the capacity for love" (Baum 36).[2] As the "loving" Compson, she is seen as the

The Faulkner Journal, Volume 12, Number 2 (1997): pp. 3–22.

victim, harmed by those who lack the capacity to love—most notably, Jason and Mrs. Compson. But reading Caddy solely as a passive victim throughout her life oversimplifies her identity that originates in her family of origin, especially as she transposes that role-structure into her adulthood when she becomes a mother. Caddy makes self-destructive choices predicated upon her family's role-formation. Most seriously, Caddy utterly abandons her only child to the horrific household that she herself escaped, and although she sends money for support, she sees her daughter only twice in the novel. Emphasizing her victimization—and as a corollary, her lack of freedom—is to diminish and distort her character, and to transform her profoundly tragic plot into one based on mere pathos. What are the triggers of Caddy's behavior, both in her childhood and adulthood?

By discovering her role within the Compson alcoholic family system, and by discerning the repetition of the patterns she learned as the daughter of an alcoholic, it is possible to understand her childhood parenting of Benjy and Quentin; her adolescent "rebellion," especially her sexual behavior, her pregnancy, marriage, and divorce, and finally her abandonment of Miss Quentin—all as her responses to unwritten and unspoken family rules and codes, regulatory behavior created by the entire family for protection against domestic disorder and suffering. Caddy, as an adult child of an alcoholic, predictably chooses what is most familiar in her life, and thereby unknowingly reproduces alcoholic family patterns in her adulthood.

I

"it will be better for me for all of us": Family Systems Theory and the Compson Family

Faulkner, himself an adult child of an alcoholic and a developing alcoholic when he wrote the novel, knew well that an alcoholic parent's behavior has psychological repercussions in the family far beyond his own chemical dependency; and that, given the terrific compulsions, abuse, and exploitation in the alcoholic home, alcoholic life patterns become an enduring feature of the children's lives as they mature into adulthood.[3] Revealing the psychic patterns of alcoholism is probably not deliberate. Faulkner himself was skeptical of psychiatrists and said, "what little of psychology I know the characters I have invented and playing poker have taught me. Freud I'm not familiar with" (Gwynn and Blotner 268). But as Lee Jenkins writes, Faulkner had "an intuitive perception of the depth and character of mental aberration and the various modes of mental functioning—as they appear in his characters" (148). Despite his persistent denial of his own alcoholism and its effects on his family, Faulkner understood at an intuitive level the bitter consequences of drinking on the family, and on the future possibilities of the alcoholic's children.

These consequences are dramatized in his first great novel, *The Sound and the Fury,* which focuses on the children who endure Mr. Compson's alcoholism. The Compson family is ensnared in an "infinite loop" organized around Mr. Compson's alcoholism.[4] The concept of the "infinite loop" comes from computer science and defines a programming error that causes the perpetual but unsuccessful recapitulation of an algorithm (i.e., a problem-solving strategy). This becomes an apt metaphor for the Compson family children, each of whom, as a childhood legacy, is deeply attracted to life patterns discovered or invented in childhood to cope with alcoholism. The Compsons are, in the terminology of researchers of alcoholism, "an *Alcoholic Family,* a family in which alcoholism has become a central organizing principle" (Steinglass 9). In the succinct words of John Earl Bassett, the novel "reveals a family both physically and mentally sick" (410). But "sickness," even understood colloquially, distorts the Compson family situation; the behaviors of all the Compson children—rescuing, retreating, fighting, hiding—begin as adaptive mechanisms during their childhood but become destructive of self and others in adulthood. As researcher of alcoholism Michael Elkin writes, "[Alcohol] can homogenize and organize very diverse people in predictable patterns" (71).

Family systems models have disclosed the enmeshment of children with the alcoholic parent, especially when the affected parent is the father. The model used in this essay derives from an analytic concept created by "the Gregory Bateson Group" in the 1950s. "Family Sys-terns theory," evolving from Bateson's research at Palo Alto, studies how the individual discovers a role in a family unit, and how the structure of the family of origin perpetuates itself even beyond childhood. Systems theory, unlike Freudian/Lacanian theory, focuses on how families as entities attempt collectively to maintain stability and unity—sometimes even at the expense of one scapegoated member's happiness. Rather than discover intrapsychic drives, systems theory discovers how interfamilial relations map personal roles. According to family systems theory, what is at stake in family actions and decisions is ultimately the coherence and stability of the family system itself for the long term, regardless of the individual suffering of the members that this final goal may cause. All of the Compson children suffer, they believe, for the sake of their family. Quentin, for example, threatens to commit suicide and tells his father that "it will be better for me for all of us" (178); even his own death, he believes, will be for his family's benefit. Mr. Compson—astonishingly—does not attempt to dissuade his son, nor does he entirely disagree with his son's reasoning: "but let no man prescribe for another mans wellbeing" (178). The Compson "dysfunctionality," so often noted in criticism, in actuality ensures family stability and coherence.

For the family systems model, individual behavior has its origin in the patterned and systemic interactions of all family members. Identity-creation, however, is especially problematic in an alcoholic home. Research suggests that children learn to fulfill specific roles in the process of adjusting to the alcoholic family environment.[5] The unpredictability of the family itself is so overwhelming, and the vulnerability of children so acute, that they seldom have any chance to escape their assigned identities within the family structure. The children's behavior patterns are often carried into adulthood and played again and again, in the futile effort to release themselves from chaos and emotional pain that originates in their alcoholic families, though the afflicted individuals seldom recognize the true source of their behavior.

Systems theory attempts to account for any family dynamic—alcoholism, hypochondria, suicide, excessive or indiscriminate sexual activity, or sadomasochism (the Compson pathologies)—in terms of what ultimate purpose these seemingly "individual" choices serve in the family's behalf. Family systems theory avoids an attempt to establish a neat, linear, cause-effect relationship for an individual's behavior, or to assign exclusive blame to an individual operating within the system. The concept of linear "causality" is replaced by an accounting of the family's interactional process—circular, self-generating, and self-reinforcing. A family systems view, therefore, accentuates the Compson family network as a complex, corporate whole, where each individual's behavior is a result of interpersonal forces operating to maintain their unique family system, and not simply the good or bad actions of a particularly neurotic or villainous family member.

Substance abuse cannot be separated from the operation of the family as a unit, and each member makes allowances for (and thereby effectively supports) the alcoholic's compulsion. As Murray Bowen, leading theorist of family systems, writes,

> alcoholism is one of the common human dysfunctions. As a dysfunction, it exists in the context of an imbalance in functioning in the total family system . . . every important family member plays a part in the dysfunction of the dysfunctional member. (262)

The entire family, then, becomes implicated in Mr. Compson's alcoholism; each person "plays a part" to sustain him. As we shall see, Caddy, the only Compson daughter, plays a unique role in enabling her father to continue drinking. Her family assignment, unwittingly created when she was a child and voluntarily—though unknowingly—continued in her adulthood, is to serve as the family's principle of coherence, even at her and her daughter's expense. Quentin's credo—"it will be better for me for all of us"—is Caddy's as well, into her adolescence and throughout her adulthood.

II

"Father was there.... The way he looked said Hush": The Rule of Silence in the Compson Household

At the shrouded center of the Compson world is Mr. Compson's alcoholism. It is a truism in Faulkner criticism that Mr. Compson is "weak," "ineffectual," "impotent," or otherwise powerless within the family. André Bleikasten summarizes the consensus of the novel's critics: "To start with the most obvious, Mr. Compson turns out to be an extremely weak and ineffectual father. What authority he possesses is the authority of failure" ("Fathers" 126). If it is axiomatic that Mr. Compson is not an "effectual" father, it does not follow that he lacks control and authority. Bleikasten and other critics blur the issue of control as it manifests itself in the Compson household. The fundamental issue of an alcoholic family is not obedience to the alcoholic's explicit decree or his paternal domination—in his capacity "as lawgiver" (*Splendid* 113), or as his wish to provide "blueprints for behavior" (Weinstein, *Love* 106)—but the unspoken and much more subtle psychological control that the alcoholic exerts over his family. It is paradoxical that, given Mr. Compson's literal weakness (alcoholism), he is in fact committed to exert his own willpower against the world and himself, a patterned action that is at the core of his worldview. As Gregory Bateson writes, "The so-called pride of the alcoholic is in some degree ironic. It is a determined effort to test something like 'self-control' with an ulterior but unstateable purpose of proving that 'self-control' is ineffectual and absurd" (327). Mr. Compson's primary concern is to maintain his drunkenness in the family, with no reprisals or criticisms from other family members.

His control over the family is manifested in his dismissal of all emotions in the family. This repression is enacted by his advocating philosophical stoicism throughout the novel—"Whether or not you consider [an act] courageous is of more importance than the act itself than any act" (176). For Mr. Compson, his children's emotions are random, accidental, and untrustworthy as guides: "A love or a sorrow is a bond purchased without design and . . . matures willynilly and is recalled without warning to be replaced by whatever issue the gods happen to be floating at the time" (178). This devaluation of emotions (ironically phrased in the financial metaphors of bonds and brokerage that he apparently disavows), in favor of stern self-control and rationalism, is typical of his alcoholic behavior. His control acts in service of his denial, his coercive suppression of his family's pain disguised as his counsel and support.[6] If seen within the context of the alcoholic family, then, Mr. Compson's philosophical discourse is his regulatory strategy enfeebling the family; at stake is not only his own alcoholism, but the consistency of his family that enables it.

"Hushing" becomes his major weapon of control of the other family members. His very appearance cuts off his family's speech: "Father was there, in his shirt sleeves. The way he looked said Hush" (61). They cannot speak of their feelings, given his strategic commitment to stoicism. The silence maintained, the "hushing" of all family members, is a fundamental family rule, created to repress their relational problems. Caroline, Quentin, Caddy, and Jason cannot express their anger with him. Benjy's observation that "he drank" (43) punctuates the novel, but the alcoholic's compulsion that Benjy notices (but cannot express) is not commented upon by family members in Mr. Compson's presence. The alcoholic's denial of his problem, which Faulkner personally manifested,[7] afflicts the entire Compson family.

Far from acting as the "absent father" many critics claim him to be, Mr. Compson is the epicenter of the Compson family dynamics. A gauge of his importance is how his children reflect their own identities in his, even after his death. It is to the father, either alive or dead, that his children turn throughout their lives for confirmation of their own fragile sense of selves. It is his judgment that serves as a final confirmation of their own actions: Quentin, who reviews his dialogue with his father shortly before his suicide; Caddy, who sacrifices herself in a loveless marriage in the vain hope that Jason will be financially secure in his old age; and his namesake son Jason IV, who uses him as an ironic model of a complete failure as he matures, but who duplicates his father's perverse, self-destructive choices, even sending Maury money. Though Mr. Compson seems powerless in the world outside the family confines, he wields immense control, living and dead, in a household sealed from that wider world.

Mr. Compson's coercive speech, disguised as philosophy, forms the principal mechanism of expelling a world that might criticize his drunkenness. If he proclaims the "external" world as vain, meaningless, and futile, he can justify his alcoholism as an appropriate response to the world's endless emptiness, a peculiarly "modernist" world view.[8] The social world, with its shared meanings, customs, and rituals (e.g., the Easter church service of 1928) then becomes a part of the "outside" version of the world that must be suppressed in favor of the "inside" family's perspective that cannot confront his alcoholism. His drinking, resulting in the family's shame within the bustling world of Jefferson, leads the Compsons to cut off all ties with their own community. The Compsons' isolation, so often remarked upon in criticism, is merely typical of families marked by substance abuse. In order to protect the afflicted (and shamed) parent, the entire family creates an alliance against the wider, social environment to defend an embattled family structure. In family systems theoretics, the Compsons create a "closed system," a family organization that discourages any interaction with a possibly critical social environment, to reinforce and enable Mr. Compson's drinking. As psychologist Gail

S. Lederer writes, "Relationally, alcoholic systems tend to be closed systems with rigid family rules" (219).

Mr. Compson's drinking is the source of a fundamental division between the family and the world. For the Compsons, space becomes metaphorical. The Compson family unit becomes the "insiders" in a closed system; society external to the family are the "outsiders."[9] The symbolic dichotomy between the "inside" family and the "outside" social world maintains the Compson marriage and organizes the children's lives. A systemic exploration of the Compson family must include the parents' marital relationship. Central to the family systems approach is the notion of power and control that constantly shifts between family members, and that quest for power is at the center of Jason and Caroline's interactions. Their debilitation is reciprocal; each partner acts in concert with the other to attain an equal incapacitation, which ironically is intended to demonstrate power by directing the sympathies of others. Mr. Compson's drinking is mirrored by Mrs. Compson's affliction (hypochondria) in her upstairs bedroom.

Ironically, Caroline's strategy for dominance is in inverse relation to Jason's own. Mr. Compson suffers from alcoholism and appears paralytic before the demands of the marketplace, which he appears to banish as irrelevant and pointless. Caroline's "paralysis," no less real than her husband's, is her response to the demands of domesticity. In compensation for her husband, Caroline strikes a balance: If her husband attempts to rule by inactivity, she will challenge him in good measure. So it happens that Caroline retreats to her bed as he escapes to his office, and she organizes family activity around her various undiagnosed illnesses just as he attempts to control his children's perspectives on the world with his drinking. Rather than speak honestly and forthrightly about her husband's drinking; rather than confront herself with her disastrous marriage; rather than take decisive action that might save her present life and her children's, Caroline avoids the truths that such self-scrutiny will bring. To confront these truths would jeopardize the marriage and perhaps end it. Instead, she manufactures a role for herself that will be reciprocal with her husband, and thereby attempts to manage him and her family. As psychotherapist Susan Baur writes, "Seen in the family setting, hypochondria . . . provides a complicated way of avoiding the dangers—and benefits—of honest expression, and as long as the family's transactions are regulated by hypochondria, the hypochondriac and spouse and children are likely to go nowhere and do nothing" (91–92). Although each embattles the other, both Mr. and Mrs. Compson cooperate in excluding the social world to preserve their relationship and their family.

As the family patriarch, Mr. Compson nears the end of his family's distinguished lineage, and it is his inheritance that is the sole source of the family's ever-dwindling assets. He maintains his power in the household primarily by controlling the checkbook. His decisions determine all family expenditures, a fact he emphasizes. It is he who agrees to the sale of Benjy's pasture for Quentin's year at Harvard, though he professes uninterest in Quentin's education.

Most significantly for the dynamics of alcoholism within the family, he has tolerated his brother-in-law Maury Bascomb living with the family, though they can ill afford such a generosity. But this choice too seems deliberate and manipulative, designed to set him off as the superior drunk, to demonstrate to his family that his alcoholism is not so bad. "I admire Maury," says Mr. Compson ironically. "He is invaluable to my own sense of racial superiority. I wouldn't swap Maury for a matched team" (43). The Compsons thus enable not only Mr. Compson but his brother-in-law whom he scorns. In this way, Maury anchors alcoholism within the home. Maury acts as Jason's own ironic foil within the family cluster, for Maury is an indolent, self-indulgent, indigent, nonworking alcoholic, with his toddys and hidden bottles, but without the redemption of a distinguished family name or a legacy. Accommodating Maury as outsider within the family—without wife, job, education, station, or family—solidifies Mr. Compson's identity by accentuating Maury's difference. The invitation to Maury therefore serves the purpose of shoring up Jason's sense of self, evidence to other family members that the social decline of the Compsons is momentarily forestalled.

Though Mr. Compson attempts to establish his control in his role as the exchequer of the family treasury, doling out his cash and his sarcasm, Caroline stabilizes his influence by her passivity, her self-pity, and her bitter irony, usually directed against her own children. Yet her speech, because it is centered on her self-delusory needs (e.g., respectability), fails to reveal to the family their shared misery. Countering her husband's alienation, Caroline finds justification for maintaining her paralysis throughout her life by lamenting the loveless marriage in which she believes she is entrapped. Even after her husband's death, Caroline can pretend powerlessness by assigning blame to her husband's negligence. Conversely, by condemning his wife and all women, Mr. Compson can justify and rationalize his own escape from his home's hostile environment into alcoholism and an early death. Together, within the family drama of shifting power and psychological control, Mr. and Mrs. Compson can rationalize their self-destructive behaviors. Caroline and Jason represent opposing human tendencies that only together can be seen as a consistent whole; each unconsciously conspires to reinforce the other's behavior patterns, until their choices have become habitual and serve as a rationale for their marital unhappiness.

Routine events—the "rigid family rules" of the alcoholic system (Lederer 219)—are the best indicators of marital conventions. One relatively commonplace incident in Compson family functioning illustrates the family's rigidified laws. Shortly after Damuddy's funeral, the children prepare for bedtime, but without their parents' assistance: *"Mother's sick, Father said. Dilsey will put you to bed"* (62). Instead of acting as parent and putting the children to bed himself, Mr. Compson delegates this role to Dilsey. But the incident also reveals to the children a dynamic of the Compson marriage and parenting. He tells the children that Mother is "sick" (but not "very" sick [75]), thereby enabling her "frailty," but also disclosing that Dilsey must occupy the role of caretaker.

The children, especially Caddy, have understood this unwritten family code. Later in the novel, Caddy attempts to "comfort" Caroline, who weeps in general despair of her life, and insidiously manipulates Caddy into extending comfort to her mother (i.e., parenting her and, like her father, accepting and enabling her hypochondria):

> Mother caught me in her arms and began to cry, and I cried. . . . Mother lay crying against the red and yellow cushion.
>
> "Hush, Mother." Caddy said. "You go up stairs and lay down, so you can be sick. I'll go get Dilsey." (64)

Caddy imitates her father's "hushing" of her mother's feigned distress, for she intuitively comprehends the scripted sequence of events in the family's code, the "rigid rules" she is compelled to enforce. Though she acknowledges her mother, she also recognizes that Mother's "suffering" is only pretended ("so you can be sick"), and silences her ("Hush, Mother"). Caddy understands that Caroline's crying is not taking place at the proper symbolic space ("You go up stairs") and that Mrs. Compson's "rest" (her incapacity) is somehow essential to proper family functioning. Not calling upon her father, she calls upon Dilsey instead to intervene on Benjy's behalf. Unawares, she has absorbed the family protocol: Family members are to be "hushed" when disturbed or distressed, and Dilsey rather than another family member should be called to contain emotional outbursts.

The most significant battle for marital control occurs only two months before Mr. Compson's death. Mrs. Compson has helped engineer Caddy's marriage to Herbert Head, an event to which Mr. Compson acceded and perhaps even secretly promoted with his anxiety over Caddy's pregnancy. Caddy's purpose in marrying Head resembles her mother's in marrying Mr. Compson: to marry for established money. Caddy's purpose, of course, is redemptive; she wishes to provide for her father and Benjy. There is no evidence that Mr. Compson attempted to prevent his daughter's sacrifice; in fact, he shares Caroline's shock and embarrassment over her pregnancy, as we shall see. But if her perception of his financial need leads to her marriage, his psychological need for control of his daughter leads to her divorce. Presumably realizing that his own death is near, Mr. Compson reveals to Herbert Head that Caddy's child is another man's (Ross and Polk 160). In doing so, he also decides momentously to bring Miss Quentin home, take her away from Caddy, and condemn her to life with Jason and Mrs. Compson:

> Father went up there and got it [Miss Quentin] and brought it home and wouldn't tell anything about where she [Caddy] was or anything and Mother crying and saying "And you didn't even see him? You didn't even try to get him to make any provision for it?" and Father says "No she shall not touch his money not one cent of it" and Mother says "He can be forced to by law. He can prove nothing, unless—Jason Compson," she says. "Were you fool enough to tell—"
>
> "Hush, Caroline," Father says. (197–198)

For once, "hushing" among the Compsons does not cloak the truth of Mr. Compson's control. When Caroline realizes that her husband has revealed the truth to Herbert, she also realizes that he has relieved Herbert of any financial responsibility for Caddy and Miss Quentin. She realizes that Mr. Compson, by his own speech, destroys his daughter's marriage, and consigns her to her fate as a penniless, unmarried mother. He undermines Caddy's plans for him and Benjy, ruins his son's job prospects in the bank, and condemns Miss Quentin to her future misery growing up in Jason's household. Whatever Miss Quentin's fate with Caddy, a single mother, it could not have been worse than living with Jason and Caroline.

It cannot be argued that Mr. Compson could not foresee the effects of his decision; on the contrary, he knew only too well the torment his wife and his son could inflict upon his only granddaughter. Nor can it be argued that Mr. Compson's contempt for Herbert's money implies his honor. He was not above collaborating in Caddy's engagement, as implied by the wedding engagement that Quentin obsessively remembers; nor does he resist Herbert during Herbert's visit to Jefferson (as does Quentin). On the contrary, Caddy's marriage and divorce represent psychic victories for Mr. Compson. Her sacrificial marriage is her tragic acknowledgment of his control over his family during his lifetime, her last opportunity of proving her commitment to him and the rest of the Compsons. But his final act of control is performed from beyond his grave: after his death, Caroline and Jason are delegated with the responsibility of degrading and destroying Miss Quentin.

III

"He's Not Too Heavy. I Can Carry Him": Caddy as the Little Parent

If the family system contained only Jason's and Caroline's polarities, it would finally splinter and collapse. How, then, does the Compson family maintain itself? The Compsons establish their homeostasis, their stability, through an emotional enmeshment with their children. (Faulkner hints that this pattern had been established in previous generations, in the Bascomb family, with the closeness of Maury and Caroline.) Consistently, the Compson parents lose their own emotional boundaries and become entangled in the emotional lives of their children. Marital surrogacy, vicarious expression of sexuality, class standing, and materialistic achievement: these are the goals assigned to Quentin, Jason, and Caddy. Their behaviors are the connective elements that preserve the family's systemic configuration. If Mr. Compson's alcoholism produces Caroline's dissatisfaction, and if Caroline's pietistic disavowals and hypochondria enable Mr. Compson's drinking, then the children too have their part to play to protect the family's unity. In their lives, they provide what each parent secretly hungers for—their own fulfillment—but can never have.

Sigmund Freud wrote of how children become "narcissistic objects," as their parents refashion their children's identities in order to revise and redefine their own identities:

> Illness, death, renunciation of enjoyment, restrictions on his own will, shall not touch him; the laws of nature and society shall be abrogated in his favor; he shall once more really be the center and the core of creation—"His majesty the Baby," as we once fancied ourselves. The child shall fulfill those wishful dreams of the parents which they never carried out—the boy shall become a great man and a hero in his father's place, and the girl shall marry a prince as a tardy compensation for her mother. ("On Narcissism" 72)

Freud's description of the parents' "overestimation" (72) of the child is but one of many possible roles parents may create for their children in compensation for their own fantasy lives. The parents may also devise a fictive "underestimation" of their offspring so as to live vicariously in some forbidden domain, as the parents disavow some despised aspect of themselves and project it onto their children. As such, the child inhabits a space that the parents ostensibly renounce but secretly desire; as Freud argues, the child lives out the parents' own wished-for lives by proxy.[10] So it happens that a sexually repressed and supposedly prudish family like the Compsons will produce a sexually reckless person like Caddy; or that a family seemingly indifferent to financial affairs and hard work will spin off an obsessively penurious son like Jason, who believes himself to be the embodiment of hard work.

As the only daughter, Caddy is the most important child in the family because in her character, rather than in the sons' characters, the family can resolve the conflict between "outside" and "inside," between the family circle and the social world. To some extent, her role is gendered, for in her childhood she acts as a maternal force securing the closed family system; but in her adolescence, she resembles her father in her intemperance and self-indulgence. Because she complements both her parents, her family position is equivocal, and her complementarity must be double to accommodate both Mr. and Mrs. Compson. She becomes the delegate who ventures outside the family (and as a consequence contaminates herself with the excess the world symbolizes for the family) but who also defines and supports the family boundaries that resist the world. It is her equivocal and alternating position within the family that complicates her character.

Caddy is often praised for her "selfless love," a comment presumably arising from Faulkner's own statement that she is his "heart's darling" (Gwynn and Blotner 6). But her constant "loving" is in reality a delegation of obligations within the family. Their exploitation of Caddy, disguised as allowing Caddy to express her natural love freely, requires that she become something that she cannot—a parenting adult—and that she put aside her own childhood needs in favor of maintaining the family structure. The duty of "loving" others is foisted onto Caddy; she acts out her parents' roles as a surrogate, not only to Benjy but to her brothers as well. As criticism of the novel has amply demonstrated, Caddy assumes the role of the little parent in the Compson family.[11] Caddy, in diametric contrast to her mother, is responsible, loving, selfless, and capable as a parentified child, devoting herself to Benjy as if he were her own child. She exclaims to her mother, "He's not too heavy. I can carry him" (61). The disruption of her own childhood, when she is coerced by both parents to be a nurturing rather than a nurtured child, leads her to become an active instrument of her family's will, an unconscious role-player who inevitably renounces her own best interests throughout her life for the sake of consolidating an unreal identity created for her by her family.

But Caddy as "little parent" represents only one aspect of her character. As her family's central character, she stands as a locus of opposing forces. Caddy oscillates between her family and society throughout the novel, in her twin roles as Little Parent and Wild Thing. The family's splitting of the world into "inside" and "outside" has been essential for the survival of the alcoholic family, and it is Caddy who symbolically ties together these bifurcated worlds. Her identity as child-mother serves to sustain domesticity in the Compson home; but she also coalesces in her character the world outside the closed family system which she achieves through her active sexuality. Caddy's character synthesizes the antithetical impulses of self-denial on the one hand (Caddy as Little Parent) and sensual self-indulgence (Caddy as Wild Thing) on the other. The inherent contradictions of her family role are ultimately destructive, for both her mothering of her brothers and her expression of her sexuality are symptomatic of the family's dysfunctionality.

Because she alternates in her allegiances to both the social and domestic world in the novel, she is at once her brothers' capable nurse but also her parents' persecutor. As a child, she is the family's loyal servant; but as an adolescent, she is the contemptible family traitor. Certainly it is objectionable to label Caddy as a "promiscuous nymphomaniac" (Anderson 57), or to construct her identity, on the basis of her gender, as a symbolic representation of "the libido" (Collins 3). Such language reinscribes the sexist "double standard" of sexual activity; no reader should be insensitive to the rigid prohibitions imposed on women during the 1920s in the South.

Nevertheless, Caddy's sexual involvement with men is rendered by Faulkner as decidedly problematic, for it apparently never brings her any kind of personal satisfaction but only pain, loss, and grief. Far from rebelling against repressive sexual codes, she has internalized them, feeling repugnance for her own sexuality: "*There was something terrible in me sometimes at night I could see it grinning at me I could see it through them grinning at me through their faces*" (112). As if to perversely satisfy her family's covert desire that she mature early so that she can mother them, she becomes a mother in actuality, to Miss Quentin. A child acting as a parent throughout her childhood, Caddy becomes, an actual mother too soon with Miss Quentin.

Her compulsive sexual activity mirrors her father and mother's complementarity within the family system. She has sexual relations with men she despises; she tells Quentin: "When they touched me I died" (149). Even granting that Quentin's account may be distorted by his own fear of sex, the text implies her eroticized self is a product of her alcoholic home. The two men whom Faulkner dramatizes, Dalton Ames and Herbert Head, seem refractions of her father. The hypermasculinized lover she sends away, Dalton seems an unconscious repetition of Mr. Compson's contempt for all women ("theyre all bitches" [160]). Her choice of a husband, Herbert Head, reproduces her father's relationship with the Compson family. Like Mr. Compson, Herbert is supposed to be the source of cash and control, but cannot be depended on for love. Just as her mother abandons her own emotional needs in favor of status, Caddy betrays her own need for love when she sends Dalton away to sustain her role as Little Parent to Quentin, then marries a man for financial and social security. As if to duplicate her father's own distant parenting and her mother's neglect, she abandons her own daughter to Jason and Caroline—regretfully, but with little resistance.

If Caddy's childhood role as maternal figure serves to reduce stress in the family system because she replaces her mother, becoming an actual mother increases tension because she threatens her father. Although most criticism of the novel focuses exclusively on Caroline's excessive response to Caddy's pregnancy, close examination of the text reveals that Caddy herself is more concerned about Mr. Compson's exaggerated grief over her pregnancy—which supposedly precipitates a severe bout of his drinking. Caddy, like Mrs. Compson, is deeply enmeshed in her father's drinking. During Caddy and Quentin's conversation at the branch, Caddy implores Quentin to "look after Benjy and Father" (123) and their needs, since after her marriage she knows that she will no longer be in the family to help regulate Mr. Compson's drinking (she supposes), or to protect Benjy from Jason's malevolence and Caroline's neglect.

Caddy's feelings of guilt derive from her unfounded belief that she is responsible for the quantity and duration of her father's drinking. She mistakenly believes that she has secretly caused his latest bout with her illegitimate pregnancy: "Father will be dead in a year they say if he doesn't stop drinking and he wont stop he cant stop since I since last summer and then they'll send Benjy to Jackson I cant cry I cant even cry one minute" (124). What is notable here is that Caddy is assuming responsibility for her father, and as a secondary effect, for Benjy's fate.

Of course, Mr. Compson is responsible for his own alcoholism. But her assumption that her behavior causes her father's drunkenness is shared by Quentin, and presumably by Caroline and Jason. Quentin intuitively understands that her loss of control outside the family boundaries in some sense provides emotional justification for the father's drunkenness, relieving Mr. Compson of his own responsibility. In short, Quentin too believes that she is responsible for Mr. Compson's drinking. He rebukes her: "If they need any looking after it's because of you" (111.). Caddy, like many daughters of alcoholics, takes full responsibility for her father's behavior, but does so as if on cue, with a supporting cast (Quentin) who affirms her false self-incriminations.[12]

Caddy's tortured sense of guilt reveals that Mr. Compson is *not* indifferent to the "outside" world but slavishly dependent upon it, even willing to sacrifice his only daughter to maintain the Compson "honor" in the wider community of Jefferson. Like Quentin, Mr. Compson invests his family's honor in Caddy's virginity, despite his proclamation to the contrary. When he speaks with Quentin, Mr. Compson assures him that "Women are never virgins. Purity is a negative state and therefore contrary to nature" (116); that, born with "an affinity for evil" (96), women are "periodic filth between two moons balanced" (128). Nevertheless, when Caddy becomes pregnant, Mr. Compson's erstwhile stoicism is shattered. Not only does he increase his drinking, but he anguishes over what the townspeople might say about the Compsons. He tells Caroline to take Caddy to French Lick, "then all the talk will die away" (102)—as if to extend his "hushing" to Jefferson itself.

At this point in her life, the parent-child cycle within the Compson family begins again, but with different players. In shamefully playing out her family role as Wild Thing, providing her father with an excuse for drinking but also duplicating his excess, Caddy accepts the punishment she thinks she deserves. With Mrs. Compson, Quentin, and Jason all judging her as guilty of betrayal (but each in different ways), she must be cast out of the family and into the world, the defined arena of self-indulgence and sensuality for the Compson system. With her passing, another scapegoat must take her place: Miss Quentin.

Caddy was taught by her alcoholic family to envision only two choices available in any situation—desert either her family (the insiders) or her lovers (the outsiders). She learns the family rule well: Abandonment and relinquishment are inevitable, and whom to abandon and what to relinquish are the only questions. Because Caddy has never experienced her own childhood; because she learns from her father and mother models of parenting that mean making someone else do the job; because her own systemic behavior of self-denial has become inflexibly habitual, Caddy refuses to raise her own child, though she desperately wishes to do so. Instead, she abandons Miss Quentin (ironically, now the most recent "insider," the newest Compson) deliberately with unstable Caroline and her malicious brother Jason (the surviving "insiders," her family of origin) and disappears into the vast "outside" of excess and extravagance. In deserting her daughter, she unknowingly repeats her mother's desertion of her. Caddy also unconsciously echoes her father's parenting, for sending Jason a monthly check for Miss Quentin's care is a thinly veiled repetition of her father's monetary (but impersonal, distanced) caretaking. The dysfunctionality of Caddy's relationship with her mother and father is thus repeated and perpetuated.

Caddy gives no convincing reason why she cannot raise her daughter by herself, but falls back upon the Compson doctrines of helplessness and meaninglessness, family codes inculcated by Mr. and Mrs. Compson during her childhood. One pathetic scene clarifies the tragic Compson pattern of abdication and self-delusion. Caddy returns to Jefferson, now the repudiated "outsider," to visit her daughter. In tragic repetition of her mother's paralysis and her father's nihilism, Caddy pleads with Jason, asking to take Miss Quentin back in exchange for a thousand dollars:

> "And I know how you'll get it," I says, "You'll get it the same way you got her. And when she gets big enough—" Then I thought she really was going to hit at me. . . . She acted for a minute like some kind of toy that's wound up too tight and about to burst all to pieces.
>
> "Oh, I'm crazy," she says. "I'm Insane. I can't take her. Keep her. What am I thinking of. . . . No. I have nothing at stake," she says, making that noise, putting her hands to her mouth, "Nuh-nuh-nothing," she says.
>
> "Here," I says. "Stop that!" (209–210)

The emotional power of this scene, and the spectacle of Caddy's loss of Miss Quentin, must not blind the reader to Caddy's own capacity for self-deception and its great psychic cost to her and her daughter. Caddy is reduced to inarticulateness—silence, "hushed" by Jason with the sarcasm he has learned since childhood. Evident here once again is Caddy's propensity for self-sacrifice and her willingness to accept losses for the "benefit" of the family. In a sense, Caddy's action echoes Quentin's words: "it will be better for me for all of us" (178).

But in adulthood, Caddy's self-sacrifice is tied paradoxically to a disavowal of her own responsibility to herself and her daughter. To "save" her daughter from the world she herself inhabits, she must desert Miss Quentin, and relinquish her to Jason's cruelty that she describes with prescience: "Just promise that she'll—that she—You can do that. Things for her. Be kind to her. Little things that I cant, they wont let. . . . But you wont. You never had a drop of warm blood in you" (209). She is capable of deluding herself into believing that she is acting wholly on Miss Quentin's behalf, and at her own expense—a thoroughly acceptable sacrifice within the Compson family ideology. Caddy, of course, wants to be with her own infant daughter. Understandably, she wishes to nurture her own offspring, being kind to her, giving her "little things." She must now convince herself that she cannot have her daughter; that she must give up what she most wants for herself, and what her daughter needs most. And so, with bitter irony, she invokes her father's own favorite word ("nothing"), that will justify her final, terrible loss.

Notes

1. Some critics suggest that the Compson family is a reflection of Faulkner's own family of origin, where Maud, trapped in an unhappy marriage to Murry Faulkner, was aloof from her children, leaving Mammy Callie Barr to provide love and attention. See Sensibar (50–53), Minter (91–100), and Wittenberg (73–88). Approaching the novel from a Freudian/Lacanian perspective, Fowler discovers in Caddy Faulkner's own psychic investment, "the projected image of his own unconscious" (19).

2. Jason (whom Faulkner himself termed his "worst villain") and Caroline Compson (the archetypal Bad Mother) receive the most vilification in published contemporary criticism (and perhaps in classroom discussions of the novel as well). For a defense of Jason, see Wagner and David Aiken; for a formidable argument for Caroline, see Williams. In an attempt to explain Mrs. Compson rather than vindicate her, Trouard argues "the possibility that [Mrs. Compson] is trapped in her roles too" (40). Gwin recovers Caddy's suppressed narrative voice to "hear Caddy's articulation of how ego boundaries may come to evaporate in a maternal space in which self and other are indistinguishable" (27). No obvious victim, Caddy becomes the textual rebel. For Gwin, Caddy represents a rebellious "counter-narrative" to recover "maternal space" against a masculine, commodified world (49). Gwin, however, falls back on the familiar argument that Caddy in her adulthood is solely

the victim of others' cruelty: "Caddy is [the] ideal victim because of her willingness to give excessively" (56).

3. Blotner treats Faulkner's bouts with drinking extensively throughout his biography (esp. 717–721), as does Karl (129–132), but neither comments extensively on Mr. Compson's alcoholism as an organizing principle in the novel. Blotner implies that Faulkner's drinking became especially prominent during 1928, the year of writing *The Sound and the Fury* (591). For Karl, alcoholism is underestimated as a force in the novel, represented more as the father's unattractive feature but not as a power that controls family behavior. Karl's lack of emphasis on alcoholism as a controlling factor in the Compsons is revealed in his contention that *Pylon* was "the first novel in which Faulkner tried to get inside the world of booze—where drinking, heavily and steadily, becomes part of the story line" (531). In fact, "the world of booze" in the Compsons is inclusive, "family-centered," but not solitary. Karl's assertion inaccurately relegates "the world of booze" to the isolated drinker, severing the alcoholic from the often supportive, enabling, though suffering, family.

4. The metaphor "infinite loop" was first applied to adult children of alcoholics by Wood (7).

5. The conceptualization of role-playing is pervasive in discussions of alcoholic homes; see Seixas and Youcha as representative. Goodman, however, warns against broadly labeling alcoholic families: "[I]t should not be assumed that all ACOAs (Adult Children of Alcoholics) have been affected by their experience in the same way, that such effects are always negative, or that all ACOAs need counseling" (162). Significantly, Goodman writes that honest discussion of the parent's alcoholism within the home lessens the family's dysfunctionality. For a discussion of Jason's role, see my "Jason's Role-Slippage: The Dynamics of Alcoholism in *The Sound and the Fury*."

6. Despite their disapproval of Mr. Compson, many critics equivocate in their assessment of him. Wadlington, for example, calls him "well-meaning" (73); Blelkasten, wise and "indeed right" ("Fathers" 128); Weinstein, "shrewd" and having "considerable appeal" ("Mother" 31), and "infused with tenderness" (*Love* 106); Brooks, "possessed of love and compassion" and "a force for order in the household" (128). Irwin correctly sees Compson's problems within the context of multigenerational family patterns: "Mr. Compson would, then, transfer onto Quentin the resentment that he harbored against his own father for the failure and defeatism that General Compson passed on to him" (67).

7. Faulkner denied his own alcoholism, saying, "I consider drinking a normal instinct, not a hobby. A normal and a healthy instinct" (*LG* 149). The South at the turn of the century recognized hard drinking as a masculine prerogative, but such a view was neither universal nor absolute. Williamson, for example, discusses the uproar in Oxford, Mississippi, against alcoholism and drinking establishments ("blind tigers"), the temperance movement, and the acrimony Murry's drinking caused within the family when Faulkner was a child (150–152; 160–161).

8. Crowley argues that alcoholism gradually becomes identified with The Modern Temper through what he calls "the drunk narrative": "A mode of fiction that expresses the conjunction of modernism and alcoholism in a pervasive ideology of despair" (x).

9. Wadlington notes the creation of binaries and embattlement of opposites within the Compson household: "As in the novel's first scene, the [Compson] mental

landscape is without middle ground or nuance; there is only this side of the fence or that side of the fence" (69–70).

10. Psychoanalyst Helm Stierlin argues that parents send their children into the world as "delegates"—envoys acting out the parents' own repressed and highly conflictual inclinations: "the delegating mode comes into play when a parent enlists an adolescent son to resolve his own conflicts over delinquent tendencies. This parent covertly encourages his son to become a delinquent and then attacks him for doing so" (76). Matthews also argues that Caroline's disapproval of Caddy reveals her own sexual repression, enacted as if by a sexual delegate: "Perhaps Mrs. Compson's abnormal overevaluation of virginity for her daughter Caddy unconsciously expresses her own discontentment with the narrow categories society allowed women. . . . Caddy's and her mother's antagonism conceals their profoundly kindred suffering" (96).

11. For Caddy as surrogate parent, see Weinstein: "Refusing to be a wife, Caroline Bascomb refuses to be a mother, and Caddy must therefore—and finally—play that role for her brothers" ("Mother" 5).

12. Interestingly, critics have also implicitly accused Caddy of causing Mr. Compson's drinking. Brooks writes, "The attentive reader will have noticed that even in his drinking, Mr. Compson has evidently gone from better to worse. . . . Evidently, the knowledge of his daughter's wantonness had hit Mr. Compson hard" (128). More recently, Weinstein writes, "[Caddy's] exit from Compson mores is steadily driving him to suicidal drink" (*Love* 107).

Works Cited

Aiken, David, "The 'Sojer Face' Defiance of Jason Compson." *Thought* 52 (1977): 188–213.

Anderson, Charles. "Faulkner's Moral Center." *Etudes Anglaises* 7 (1954): 48–58.

Bassett, John Earl. "Family Conflict in *The Sound and the Fury*." *Critical Essays on William Faulkner: The Compson Family*. ed. Arthur F. Kinney. Boston: G. K. Hall, 1982. 408–424.

Baleson, Gregory. *Steps to an Ecology of the Mind*. New York: Ballantine, 1972.

Baum, Catherine B. "'The Beautiful One': Caddy Compson as Heroine of *The Sound and the Fury*." *Modern Fiction Studies* 13.1 (1967): 33–44.

Baur, Susan. *Hypochondria: Woeful Imaginations*. Berkeley: University of California Press, 1988.

Bleikasten, André. *The Most Splendid Failure: Faulkner's The Sound and the Fury*. Bloomington: Indiana University Press, 1976.

———. "Fathers in Faulkner." *The Fictional Father: Lacanian Readings of the Text*. Ed. Robert Con Davis. University of Massachusetts Press, 1981. 115–146.

Blotner, Joseph. *Faulkner: A Biography*. Two volumes. New York: Random, 1974.

Bowen, Murray. *Family Therapy in Clinical Practice*. New York: Jason Aronson, 1978.

Brooks, Cleanth. "The Breakup of the Compsons." *Critical Essays on William Faulkner: The Compson Family*. Ed. Arthur F. Kinney. Boston: G.K. Hall, 1982. 127–138.

Collins, Carvel. "A Conscious Literary Use of Freud? *Literature and Psychology* 3 (1953): 2–3.

Crowley, John W. *The White Logic: Alcoholism and Gender in American Modernist Fiction*. Amherst: University of Massachusetts Press, 1994.

Elkin, Michael. *Families Under the Influence: Changing Alcoholic Patterns*. New York: Norton, 1984.

Faulkner, William. *Lion in the Garden: Interviews with William Faulkner, 1926–1962.* Eds. James B. Meriwether and Michael Millgate. NewYork: Random, 1968.

———. *The Sound and the Fury: The Corrected Text.* New York: Random, 1984.

Fowler, Doreen. "'Little Sister Death': *The Sound and the Fury* and the Denied Unconscious." *Faulkner and Psychology: Faulkner and Yoknapatawpha, 1991.* Eds. Donald M. Kartiganer and Ann J. Abadie. Jackson: University Press of Mississippi, 1994. 3–20.

Freud, Sigmund. "On Narcissism: An Introduction." *General Psychological Theory: Papers on Metapsychology.* New York: Collier, 1963. 56–82.

Goodman, Ronald W. "Adult Children of Alcoholics." *Journal of Counseling and Development* 66 (1987): 156–162.

Gwin, Minrose C. *The Feminine and Faulkner: Reading (Beyond) Sexual Difference.* Knoxville: University of Tennessee Press, 1990.

Gwynn, Frederick L. and Joseph Blotner, eds. *Faulkner in the University.* Charlottesville: University Press of Virginia, 1995.

Irwin, John T. *Doubling and Incest / Repetition and Revenge. A Speculative Reading of Faulkner.* Baltimore: Johns Hopkins University Press, 1975.

Jenkins, Lee. *Faulkner and Black-White Relations: A Psychoanalytic Approach.* New York: Columbia University Press, 1981.

Karl, Frederick R. *William Faulkner: American Writer.* New York: Weidenfeld and Nicolson, 1989.

Kinney, Arthur F. "The Family-Centered Nature of Faulkner's World." *College Literature* 16.1 (1989): 83–102.

Lederer, Gail S. "Alcohol in the Family System." *Reweaving the Family Tapestry: A Multigenerational Approach to Families.* Ed. Fredda Herz Brown. New York: Norton, 1991. 219–241.

Matthews, John T. *The Sound and the Fury: Faulkner and the Lost Cause.* Boston: Twayne, 1991.

Minter, David. *William Faulkner: His Life and Work.* Baltimore: Johns Hopkins University Press, 1980.

Ross, Stephen M. and Noel Polk. *Reading Faulkner: The Sound and the Fury.* Jackson: University Press of Mississippi, 1996.

Seixas, J.S, and G. Youcha. *Children of Alcoholism.* New York: Crown, 1985.

Sensibar. Judith. L. *The Origins of Faulkner's Art.* Austin: University of Texas Press, 1984.

Stierlin, Helm. *Separating Parents and Adolescents: A Perspective on Running Away, Schizophrenia, and Waywardness,* New York: Quadrangle/New York Times, 1974.

Steinglass, Peter, et al. *The Alcoholic Family.* New York: Basic, 1987.

Storhoff, Gary. "Jason's Role-Slippage: The Dynamics of Alcoholism in *The Sound and the Fury.*" *Mississippi Quarterly* 49.3 (1996): 519–535.

Trouard, Dawn. "Faulkner's Text Which Is Not One." *New Essays on The Sound and the Fury.* Ed. Noel Polk. Cambridge: Cambridge University Press, 1993. 23–69.

Wallington, Warwick. *Reading Faulknerian Tragedy.* Ithaca: Cornell University Press, 1987,

Wagner, Linda W. "Jason Compson: The Demands of Honor." *Sewanee Review* 79 (1971): 554–575.

Weinstein, Phillip. "'If I Could Say Mother': Construing the Unsayable about Faulknerian Maternity." *Faulkner's Discourse: An International Symposium.* Ed. Lothar Hönninghausen. Tubingen: Niemeyer, 1989. 3–15.

———. *What Else But Love? The Ordeal of Race in Faulkner and Morrison.* New York: Columbia University Press, 1996.

Williams, Joan. "In Defense of Caroline Compson." *Critical Essays on William Faulkner: The Compson Family.* Ed. Arthur F. Kinney. Boston: G. K. Hall, 1982. 402–407.

Williamson, Joel. *William Faulkner and Southern History.* New York: Oxford University Press, 1993.

Wittenberg, Judith Bryant. *Faulkner: The Transfiguration of Biography.* Lincoln: University of Nebraska Press, 1979.

Wood, Barbara L. *Children of Alcoholism: The Struggle for Self and Intimacy in Adult Life.* New York: New York University Press, 1987.

MARGARET D. BAUER

"I Have Sinned in That I Have Betrayed the Innocent Blood": Quentin's Recognition of His Guilt

> Then I remembered bread my flesh had eaten,
> The kiss that ate my flesh . . .
>
> —James Wright, "Saint Judas"

The three scenes replayed after Quentin Compson is knocked unconscious by Gerald Bland have each been suggested as the climax of the second section of William Faulkner's *The Sound and the Fury.* Because all three scenes involve Quentin's discovery of Caddy's sexual relationship with Dalton Ames, it is generally agreed that the reason for Quentin's suicide at the end of his section is related to his sister's loss of virginity. Most critics draw their theories about Quentin's motivations from one of the first two scenes played out while Quentin is unconscious: the scene with Caddy at the branch when Quentin proposes either incest or a double suicide, and the confrontation between Quentin and Dalton on the bridge. Theories vary, however, regarding what exactly it is about Caddy's relationship with Dalton that is so devastating to Quentin: there are those who believe it is Caddy's lost virginity, the symbol of their family's honor; some think it is losing Caddy to another man; others argue that it is Quentin's fear of forgetting his grief over Caddy's actions; and still others reason that it is the discovery of his own impotence and the impotence of the codes he lives by. This essay will not discount these theories but, rather add another, first proposing that

Southern Literary Journal, Volume 32, Number 2 (2000): pp. 70–89.

it is the third scene in this flashback, Quentin's last extended memory of himself and Caddy before his suicide, which is the climactic moment of the section. This recollection is particularly agonizing to Quentin because it reminds him of his own culpability regarding Caddy's destruction. Once this memory surfaces, Quentin can no longer escape the fact that for him his sister gave up a *chance,* however slight it may have been, of leading a "normal" life: concerned about her brother, Caddy did not go after her lover to stop him from leaving, the consequence of which was promiscuity, which led to pregnancy and a hurried, deceptive marriage to a man Quentin finds repugnant. Quentin's inability to live any longer with this guilt, then, can be seen as another reason for his suicide. Given that its disclosure comes so close to his jump off the bridge, I propose here that it may very well be the deciding reason.

This reading not only confirms Quentin's recognition of his betrayal of the sister whose love for him is unqualified, it also provides a further explanation of the novel's Easter weekend structure. Quentin's suicide at the end of the Maundy Thursday of the novel is reminiscent of the death of Judas, who also betrayed one who loved unconditionally and then, "when he saw that he was condemned, repented . . . and went and hanged himself" (Matthew 27:3, 5). Therefore, this reading leads to a view of Caddy—more so than Benjy, Quentin, or Miss Quentin—as the Christ figure of the novel. Because of his age at the time of three of the four sections of the novel (thirty-three), blonde hair, blue-eyes, and innocence, Benjy has often been viewed as the novel's Christ figure. As will be further remarked upon in do paper's conclusion, at least one reader, James Dean Young, sees parallels between Quentin and Christ. More convincing than either of these are the arguments for Miss Quentin as Christ-like in her role in the novel. She is the character who has the capacity for redeeming the Compsons, if they would only have made up for their treatment of Caddy by treating her better; she is also the one who is "tortured" on Good Friday (by Jason) and "resurrected"—or at least she escapes—on Easter Sunday. The case I will make for Caddy as a Christ figure is, I believe, even more convincing than the case for Miss Quentin in that not only is Caddy's fate Christ-like, but so is, to a greater extent than Miss Quentin's, her character. Her selfless love and sacrificed life are particularly illuminated in the memories of her older brother in his section of the novel. Of course, regardless of which character is viewed as the novel's Christ figure, there is no promise of salvation in the end. Benjy is, after all, still a tormented imbecile the last we see him in the novel and, according to the novel's appendix, is eventually sent to the state asylum in Jackson. Quentin's death is followed by no promise of a better life for those he leaves behind, and we are not told what kind of life Miss Quentin lived after her escape/resurrection. Caddy's fate on and following the novel's Easter Sunday will be discussed later. Suffice it to say for now that she does not pass from the Compson world to any paradise.

Throughout the day on which the Quentin section takes place Quentin's thoughts move towards recognizing his responsibly for Caddy's behavior and current situation: pregnant out of wedlock, then married to someone she does not love. Although the events of the physical world through which Quentin wanders as he passes the day of his suicide do have some part in calling up certain memories, critics have often noted that the order of Quentin's memories is also somewhat related to their degree of painfulness to him. I would add to this observation that the degree of painfulness of each memory is in direct proportion to the degree of guilt he feels for his actions during the recalled event. In the beginning of the section, fragments of memories pop into and out of Quentin's mind, some provoked by analogous occurrences happening around him, others slipping in while he is walking aimlessly. In either case, his preoccupation with the past is unmistakable. He is reliving those memories that trouble his conscience, and he slowly comes to realize the source of the disturbance; guilt over the subconscious knowledge that he, along with other members of his family, participated in the treatment of Caddy that has resulted in her misfortune.

Quentin's gradual acceptance of his guilt is reflected in the increasing duration and intensity, from fragmented thoughts to whole scenes recalled, of significant memories as the day wears on.[1] The first of the whole scenes he relives is his mother's self-pitying monologue, which epitomizes the atmosphere of the Compson household (102–104). In particular, Mrs. Compson's tirade reveals not only her condemnation of Caddy's recent promiscuous behavior but also her inability to offer love or affection to any of her children besides Jason, and that of course, includes Quentin as well as Caddy. This scene and the scene that follows involving Herbert Head, Caddy's fiancé, are recalled at length, but, at the same time, Quentin is still a conscious and therefore still somewhat in control of his thoughts. He can shake them away when they become too painful.[2] For example, in the first of these extended memories he cuts his mother's voice off just after she has mentioned wanting to "escape this curse [and] try to forget that the others ever were" (104). Significantly, Quentin thereby halts the flow of memory just after recalling his mother's implicit rejection of him, which places him in the position of victim along with Caddy (and of course Benjy). As Lawrence Thompson notes, "The central irony in Quentin's death-day monologue is provided by the stubborn manner in which he censors all the attempts of his conscience to make him see that he shares with the other Compsons the moral responsibility for what happened to Caddy" (41). In other words, although he recalls his mother's rejection of him, he does not allow himself at this point to see that it compares with his own rejection of Caddy, which, indeed, repeats his mother's condemnation of her: both consider Caddy tainted by her sexuality. Indeed Mrs. Compson's words, quoted above, are later echoed by Quentin when he shares with Caddy his belief that their family is cursed (158).

Although painful enough as a reminder that his mother does not seem to love him, the memory described above, if allowed to play through, would also lead to an uncomfortable recollection of his own shortcomings with Caddy (who does seem to love him) regarding his failure to express to his family his disapproval of his mother's idea of finding a husband for Caddy, as well as of her later choice of Herbert Head. The reader recalls that earlier in this memory sequence Quentin had recalled Mr. Compson's advice after the discovery of Caddy's pregnancy that, rather than take Jason and leave her family, Mrs. Compson should take Caddy away to French Lick for a while until they can figure out what to do about her shameful condition. Agreeing to do so, Mrs. Compson suggests that she might even find a husband for Caddy there so that she can be married off before her condition is even known. Karl F. Zender argues that Quentin "view[s] the journey to find a husband for Caddy as an interring of his sister within the death-in-life of Mrs. Compson's obsession with respectability" (111). However, Quentin makes no effort to put a stop to Mrs. Compson's scheme beyond asking Caddy not to marry Herbert. If he is aware of the consequences ("death-in-life") of coercing Caddy into a loveless and treacherous marriage, then his failure to speak up to his parents on Caddy's behalf is a betrayal of his sister. Furthermore, it reveals his mixed-up priorities: Caddy's—and even his own—feelings for Herbert are less important than the fact that Caddy is pregnant and must marry to save the family from shame. Although Quentin does not analyze his memories (he does not, in other words, consciously make the connections I have noted above), in contrast to his youngest sibling who is retarded, he is *capable* of doing so; therefore, one can conclude that at some subconscious level he is recognizing the significance of these memories, as evidenced by the very fact that he stops them short of illuminating his partial but crucial responsibility for Caddy's fate.

When the next long memory, involving the subject of Caddy's marriage becomes too discomforting, Quentin cuts it off as well, not wanting to face that which he apparently is on the verge of recognizing the effect that the Compsons, including himself, have had on Caddy, a net realization would culminate in the fact that she married Herbert Head largely for Quentin's sake. After recalling his first meeting with Herbert Quentin remembers begging Caddy not to marry "that blackguard" (111).[3] Caddy's bitter tone and harsh admonishment—"You're meddling in my business again didn't you get enough of that last summer" (111) reflects the effect that her family's unmerciful treatment has had on her usually affectionate nature. At the same time, Quentin is reminded of her more natural compassion by her request that he take care of their father and Benjy in her absence. He should realize, too, if not at the time, then perhaps upon recollection, that her acceptance of his view of her as corrupted by her loss of virginity has broken her spirit. Although she can still love, she can no longer fight. Had he been capable of truly loving his sister he would have fought for her against the family's arranged marriage.

Caddy does not take up for her fiancé during this conversation; rather, she merely reminds Quentin that she has "to marry somebody" (113) because of a condition that if revealed before she weds would be particularly destructive to her brother's precious family name. Quentin abruptly switches his focus back to the present after his sister alludes to her pregnancy but not before an earlier memory slips in: *"told me the bone would have to be broken again"* (113). This seemingly vagrant thought reveals a realization that he has habitually brought on his own pain and thus supports the argument that Quentin is moving towards a recognition of his guilt. He may not stop to analyze the significance of these memories, but their juxtaposition reveals that at some level he makes a connection between them. Just as his obsession with Caddy as representative of family honor has been partly responsible for her having to get married, creating a situation emotionally painful to him, so also a similar concern about his sister's honor once resulted in his suffering physical pain when, trying to chase away one of her early admirers, he had moved around too much on a broken leg, causing it to mend incorrectly and, consequently, to have to be re-broken and reset.[4] Again, Quentin does not analyze the parallel; rather, as before, he focuses his senses on the physical present.

Although he cannot keep his mind from wandering, Quentin does not allow himself to get lost in the past again; apparently he is resisting, which also implies that he is recognizing the truth these memories reveal to him about himself. The next extensive replay of the past occurs only after he has been knocked unconscious by Gerald Bland. According to Kathryn Gibbs Gibbons, "Quentin's unconsciousness is a device by the author analogous to a hypnosis situation in which the patient becomes unconscious so that the psychologist can discover the source of illness more quickly. Quentin's unconscious 'talks' about what bothers him!" (18). The transition into this long memory is abrupt, just as it would be if he were suddenly knocked out, and, examining the type of the text, one realizes that Quentin has indeed been rendered unconscious, as Gibbons as well as Lawrence Bowling (133) and Noel Polk (151) have noted. Just before Quentin is knocked out, his thoughts of the past are represented in italics and interspersed into the dialogue going on around him, which is printed in regular type and properly punctuated. Abruptly, then, Faulkner switches to standard type without punctuation or capitalization for the flashback.[5] This change indicates that Quentin is knocked out just after he recalls asking Caddy, *"Did you love them Caddy did you love them,"* and hears her reply, *"When they touched me I died"* (149). This answer, with its Elizabethan view of sex a "a little death," suggests the reason Caddy has become promiscuous: through her sexual encounters she can escape, for a little while at least, the physical world that oppresses her.[6] This is the same answer she gave when Quentin asked if she loved Dalton, the recollection of which, then, would remind Quentin of the chance of escape from her family that Caddy had with Dalton, a chance ruined by Quentin, as will be shown with an analysis of the long flashback he experiences while unconscious. His subconscious guilt, the source of which he has not fully understood, has been driving him to suicide. When the guilt becomes clear to him via the recollection of the third significant event in the "dream sequence," he goes through with the act.

This "dream sequence" is the flashback containing the three most crucial scenes of Quentin's section. The first scene of this sequence involves the revelation to Quentin of Caddy's loss of virginity, which many critics believe is what drives him to commit suicide. Though devastating to the youth, who considers Caddy's virginity to be a symbol of his family's honor, it is still not *the* revelation that decides Quentin's fate, as I will soon argue. The scene begins just after Caddy returns from meeting with Dalton, when Benjy's unceasing bellows reveal that he notices a significant difference in her. (She cannot calm him by washing her mouth this time.) Caddy leaves the house and Quentin finds her sitting in the branch. Seeing her, he realizes the reason for Benjy's bellows: Caddy has lost her virginity. The long memory extends through the confrontation between Quentin and Dalton to another scene with Caddy. I argue that it is this third scene in the sequence that ultimately determines Quentin's fate.

Arnold Weinstein comments on the length and significance of the whole memory: "No longer through elliptic glimpses and spurts, the final revelation now comes to us with crushing and imperious finality. In this last encounter the present completely vanishes and we witness the most direct and moving confrontation between Quentin and Caddy." Weinstein is mainly referring to the first scene of this memory. He is one of the critics who sees it as the section's climax: "Here Caddy outspokenly asserts her sexuality and love for Dalton Ames as well as the willingness to grant Quentin whatever he may ask of her. It's very length is an index of its paralyzing and enduring hold on Quentin" (127). According to Melvin Backman, "The disclosure of [Quentin's] impotence, in the scene with Caddy at the branch and [the second scene] with Dalton at the bridge, is the climax of the Quentin section" (23); more recently, Noel Polk has linked these two scenes—"the one recounting Caddy's love affair with Dalton Ames and [Quentin's] ineffectual efforts to stop it"—and called them "crucial" (149–150). In preparation for my contention that neither of these scenes is the source of realizations so devastating that Quentin must kill himself to escape them, I first point out that Quentin has allowed fragments of both of these memories into his consciousness earlier in the section—while he still maintained some control over his thoughts. In contrast, the third scene in the sequence, the final recalled conversation with Caddy from which he snaps back into consciousness, is the only memory that is not found—even fragmented—earlier or later in his section of the novel. Noel Polk his pointed out that Quentin's memories "exist in degrees of intensity, of psychic pain" (149). I would argue that the depth of this scene's repression indicates that its degree of painfulness to Quentin is unmatched even by these other extensive scenes. This is not to say that these other scenes are not relevant to Quentin's suicide. Their revelation to Quentin of the extremity of his weakness and the confirmation of Caddy's loss of virginity are, of course, significant to his *plans* to end his life. He must prove that he is strong enough to die for his codes in order to make Caddy see that they are more important than love. But he had tried to commit suicide before, as will be discussed subsequently, at the branch scene mentioned previously, and he had been unable to go through with it. What pushes him to carry out his plan this time is his realization that he and his codes have helped to ruin Caddy's life.

Polk describes Quentin's section as "his effort to sort out, analyze, and come to terms with those scenes of pain that he *can* handle, and to evade, to repress, those he cannot. He is trying to shape his memory into an acceptable version of his life that will both explain his present misery and justify his decision to commit suicide" (150). In contrast, I argue that although Quentin has successfully "evaded and repressed" his most painful memories in the past, on the day of his death, he ultimately relives them, too, and through doing so achieves insight about his own behavior with which Polk does not seem to credit him. Yes, Quentin has planned to commit suicide all along, but I argue that he is looking for a reason *not to,* examining his memories in hopes that they will not reveal what he is beginning to realize: his true, rather than imagined, role in Caddy's destruction.

In the first crucial scene of this flashback, the branch scene with Caddy, the connection between intercourse and death is reiterated when Caddy tells Quentin, "I would die for [Dalton] Ive already died for him" (151). Here, too, then, Caddy's choice of words suggests that orgasm, which allows one to transcend the self, has provided brief escapes from her oppression, the source of which includes her older brother's codes of honor and morality. Following this admission of having engaged in and even, in spite of her word choice, enjoyed sexual relations, Caddy asks Quentin, "youve never done that have you" (151). As already noted, some critics believe that Quentin's realization of Caddy's active sexuality, compounded by his own fear of sexuality, is the climactic moment of the section. But, as noted previously, Quentin has recalled this part of their conversation earlier in the novel: shortly *before* he is knocked unconscious, he hears Caddy's voice repeating, *"Have you ever done that"* and *"Poor Quentin youve never done that have you"* (148). Unconscious now, he relives the whole scene, and it surprisingly plays out to a somewhat encouraging (to him) conclusion. After Caddy asks him this question, Quentin draws his knife on her, in act perceived by many critics as his asking her to commit incest with him, given the language of the dialogue and the earlier connections made between sex and death. Therefore, Quentin's alleged proposition to Caddy has also been alluded to throughout this section of the novel whenever Quentin recalls or imagines telling his father that he and Caddy committed incest. In fact, as early as the fifth paragraph of his section, the words, "I have committed incest, Father," enter Quentin's mind (77).

That Quentin has earlier recalled fragments of this memory indicates that it is not as painful to him as the scene he has completely repressed. Furthermore, the knife scene read literally becomes an ironically protective memory for Quentin in comparison to the later scene with Caddy. Caddy's willingness to either die or have sex with him in this scene depending on how the reader—or Quentin—chooses to interpret their dialogue, attests too her love for him as well as, perhaps, a beginning acceptance of his values, perverted though they may be (i.e., his notion that sex with him is somehow more acceptable than with Dalton Ames who is apparently not a member of the southern aristocracy). In addition, Caddy's willingness to surrender to Quentin's desires puts him on a level with Dalton, in that she thereby shows that her love for Quentin is proportionate to her feelings for Dalton. Of course, the knife scene is still to a great extent a painful memory, since Quentin's inability to go through with the suicide pact/sexual proposition reveals his cowardice and impotence and would also remind him of Caddy's ultimate rejection of her brother: after Quentin drops the knife she gets up and goes to her lover, a man who *is* able to carry out propositions.

Melvin Backman sees this choice of the "sexual[ly] poten[t]" Dalton over Quentin as "the ultimate reason for Quentin's suicide" (27). But Quentin has recalled his realization of Dalton's superior virility before, too, which suggests that it, too, is a less painful memory than the one that he has completely repressed. While riding with the Blands earlier, he had thought about how, the first time he saw Dalton (when, at the end of the same scene described above, Caddy left her brother to go with her lover), he noticed the man's strength: "with one hand he [Dalton] could lift her to his shoulder and run with her" (148). Now, recalling the scene while unconscious, Quentin notices how, as Dalton extends his hand to shake Quentin's, "he held [Caddy] in one arm like she was no bigger than a child" (155). Ironically, the recollection of Dalton's strength is in one sense another strangely positive memory, for it supports Quentin's hope, expressed earlier in the scene, that Dalton *forced* Caddy to have sex with him: "did he make you then he made you do it . . . he was stronger than you" (150)[8]. Finally, the strangely positive nature of this memory is supported at the end of the scene, too, when Caddy returns from her tryst with Dalton and seems to offer herself to her brother again. Her response to Quentin's command that she go home is as sexually suggestive as their earlier conversation over and about the knife (though in contrast to the critical analysis of the sexual nature of Quentin's request in that scene, critics have overlooked Caddy's sexual innuendo in this one)[9]:

> [CADDY, in response to Quentin's command to go home:] yes I will if you want me to I will
> . . .
> [QUENTIN:] go on to the house like I told you
> [CADDY:] yes Ill do anything you want me to anything yes
> [QUENTIN, to himself:] she didn't even look at me I caught her shoulder and shook her hard
> [QUENTIN, to Caddy:] you shut up (156)

Although Quentin is apparently not comfortable with the possibility that his sister is accepting the very proposition he is afraid to make, the memory of her offer would undermine the painfulness of the first part of this scene through its suggestion that, even after meeting with Dalton, she is still willing to have sexual relations with Quentin—or do whatever Quentin asks of her.[10] Indeed, she tells Quentin at this time that she "do[es]nt know" if she loves Dalton and again shows an acceptance of Quentin's views of her as tainted by her sexuality: "dont cry," she tells her brother, "Im bad anyway you cant help it" (158). Thus, there is not only the possibility of Caddy's preference for him; Quentin also still has hope at this point that he can bring his sister to accept his code of ethics.

But first he must get rid of Dalton. Quentin's unconscious reminiscing switches abruptly to his encounter with his sister's seducer. This scene, too, has been recalled very early in his section; while dressing on the morning of his suicide, he had remembered "when he [Dalton] put the pistol in my hand" (179). While unconscious after his beating from Gerald, Quentin relives the humiliation of fainting after refusing Dalton's offer of the gun. He has realized he was no match for Dalton, and the truth of his weakness compounds the damage done to his ego in the preceding scene when Caddy left him to go to Dalton. Quentin remembers thinking, "I had just passed out like a girl but even that didn't matter anymore" (162). He seems to be relieved that he knows the nature of Caddy's relationship with Dalton and thus no longer has to wonder what his sister is doing when she is out of his sight He remembers that he "felt almost good after all those days and the nights with honeysuckle [which he associates with Caddy's sexuality] coming up out of the darkness into my room where I was trying to sleep" (162). He may be unable to get rid of the man, but at least as long as Dalton is around, he knows where Caddy is when she disappears. Therefore, here again the memory's painfulness is subdued by a way to view it optimistically. Another positive note can be found in Quentin's earlier recollection that when he saw Dalton at the bridge, he had noted that his shirt was "of heavy Chinese silk or finest flannel." Saying the name "Dalton Ames" to himself, then, he had thought, "It just missed gentility" (92). Taken with his relief expressed at the end of the whole memory, the thought suggests that Quentin was toying with the idea that Dalton might be a suitable mate for Caddy after all. Donald M. Kartiganer suggests that Quentin creates Dalton, like a character in a romance, in his recollections of the man (85–86). I would add, then, that he now begins to recreate this character—from rake to knight in shining armor.

His peace of mind is short-lived, however, for in the next scene, when Caddy does choose him over Dalton, she gives up a *chance* for reciprocated love, which I argue is the crucial recollection/realization in this sequence of memories. Quentin has successfully suppressed recalling Caddy's sacrifice for him until he is unconscious: no part of this conversation with Caddy can be found anywhere else in the section. However, now that he is unconscious and thus no longer able to control his subconscious, he cannot stop his mind from proceeding through this painful memory, thereby revealing to him the truth of his responsibility for Caddy's destruction. The memory begins as Caddy runs up to Quentin after hearing the pistol shots. On the way, she apparently met Dalton and, thinking he had shot her brother, sent him away, telling him she never wanted to see him again. This encounter with Dalton is suggested when, upon finding her brother unharmed, she tells Quentin that she must hurry and rectify her mistake in sending Dalton away. But Quentin holds her back. Concerned about her brother, she stays, and, as far as the reader knows, never sees Dalton Ames again.

I contend that Quentin has come too view Dalton Ames as Caddy's missed opportunity for a happy, or at least less destructive, life. Although there is no proof in the novel that Dalton would eventually have married Caddy and taken her away from her family, Quentin must wonder what might have been if he had let Caddy go to her lover. He has earlier recalled that when he told Dalton to meet him at the bridge, Dalton asked if Caddy was "all right" and if "she need[ed him] for anything now" (158–159); and later, at the start of the confrontation between the two young men on the bridge, Dalton again expressed concern for Caddy: "listen save this for a while I want to know if she's all right have they been bothering her up there" (159). In light of this concern, which is certainly more concern than any expressed by the Compson family members for Caddy, Dalton's seemingly insulting advice to Quentin about his sister—"no good taking it so hard its not your fault kid it would have been some other fellow" (160)—may reflect, rather than disrespect for Caddy, an understanding of her situation. Knowing Caddy so intimately, perhaps

Dalton has recognized that her desire for love, which has not been fulfilled at home, would inevitably lead her to look elsewhere for it. In any case, Dalton's concern for Caddy's well-being, together with Caddy's "surge of blood" (163) when she hears her lover's name, reveals to Quentin that, regardless of what she may *not* be to Dalton, she *is* to him a human being, rather than just a symbol, as she is to her family. Therefore, once she lost this man who saw her as more than an *idea,* thereby giving her life, Caddy began to seek such rejuvenation (as well as the aforementioned sense of escape achieved through sexual relations) with other men who come along. Quentin realizes, then, that by keeping her from making amends with her first lover that day, he is in large part responsible for Caddy's sequential promiscuity, if not also for the missed chance to spend her life with a man whom she loves.[11]

Upon Quentin's regaining consciousness after reliving this whole experience (indicated by the return to proper punctuation and capitalization for the narrative and italics for the echoes from the past), his roommate Shreve reveals the sequence of events leading to the altercation between Gerald and Quentin, which ultimately shows that Quentin is seeking to be punished for his treatment of his sister. The reader can see how Gerald's story of a woman he once left waiting for him may have been an uncomfortable reminder to Quentin of Caddy's loss of Dalton. Shreve goes on to report "how [Gerald] lay there being sorry for [the woman] waiting on the pier for him, without him there to give her what she wanted" and how Gerald had commented about "how tough women have it, without anything else they can do except lie on their backs" (167). Quentin's assault of Gerald at this point is evidence that he perceives the sad parallel between Gerald's callous treatment and opinion of women and Caddy's loss of Dalton Ames and subsequent self-destructive promiscuity.

Although Caddy had thought that she could make amends with Dalton—"I can tell him [apologize to Dalton for sending him away] I can make him believe anytime" (163)—apparently, for whatever reason, this was not the case. And so, the suppressed memory of how she stayed behind with Quentin while her lover, having been dismissed by her, left town resurfaces while Quentin is unconscious. Surely Quentin's guilt over his responsibility for Caddy's loss, which led to her later promiscuity; would be of greater anguish to him than his realization of Caddy's sexuality or his weakness. He has lived with knowledge of the latter two facts since the earliest recorded event in the novel the branch scene from their childhood when Caddy, oblivious to propriety, took off her dress to keep it from getting wet, and, oblivious to her father's forbidding it, climbed the tree to find out about their grandmother's death. But when he realizes his part in Caddy's promiscuity, which resulted in pregnancy and her marriage to an unworthy husband who took her away from him, Quentin is overcome with grief and strikes out at another man for whom he knows he is no match: Gerald Bland.[12]A beating is not enough punishment to assuage his guilt, however. Having grown up in the Calvinistic South, Quentin feels he must pay "an eye for an eye" for his crime of destroying Caddy's life, he must sacrifice his own life.

The argument that Quentin realizes his responsibility refutes Lawrence Bowling and other critics who deny that Quentin ever accepts his part in Caddy's destruction. Bowling writes that the outside world "passes [Quentin's] life before him in review, in order that he may discover his error . . . but Quentin . . . remains impenitent, rejects life, and dies without ever achieving any significant understanding, either of himself or of the world in which he has refused to live" (139).[13] Bowling supports this theory with other events occurring in the physical present of 2 June 1910 that parallel events being recalled in Quentin's mind. Hearing the boys fishing for the prize trout, Quentin thinks of their already spending money not yet won, "making of unreality a possibility, then it probability, then an incontrovertible fact, as people will when their desires become words" (117). Bowling says that Quentin "apparently does not realize that the tragedy of his own life has stemmed from the same basic error in thinking. Repeatedly, Quentin has ignored reality and attempted to will his personal desire into 'incontrovertible fact'" (131). It is also possible, however, that these thoughts, since they are worded so that they could also apply to his own desire to tell his father he and Caddy committed incest, do indicate a realization of the parallel between these boys' foolishness and his own.

I would also argue that Quentin recognizes the parallels between the little Italian girl and Caddy. Although Lawrence Bowling notes the echo of the past in the closing events of Quentin's adventure with the little Italian girl—"like Quentin's proposal for 'saving' Caddy by their committing incest, Julio's beating his sister would have been more injurious than any harm the sister had received from anybody else"—in contrast to Stephen Ross (182), John Matthews (*Play* 89, *Sound* 60), and myself, Bowling believes that "from Quentin's reporting of the incident there is no indication that he perceives either the irony of Julio's actions or the basic similarity between Julio and himself" (132). Since meeting the girl, however, Quentin his called her "sister" and is thereby connecting her consciously or unconsciously, with Caddy, as Ross and Matthews have asserted. Furthermore, at one point Quentin says, "Goodbye, sister," and runs from her. Looking back he describes her as "a small figure clasping the loaf of bread to her filthy little dress, her eyes still and black and unwinking" (133), and he runs again. The child's dirty dress is reminiscent of the aforementioned memory of the child Caddy, and Quentin's futile running recalls the way he tried to run away from the knowledge of the nature of Caddy's relationship with Dalton: when Caddy leaves with Dalton after the scene at the branch, Quentin runs across the pasture (156). Also, the little girl's sudden reappearance parallels Caddy finding Quentin after this particular liaison with Dalton. He can shake neither female: like the little

Italian girl, Caddy remains "unwinking" in Quentin's consciousness. When the girl shows up again he begins to think more and more of Caddy. All of these connections would indicate that he does associate the girl with Caddy. That he wants to lose the girl reinforces the notion that she provokes painful memories of Caddy, whose memory follows him as well. As Wolfgang Iser proposes, "the desire to get rid of the child awakens in Quentin the memory of how he once used to worry about his sister Caddy; at the time he wanted to win Caddy's love, [whereas] now he wants to be free of the child"—i.e., free of Caddy's memory, which awakens his guilt and drives him to his death. But the child is a "dumb[ly] persisten[t]" as the memory of "the painful relationship with the sister" (147).

Bowling believes that Quentin's "endeavor to help the little Italian girl find her way home . . . is . . . the first truly unselfish act of his life, his first act of love, compassion, and sacrifice" (133). Here, too, Bowling provides evidence against his own argument that Quentin does not make any connections between the day's events and his memories from the past: if one views Quentin's care for the girl as an attempt to pay for his crimes of selfishness and insensitivity against Caddy, this would indicate that Quentin *does* make the connection between the two girls and *does* realize he made mistakes in his treatment of Caddy, for which he must somehow make up. Finally, Quentin's hysterical laughter upon being accused of "stealing" the Italian's sister indicates that he notices the irony of the accusation: he already has a sister whose memory he has been trying all day to escape. Why would he want another? Charged with molesting the child, his hysteria increases, further indicating a realization of the parallel between the child and Caddy. His being blamed for the crime he did not commit is ironic, poetic justice, for the crime he did commit against his sister, in part because of *not* being able to commit incest with her.[14] But once again Quentin is not allowed to pay enough for his crime. One dollar to the girl's brother and six dollars to the sheriff will not appease Quentin's conscience. He must go through with his suicide plan. His last view of the child brings up another bout of uncontrollable laughter; this time, though, Quentin thinks "that if [he] tried too hard to stop it [he]'d be crying" (147). Perhaps he realizes at this point that this last view of "Sister" is in a way his last view of his sister, for he will soon be dead.

As has been shown, at least a subconscious perception of his responsibility for Caddy's destruction can be found in Quentin's abrupt discontinuance of those memories that lead him to recognize his guilt, the poignant scenes he relives while unconscious, and the connections he recognizes between the people and events in the physical world and those in his psyche. Looking back, then, to the end of the very first paragraph of the Quentin section—when Quentin recalls his father telling him, "The field only reveals to man his own folly and despair, and victory is an illusion of philosophers and fools" (161)—one can find even further evidence that guilt pushes Quentin to his decision to commit suicide. Contemplating "the field" of his experiences, Quentin realizes "his own folly and despair," i.e., his responsibility for Caddy's predicament. Whereas he did succeed in getting rid of Dalton Ames, the "victory" was only "an illusion of philosophers and fools"—with Quentin qualifying as both since the "philosopher's" ideals, which made Caddy a symbol rather than a human being who needed to be loved, pushed the "fool's" sister into looking for a love that acknowledged her physical being. His foolish defense, then, of her honor resulted in her promiscuity, pregnancy, and loveless marriage. His "victory," ironically is, manifested in the ruin of the only person in his family who had the chance to break free from the Compsons' destructive codes and to live a less restricted life. Quentin's other memories during this day recall the aspiring as well as loving girl he helped to destroy: the only Compson child willing to chance punishment for knowledge (when she climbed the tree to find out about Damuddy's death); a girl who scorned the double standards set by men for women (evidenced in her anger at catching Quentin with Natalie after he has been harassing her about the boys she kissed); a young woman who gave love to a family incapable of returning it (the extent of her love reflected in her marrying a man she cared nothing for in order to save the Compsons from shame). Quentin betrayed this love and can no longer live with the guilt. He would perhaps like to believe that his inept parents or his unlikable brother Jason (who spied an Caddy for their mother) are to blame for his sister's fate, while he is innocent, but he was present at each of these crucial testimonials to Caddy's generous and admirable nature, and it was his voice that criticized loudest against her defiance of society's standards. Consequently, this girl who would be king—"*You know what I'd do if I were King?* she never was queen or a fairy she was always a king or a giant or a general" (173)—has come to accept Quentin's view that she is damned. The loss of her spirit reflected in this acceptance is tragic—and another painful burden for Quentin's conscience.

After his recollection of the crucial scene in which Caddy gave up her stimulating relationship with Dalton Ames out of concern for her brother, Quentin holds an imaginary debate with his father over the value of his codes of honor and morality in one last attempt to exorcise his guilt by establishing that his ideals in more important than Caddy's life. But he rejects his father's view of humanity a "dolls stuffed with sawdust" (175), thereby indicating his recognition of the value of human life. Therefore, his despair at the realization of the "temporary" nature of this life can be connected to a recognition that one should make the best of the short amount of time allotted him or her. Again, then, his guilt is compounded for what he has done to ruin Caddy's brief, though long-suffering, life.

Faulkner's setting the Quentin section on the Maundy Thursday of the novel's Easter Week structure is evidence that the author intended guilt as a crucial motivation for Quentin's suicide. Maundy Thursday is the day not only of the Last Supper but also of Judas's betrayal of Christ. In his article on "Quentin's Maundy Thursday," James Dean Young compares what happens to Quentin during this day with, surprisingly, what happened to Christ on Maundy Thursday. My essay has shown, however, that Quentin's recollections of his behavior towards his sister equate him with Judas, the betrayer, and Caddy with Christ, the betrayed.[15] During the Last Supper, Christ spoke of dying so that men could live. It is Caddy, not Quentin, who has sacrificed her life for others. Quentin, on the other hand, has repeatedly betrayed Caddy's love for him. Apparently Quentin does not see himself as a Christ figure, as is evident in the beginning of the section when he thinks "that Christ was not crucified: he was worn away by a minute clicking of little wheels. That had no sister" (77). Indeed, the idea of Christ being "worn away" reinforces the parallel just made between Christ and Caddy, who may sacrifice herself for others, but does not die. The end of this quotation can be interpreted as meaning that Christ was innocent . . . he had not betrayed a sister. Quentin is thereby denying any connection between himself and Christ.

In Matthew 27:4, Judas says. "I have sinned in that I have betrayed the innocent blood." Like the traitor Judas, Quentin kills himself after recognizing the extent of his guilt. But, just as Christ still had to withstand his torture and bear his cross, Caddy must go on living the life of selflessness Quentin has pushed her into, beginning with a loveless marriage and then apparent prostitution, whereby she repeatedly sacrifices herself for the pleasure of others. Unlike Christ, then, Caddy is not so "fortunate" as to die the day after Quentin's betrayal. She continues to endure the misery of this world, at least until 1943 when, according to Faulkner's appendix to the novel, she is spied in a magazine by a Jefferson librarian. Quentin kills himself at the end of a fateful Thursday, but not in the rejuvenating month of April and not in the same year that the rest of the novel takes place. Caddy's trial goes on: the novel's Good Friday does not come for eighteen years, and, even after its Enter Sunday two days later, Caddy is not rewarded for her sacrifices with a resurrection. As revealed by the photograph of her with the Nazi general, she has "descended into hell" and lived among the damned for at least fifteen years past Easter.[16]

Notes

1. See Melvin Backman's detailed explanation of this progression (16–17).

2. Stephen M. Ross also discusses Quentin's fluctuating control over his story. Although, as I suggest above, Quentin has the power, while he is conscious, to cut

off his recollection of painful memories, as Ross points out, he cannot stop them from entering his mind in the first place (173).

3. Also relevant to the issue of Quentin's control over his memories is Arnold L. Weinstein's discussion of the conversation Quentin has with Herbert, after which, he points out; Quentin begins lose control over his memories (123).

4. Arnold Weinstein calls this reference to Quentin's broken leg "the objective correlative of the suffering which Caddy has caused and which he can no longer repress" (123). I argue, rather, that it reminds him of his own responsibility for his own and Caddy's suffering.

5. Stephen Ross also comments on absence of punctuation in these scenes, relating it to Quentin's lack of control over his memories. He too suggests these memories' particular painfulness to Quentin, although he does not note that these scenes take place while Quentin is unconscious.

6. John T. Matthews (*Sound* 46) and Dawn Trouard (43) explain Caddy's association of sex and death similarly. My interpretation is a more positive reading than, for example, Doreen Fowler's belief that Caddy's words reflect the influence of her mother, who also "pair[ed] sex and death" when she dressed in mourning after witnessing Caddy kissing a boy (144).

7. It seems that Quentin's reasons for contemplating a sexual relationship with Caddy may go back to some historical allowances for incest, as listed by Constance Hill Hall, including "a privilege . . . reserved for royalty" (6). One is reminded here of events in *Absolom! Absolom!,* as recreated, significantly, by Quentin and his roommate Shreve: Henry Sutpen, with whom Quentin has seemed to identify since first hearing that ultimately Henry killed his sister's fiancé, had at one point made his peace with allowing his half-brother Charles Bon to marry their sister with the assertion that "kings have done it! Even dukes!" (273). In theories similar to Hall's, Warwick Wadlington describes "Quentin's desperate fantasy of incest" as "a rigorous extension of the inbreeding attitude of a household that feels itself surrounded by relative nonentities" (416); and André Bleikasten explains that "in sociohistorical terms, [Quentin's] obsession with incest any reflect the panic of a declining social class which struggles for survival but refuses any influx of outside blood" (227). In this light, in spite of his puritanical nature, Quentin would view the notion of Caddy committing incest with him a more acceptable than sexual relations between Caddy and Dalton Ames, whom he probably would classify "poor white trash."

8. Referring to this as well as other examples of Quentin's self-deception, André Bleikasten comments on his tendency to deny or "twist" the truth "when faced with unpleasant facts . . . so as to minimize their significance" (207).

9. Richard Godden has offered a provocative reading of an earlier scene after Quentin and Caddy seem to consider a double suicide (or committing incest) and just before Dolton arrives and Caddy introduces him to Quentin. Godden points out how Caddy seems as aroused as Quentin during that interaction following the knife scene (125).

10. In support of this reading of Caddy's offer to her brother is, first, Herbert Head's remarks to Quentin, recalled earlier, regarding how much Caddy talked about her brother to him (107–108). Second, in Jason's section Mrs. Compson remarks to Jason, "when Quentin started to school we had to let her go the next year, so she could be with him." She believes that Quentin, had he not committed suicide, "could have controlled" Caddy because "he seemed to be the only person she had any consideration for" (261). Herbert and Mrs. Compson, though not the

most reliable of sources, both suggest that Caddy's devotion to—perhaps obsession with—Quentin is as strong as his for her. Again, one might also read Richard Godden's analysis, referenced in the preceding note, for another critic's view that the incestuous attraction was not one-sided.

11. As I will continue to develop it, my reading of Quentin's growing understanding of his responsibility for Caddy's promiscuity differs from Giles Gunn's view of Quentin as "idealistic" and "romantic" attempt *"to take the responsibility of Caddy's promiscuity upon himself"* by implying that it was caused by an initial and initiating, act of incest (57; emphasis added). I argue that in the course of the day, Quentin ultimately—and *rightly*—accepts his *actual,* rather than imagined, responsibility for Caddy's destruction, her promiscuity being only assumption of which—not in his fantasy role as her lover but his very real role as her brother—and that it is that acceptance that drives him to commit suicide.

12. Richard Feldstein makes the same argument for why Quentin provokes Gerald (7). However, Feldstein is not referring to the same offense against Caddy that this paper argues drives Quentin to seek punishment; rather, he believes Quentin wants to be punished for his cowardly behavior during his meeting with Dalton Ames.

13. Edmond Volpe apparently disagrees with Bowling on this point, for he believes that Quentin *"makes judgments, establishes relationships, derives significances* from remembered scenes and from the situations he becomes involved in as he wanders during his final day." However, Volpe adds that "the significance of these memories for Quentin is not necessarily their real significance" thereby making his position about Quentin's perception of the parallels ambiguous (92–93; emphasis added).

14. Philip Weinstein also discusses the parallels between the two situations in such a way as to suggest that Quentin recognizes that is "implicated in Caddy's experience" (48).

15. John Matthews also suggests that Caddy is the novel's Christ figure (*Play* 109)

16. Interestingly, when asked about the chances "of getting [Caddy] back from the clutches of the Nazis," Faulkner commented on Caddy's tragedy in terms of her not being "resurrected" (Gwynn and Blotner 1). Also noting the absence of a positive resurrection, Gary Lee Stonum remarks upon Reverend Shegog's sermon, which "is curiously lacking in emphasis on the Resurrection. [Reverend Shegog] dwells instead on suffering in the temporal world and on the generations passing away" (54).

Works Cited

Backman, Melvin. *Faulkner, The Major Years: A Critical Study.* Bloomington: Indiana University Press. 1966.

Bleikasten, André. *The Most Splendid Failure: Faulkner's The Sound and the Fury.* Bloomington: Indiana University Press, 1976.

Bowling, Lawrence. "Faulkner: The Theme of Pride in *The Sound and the Fury,*" *Modern Fiction* Studies 11 (1965): 129–139.

Faulkner, William. *Absolom! Absolom!.* 1936. Corrected ed. New York: Random. 1986.

———. *The Sound and the Fury.* 1929 New, Corrected ed. New York: Random. 1984.

Feldstein, Richard. "Gerald Bland's Shadow," *Literature and Psychology* 31.4 (1981): 4–12.

Fowler, Doreen. "Eleusinian Mysteries in *The Sound and the Fury*," *Faulkner and Religion: Faulkner and Yoknapatawpha, 1984*. Jackson: University Press of Mississippi, 1991, 140–156.

Gibbons, Kathryn Gibbs. "Quentin's Shadow," *Literature and Psychology* 12.1 (1962): 16–24.

Godden, Richard. "Quentin Compson: Tyrrhenian Vase or Crucible of Race?" *New Essays on The Sound and the Fury*, American Novel series. Ed. Noel Polk. New York: Cambridge University Press, 1993, 99–137.

Gunn, Giles. "Faith and Family in *The Sound and the Fury*." *Faulkner and Religion: Faulkner and Yoknapatawpha, 1984*. Jackson: University Press of Mississippi, 1991, 44–64.

Gwynn, Frederick L, and Joseph L Blotner, eds. *Faulkner in University: Class Conferences at the University of Virginia, 1957–1958*. Charlottesville: University of Virginia Press, 1959.

Hall, Constance Hill. *Incest in Faulkner: A Metaphor for the Fall*. Ann Arbor: University of Michigan Research Press, 1983.

Iser, Wolfgang. *The Implied Reader: Patterns of Communication in Prose Fiction from Bunyan to Beckett*. Baltimore: Johns Hopkins University Press, 1974.

Kartiganer, Donald M. "'Now I Can Write': Faulkner's Novel of Invention." *New Essays on The Sound and the Fury*. American Novel series. Ed. Noel Polk. New York: Cambridge University Press, 1993, 71–97.

Matthews, John T. *The Play of Faulkner's Language*. Ithaca: Cornell University Press, 1982.

———. *The Sound and the Fury: Faulkner and the Lost Cause*. Twayne's Masterwork Studies, series 61. Boston: Twayne, 1990.

Polk, Noel, ed. *New Essays on The Sound and the Fury*. American Novel series. New York: Cambridge University Press, 1993.

———. "Trying Not to Say: A Primer on the Language of *The Sound and the Fury*." *New Essays on The Sound and the Fury*. American Novel series, Ed. Noel Polk. New York: Cambridge University Press, 1993, 139–175.

Ross, Stephen M. *Fiction's Inexhaustible Voice: Speech and Writing in Faulkner*. Athens: University of Georgia Press, 1989.

Stonum, Gary Lee. "*The Sound and the Fury:* The Search for a Narrative Method," William Faulkner's *The Sound and the Fury*. Modern Critical Interpretations series Ed. Harold Bloom New York: Chelsea, 1988, 39–56.

Thompson, Lawrence R. *William Faulkner: An Introduction and Interpretation*. 2nd ed. New York: Holt, 1967.

Trouard, Dawn. "Faulkner's Text Which Is Not One," *New Essays on The Sound and the Fury*. American Novel series. Ed. Noel Polk. New York: Cambridge University Press, 1993, 23–69.

Volpe, Edmond L. *A Reader's Guide to William Faulkner*. New York: Farrar, 1964.

Wadlington, Warwick. "*The Sound and the Fury:* A Logical Tragedy." *American Literature* 53 (1981): 409–423.

Weinstein, Arnold L. *Vision and Response in Modern Fiction*. Cornell University Press, 1974.

Young, James Dean. "Quentin's Maundy Thursday." *Tulane Studies in English* 10 (1960): 143–151.

Zender, Karl F. *The Crossing of the Ways: William Faulkner, the South and the Modern World*. New Brunswick: Rutgers University Press, 1989.

THOMAS L. MCHANEY

Themes in The Sound and the Fury

The Decline of the Compsons

Since *The Sound and the Fury* is a modernist variation upon the family chronicle novel, its themes are consonant with that form, and one of Faulkner's models was his own novel of the same year, originally to be called "Flags in the Dust" but published in January 1929 as *Sartoris,* the name of a family whose decline is traced throughout the book. A model for both is the German modernist Thomas Mann's *Buddenbrooks,* also named for the family that forms the subject of the novel, and subtitled *The Decline of a Family.* The major theme of such novels is, obviously, decline: the falling fortunes—economical, spiritual, and even physical—of a family through just a few generations from the time of a powerful and successful patriarch. Faulkner's own family, he could see clearly, had lived out such a pattern from the days of his self-made great-grandfather Col. William C. Falkner, through his eccentric but generally successful grandfather, his often-defeated father, and on to himself, the ne'er-do-well artist—the sensitive aesthete often seen, in nineteenth-century psychology, as one of the common results in the last phase of a four-generation family cycle. J. P. Stern explains the matter with regard to *Buddenbrooks* usefully. In Mann's novel the members of the Buddenbrooks family are north German merchants and shippers, just as Faulkner's forebears were north Mississippi merchants and shippers. "The decline of the fortunes of the [Buddenbrooks] family firm," Stern writes, "is traced out

Literary Masterpieces, Volume 6: The Sound and the Fury (Framington Hills, MI: The Gale Group, 2000): pp. 61–100.

over three-and-a-half generations, and is given its partial and proximate cause in the Buddenbrooks's inability to adjust to the changes from mercantilism to financial capitalism which are taking place around them. Hand in hand with their economic decline goes a gradual loss of physical stamina and moral fibre."[1] These themes in Faulkner's novel are clear: Quentin's frailty, impotence, and unreadiness for living; Jason's immorality; and even Caddy's promiscuity follow upon their father's economic failure and alcoholism in a South that had changed drastically, first from losing the Civil War and the destruction of the economic system of the Old South, and now, in the 1920s, from the impact of further changes in the American economy. Jason speculates on the cotton futures market, and the family's attempt to have Quentin educated at an elite northeastern university, Harvard, results only in the loss of their pasture and Quentin's suicide.

The two great human subjects, Sigmund Freud taught, are sex and death, and they play perhaps the most poignant role in *The Sound and the Fury.* Since the germinal anecdote for the novel concerns a death—the children's discovery, from a position of innocence, of the arrival of death in their household—it is not surprising that the pattern of the novel is punctuated with several other deaths: Quentin's suicide, his father's death, and the death of Roskus are all significant transition points in the book, but the theme is underscored by such small details as the death of one of the family's horses, Nancy, and of the pigs that are being slaughtered for food in an early scene, and by such large details as the setting of the novel on Easter weekend and the employment of analogies to the classical myth of Persephone's abduction by Hades, lord of the underworld, the abode of the dead.

The power, misuse, and misperception of sex are equally apparent as recurrent themes: not merely Caddy's problems with her sexual coming of age in a repressive and ignorant household or her daughter's sexuality and its consequences, but also the implications of impotence and obsession with sex manifested in her brothers. As a child Caddy catches her brother Quentin playing innocent sexual games—seeking knowledge—with a girl named Natalie; Caddy slaps the girl and sends her home, and then she and Quentin have a fight in the hog wallow, covering one another with the filthy mud. No wonder that Quentin is thereafter sexually impotent, doubtless sublimating the experience that sex is something dirty. Benjy's longing for his sister is characterized as that of a child for a mother figure, but in a Freudian world such longing is no longer innocent, touching as it does the Oedipal longing for sexual possession. Both Caddy's and Benjy's coming of age are portrayed in the novel as problematical; eventually, Benjy is castrated because he is believed to have attempted a sexual assault on a little girl. While this is not true—Benjy confuses the schoolgirl with a memory of Caddy as a girl coming home from school—Jason's complicity in arranging the castration repeats another variation of the Oedipal struggle between son and father, one masked in the competition of brothers for the sole possession of a mother or a sister.[2]

Other important themes that relate to the problems in the Compson household have to do with religion—specifically, the loss of Christian values and thus of human love and mercy—and with the philosophical conception of time. These themes are used in a manner that suggests Faulkner's awareness that they are in some respects antithetical in the modern era. Belief in divinity and in an absolute sense of time—a beginning and an ending, a creation and a last judgment—as well as immortality have endured many challenges from modern science and philosophy, as has the commonsense notion of time and the idea of the uncorrupted recovery of time through memory. In the American South, thought to be a culture of noble memory and firm religious belief, the Compsons prove a poor example of lost ideals. Each of the sons has a problem with religion: none of them is, in fact, religious; each of them fails miserably to match up to the Christian qualities their faithful servant Dilsey espouses; and each of them, on the day Faulkner has assigned them a monologue, enacts an ironic parody of the life of Jesus on the equivalent days of his trial, crucifixion, death, and resurrection. The sons likewise have a problem with time: Quentin wants to stop it, but he cannot even stop its mechanical representation on the false faces of watches and clocks, and in fact the events he wants to stop have already occurred. Benjy cannot understand the passage of time: in his undeveloped consciousness, all events can be repeated in memory without change, because he is a creature of pure instinct, without language and therefore without the power of reflection and interpretation of the past. Jason wants to defeat time by creating a powerful future for himself, but he is in fact always late, regarding the Southern past with nothing but disdain. All the themes in the novel are interwoven, and so the theme of Southern honor, voiced by the older Jason Compson ("no compson [sic] has ever disappointed a lady" [113]), touches affairs of sex, matters of religion, and the family's decline. Compson's stoicism leads to cynicism, despair, and ultimately nihilism ("no battle is ever won he said. They are not even fought" [481]).

The theme of race is not foregrounded in the novel, yet its presence is unmistakable in the parallel portraits of the Compson and Gibson family members, in Quentin's reflections on race as a Southerner in Massachusetts and his dealings with the canny figure of Deacon at Harvard, in the relationship between Jason and the wise old Job who works in the hardware store, and in the portraits of African American life as conduced at a remove from white observation: the women at the water hazard on the golf course and the participants in the Easter service at Dilsey's church. As the caring, sometimes outspoken but self-sacrificing servant, Dilsey in some respects resembles far more idealized figures in Southern plantation fiction,[3] but like other characters in the novel she is presented through the eyes of others. The argument can be made that in *The Sound and the Fury* Faulkner addresses the race issue seriously for the first time in a novel, even if as a side story to the decline of the Compsons. While not everyone has agreed on this matter, many critics, including African American scholars and writers, perceive both a fictionist's imagination and a critical intelligence at work in Faulkner's demythologizing of Southern stereotypes concerning race and relationships between the races in the South.[4]

It may seem obvious now that someone with Dilsey's work ethic, religious devotion, family values, and diplomatic skills should not be doomed to a thankless and unremunerative job serving people who do not deserve her loyalty, but at the time Faulkner wrote the novel, and well into the 1960s in the South, only a thoughtful and liberal-minded person might have questioned this condition. Social customs supported by city and state legal codes and bolstered by religious arguments from established orthodoxies supported a system of racial separation and subservience for African Americans. Women's lives in general were similarly constrained, though not to the almost absolute degree that applied to African Americans. Faulkner did not write *The Sound and the Fury* as a tract—though he wrote several tracts in the 1950s, outside of his work as a novelist—but the situation he portrayed certifies his increasing understanding of, and sympathy for, the plight of African Americans in his state and region. He observed their condition firsthand, not only as witness to racial violence in his hometown but also as a dependent of and friend to several African Americans who worked for his parents and grandparents, including his grandfather's driver, Chester Carothers, and his own childhood nurse, Caroline "Callie" Barr, for whom he provided completely through the end of her long life and whose funeral he held in his house, speaking a moving eulogy in 1940.[5]

Quentin Compson's experience with race, Southern snobbery, and male chauvinism occurs not in Jefferson, Mississippi, but in Cambridge, Massachusetts, where his section of the novel takes place. Away from his provincial home for the first time, Quentin wonders how he will react to the changed racial customs of the north. He finds himself in a city where people of African descent ride streetcars freely, march in parades, and have white boys for helpers when they show up at the train station to carry a Southern student's baggage. When the train on which he rides at Christmas stops at a crossing where an elderly African American sits on a mule, Quentin renews old customs learned from the servants and realizes for the first time how much he misses "them"—not his family but Roskus, Dilsey, and others of their race (55).

Quentin's day raises, however, a theme more crucial to his life and death than race. It is a theme that Faulkner worked with a great deal in early poetry, a play, and an allegorical prose tale titled *Mayday,* written in 1926. The theme is the perceived betrayal of idealistic and enraptured young men by nymph-like young women who lure them into cloying relationships that effectively drown their spirits.[6] This theme, which Faulkner portrayed with comic distance in such works as the unfinished *Elmer* (published posthumously in 1984), *The Hamlet,* and a splendid story about Native Americans, "A Courtship," derives from several romantic disappointments in Faulkner's life but is supported, of course, by an extensive tradition of poetry, prose, and drama by many authors.

The obverse of the theme of female betrayal is actually more important in *The Sound and the Fury,* for as with the issue of race, Faulkner developed a highly sensitive portrait of conditions taken for granted or misunderstood by a puritanical and patriarchal white society with a hypocritical code of honor. This obverse theme is, of course, that of female diminishment and subjugation, the imposition of the "double standard" by which women were judged and men exculpated for sexual dalliance, and the commodification of the female body, even the female life. Each Compson boy wants from Caddy maternal solace or material value she should not be asked to provide. Their demands begin when she is quite young and continue through her banishment and exile. Thus, *The Sound and the Fury* is not about female betrayal but misplaced male anger and disappointment, all from males who cannot, or will not, simply proceed with their own lives in their own way. Even the portrait of Caroline Compson as a whining, neurasthenic, selfish mother and falsely proud social climber may be explained, if not excused, by reference to codes of behavior socially imposed on Southern women of her time.[7]

The Sound and the Fury, which begins with the threshold experience of Benjy regarding a lost world through an iron fence (the Compsons' former pasture, now a golf course), ends with his contented regard of thresholds on the town square of Jefferson, Mississippi, his hometown: "cornice and facade . . . post and tree, window and door and signboard" are "each in its ordered place" (199). If he were making his customary carriage ride, he would be bound to the ultimate human threshold represented by the graves of the dead Compsons in a fenced circle of cedars in the town cemetery. The prose at the end of the novel is straightforward, rhythmic, and calm, appropriate for closure. If Benjy were indeed an "idiot" and the teller of the whole tale, perhaps *The Sound and the Fury* would signify nothing, or nothingness, but there are many tales in the novel, and many tellers. Within the remembered lives of the three Compson brothers are reports of several stories from the lips of others: the older Jason Compson; Roskus; Versh; T. P.; Luster; Dilsey; Frony; Quentin's Harvard roommate, Shreve; the fishing boys near Harvard who tell Quentin about the legendary trout that "was a neighbourhoood character" (74); and Job, the old man who works in Earl's hardware store. The debate on the meaning of the novel is, of course, open, as is proven by the critical essays in this volume and the entire critical record concerning the book. Still, the novel has signified *something* to almost everyone who has read it.

The title is nonetheless apt, for all that Benjy Compson is apparently not a damaged consciousness, although he has a damaged mind. Unable to speak, he nevertheless does tell a tale, and his version and those of his brothers—one a walking shadow and the other a poor player who struts and frets—required a writer who had felt and mastered the contradictory emotions out of which the novel was composed. Like one of Pablo Picasso's Cubist "deconstructions" of pictorial expectation, or T. S. Eliot's multilingual poem *The Waste Land* (1922), made of poetic fragments, this modernist novel signifies far more than its shattered form or ill-fated families literally represent, so rich and deliberate is its symbolism within the tradition of what Eliot called "the mythical method."

The human plot of *The Sound and the Fury* is about a family gone wrong: normal-seeming children who become neurotic, psychotic, or banished—all by identifiable forces both within and beyond the control of their parents. Caroline and Jason Compson, however, have had to endure psychological mismanagement in their own upbringing, events about which the novel provides only hints, but significant ones: Mr. Compson's father was "always right," Quentin remembers (111), and Mrs. Compson's brother Maury is a leech on the family, a philanderer who uses small children to further his adulterous relations and repeatedly sends the children away, closeting himself and his sister and giving her a drink of whiskey. Caroline's sense that Benjy, whom she originally named for her brother, is a curse on her hints at guilt feelings rooted in the same ignorant psychology that causes people to regard Benjy as an idiot. The taint of incest is thus evoked in her generation as found peculiar ways of giving order where uncertainty or at best constant flux seemed to rule, but almost all of them depended upon the repetition of themes, images, allusions, and metaphorical or symbolic expression to replace the old order of chronological events and straight-forward causality in the plot.

The Sound and the Fury exhibits all of these broad features of modernist fiction, but the feature with which the reader may need the most help is what British critic and novelist David Lodge has called that mode of "aesthetic ordering" that employs "allusion to or imitation of literary models, or mythical archetypes; or repetition-with-variation of motifs, images, symbols. . . ."[11] It was this device to which Eliot, having already used it himself in *The Waste Land,* gave the name "the mythical method" as he reviewed Joyce's *Ulysses* in 1923. *Ulysses* was a book, Eliot wrote, that "has given me all the surprise, delight, and terror that I can require," and "a book to which we are all indebted, and from which none of us can escape." The aspect of the novel with which Eliot was most taken, apparently, was "using the myth [of Odysseus as a foundation for the modern story], in manipulating a continuous parallel between contemporaneity and antiquity . . . a way of controlling, of ordering, of giving a shape and a significance to the immense panorama of futility and anarchy which is contemporary history." What made Joyce's achievement possible, Eliot wrote, was "Psychology (such as it is, and whether our reaction to it be comic or serious), ethnology, and *The Golden Bough*"—so that "Instead of narrative method, we may now use the mythical method." It was this method that Faulkner used to provide foundations of order for the severely fractured plot of *The Sound and the Fury*.

There is a narrative plot to *The Sound and the Fury*, but the reader is forced to construct it by recalling and putting together scenes, speeches, images, motifs, and themes that are often separated by many pages and not in chronological or causal order. Summarized one way, the surface plot might be told like this: In the first section a thirty-three-year-old idiot spends his birthday with a mischievous boy, the grandson of the family's major caretaker; in the second section a freshman at Harvard ends his year at college by searching for an inconspicuous place to drown himself; in the third section a blustery small-town cotton speculator delivers a mordant monologue of complaint against his family, especially the women; and in the fourth section, on Easter Sunday, a loyal and much-abused family servant takes her daughter, grandson, and the idiot son of the white family she serves to a moving service in her segregated church, while the idiot's cruel older brother searches unsuccessfully for the runaway niece who has stolen his savings. Afterward the servant's grandson drives the idiot toward the town's graveyard in order to get him out of the house, but he turns the wrong way around the courthouse square, encountering the mean older brother, who straightens things out.

This plot synopsis, as anyone who has read the novel can see, is a completely inadequate summary of the novel, though it mentions many of the principal events that happen in the present time of each of the four sections. Randomly recalled memories of past actions and feelings constitute the bulk of Faulkner's story of a once prosperous and prominent family in Jefferson, Mississippi, as it descends into tragic dissolution and loss. The tragedy of the Compsons is underscored in several ways through elaborated patterns of motif, theme, and allusion or literary reference.

Twilight

Faulkner's manuscript draft of the Compson novel carried at the top of the first page of the first section the title "Twilight," an appropriate reference to the decline of the Compson family, to the dawn of waking or the dusk of going to sleep that figures in the Benjy and Quentin sections, to the part of the day during which the Compson children were sent away from the house on the occasion of their grandmother's death, and even to what critic Michael Millgate has called "the half world" of Benjy Compson's state of being, his "timeless suspension between the light and the dark, comprehension and incomprehension, between the human and the animal."[13] The word may allude to "The Twilight of the Gods," the English translation of *Götterdämmerung,* the title of the final opera in nineteenth-century German composer Richard Wagner's monumental cycle of operas, *Der Ring des Nibelungen* (The Ring of the Nibelungs), four interwoven musical dramas about conflict within the family of the old Germanic gods and their decline and fall. Wagner developed the device of using recurrent musical phrases that announced individual characters and important symbolic objects, and fiction writers of a later generation picked up the device, which has been called the *leitmotiv,* in their own way. Mann, whom Faulkner admired, used leitmotivs in *Buddenbrooks* and other works, and Faulkner uses them in *The Sound and the Fury* ("Did you ever have a sister?"; "Once a bitch always a bitch"; and "Caddy smelled like trees," which identify Quentin, Jason, and Benjy, respectively). Whether or not the word *twilight* alludes to Wagner's opera, it is a repeated thematic motif in Faulkner's novel, where it appears, in one form or another, more than a dozen times (the word *dawn,* in contrast, appears only twice).

The twilight motif may also be regarded as an allusion to Faulkner's apprentice writing, especially to his early career as poet—when he admired and imitated poetry by many other writers, including Joyce, that was suffused with twilight—and to two apprentice texts, the play *Marionettes,* written in 1920, and the allegorical tale *Mayday,* written in 1926. More than one poem in Faulkner's first book, the poetry collection *The Marble Faun* (1924), speaks of twilight in some way. The title character and narrative voice is a twilight consciousness, a half-animal, half-human faun frozen in marble in a living garden where nymphs cavort provocatively. Several poems in the collection display language that would not be inappropriate for Quentin Compson: "I am sad, nor yet can I, / For all my questing, reason why; / And now as night falls I will go / Where two breezes joining flow / Above a stream," laments the faun at one point.[14] Poem X of *A Green Bough* (1933), originally titled "Twilight" and derived from a poem and a prose sketch written in the mid 1920s, features a young man returning home at twilight, thinking of "his circling / Sinister shadow about his head" as he works during the day and how in his night's sleep he will forget "his father, Death; Derision / His mother, forgotten by her at last."[15]

Marionettes and *Mayday,* for which Faulkner made handsome symbolist drawings, both depict rejected lovers as heroes. In *Marionettes* Pierrot is drunk and dreams the play in which his Shade plays his role—a stagecraft version of stream-of-consciousness—and in *Mayday* Sir Galwyn drowns. Both young men are flanked, in the drawings accompanying the texts, by symbolic abstractions: the Shade of Pierrot is flanked by a Grey Figure and a Lilac Figure—dawn and dusk, the twilight poles—and Sir Galwyn is followed by a shadow and flanked by figures who represent Hunger and Pain. The concept of the shadow prefigures Quentin, who cannot evade his shadow in a monologue literally flanked by the monologues of Benjy and Jason, one expressive of hunger and one of pain.[16]

Macbeth

The title of Faulkner's fourth novel has sent readers and scholars to William Shakespeare's *Macbeth,* if only to recall the speech by the tragic hero from which the phrase "sound and fury" comes:

> SEYTON: The queen, my lord, is dead.
> MACBETH: She should have died hereafter;
> There would have been a time for such a word.
> To-morrow, and to-morrow, and to-morrow,
> Creeps in this petty pace from day to day
> To the last syllable of recorded time,
> And all our yesterdays have lighted fools
> The way to dusty death. Out, out, brief candle!
> Life's but a walking shadow, a poor player
> That struts and frets his hour upon the stage
> And then is heard no more: it is a tale
> Told by an idiot, full of sound and fury,
> Signifying nothing. (act 5, scene 5, 16–28)

When Faulkner changed his title from "Twilight" to *The Sound and the Fury,* he may have felt prompted by the presence of the "idiot" Benjy as the narrative point of view in the first section. Since shadow images and characters somewhat like Quentin appeared in the novelist's writing long before he began *The Sound and the Fury,* Quentin's association with the "walking shadow" of Macbeth's speech may also have led Faulkner to the speech for his title. However or whenever he made the choice, the selection was a great stroke of imagination, for the title itself, with its rhythm altered by the addition of "the" twice, and Macbeth's familiar speech, which so many schoolchildren have had to learn, provide an excellent overture to the novel. *Macbeth* is a Scottish play, and the Compsons are descended from Scots. Macbeth's soliloquy—a kind of interior monologue—comes just after he is informed of Lady Macbeth's suicide, and his entire speech is in accord with the three monologues given the Compson boys. Macbeth's evocation of time—"She should have died hereafter" (meaning either "she would have died anyway" or "she should have died at a less tumultuous time")—leads to his wish, like Quentin's, to control it: "There would have been a time for such a word" (meaning, perhaps, that death would come better in old age). This wish leads in turn to Macbeth's sad meditation upon Time's hopeless and inexorable march into nothingness. The tone is similar to some of the older Jason Compson's pessimistic observations about the meaning of existence, and the three metaphors for life—"a walking shadow," "a poor player who struts and frets," and "a tale told by an idiot"—fit the three Compson brothers well.

Easter

In terms of Faulkner's application of the "mythical method" that Eliot praised in Joyce's *Ulysses,* one of the two main examples in *The Sound and the Fury* is the elaborate use of the biblical account of Jesus' life, and especially his last days, and of the ritual and folklore associated with the celebration of Easter in Christian churches. Faulkner's choice of Easter 1928, the year in which he also wrote the book, may have taken inspiration from the fact that this specific Easter occurred on what modern Bible editions commonly calculate as exactly the same days as the events that lie behind the Christian celebration of Easter: the period of Jesus' entry into Jerusalem at the Jewish Passover, his Last Supper, trial, crucifixion, death, and burial. According to a typical "Harmony of the Gospels" found as an appendix to common editions of the Bible, the original events took place, for example, on 5 April (Maundy Thursday), 6 April (Good Friday), 7 April (Holy Saturday), and 8 April (Easter Sunday).[17] The Easter of *The Sound and the Fury* corresponds exactly to this "first" Easter, with two exceptions: the "Harmony of the Gospels" uses the Jewish calendar, and so a day begins at sundown—twilight, not midnight—and ends at sundown. Thus, events on Faulkner's 7 April, for example, correspond to Bible events recorded as commencing after sundown on the night of 6 April and before sunset on 7 April; and, of course, Faulkner places his Maundy Thursday on 2 June 1910, too late a date for Easter week but a day on which Quentin's movements around Cambridge and Boston parody the life of Jesus on Thursday 6 April.

Because of changes in the Western calendar from the Julian to the Gregorian, as well as changes in the ecclesiastical calendar, a naive reader may perceive the modern "Harmony of the Gospels" to show time as much out of joint as it appears to be in *The Sound and the Fury.* Jesus' birth is recorded as occurring in 5 B.C.—that is, five years before the date traditionally marking the beginning of the Christian Era; in A.D. 9, at the age of thirteen, he attends Passover and astounds the "Doctors" in the temple with his wisdom. Then he "retires" for eighteen years to prepare for his ministry, which begins when he is thirty, in A.D. 26. The major events thereafter are his baptism in the River Jordan, his time in the desert where Satan tempts him, his gathering of the first disciples, his first miracle (changing water to wine during a marriage at Cana), and then the start of his public ministry when he drives the money changers from the temple at Passover in Jerusalem. Thereafter Jesus returns to Jerusalem for Passover and carries his ministry to Galilee, where the miracles increase in number: he cures an infirm man at Bethesda pool, causes a remarkably great catch of fishes, casts out a demon, raises the dead, and heals many, including a "blind and dumb demoniac." His "kinsfolk try to lay hold on him as mad," but he continues to heal the sick, including a woman "with an issue of blood," and perform miracles, feeding multitudes with a magnification of bread and fishes, walking on the water at the Sea of Galilee, and foretelling his death and resurrection. King Herod, who has murdered John the Baptist, Jesus' teacher and initiator into the religious life, "fears that Jesus is John risen from the dead" and initiates plots against him.[18] Jesus continues to teach, cure the sick and dumb, and preach with parables—simple illustrative anecdotes—such as the parable of "the lost coin" or "the rich fool" or "the importunate widow." Jesus' crucifixion occurs in A.D. 30, according to the "Harmony of the Gospels," and with his birth recorded as 5 B.C., this would make him thirty-four at the time of his crucifixion instead of the traditionally accepted age of thirty-three.

A reader of *The Sound and the Fury* should be able to identify many of the events taken from "Harmony of the Gospels" as having counterpart events in the novel: Quentin's encounter with the boys who are fishing or his buying bread for the little Italian girl; T. P.'s making Benjy drunk on champagne, which he thinks is just soda water at Caddy's wedding; Luster and Benjy wading where the women do washing; and Benjy's dumbness and his torment by the devilish Luster. Jesus' parables are parodied in Luster's searching for his coin, Jason's performance as the "rich fool," and Caroline Compson's whining as the importunate widow. Jason's foolishness is manifest, but an interesting example is his being wrong about baseball. In 1928, Babe Ruth's greatest year, Jason announces that he would never bet on a team that included "that fellow Ruth" (157), an anecdote that serves as a Christian parable on its own: Jason wants nothing to do with "ruth," a word that means compassion for others or mercy, a Christian virtue. Herod's fear that Jesus is the murdered John come back from the dead is touched on in *The Sound and the Fury* obliquely when Luster worries about his father's ghost (22) and when it is mentioned that T. P., who is missing, has "gwine out to St John's today" (197).

The eighteen years between Quentin's June 1910 and the Easter 1928 of the novel's present constitute a parody of the eighteen years in which Jesus retired before starting his ministry. The ambiguity about dates in the Christian story is reflected by Faulkner's own practice with dates in his fiction, which he liked to call his "apocrypha"—that is, writings of questionable authenticity, like those scriptural writings excluded from the Jewish and Protestant canons of the Old Testament. There are many instances in Faulkner's work in which dates simply do not add up correctly. Between works, even between the novels of his Snopes trilogy (*The Hamlet,* 1940; *The Town,* 1957; and *The Mansion,* 1959), consistency was not something he cared for at all. In his 1932 novel *Light in August* he makes a point of confusing the issue of whether Joe Christmas, who is given parodic attributes of Jesus, is thirty or thirty-three when he returns to a place near where he was raised to meet his martyrdom. Faulkner's notes for *The Sound and the Fury* give Benjy's birth year as 1897, the author's own birth year, making him the age of three—and possibly still normal—when Damuddy dies in 1900. But that Benjy is thirty-three in 1928 requires that he is born in 1895, and is thus five in 1900. It appears, however, that he is five when his disability is discovered and his name is changed. This does not appear to be the same year that Damuddy dies. A passion for fact and strict chronological accuracy would force a resolution of this issue, but Faulkner's knowledge of the Bible suggests another: he may have conceived of Benjy as being three at Damuddy's death, when quite reasonably no one regarded the child as brain-damaged and his name is still Maury. His name is changed when he is five, possibly after a bout of measles is neglected and he suffers brain damage that renders him dumb. Perhaps in 1928 Benjy is thirty-three, or perhaps, as Jesus might have been in A.D. 30 if he were born in 5 B.C., he is thirty-four. Since 1928 is the only clearly stated date in the novel, Faulkner is apparently willing to let the rest remain ambiguous.

Many events that occur during the ministry and the final days of the life of Jesus recounted in the Gospels of Matthew, Mark, Luke, and John in the New Testament are touched upon parodically in the four sections of *The Sound and the Fury*, and it does not seem to be a coincidence that both the New Testament and Faulkner's novel include four versions of the story. Faulkner's novel, however, does not move through Easter week in the expected order. The first section of the novel is set on 7 April 1928, a Saturday. Quentin's section, set on 2 June 1910, is not only eighteen years previous to the present time of the story, it could never lie within the moveable feast of Easter. This day is nevertheless a Thursday, and in the strangeness of modernist fiction, this "fact" and the parodic elements of the section are more than enough to connect it as parallel to Easter events and put it in strange accord with the disordered Saturday, Friday, and Sunday of the other sections of the novel. It is not the calendar's but, as one critic has written, "Quentin's Maundy Thursday."[19]

The first day of the novel is Holy Saturday (Benjy's section). Holy Saturday is the day after Christ's crucifixion and entombment, a day when, Christian tradition has it, Jesus descended into Hell in order to "harrow" or rob it, that is, to bring up to Heaven the worthy Old Testament patriarchs who would otherwise, by historical accident, be denied Salvation since they lived before the time of God's new covenant and the acts of Christ. This is Benjy's day, and it duplicates many details from the biblical account and Christian lore of the acts of Jesus on that day. The second section is Quentin's Maundy Thursday, and the third is Good Friday, the day of Jesus' crucifixion, death, and entombment. The modern church has made ritual of the belief that Jesus spent the hours of noon to three o'clock on the cross, and these hours are honored in Faulkner's imagination. First, the Compson clock chimes five times when it is eight o'clock, indicating three missing hours. Then Jason, whose cross in life is his family and whose father has bequeathed him a bitter cup (by drinking himself to death), is, in his view, tormented and ruined by the Jews, the commodity brokers in New York with whom he speculates on the future—cotton futures, to be exact. On Easter Sunday in *The Sound and the Fury,* it is not the tomb of Jesus that is empty but both Miss Quentin's room and Jason's money box. Miss Quentin, thus, has harrowed Hell herself—plundering the devilish Compson household and escaping with its hidden wealth (a reminder, as with Herbert Head's profession as banker, that Pluto as god of the underworld is characterized as the god of hidden wealth, hence the term *plutocracy* for a society ruled by the rich).

As Mary and Martha stand at the tomb of Jesus and hear the angel say "He is risen," Caroline Compson and Dilsey stand at the open door listening to Jason's tirade.

The parallels to Easter lore and ritual in *The Sound and the Fury* are many, and they function just as Eliot said the parallels to the *Odyssey* function in Joyce's *Ulysses:* they control, order, and give shape and significance to the futility and anarchy that seem to prevail in the Compson household and family history and especially in the daily mental life of the three sons. Because the parallels underscore the absence of love and compassion among most of the Compsons, the structuring story of the life and passion of Jesus fulfilled at Easter, to those who know it, offers an alternative to the life of the Compsons, and thus perhaps to faithless modern life as well.

What happens on these four crucial days, though imaginary, topsy-turvy, and assigned to unlikely characters, is not just a parody of Holy Week in the Christian calendar, it is also a passion week of the heart. This is a concept Faulkner developed from such works as Herman Melville's *Moby-Dick* (1851), in which Captain Ahab's monomaniacal quest for the whale causes him to have "a crucifixion" in his face and to clench his hands so tightly that he drives his "nails" into his own palms. Writing about *Moby-Dick* in 1927, just a year before he wrote *The Sound and the Fury,* Faulkner described it as a "sort of Golgotha of the heart," a reference to the site of the Crucifixion as a symbol of suffering, shame, redemption, and renewal.[20] Faulkner's friend and mentor Sherwood Anderson had also written a work in which a similar idea is expressed; in "The Philosopher," from his 1919 story collection *Winesburg, Ohio,* Doctor Parcival explains it to George Willard, the recurrent young character who appears in many stories in the book. "The idea is very simple," Parcival says, hoping Willard "will be able to write the book that I may never get written." It is "that everyone in the world is Christ and they are all crucified."[21] In Faulkner's second novel, *Mosquitoes,* published in the same year that he analyzed *Moby-Dick* for the *Chicago Tribune,* he paid homage to Anderson by creating a genial and wise character named Dawson Fairchild who, in Anderson's groping style, tries to explain what creativity really is. "Genius," the character tells a companion at the end of an evening of drinking and wandering he New Orleans French Quarter,

> People confuse it so, you see. They have got it now to where it signifies only an active state of the mind in which a picture is painted or a poem is written. When it is not that at all. It is that Passion Week of the heart, that instant of timeless beatitude which some never know, which some, I suppose, gain at will, which others gain through an outside agency like alcohol . . . that passive state of the heart with which the mind, the brain, has nothing to do at all, in which the hackneyed accidents which make up this world—love and life and death and sex and sorrow—brought together by chance in perfect proportions, take on a kind of splendid and timeless beauty.[22]

Ironically, in composing *The Sound and the Fury* at a time when he felt that all publishers' doors were closed to him, so that he could write straight from his heart, Faulkner appears to have experienced the condition as his character Fairchild explains it, bringing together "love and life and death and sex and sorrow . . . by chance in perfect proportions" in what he may have remembered as "Passion Week," though technically, Passion Week is the week leading up to Palm Sunday and Holy Week leads up to Easter.

The important matter for reading *The Sound and the Fury,* of course, is not whether Faulkner misconstrued "Passion Week" as the week of the crucifixion, but the meaning and purpose of the concept: Faulkner's passion week of the heart in this novel is a replaying of the last days of the Easter story, the Passion of Jesus of Nazareth, in the unlikely lives of a peculiar trinity: Benjy, Quentin, and Jason Compson of Jefferson, Mississippi, the first considered an idiot, the second a suicide who has been dead for eighteen years, and the third the meanest and most diabolically humorous character Faulkner ever created. The reader who wishes to get the most from Faulkner's book will benefit from comparing the days of the characters' lives with the actions or fate of Christ on the equivalent days now celebrated by Christian churches: what are called Maundy Thursday, Good Friday, and Holy Saturday. Easter Sunday in the novel belongs to an interesting omniscient narrator, as if God himself stepped in to clarify what is going on after the preceding three tortured, subjective sections. It is often called the "Dilsey Section" because it starts with her and concerns many of her actions. But like Caddy, Caroline Compson, and Miss Quentin, Dilsey is another woman in the novel who does not have a "voice" of her own, though they all have identifiable roles in the parody of the Christian story: mother, sister, female witness at the empty tomb, Mary Magdalene even if, as Jason suspects, Caddy has indeed been forced to turn to prostitution. By way of compensation, Faulkner reserved yet another "mythical method" for these characters.

Persephone

The narrative of the life of Jesus, twisted topsy-turvy and assigned in fragments to the Compson sons, is only one of the submerged plots of *The Sound and the Fury*. Yet another is assigned to the silent, absent, or suppressed female characters of the novel, an older story of death and resurrection—or at least descent into Hell and return to a world temporarily renewed. This is the story of the maiden Persephone or Proserpine, the daughter of the goddess of grain, fertility, and child-bearing, Demeter (in the Greek) or Ceres (in the Latin: hence the English word *cereal*). Parallels to the plot of this story are assigned to the Compson women—Caddy, Caroline Compson, and Miss Quentin—and to Dilsey. Persephone is a lovely girl picking flowers in a field when Hades (also called Pluto), lord of the underworld, abducts her in his golden carriage and carries her off. The world becomes barren because her mother, goddess of the harvest, is distraught. But Demeter does not simply mourn; she puts on a veil because as a goddess her face is too dazzling for humankind to look upon, and she sets out to find her daughter. She meets a swineherd named Eubuleus who saw the abduction, and he remembers the event because some of his pigs fell into the chasm through which Hades carried Persephone to the underworld. Demeter persuades Hades to give her daughter back, an agreement he will honor if Persephone has eaten nothing in his realm. As he conducts her back to the land of the living, he offers her a pomegranate, and she eats a few of the bright red seeds. This seals her fate: thenceforth, she must spend six months in the underworld and six above, her departure signaling the dying of the year, her return the spring. Associated with Persephone is another figure besides her fertile mother, Demeter: Hecate, a fertility goddess from an older tradition who reigns with Persephone as Queen of Hell and who in the Christian era was interpreted as a witch. As a goddess of witchcraft, she has a role in *Macbeth* with the three "weird sisters," the witches who predict Macbeth's fate in the first act of the play. In the ancient world Persephone, Demeter, and Hecate are an interesting female trinity; they represent the triune aspect of womankind symbolized in the phases of the moon (the celestial object often associated with the feminine)—maiden, mother, and wise old woman; new moon, full moon, and waning moon.

Caddy, her mother, and Dilsey represent an ironic repetition of the mythological roles of these three figures: Caddy is a maiden and abductee; Caroline is a mother, yet terrible in the role; and Dilsey is a wise old woman relegated to an inferior position because of the racist society in which she serves. In a second repetition, matters are made worse: Miss Quentin is supposed to be a maiden, though an empty condom pack in the yard belies that; Caddy is a mother, yet absent; and Caroline in her imitation of helplessness is a wise old woman. Just as ironic reversals and inversions occur in the Compson boys' lives, which parody the life of Jesus, the story of Persephone is reversed and inverted in several ways through association with the women of the Compson household. Caddy's pregnancy precedes her abduction, so she is no longer a maiden. Her mother dons a veil to mourn what she intuits is Caddy's loss of virginity and orchestrates her "abduction," demanding that her husband take Caddy to French Lick, Indiana, where in actual fact the hot springs that fed the spa and produced a purgative known as "Pluto Water" were called "Pluto's Well" and "Persephone's Well." There she meets Herbert Head, a dishonest gambler and banker (his profession suiting the name *Pluto,* associated with wealth). Head's initials associate him with the name *Hades,* which is applied both to the abode of the dead and to the deity who presides over it. He brings Caddy an expensive automobile as a wedding present in which he will carry her back to his home in Indiana, a state ironically named for the Native American, the "red man" whom the Puritans had associated with the Devil. The Compson household is indeed barren in Caddy's absence; the pasture that sustained livestock and doubtless a kitchen garden is gone. In Benjy's and Quentin's sections aspects of Persephone's story are evoked pointedly: Caddy comments about the death of some pigs (9), and the animals are referred to several times in various contexts. Quentin recalls the myth itself, although only in fragments—"the swine of Euboeleus [*sic*] running coupled" (93), and "swine untethered in pairs rushing coupled into the sea" (112)—that connect the abduction of Persephone, when Eubuleus's swine fall into the hole made by Hades, to Jesus' miracle of casting out devils from two men of the Gergesenes into a flock of pigs that then rush over a cliff into the sea (Matthew 8: 28–32, Luke 8: 26–34).

Miss Quentin repeats her mother's fate, unmourned. Fleeing the devil that is Jason, she goes away in the car owned by the carnival man with the red bow tie. Unlike in her mother's case, her absence from the Compson house will not change anything.

Tamar

The Absalom-Tamar story in the Bible (2 Samuel) appears in *The Sound and the Fury* in certain ways and was the basis for Faulkner's reuse of Quentin,

Shreve, and the older Jason Compson in his 1936 novel, *Absalom, Absalom!* The Bible story about King David's children concerns his daughter Tamar, who is raped by her brother Amnon and avenged by another brother, Absalom. Absalom becomes a rebel and is killed, causing David's lament, "O my son Absalom, my son, my son Absalom! Would God I had died for thee, O Absalom, my son, my son!" (2 Samuel 18:33). Faulkner certainly knew this Bible story and in both *The Sound and the Fury* and *Absalom, Absalom!* alluded to many of its elements as recorded in the Bible and in a contemporary poem. But both books also are indebted for material—character, plot, theme, and image—to a rich poetical treatment of the Absalom story by a once-well-known American poet, Robinson Jeffers (1887–1962). Jeffers's "Tamar" is a narrative poem of some eighteen hundred lines published in 1925 by Anderson's publisher, Boni and Liveright (the firm that became Faulkner's publisher the following year). It tells a modern story of two generations of incest and tragedy in the family of old David Cauldwell of California. The family includes an "idiot," Jinny, "the old woman with a child's mind," who finds peace in staring at a candle flame; a bitter aunt, Stella; and Cauldwell's two children, a wild boy, Lee, and a passionate daughter, Tamar. The voice of David's dead sister Helen speaks through the idiot to Tamar, saying that David committed incest with her; eventually, Tamar and Lee themselves make love and Tamar—her aunt says she has a "luckless" name—becomes pregnant. Seeking a father for her incestuous child, she gives herself to another man, and the experience is so loathsome that she longs for death. Her mother, in turn, torments her, asking "Slut, how many?" and she replies, "I am still sick," much as Caddy replies to Quentin (71). Tamar even thinks a line that could have inspired Faulkner to adopt the title and the narrative stance of the first section of *The Sound and the Fury.* With her mind on the idiot in the family and her nightly babbling of strange dreams, she "lay thinking with vacant wonder / That life is always an old story, repeating itself always like the leaves of a tree / Or the lips of an idiot."[23]

Freud

Faulkner was more interested in and familiar with the concepts of Freud than his statements on the matter reveal; in fact, as he did concerning his familiarity with Joyce's *Ulysses*—a 1924 copy of which he owned and had his wife read so she could better understand his own fiction—he tended to play down any direct knowledge of Freud's ideas. But *Soldiers' Pay,* Faulkner's first novel, owes a major scene in the second chapter to the section on misquotation in Freud's *The Psychopathology of Everyday Life* (1904). *Mosquitoes* is replete with play on Freud's theories of sexuality, and what might have been Faulkner's third novel, had he completed it—the parodic self-portrait *Elmer*—also uses allusions to Freud for comedy. Thus, in his early career as novelist Faulkner found psychology useful for the mythical method, too, just as Eliot had suggested ("whether our reaction to it be comic or serious," Eliot had written in his review of Joyce's novel, "*Ulysses,* Order and Myth"[24]). Some of the images and thematic use Faulkner made of Freud's ideas about infantile sexuality and adolescence, especially the fascination of young men with phallic objects, moved from *Elmer* into *The Sound and the Fury:* Benjy's castration is the most serious example; Jason's keeping hands in his pockets—"'Jason going to be a rich man,' Versh said. 'He holding his money all the time'" (23)—is a comic sexual reference that also evokes Christ's parable of the rich fool. Similarly, Quentin is obsessed with smokestacks, a variation on Elmer's more obvious fascination with smokestacks, buggy whips, shower heads, screwdrivers, and cigar butts in the street.[25]

In other ways *The Sound and the Fury* shows the influence of Freud, too, especially the elaborations of the Oedipus complex and the development and redevelopment of some of the themes and images already discussed as classical Freudian "repetitions" of repressed psychic material.[26] The possibility of another Freudian pattern was raised early in the criticism of the novel: Carvel Collins suggested that Freud's ego-id-superego model of the unconscious mind was dramatized in the novel, with Benjy as the infantile id, Jason as the repressive superego, and Quentin as the ego itself.[27] This argument still has merit, especially given the attention Faulkner pays to Quentin's ego-sense when the young man's self-reference, the personal pronoun "I," shifts from an upper-case to a lower-case *i* as he moves closer and closer to the hour at which he plans to commit suicide. It is easy to see that each of the Compson boys exhibits one or more mental conditions for which modern psychology had new names: retardation, neurosis, psychosis, paranoia, and schizophrenia.

As with any patterns of allusion, those from psychology remain a device of the novel, like a figure of speech, not the purpose of the novel. The reader must remember that the human acts of the Compsons remain the foreground of the novel. But the topic of modern psychology is directly introduced in *The Sound and the Fury.* In the academic year 1909–1910 at Harvard, when he needs but does not seek all the help he can get, Quentin has enrolled in psychology at the home institution of William James, who wrote *Principles of Psychology* (1890), but he is cutting—in Freudian terms, *avoiding*—the class (64). (The only other class that the novel represents Quentin as taking is physics, a field that in 1909–1910 was in as great a state of renewal as psychology.[28]) In the fall of 1909, when Quentin arrived at Harvard, James's former student G. Stanley Hall (then president of Clark University in nearby Worcester, Massachusetts) arranged for Freud to come there for his one and only visit to America. Freud lectured on the development of psychoanalysis, and the meeting was attended by many famous European and American psychologists and other scholars, including James himself.

Time and Memory

Another of the psychological problems that the Compson boys appear to exhibit are that each has a demonstrable problem with the concept of time. Benjy does not recognize time's passage; Quentin wishes to stop it; and Jason avoids the past as much as possible, living for what appears to be an illusory future. Despite these characters' entrapment by or insistence upon a spatialized, scientific sense of chronological time (even when clocks are defective and watches broken), memory and irrational association are the vehicles of expression for each of the boys' monologues. These matters represent important, and timely, avenues for allusion in *The Sound and the Fury,* for the interest in time and memory, always a device for writers, had taken as much of a turn in the early twentieth century as had the interest in psychology.

The cause of this turn was the work of the French philosopher Bergson, whose writing on both time and memory as richly influenced the fabric of creative literature in the second and third decades of the century as did the psychology of Freud. Eliot attended Bergson's famous lectures at the great Paris university the Collège de France. Faulkner read Bergson and found his work not merely interesting but inspiring, as he told both a French interviewer and a young woman he courted and tutored as a writer.[29] Beginning with *Time and Free Will* in 1889, Bergson developed his understanding that the driving energy in the adverse is élan vital, a creative life force of which all partook. Memory was both the source of selfhood and the means through which an individual might understand the self through intuitive attention to the flux of being in the flow of time. Interestingly, Bergson married a cousin of the French novelist Marcel Proust, whose seven-volume novel, *Remembrance of Things Past* (1913–1927), investigated the persistent reality of past experience and concluded with the hero's discovery that human beings are "memory incarnate."

The failure to understand the true nature of time, Bergson believed, is the great flaw or error in the human condition. Time is not chronology but duration, a great stream of endless being and becoming in which all living is an enduring part. In Bergson's view, it is clear, Benjy, Quentin, and Jason suffer from this error: none of them understands the creative evolution of being nor possesses the intuitive attention one needs to devote to the shifting flux of the life that endures in order to understand self and then manifest a truly free will. Bergson might say that Dilsey exists in error too, for she sees the world from the religious perspective of the Old and New Testaments and thus accepts a first cause, the Creation, and a Last Judgment, a beginning and ending to time, but she seems to have a typically Bergsonian experience in her small church under the influence of the St. Louis preacher Reverend Shegog, who moves the congregation into an intuitive experience of self and communion. (About Dilsey and others like her, Faulkner sums up in the Compson appendix, "They endured."[30]) Bergson corresponded about the development of his ideas with other great thinkers of his time such as William James, Albert Einstein, and Freud—all of whom also appear to have a hint, or more than a hint, of a place in *The Sound and the Fury.* Bergson spent five years studying "all of the literature available in memory and especially the psychological phenomenon of aphasia, or loss of the ability to use language. According to the prevailing theories of motor psychology in his time, a brain lesion that affected the speech should also affect the "very basis of psychological power," the entire brain. Bergson showed that this was not the case, that a person so affected "understands what others have to say, knows what he himself wants to say, suffers no paralysis of the speech organs, and yet is unable to speak."[31] This of course is a perfect description of Benjy Compson, who can move about, go where he knows he will hear a forbidden name, and remember all that has happened to him. He bellows and moans in an attempt to speak but cannot. Against the empirical, positivistic bent of his age, Bergson offered another way of knowing, intuition that is "global, immediate, reaching into the heart of a thing by sympathy,"[32] and one may wonder if it was this, too that Faulkner said had "helped" him when he read the philosopher's work.[33]

The "Idiot" Theme

Faulkner knew two severely afflicted children in Oxford, Mississippi, Edwin Chandler and Margaret Brown, and his interest in them might well have piqued his interest in the most famous afflicted American of his day, another Southerner, Helen Keller of Tuscumbia, Alabama. Keller's story is well known, thanks to William Gibson's play *The Miracle Worker* (1959) and the movie made from it. Less well known, perhaps, is the similarity between Keller's disability and that of Benjy Compson. Keller had a normal birth, but a childhood illness rendered her blind, deaf, and mute. Such afflictions were common before antibiotics because many childhood illnesses could lead to severe infection, lasting high fevers, meningitis, encephalitis, and brain lesions that caused loss of speech as well as damage to optical and auditory nerves. Keller was afflicted in all three areas because she had suffered the illness that made her blind and deaf before she had learned speech. Thus, until she was nearly seven years old she remained mute and often behaved in an animal-like way. From her own account of her life in the "darkness," she apparently had the instincts of a domesticated animal, alert to the little that her sense brought her—smell and touch—and to the patterns of repeated events (as a dog becomes excited and expects to go outside when the word "walk" is said or a leash is picked up). But she truly had no language until her parents hired a young woman from the Boston School for the Deaf who herself had suffered from impaired eyesight as a child. At the Keller's Alabama home, Annie Sullivan worked with Helen on the alphabet, drawing letters into the girl's hand and trying to teach her the names of common things. Keller recalls in her life story that she learned these things "monkey-like," without understanding. But one day, when Helen threw a particularly violent tantrum and broke the doll Annie had given her, a peculiar thing happened: "I had not loved the doll" she wrote:

> In the still, dark world in which I lived there was no strong sentiment or tenderness. I felt my teacher sweep the fragments to one side of the hearth, and I had a sense of satisfaction that the cause of my discomfort was removed. She brought me my hat, and I know I was going out into the warm sunshine. This thought, if a wordless sensation may be called a thought, made me hop and skip with pleasure.
>
> We walked down the path to the well-house, attracted by the fragrance of the honeysuckle with which it was covered. Someone was drawing water and my teacher placed my hand under the spout. As the cool stream gushed over one hand she spelled into the other the word water, first slowly, then rapidly I stood still, my own attention fixed upon the motions of her fingers. Suddenly I felt a misty consciousness as of something forgotten—a thrill of returning thought; and somehow the mystery of language was revealed to me. I knew then that "w-a-t-e-r" meant the wonderful cool something that was flowing over my hand. That living word awakened my soul, gave it light, hope, joy, set it free![34]

Keller also felt remorse, she recalled, for the broken doll, a moral sense. From that time she developed rapidly, learning to read Braille and to write. On a visit to Wellesley, she declared that she would go to Harvard—an impossibility for a woman in those days, and so she went to Radcliffe, the women's campus affiliated with Harvard. There she received the fascinated attention of William James, who regarded her not as a novelty but as a rare being who had suddenly experienced, with self-consciousness, the discovery of mind through language. She was highly sensitive to touch and to smell; one version of her life story has a picture of her "listening to the trees" and a chapter on "Smell: The Fallen Angel."[35]

Faulkner's portrait of Benjy Compson has much in common with Keller's story of her life. Benjy's inability to speak; his apparently simple, doglike pleasure in the opportunity to go outside, which he associates with Caddy; his fascination with water and trees; and his acute sense of smell all suggest parallels with Keller. However, the Compsons do not seek help for Benjy when, at the age of five, he appears to be impaired. His mother instead regards him as a "curse," whether motivated by a misplaced puritanism or more severely troubled by a possibly incestuous relationship with her brother Maury, who is always closeting her alone in a room with him and giving her a drink of whiskey.

But is Benjy an "idiot"? This is a complicated question. Luster says he is deaf and dumb, but he is not. Only Jason and the frightened father of the little girl Benjy is supposed to have attacked use the word "idiot" to describe him. He can walk, perform simple tasks like taking a note to Mrs. Patterson for Uncle Maury, and remember that certain places offer the promise of Caddy's name or the memory of her comforting presence; he is often trying to "say." It thus seems likely that the measles discussed in his section (24, 47) led to a lesion in his brain that affected his speech; half a lifetime of neglect after Caddy's departure contributed to his physical decline and the hopeless state of his mind by the time he is thirty-three. What is missing from Benjy's life is the transforming moment of discovering language, finding a relationship between mind, world, and word. One can imagine how important this moment was for Keller, an instant on which she dwells eloquently in her life story.

Faulkner surely knew other sympathetic or ironic literary treatments of "idiot" characters, including those by William Wordsworth, Melville ("Pip" in *Moby-Dick*), and Fyodor Dostoyevsky (his novel *The Idiot,* 1868). Since Faulkner had a university library close at hand for at least a decade—from his return to Oxford, Mississippi, from RAF training in 1919 until he moved from his parents' house on the Ole Miss campus in the summer of 1929, shortly after he completed *The Sound and the Fury* and married Estelle Oldham—he may even have studied the word *idiot* in a dictionary with good etymologies. If so, he would have found the remarkable coincidence that the word is related to a great many words that express themes important in his novel. Current dictionaries say that *idiot* is no longer considered appropriate and in fact represents "offensive" usage. An etymological investigation of the word, however, shows that it derives from a root that relates it to such other words important in *The Sound and the Fury* as *self, secret, seduce, sober, solitary, sullen, soliloquy, ethnic,* and *suicide.*

Considerable close study of *The Sound and the Fury* appears to offer the prospect that nothing in it signifies nothing. Faulkner, who wrote nineteen novels and more than a hundred stories, is not apt to have believed that any tale failed to signify or he would have stopped writing, an observation he himself made in defense of Albert Camus, who, Faulkner argued, could not have been a nihilist who believed life had no meaning since he kept searching for meaning in the pieces that he wrote.[36]

The perception of Benjy as an "idiot" and the last words of Macbeth's soliloquy that supplied the title of the novel have tempted critics to focus on the nihilistic closure created by the final scene. Certainly, Benjy's losses will never be restored. As Faulkner put it, he understood "that Benjy must never grow beyond this moment; that for him all knowing must begin and end with that fierce, panting, paused and stooped wet figure which smelled like trees. That he must never grow up to where the grief of bereavement could be leavened with understanding and hence the alleviation of rage as in the case of Jason, and of oblivion as in the case of Quentin."[37] Jason's vicious restoration of an idiot's pitiful and momentary sense of false order in the scene that follows the episode at the Easter church is seen as anything but a restoration of order. If Benjy is calmed because now the carriage turns in its customary direction and the colorful facades of the buildings around the courthouse square flow past in a pattern that he recognizes from long habit, it may be simply an idiot's order, signifying nothing. To draw on Macbeth's speech again, Benjy's tomorrows must be exactly like his yesterdays, and his trip is in fact a visit to "dusty death," for the only trip he takes away from home is to the cemetery where his alcoholic father and suicide brother, along with their more illustrious predecessors, are buried. The Compsons, Scottish and Protestant, apparently do not take joy rides.

John Hagopian finds this scene's placement as closure to be Faulkner's stamp of intention on the novel, an indication that the family life portrayed in the book is indeed a tale told by an idiot, signifying nothing. In a sense the point is moot, however, for even a novel that deliberately signifies "nothing" paradoxically signifies "something," and the continued life of Faulkner's novel in the hands of common readers, students, scholars, critics, and other writers of fiction would seem to counter any opinion that reduced it to the nihilistic. *Tragic*, and as rich in the texture of its tragic progress as a Shakespearean play, would seem to be a better characterization, thus justifying in a different way the paraphrase of *Macbeth* in the title. Replying to the author of a trio of favorable essays on his work in 1941, Faulkner admitted that he preferred reading "Shakespeare, bad puns, bad history, taste and all, than [the Victorian aesthete Walter] Pater, and that I had a damn sight rather fail at trying to write Shakespeare than to write all of Pater over again so he couldn't have told it himself if you fired it point blank at him through an amplifier."[38]

The Relationship of Faulkner's Themes to His Life

Children, of course, do not reflect upon their times in abstractions, but they do reflect their times, and, as the Georgia novelist and short-story writer Flannery O'Connor asserted, "The fact is that anybody who has survived his childhood has enough information about life to last him the rest of his days."[39] *The Sound and the Fury* supports O'Connor's assertion, although she would be the first to recognize that it is Faulkner's bold conception and his technical virtuosity with language, not his memories, that make the novel one of his most widely taught and analyzed works. Nonetheless, his memories of childhood and young manhood lie relatively visible beneath the surface of the novel for anyone familiar with the details of his life.

Faulkner and his two brothers lost both their grandmothers to lingering battles with cancer when he was about the age of Quentin at the time of Damuddy's death in the novel. His young cousin Sallie Murry Wilkins, who had already lost her father to illness, was a part of that family circle. Like the Faulkner boys, she lived in the same house with a grandmother who died. The boys' maternal grandmother, Leila Dean Swift Butler, died on 1 June 1907. It is quite possible that events like those recalled in the novel—children sent away from the house while a funeral is going on—took place on 2 June, the same day as Quentin's section. The boys' paternal grandmother, Sallie Murry Faulkner, for whom Faulkner's cousin Sallie was named, died on 21 December 1907. From these events—the details of which are not recorded in letters or any biography—Faulkner began his novel, and the anecdote of the children being sent away during the funeral blossomed into a set of fictional details that carry philosophical, psychological, and symbolic implications for several of the themes in the novel. Though Faulkner disliked explaining himself, having discovered that explanation was antithetical to the kind of unfolding of experience he wished to create in his books, he did write a revealing passage or two on *The Sound and the Fury* when attempting an introductory essay for a limited edition of the novel that never materialized. By virtue of obvious and sometimes subtle allusions to the New Testament of the Bible, to classical, Renaissance, and modern literature, and to philosophical and psychological texts contemporaneous with the period when he was writing the novel, he demonstrated how the actual is transformed by the prepared writer into the highly charged symbolic text that nonetheless looks, in a certain light, "real."

Thus, just as the two deaths in Falkner households, six months apart when the writer and his brothers were at an impressionable and doubtless innocent age, fuse with many other matters into the anecdote with which Faulkner's account of the fall of the Compsons begins, so the figure of Dilsey owes something both to Callie Barr, the woman who nursed the Faulkner boys through their childhood, and to his symbolic imagination. As the African American cultural critic Albert Murray has observed, Dilsey represents, among other things, the possibility of redemption, not just for herself but for anyone who has the proper disposition to seek and accept redemption, a condition unfortunately rare in *The Sound and the Fury,* in which Benjy is lost in the darkness of untreated disability, Caroline Compson whines, her husband drinks himself to death, Quentin commits suicide, and Jason plans a future based on revenge that requires a relatively constant meanness.

The marriage in 1918 of Cornell Franklin and Estelle Oldham, a childhood sweetheart to whom Faulkner had turned increasingly as he matured, lies behind Quentin's—and Benjy's—anguish regarding the marriage of Caddy. Estelle's impending marriage in 1918 apparently provoked such dangerous talk from Faulkner that both her family and his thought it best to get him out of town, and so, like Quentin, and at approximately the same age that Faulkner made Quentin during his section of the novel, Faulkner left home for the first extended sojourn in his life. He went to New Haven, Connecticut, where his friend Phil Stone was a law student at Yale, and he doubtless brooded on sex and death as he lamented Estelle's marriage. In New Haven, Faulkner plotted for a commission as an RAF pilot who might perish gloriously in the skies over Europe, but he also met an intelligent group of like-minded young men, including the already famous student poet Stephen Vincent Benét, frequented a great bookstore, and wrote his parents typically collegiate letters asking for money, requesting fresh clothes, offering thanks for gifts of food, and detailing the pleasures and sometimes the peculiarities, to his innocent eyes, of life in the North.

Quentin's Harvard owes nearly everything to Faulkner's 1918 sojourn in New Haven. Faulkner's stay there turned out to be one of the happiest periods of his life, second only to his time in New Orleans in 1925. In New Haven he had a job in a firearms factory, so he was part of the war effort; he had Stone's conviviality and love of books and literature to share and enjoy. He made some lifelong friends, and he wrote his brother a letter, dated 2 June—the possible anniversary of Damuddy's funeral—in which he records having done happily most of the things Quentin does leading up to his suicide.[40] There can be little doubt, from the biographical evidence, that Faulkner was dangerously unhappy about Estelle's marriage, and some of his letters from New Haven maybe designed to allay his parents' worries, yet he advanced his art while in New Haven, made plans, and achieved goals. The experience, coupled with his longtime acquaintance with the small university campus he frequented—and his parents for a time lived on—in Oxford, Mississippi, helped him capture the flavor of collegiate life in Quentin's section, though he turns everything into material germane to his main fictional concerns. So collegiate pranks and talk, where sex is in the forefront, strike bitter chords in Quentin, obsessed as he is with his sister's sexual coming of age. The theme of innocence lost in the garden that is the Compson pasture has both biblical and psychological undertones, the discovery of death but also the shame of sex.

As with any likely young provincial American writer of the early modernist era, Faulkner responded with excitement and remarkable writing to the sudden deluge of new ideas that gave a different slant on all the oldest of human experiences: death, sex, time, family, society, money, the inner life, and many other matters that endured, transforming reinterpretations. The title of early books by Ernest Hemingway (*In Our Time,* 1924) and F. Scott Fitzgerald (*This Side of Paradise,* 1920) expressed it obliquely, and Eliot's *The Waste Land* caught the sense of it all. When the present changes, the past changes, as Faulkner came to understand better than most, but he was a writer of his time, and his themes were those of his contemporaries and of his age.

Faulkner and the Themes of the Era

Though Faulkner moved ahead of most of his novelist contemporaries, on the race issue for example, many themes expressed in *The Sound and the Fury,* major and minor, were common concerns of writers in the 1920s: materialism and its consequences, spiritual disillusionment, the cultural impact of World War I and of the automobile, the negative effect of small-town narrow-mindedness on the healthy development of individuals and society itself, and the impact of new ideas in psychology. Faulkner handled these themes not merely with character and plot, but with highly allusive substructures buried beneath the everyday lives depicted in the novel, using the "mythical method" that Eliot praised so much in Joyce's triumph, through fiction, over the futility and anarchy of the modern era. Faulkner's borrowings from Freud, Bergson, mythology, contemporary poetry, the history and rituals of Christianity, and the cultural expression of his time appear to be intentional, though the climate of ideas in this period was so rich and pervasive that they need not have been as deliberately orchestrated by Faulkner as they are, for example, in the major works of Joyce and Eliot.

The Sound and the Fury appeared at the end of a remarkable postwar decade of American achievement in the art of fiction. In 1930, the year after the novel was published, an American, Sinclair Lewis, became the first of his countrymen to win the coveted Nobel Prize in literature that Faulkner himself would receive twenty years later. In accepting the prize, Lewis praised the work of writers who had published singular works in the preceding year: Hemingway *(A Farewell to Arms),* Thomas Wolfe *(Look Homeward, Angel),* and Faulkner. Lewis had satirized the restrictive narrow-mindedness of small-town American life in *Main Street* (1920) and the crassness of American materialism in *Babbitt* (1922), the title character of which became synonymous with middle-class booster-ism, much as Faulkner later immortalized a rapacious and pleasureless class of redneck materialists with the family name Snopes. Faulkner's Jason Compson speaks like a character in Lewis's *The Man Who Knew Coolidge,* which came out in 1928, the year Faulkner was writing *The Sound and the Fury.* Jason is a vicious version of Lewis's George Babbitt, right down to the pride he takes in his Ford.

Sherwood Anderson, with whom Faulkner had a brief but highly important close friendship, was, before Lewis's ascent, one of the most important writers in America, and his *Winesburg, Ohio* might be said to have launched the remarkable decade of writing that ends with those novels Lewis singled out in 1930—and with the heating up of the Great Depression. Anderson's friendship with Faulkner in New Orleans in 1925 and 1926 proceeded in part from the common small-town backgrounds the two writers shared, but also from Anderson's generosity toward writers of talent. He gave Faulkner some crucial advice about the technical aspects of writing novels, but more importantly for a discussion of how Faulkner's themes are those of his age, Anderson demonstrated in his own work the application of the new psychology. Like Faulkner, Anderson tended to deny influence, but he was called by one of his friends "the phallic Chekhov,"[41] a witty phrase that placed Anderson squarely in the camp of Freud.

Winesburg, Ohio was said to have given the dignity of complex psychological lives to obscure and ordinary-seeming people in backwater communities,[42] an improvement on the "Main Street" school of Midwestern satirical realism practiced by Lewis.

In addition to Anderson, Lewis, Fitzgerald, Hemingway, and Eliot, writers such as John Dos Passos, Jeffers, and the playwright Eugene O'Neill took up the themes of family and psychology in new and striking ways that Faulkner attempted to imitate in earlier work and had fully absorbed by the time he wrote *The Sound and the Fury*. There is even a hint in *The Sound and the Fury* of the "portrait of the artist" that such writers as Joyce, Proust, and Mann, especially, had revived from the German *bildungsroman* (the novel of a young man's education or apprenticeship to life) and *kunstlerroman* (the novel of the artist's development) of earlier eras to which the moderns had given a psychological and mythological slant. That is, Quentin, a somewhat autobiographical character, is a sensitive and reflective young man living in an intellectual environment, with friends as unusual as those of Stephen Dedalus in *Ulysses*, but Faulkner wisely restrained himself from self-absorption with the problems of the artist. He had attacked that problem with humor in the unfinished *Elmer*, written in New Orleans and Paris in 1925 (a shorter version even lad the working title "Portrait of Elmer Hodge"), about a sharecropper boy who tries to become a painter. Quentin's potential as an artist figure is expressed ironically when he appears later in *Absalom, Absalom!*, in which the bitter spinster-poet Rosa Coldfield explains that she wants to share her story with him because

> you are going off to attend the college at Harvard they tell me. . . . So I don't imagine you will ever come back here and settle down as a country lawyer in a little town like Jefferson. . . . So maybe you will enter the literary profession as so many Southern gentlemen and gentlewomen too are doing now and maybe some day you will remember this and write about it. You will be married then I expect and perhaps your wife will want a new gown or a new chair for the house and you can write this and submit it to the magazines.[43]

Despite his increasing resistance to intellectualizing about his work or even to being identified as a literary man, Faulkner at one time or another acknowledged most of the influences on his work, including titans such as Mann and Joyce. They were, he told one interviewer, the "two great men in my time," and to a young French interviewer he said, "I feel very close to Proust."[44]

Notes

1. J. R Stem, "The Theme of Consciousness: Thomas Mann," in *Modernism: 1890–1930,* edited by Malcolm Bradbury and James McFarlane (London: Penguin, 1991), p. 417.

2. John Irwin has convincingly demonstrated many variations upon the Oedipal story in his excellent study of Freudian implications in Faulkner's novel, *Doubling and Incest, Repetition and Revenge* (Baltimore: Johns Hopkins University Press, 1975).

3. There is a Dilsey in the once-popular *Diddie, Dumps, and Tot, or Plantation Child-Life,* by Louise-Clarke Pyrnelle (New York & London: Harper, 1882), but she is a child, and there is a Candace, too, also of African origin. Faulkner had created a Dulcie, also a child, but white, in his strange allegorical children's tale, *The Wishing Tree,* composed in 1928, the same year he wrote *The Sound and the Fury.*

4. Cultural critic Albert Murray, who is also a jazz historian and a novelist, has observed that Faulkner could give his black characters a "greater humanity" because the Mississippi writer was steeped in the folklore and wisdom of African Americans. Northern intellectuals, he says, looked to Europe, to Freud and Marx, for interpreting black character and thus missed the essence of the black experience in America, an observation borne out by *The Sound and the Fury,* in which Freudian paradigms may rule the Compsons, but what Murray calls "the centrality of the church" speaks to and for Dilsey Gibson. See *Conversations with Albert Murray,* edited by Roberta S. Maguire (Jackson: University Press of Mississippi, 1997), p. 5. In another interview Murray points out that Dilsey represents on a universal scale "the possibility of redemption" (157). Novelist Ralph Ellison observed as early as 1953 that Faulkner "has explored perhaps more successfully than anyone else, either white or black, certain forms of Negro humanity." See "Twentieth-Century Fiction and the Black Mask of Humanity," in Ellison's *Shadow and Act* (New York: New American Library, 1966), p. 47.

5. For Chester Carothers, see *Thinking of Home: William Faulkner's Letters to His Mother and Father, 1918–1925,* edited by James G. Watson (New York & London: Norton, 1992), p. 40; and Joseph Blotner, *Faulkner: A Biography, 2 volumes* (New York: Random House, 1974), I: 133. For Callie Barr, see Blotner's biography and "Funeral Sermon for Mammy Caroline Barr, 1940," in *William Faulkner: Essays, Speeches & Public Letters,* edited by James B. Meriwether (New York: Random House, 1965), pp. 117–118.

6. The novelist Edith Wharton called it the *noyade,* the drowning, of marriage in *The Custom of the Country* (New York: Appleton, 1913). The novel tells a story of modern love in which a socially ambitious girl from upstate New York does not so much conquer New York society as ruin one of its finest, a poetic chap named Ralph Marvell, whose subsequent death by pneumonia is a sort of drowning.

7. Ann Douglas's *The Feminization of American Culture* (New York: Knopf, 1977) provides a good survey of the forces in popular culture and custom that disestablished women and provoked many of them to enforce upon men the stereotypes of helplessness that had been imposed upon them: that is, through a pose of helplessness, women exerted an oblique power.

8. William Faulkner, "Address upon Receiving the Nobel Prize for Literature," in *Essays, Speeches & Public Letters,* edited by James B. Meriwether (New York: Random House, 1965), p. 120.

9. Excellent summaries and explanations of the characteristics of the modernist novel appear in essays by British novelists Malcolm Bradbury and David Lodge, both of whom are novelists as well as brilliant literary historians, in *Modernism: 1890–1930,* edited by Bradbury and James McFarlane (London: Penguin, 1991); in American literary critic J. Hillis Miller's *Fiction and Repetition: Seven English Novels* (Cambridge, Mass.: Harvard University Press, 1982); and in *The Modern Temper: Backgrounds of Modern Literature,* edited by Richard Ellmann and Charles Feidelson Jr. (New York: Oxford University Press, 1965).

10. Bradbury and McFarlane, "The Name and Nature of Modernism," in *Modernism: 1890– 1930,* p. 27.

11. David Lodge, "The Language of Modernist Fiction: Metaphor and Metonymy," in *Modernism: 1890–1930,* p. 481.

12. T. S. Eliot, "*Ulysses,* Order, and Myth," *Dial,* 74 (May 1923): 483.

13. Michael Millgate, *The Achievement of William Faulkner* (New York: Random House, 1966), p. 86. Millgate speculates that "Twilight" might also have been the title of the short story, presumably concentrating on the Compson children and the discovery of Damuddy's death, from which Benjy's section and the rest of the novel developed. Millgate notes the thematic relationship of the title "Twilight" to that of Faulkner's short story "That Evening Sun Go Down" (1931; republished as "That Evening Sun"), another story of the Compson children and death, with the title taken from W C. Handy's song "St. Louis Blues."

14. Faulkner, *The Marble Faun,* p. 30, in *The Marble Faun and A Green Bough* (New York: Random House, 1965).

15. Faulkner, poem X, in *A Green Bough,* p. 30, in *The Marble Faun and A Green Bough.*

16. A thorough discussion of many such transformations of elements from Faulkner's apprentice work into elements of *The Sound and the Fury* is found in Martin Kreiswirth's *William Faulkner: The Making of A Novelist* (Athens: University of Georgia Press, 1983).

17. *The Holy Bible* (King James Version). Cleveland & New York: World, n.d. This edition contains a separately paginated text, *The Bible Readers' Aids and a New and Practical Plan of Self-Pronunciation, Being Brief Treatises Upon and Outlines of Topics Related to the Study and Understanding of the Holy Scriptures,* edited by Rev. Charles H. H. Wright, D.D., copyright 1924. "Harmony of the Gospels" is on pages 43–49 of this text; a section on parables and miracles of Jesus is on pages 51–52.

18. "Harmony of the Gospels," p. 44.

19. James Dean Young, "Quentin's Maundy Thursday," *Tulane Studies in English,* 10 (1960): 143–151.

20. Faulkner, "To the Book Editor of the *Chicago Tribune,*" in *Essays, Speeches & Public Letters,* p. 197.

21. Sherwood Anderson, "The Philosopher," in *Winesburg, Ohio,* edited by Ray Lewis White (Athens: Ohio University Press, 1997), p. 35.

22. Faulkner, *Mosquitoes* (New York: Boni & Liveright, 1927), p. 339.

23. Robinson Jeffers, *Roan Stallion, Tamar, and Other Poems* (New York: Boni & Liveright, 1925), pp. 116, 136, 155. For a survey of Jeffers's impact on Faulkner, see Thomas L. McHaney, "Robinson Jeffers' 'Tamar' and *The Sound and the Fury*," *Mississippi Quarterly,* 22 (Summer 1969): 261–263; Beth Haury, "The Influence of Robinson Jeffers' 'Tamar' on Faulkner's *Absalom, Absalom!*" *Mississippi Quarterly,* 25 (Summer 1972): 356–358; and McHaney, "'Tamar' and Faulkner's *The Wild Palms,*" *Robinson Jeffers Newsletter* (August 1971): 16–18.

24. Eliot, "*Ulysses,* Order, and Myth," p. 483.

25. See McHaney, "The Elmer Papers: Faulkner's Comic Portraits of the Artist," *Mississippi Quarterly,* 26 (Summer 1973): 281–311, and "At Play in the Fields of Freud: Faulkner and Misquotation," in *Faulkner, His Contemporaries, and His Posterity,* edited by Waldemar Zacharasiewicz (Tiabingen & Basel: Francke, 1993), pp. 64–76.

26. These aspects of Freudianism in *The Sound and the Fury* are discussed in John Irwin, *Doubling and Incest, Repetition and Revenge* (Baltimore: Johns Hopkins University Press, 1975; enlarged, 1996).

27. Carvel Collins, "The Interior Monologues of *The Sound and the Fury,*" in *English Institute Essays: 1952,* edited by Alan S. Downer (New York: Columbia University Press, 1954), pp. 29–56.

28. See Julie Johnson, "The Theory of Relativity in Modem Literature: An Overview and *The Sound and the Fury,*" *Journal of Modern Literature,* 10 (June 1983): 217–230.

29. Joseph Blower, *Faulkner: A Biography, 2 volumes* (New York: Random House, 1974), II: 1219, 1302, 1441.

30. Faulkner, "Appendix: Compson, 1699–1945," in *The Sound and the Fury: An Authoritative Text, Backgrounds and Contexts, Criticism,* p. 215.

31. "Bergson, Henri (Louis)," *The New Encyclopaedia Britannica,* 15th edition, volume 2 (Chicago: Encyclopedia Britannica, 1989), p. 130.

32. Ibid.

33. Blotner, *Faulkner. A Biography,* II: 1302.

34. Helen Keller, *The Story of My Life* (1903) (1902; reprint, Cutchogue, N.Y.: Buccaneer Books, 1976), pp. 35–36.

35. Keller, *The World I Live In* (New York: Century, 1906), pp. 64ff.

36. Faulkner, "Albert Camus," in *Essays, Speeches & Public Letters,* pp. 113–114.

37. Faulkner, "An Introduction to *The Sound and the Fury,*" *Mississippi Quarterly,* 26 (Summer 1973): 413.

38. Faulkner to Warren Beck, 6 July 1941, in *Selected Letters of William Faulkner,* edited by Blotner (New York: Random House, 1977), p. 142.

39. Flannery O'Connor, "The Nature and Aim of Fiction," in her *Mystery and Manners,* edited by Sally and Robert Fitzgerald (New York: Farrar, Straus & Giroux, 1969), p. 84.

40. Faulkner to Maud Butler Falkner, in *Thinking of Home,* pp. 61–62.

41. Anderson to Paul Rosenfeld, late October 1921, in *Letters of Sherwood Anderson,* edited by Howard Mumford Jones and Walter B. Rideout (Boston: Little, Brown, 1953), p. 78.

42. John Crowe Ransom, "Freud and Literature," *Saturday Review of Literature* (4 October 1924): 161–162.

43. Faulkner, *Absalom, Absalom!: The Corrected Text* (New York: Vintage, 1990), p. 5.

44. "Interview with Jean Stein vanden Heuvel," in *Lion in the Garden: Interviews with William Faulkner, 1926–1962,* edited by Meriwether and Millgate (New York: Random House, 1968), p. 250; "Interview with Loïc Bouvard," in *Lion in the Garden*, p. 72.

MICHELLE ANN ABATE

Reading Red: The Man with the (Gay) Red Tie in Faulkner's The Sound and the Fury

Since its publication in 1929, critics and commentators have analyzed William Faulkner's *The Sound and the Fury* from every perspective imaginable. Essays have been published, for instance, on everything from such oft-discussed elements as structure and time to such unexpected topics as defenses of the whining hypochondriac, Caroline Compson.[1] This sheer volume of analysis has prompted Irving Howe to remark that for good or ill "virtually every noun in *The Sound and the Fury* [has been] elevated to symbolic significance."[2] In spite of all this attention to detail, one element of the novel has largely escaped examination and especially symbolic examination: the man with the red tie. Although critics typically view this character as minor in the text, he is anything but that. A careful investigation of the man with the red tie reveals that he may not be one of Miss Quentin's boyfriends nor simply a man associated with the traveling carnival. Instead, his distinctive and oft-mentioned tie could be a symbol that announces him as a homosexual. If true, this new orientation undermines the way in which both Miss Quentin and her escape have been popularly interpreted. Rather than casting her exodus as a mere repetition of her mother's mistakes, the character's gay red tie could render it a long-awaited deliverance from them. Echoing Mikhail Bakhtin's observations about the transgressive nature and regenerative power of medieval carnivals,[3] the carnivalesque showman may

The Mississippi Quarterly, Volume 54 (2001): pp. 293–312.

help establish an entirely new order by liberating Miss Quentin from the oppressive hierarchy of the Compson home.

Although historians Jonathan Ned Katz[4] and Allan Bérubé note that homosexuality in the United States did not become widely visible until after the Second World War, lesbians and gay men certainly existed in the nation prior to this period. In the 1915 edition of his famous volume *Sexual Inversion,* for instance, sexologist Havelock Ellis discussed both the presence of and culture associated with gay American males. "The world of sexual inverts," he remarked "is, indeed, a large one in any American city, and it is a community distinctly organized—words, customs, traditions of its own. . . ."[5] One of the "traditions" the sexologist goes on to elucidate is gay men's clothing:

> . . . it is notable that of recent years there has been a fashion for a red tie to be adopted by inverts as their badge. This is especially marked among the 'fairies' (as a *fellator* is there termed) in New York. 'It is red,' writes an American correspondent, himself inverted, 'that has become almost a synonym for sexual inversion, not only in the minds of inverts themselves, but in the popular mind. . . . It is the badge of all their tribe.' (pp. 299–300)

Numerous other historians verify Ellis's observations.[6] In *Gay New York: Gender, Urban Culture and the Making of the Gay Male World, 1890–1940,*[7] George Chauncey comments on the use of red neckties as a symbol for homosexuality. Challenging assertions that homosexuals were largely marginalized prior to World War II, Chauncey argues, "gay men were highly visible in twentieth century New York, . . . in part because so many gay men boldly announced their presence by wearing red ties, bleached hair, and the era's other insignia[s] of homosexuality" (p.3). Chauncey goes on to assert that from the 1890s until the 1940s red neckties were among the most common and famous symbols used by gay males to identify themselves and others (p. 52). To men and women who did not know the meaning behind the tie, the bright object "might just be considered odd" (Chauncey, p. 52). To those who were aware of its significance, however, the tie invariably "Invited remarks from newsboys and others" (Chauncey, p. 52). In one instance, Chauncey notes, a group of street boys caught a man wearing a red tie and "sucked their fingers in imitation of fellatio" (p. 52). From its introduction, the tie was "An unconventional choice in an era of conservative colors" (p. 52). Thus, it "announced unorthodox tastes of another sort only to those in the know" (p. 52).

The link between red ties and homosexuality during this era was not limited to large urban areas such as New York. It could be found in cities throughout the country. Paul Cadmus's 1934 painting *The Fleet's In* depicts a homoerotic encounter between a civilian and a sailor. In the painting, a man offers a cigarette to the seaman. As George Chauncey observes, the gentleman has "the typical markers of a fairy [during this period]: bleached hair, tweezed eyebrows, rouged cheeks, and red tie" (p. 64). The expression Cadmus depicts on the sailor's face suggests that "he knows exactly what is being offered along with the smoke" (Chauncey, p. 64). This image implies that the use of red ties was understood not only by gay men in New York but also by homosexuals throughout the military and thus, presumably, throughout the country.

Of course, to assert truly that the red tie could announce the homosexuality of Faulkner's character, one must prove that it is not merely a "uniform" for the role he plays as a showman or pitchman. Documentation of attire worn by both circus and carnival staff during this period does not indicate that it was a convention for pitchmen, showmen or talkers to wear a red tie as a part of their professional garb. Throughout the 1920s, individual carnivals and circuses determined what kind of standardized clothing, if any, was to be worn by their staff.[8] Although these gentlemen were often outfitted in suits and ties, red ties were not employed.[9] Most sideshow men simply wore regular street suits and topped them off with a Homburg hat.

This lack of evidence about the use of red ties in circuses and carnivals is compounded by the ambiguous way in which Faulkner constructs the show in his text. The circus historians with whom I consulted concluded that the event incorporated in *The Sound and the Fury* is not a realistic circus or carnival. As the Director of Circus World Museum, Fred Dahlinger, noted, errors in the cost of ticket prices and the use of circus lingo suggest that it is not modeled on an actual traveling organization but cobbled together from the author's memories of both events. Real circus hands, for instance, would have called their rail cars "sleepers" rather than by the manufacturer's name of Pullman. In addition, at a costly quarter, the price of admission for the small, single-tent show is too high for the period. Given that none of the characters in *The Sound and the Fury* ever refers to the outfit as either a circus or a carnival, Faulkner may have been aware that the show he constructed was not a legitimate one. Throughout the lengthy text, it is simply called "that/dat show."

In light of these details, one may infer that the exact type of show in *The Sound and the Fury* is not important and neither is the precise role the man with the red tie has in it. All that is relevant is that the, show is a traveling one, that it frequents large towns and that the man with the red tie is connected to it in some way. "That/dat show" merely explains the existence of a character who would otherwise not have been in the rural Southern town. It is not meant to provide a historically accurate representation of carnivals and circuses in the 1920s.[10]

In the same way historical evidence outside of Faulkner's text links red ties with gay men, elements within *The Sound and the Fury* also point to this condition. Throughout the novel, neither the first nor the last name of the man with the red tie is mentioned. As with the refrain of "that/dat show," characters simply refer to him by his unconventional necktie. This strategy suggests that the traveling showman's attire is not only significant, but even symbolic; it contains an important detail about his personality.

In addition, many of the comments Jason Compson makes about the man with the red tie allude to the character's homosexuality and his awareness of it. Although the Compson son has lived the majority of his life in a small town, he has spent time in large cities such as Memphis. While there, he frequents the "seedy" areas where prostitutes such as his girlfriend Lorraine live. Even though Jason never mentions encountering any dandies, gay men were likely to have composed part of this marginalized sexual population. Throughout the third and fourth sections of the text, the comments Jason makes may indicate that he is "in the know" about the meaning of the red tie. The first time he spots his niece with the man, for instance, he remarks, "So when I looked around the door the first thing I saw was the red tie he had on and I was thinking what the hell kind of man would wear a red tie."[11] A few pages later, Jason adds, "I saw red. When I recognized that red tie, after all I had told her, I forgot about everything" (p. 149). During the remainder of the novel, Jason continues to utter remarks such as accusing his niece of "letting your own uncle be laughed at by a man that would wear a red tie" or of running home to "[t]ry to make her [grandmother] believe that I don't know who he was" (pp. 152, 151).

Giving further credence to this theory that such comments point to the showman's homosexuality rather than his heterosexual involvement with Miss Quentin are the expletives with which Jason curses the gentleman. Once again, these terms imply that the Compson son and, by extension, William Faulkner know exactly what the tie means. As Tom Bowden has noted, whenever Jason refers to his mother, sister or niece, Faulkner chooses the abnormal spelling of a common expletive. Instead of referring to his "damn niece" or "damn sister," the author has Jason characterize them as his "dam niece" or "dam sister." Although this alternative spelling has no effect on the word's pronunciation, it radically alters its semantics. While the word "damn" means cursed to hell, "a dam is a domesticated female animal."[12] Jason both begins and ends his section with the assertion, "Once a bitch always a bitch" (pp. 113, 165). Thus, even in the way he curses women, the Compson son reveals his belief that they are nothing more than bitch dogs.

Jason does not reserve this revealing expletive exclusively for females; he also applies it to the man with the red tie. The first time Jason chases Miss Quentin and the showman, he mutters "what kind of a dam man would wear a red tie" (p. 145). A few pages later when the man with the red tie runs into the woods with his niece, Jason asserts, "I'll make him think that dam red tie is the latch string to hell" (p. 151). Faulkner's decision to have Jason use the word "dam" instead of "damn" in these instances not only curses the gentleman but also frames him as a bitch, a female and, thus, one may infer, a homosexual.[13] Even today, the word "bitch" is still used to insult gay men.

Jason's possible knowledge of the red tie's meaning calls into question his motivation for pursuing Miss Quentin. After enduring the shame from his promiscuous sister, Caddy, the Compson son would understandably not wish to have this pattern repeated with his niece. Hence, when Miss Quentin began behaving in ways that recalled her mother's actions (skipping school, running around with boys), Jason followed her to preserve her virginity or, at least, societal perceptions of it. Upon discovering that his niece's "boyfriend" was gay, however, his interest in chasing the girl was likely to have changed. After all, if the young woman is fraternizing with a gay man, she is most likely not involved in a sexual affair with him. Nevertheless, Jason is greatly concerned with public opinions of himself and his family. Throughout his portion of the novel, in fact, the bitter character is largely obsessed with preserving the "good Compson name." Like most places in the country, the American South during the 1920s did not hold male dandies in high esteem. For most men and women, such figures were abnormal and even degenerate. While it is likely that few (if any) residents of Yoknapatawpha understand the significance of the red tie, Jason would still want to prevent the possibility of bringing shame to his niece and, by extension, himself for associating with "inverts." In addition, he may be morally and/or personally disgusted by gay men. Thus, he would strive to wrest Miss Quentin from the man with the red tie. Depending upon the amount of social stigma his community attaches to homosexuality as well as his own level of homophobia, this desire may have actually increased if he decided that, the traveling showman was gay; perhaps he would have been less adamant in his pursuit if the man were not wearing a red tie.

If true, these details contribute to Jason's intense anger upon discovering that Miss Quentin has stolen the money with the man's assistance. If the Compson son is aware of the showman's sexual orientation and his assistance in Miss Quentin's "theft," then he has been robbed not only by a woman but by someone "worse" than a woman, a homosexual. When the pair successfully eludes Jason, Faulkner's traveling show reveals that it can be a carnival in a Bakhtinian sense even though it is not one by historical standards. The "temporary liberation from the prevailing truth and the established order . . . and the suspension of all hierarchical rank, privileges, norms, and prohibitions that medieval carnivals celebrated" (Bakhtin, p. 45) is echoed in Jason's inability to persuade either the police or the traveling show's staff to help him retrieve the money. Both entities refuse to acknowledge his social, familial and even economic "rank" or to assist efforts to re-establish his order over Miss Quentin; the police doubt Jason's claim to the money while the show hands are repulsed by his violent temper and slanderous accusations. Jason is astounded by these disruptions in the social order and behaves as if he's been emasculated. As Doreen Fowler notes, the ultimate sign of this symbolic castration "is [Jason's] inability to drive his car; on the trip back to Jefferson, Jason takes the back seat, and a black man drives."[14] Realizing that he will not regain the masculine power of the stolen money (Fowler, p. 10) and, by extension, will never re-establish the former order within the Compson house, Jason must accept that he has "sunk lower" than both women and gays. The carnivalesque show has not only turned his world upside-down, but, by aiding Miss Quentin's escape, it has destroyed it.

Significantly, the showman's (gay) red tie is not the only element in *The Sound and the Fury* in particular or William Faulkner's career in general that explores gender and sexuality. As numerous critics and biographers have noted, "inversion" is a trope that runs throughout the author's life and work. While a student at the University of Mississippi, for instance, Faulkner was known to "pose" as a homosexual. Dressing as a dandy and spending most of his time engaged in the "feminine occupation" of writing poetry, "Count No 'Count," as John Duvall notes, "was perceived by his Oxford contemporaries as downright 'queer.'"[15] Faulkner's gay friend and future editor, Ben Wasson, confirmed these observations. In 1919, the aspiring author approached Wasson with a copy of Conrad Aiken's *Turns and Movies and Other Tales in Verse.* Once on campus, Faulkner selected a shady place beneath one of the many Confederate monuments. As Wasson recounts, "'We sat there together on the grass, and he read the book aloud . . . as students passed to and fro, glancing questioningly at us'" (Duvall, p. 53). Perhaps John Duvall put it best: "Small wonder that Wasson recalls questioning glances: had Wasson been a young woman, the passing students would have incorporated the moment as part of normal heterosexual courtship . . . had the students known of the frank treatment of homosexuality in Aiken's *Turns and Movies,* their glances perhaps would have been outraged" (p. 53).[16]

After leaving Ole Miss, William Faulkner became well acquainted with the gay culture of both New Orleans and Paris during what may be called the height of "the red tie period," the 1920s:

> Virtually the entire year of 1925 Faulkner spent either in New Orleans—certainly an important American site of flamboyant sexual masquerade and activity of all sorts—or in Europe, mainly in Paris. Living and traveling with his homosexual friend Bill Spratling off and on for two years during this period, Faulkner mixed with male homosexuals and lesbians at various bars and houses in the Vieux Carré in New Orleans. Other homosexual friends included Ben Wasson and Stark Young. In Paris he found a city of expatriate writers, Natalie Barney, Gertrude Stein, Reneé

> Vivien, and other homosexual artists, writers and patrons of the arts. Since the early part of the twentieth century, the city has also been the site of cross-gendered performance and parody, despite middle-class moral outrage. The 'mannish lesbian' was in vogue, and male homosexuality was, as Shari Benstock put it, 'overt, even flamboyant, and was grounded in the aesthetic of the dandy that dominated the literary and artistic culture of the period.'[17]

While William Faulkner inhabited such "queer" circles one may infer that he became acquainted with their culture and symbols. Admittedly, the appearance of gay men often varied by geographic region. Yet, as Havelock Ellis, George Chauncey, and Paul Cadmus assert, tweezed eyebrows, rouged cheeks and red ties frequently transcended such boundaries; they were likely to have been employed by "inverts" the writer encountered.

Years later, Faulkner's various associations with gay men and women found their way into his writing. As Minrose Gwin observed, "throughout his career [Faulkner's] works evince an interest in sex and sexuality, gender and gendered behavior" (p. 122). Although nearly all of his texts contain some reference to homosexuality or, at least, gender confusion, the novel he wrote just prior to *The Sound and the Fury*, his second book, *Mosquitoes,* is especially concerned with this issue.[18] Throughout the text, both lesbian and gay tensions abound. At one point, a direct reference to famed sexologist Havelock Ellis appears. In the middle of a discussion about the inherent "emotional bisexuality" of men and women, a character named Dawson mentions the work of "'Dr. Ellis and your Germans.'"[19] Although the conversation between Dawson and his companion ends shortly after this remark, its inclusion indicates Faulkner's familiarity with this individual and his desire to make readers aware of this knowledge.

As *Mosquitoes* progresses, characters do not simply make passing references to scientists investigating homosexuality. Often, they openly discuss gay and lesbian intimacy.[20] Four sections of Faulkner's novel, in fact, were removed from the original manuscript because they contained such explicit descriptions of homosexual erotica. Amazingly, these sections were not reprinted until 1994 in Minrose Gwin's "*Mosquitoes*' Missing Bite: The Four Deletions."[21] Although contemporary audiences may not find the deleted sections objectionable, 1920s audiences, less accustomed to gay men and lesbian women, would have been shocked by them. Thus, to the author's disappointment, they were cut from the published novel.

The censure *Mosquitoes* suffered for its treatment of gender and sexuality did not deter William Faulkner from continuing his exploration of these issues in his next novel, *The Sound and the Fury.* In this text, in fact, such references are more frequent, albeit more coded. According to Minrose Gwin, the writer "learned certain hard lessons from having his explorations of same-sex erotica in *Mosquitoes* at least partially purged" ("Bite," p. 33). Faulkner knew that if *The Sound and the Fury* was to be printed as he had written it, he needed to make references less direct. Hence, before the man with the red tie even enters the novel, subtle instances of gender-bending and even homoeroticism arise. The first such occurrence appears in Benjy's section. Since Benjy lacks the ability to critically analyze his surroundings, he often confuses memories, people and events. Karen Kaivola remarked that, as first-time readers of *The Sound and the Fury* "move with Benjy across the boundaries of time and space, Quentin's gender identity is not clear. Sometimes female (Miss Quentin) and sometimes male, this confusion disrupts the dichotomy of sexual difference."[22] Benjy's seamless shifts between memories of his brother Quentin Compson and his niece, Quentin Head, frustrate efforts to understand which Quentin he means or that there are even two Quentins. The confusion that arises from this blurred distinction implies that there is one hermaphroditic Quentin. Reading Benjy's section for the first time, one is tempted to see Quentin as either a gay man to whom feminine pronouns are homophobically attributed or as a lesbian with whom masculine pronouns are similarly associated. It is not until later in the novel that this uncertainty is resolved and readers learn that the name "Quentin" refers to two people.

The gender confusion surrounding Quentin in the opening pages of *The Sound and the Fury* is perpetuated in its second segment. As Bing Shao notes, Quentin Compson's narrative "problematizes rather than clarifies the gender issue."[23] Throughout this section, the young man is often framed as a homosexual or, at least, a feminine man. Quentin's fellow students at Harvard, for instance, question his relationship with his roommate, Shreve MacKenzie. At one point, one of them even teases that Shreve is Quentin's "husband" (p. 50). When Gerald Bland's mother attempts to have Shreve removed from Quentin's room because he is, in her opinion, a "fat Canadian" (p. 67), MacKenzie humorously recalls the rumors. As he exits the room one day, Shreve jokes, "'Well, I'll say a fond farewell. Cruel fate may part us, but I will never love another. Never.'" (p. 68). After the dismissal of the charge that Quentin was kidnapping the little Italian girl, Shreve behaves in a way that suggests he may not have been teasing when he made these remarks. As Quentin, Shreve, Spoade and Gerald ride in Mrs. Bland's car, Quentin notes, "Shreve's fat hand touched my knee" (p. 93). Although this act may be seen as merely an accidental brush in a crowded, bouncing car, it happens again. After moving his knee away from Shreve's hand, Quentin notes, "His hand touched my knee again. I moved my knee again" (p. 93). The repetition of this occurrence presents the possibility that Shreve's actions are not simply accidental or even homosocial. They may be homoerotic and thereby position Quentin and Shreve in the exact way their classmates were insinuating: as homosexual "husbands."

In addition to being directly treated as a homosexual, Quentin has his masculinity questioned indirectly by being feminized. Nearly every attempt the young man makes to "act like a man" backfires, framing him as an effeminate man or even a woman. Nowhere, perhaps, is this tendency more apparent than in the manly realm of sexual conquest. At the time of his death, Quentin is a timid virgin. Unlike the gender codes for Southern women, sexual inexperience causes men embarrassment and even disrespect. At one point, Quentin's father even quips, "In the South you are ashamed of being a virgin. Boys. Men. They lie about it" (p. 50).

Unable to prove his masculinity through sexual prowess, Quentin tries to assert it through the equally manly acts of fighting and weaponry. As with his failed sexual escapades, though, he is abysmally unsuccessful in these areas. In one of the most haunting moments, the youth fails to shoot Dalton Ames after promising Caddy "tomorrow I'll kill him I swear I will" (p. 95). But "[w]hen [Dalton] put the pistol in my hand," Quentin says, "I didn't [shoot him]" (p. 51). Frozen by fear, the boy simply watched as Ames skillfully—and mockingly—shot pieces of bark "no bigger than silver dollars" without even aiming (p. 102). After mustering the courage to order Dalton out of town, Quentin "passed out like a girl" (p. 103). This emasculating moment is repeated during a fight with Gerald Bland. Even though Quentin initiates the hostilities, he is quickly defeated: the classmate "boxed the hell out of" him (p. 104). When the scuffle first began, in fact, Quentin's first instinct was to slap Bland rather than make a fist and punch him (p. 102). Given the frequency of such feminizing moments, it comes as no surprise when Quentin assumes the identity of a woman, Dalton Ames's mother. "If I could have been his mother lying with open body lifted laughing, holding his father with my hand refraining, seeing, watching him die before he lived" (p. 51).

Such instances of gender transgression, of course, cannot always be equated with homosexuality. As queer theorists such as Judith Butler in her landmark *Gender Trouble* would argue, simply because Quentin often behaves in effeminate ways and is even cast as gay does not mean that he is a homosexual. The youth did symbolically violate the incest taboo by telling his father that he had been intimate with his sister. The memory of this forbidden (but purely imagined) act, in fact, is one of the primary reasons for his suicide. Haunted by this "irrecoverable memory of pleasure before the law,"[24] Quentin is so figuratively flooded by feelings of melancholy that he literally drowns; he takes his life by jumping into a river. Even though Quentin has symbolically violated the incest taboo (or, at least, parodied its violation), there is no evidence that he ever transgressed what Butler deems the second generative moment of gender identity, "the prior taboo against homosexuality" (p. 135). Thus, instances of gender confusion in Benjy's section and sexual transgression in Quentin's segment certainly point to the man with the (gay) red tie but they cannot be equated with him. The man from the traveling show is the only figure that can be characterized as "queer" in the contemporary sense of this term.

The symbolic meaning of the (gay) red tie in Faulkner's *The Sound and the Fury* complicates common, critical views of both Miss Quentin and the final sequences of the text. Since the 1929 publication of the novel numerous reviews have characterized the young girl as a degenerative version of her mother. Like Candace, Miss Quentin seems lax in her sexual mores, often behaving in ways that are more promiscuous than Caddy's: she cuts class and can be seen riding with men in broad daylight. As John Bassett noted, "even if [Caddy] 'placed no value whatever' on her virginity she at least cared for the implications of its loss to Benjy and Quentin, whereas Miss Quentin scarcely admits there is a moral issue involved in promiscuity."[25] When Benjy caught Caddy and Charlie in the outdoor swing, the young woman knew her actions were shameful and vowed never to engage in them again: "'I won't. . . . I won't anymore, ever'" (p. 81). Miss Quentin's reaction to being discovered in the same swing with the man with the red tie, however, is remarkably different. Rather than "repent" her behavior, the young woman scolds Luster for his lax supervision of Benjy. "*'You old crazy loon. . . . I'm going to tell Dilsey about the way you let him follow everywhere I go. I'm going to make her whip you good'*" (p. 31). Unlike her mother, Miss Quentin does not care if others know what she does. At one point, she even boldly announces, "'I dare anybody to know everything I do'" (p. 119). Given this brazen attitude, many have posited that the relationship between Caddy's life and that of her daughter is cyclic: Miss Quentin seems doomed to repeat the mistakes of her mother. After the young girl escapes the Compson household at the end of the novel, most presume she will follow her mother's pattern of promiscuity and prostitution.

These observations, however, hinge on two assumptions: that the man with the red tie is heterosexual and that he and Miss Quentin are involved in a sexual relationship. The historical significance of the red tie, Faulkner's probable knowledge of it, and textual evidence that suggests Jason may also be aware of its meaning call these assertions into question and thereby views of Miss Quentin and her escape as well. If the man with the red tie is, in fact, gay, then he and Miss Quentin are likely not to be involved in a sexual relationship. Giving credence to this reading, Faulkner has Luster and not the traveling showman discover the box of Agnes Mabel Becky condoms. "'Found it under this here bush,' Luster said. 'I thought for a minute it was that quarter I lost'" (p. 32). Although the man with the red tie knows what the package contains, the contraceptive does not belong to him. In an effort to ascertain its owner, the gentleman even asks, "'Who come to see her last night. . . . Damn if one of them didn't leave a track'" (pp. 32–33). Hence, Benjy may catch the young girl in the same porch swing where he saw her mother, but she is not necessarily repeating Caddy's actions. Contrary to the assumptions of Jason and countless critics, Miss Quentin may not be repeating the cycle. By fraternizing with gay men with whom she is not likely romantically involved and by cautiously using contraceptives when she is sexually active, she is attempting to break it. These details offer a possible explanation for why Miss Quentin dares anybody to know everything she does: she might not be involved in any disreputable behavior. Admittedly, the man with the red tie is part of a stigmatized minority. But, since she is not engaged in a sexual relationship with him, the liberal-minded young woman sees no need to conceal their association.[26]

This alternative reading of Miss Quentin gives new significance to one of Dilsey's most famous utterances, "I've seed de first en de last. . . . I seed de beginnin, en now I sees de endin" (p. 185). As Arthur Geffen notes, this remark already bears multiple meanings:

> It surely refers to the vision she has shared with Shegog of the beginning and end of Christ's life on earth and of two of the endpoints of Christian sacred history—the crucifixion and the judgment. Also her language duplicates that of the Book of Revelation: 'I am the Alpha and the Omega, the beginning and the ending'; 'I am Alpha and Omega. . . . the first and the last.' Her words may then indicate that she, like Shegog, has seen God face to face. However, the statements, particularly when taken in the context in which they are later uttered, appear also to be comments on the doom of the family she has served all her life.[27]

If Dilsey is aware of the red tie's meaning, then her comment acquires added authority. The black servant knows that neither Jason nor Benjy is in a position to have children: Benjy is castrated and Jason's only romantic interest is a whore he keeps in Memphis. Thus, Caddy's daughter, Quentin, was the only hope for perpetuating some aspect of the family line. If Miss Quentin has run off with a gay man, however, this possibility is largely foreclosed. The young woman is not likely to bear children and, thus, the Compson name is likely to pass. Quentin's escape ensures, as Geffen asserts, "the doom of the family [Dilsey] has served all her life" (p. 240). She has truly "seed de first en de last" Compson.

In spite of the ways in which the man with the red tie enriches the unresolved tensions in *The Sound and the Fury*, Faulkner later tried to alter this character and his implications. As Susan Donaldson observed, ". . . the whole of [Faulkner's] career is marked both by his attraction to the blurring of sexual boundaries and by his horrified response to that possibility."[28] In the Appendix that the author wrote nearly twenty years after the publication of *The Sound and the Fury,* he suggests that the man with the red tie is heterosexual by asserting that the gentleman with whom Miss Quentin escaped "was also under sentence for bigamy" (p. 214). Moreover, while outlining these accusations, Faulkner never refers to this character as "the man with the red tie." Throughout the Compson Appendix, he calls him a "pitchman." Such tactics eliminate (or, at least, try to eliminate) the badge of homosexuality previously connected with this character. They erase the queer elements within his name and his attire and, in doing so, reinforce his heterosexuality.

In spite of such efforts to make the man with the red tie heteronormative, the original 1929 text of *The Sound and the Fury* suggests otherwise. As mentioned earlier, the traveling showman is called nothing but "the man with the red tie" throughout the text. In addition, not one sentence in the novel even hints that he is married let alone has been accused of bigamy. On the contrary, the carefree way in which the man with the red tie carouses with Miss Quentin suggests an untethered spirit. Given this lack of evidence, Faulkner's remarks in the Compson Appendix seem like an attempt to redress the novel: to change the original text, alter the sexual orientation of the man with the red tie, and thereby transform Miss Quentin's escape into a repetition of her mother's mistakes.

A careful reading of the entire Compson Appendix, though, and not simply its remarks about the man with the red tie, suggests that accusing Faulkner of intentionally redressing the novel may be at least somewhat unfair. Written eighteen years after the publication of *The Sound and the Fury*, the Appendix is littered with "misremembrances" about the text. In one of the most glaring, the author discusses the "rainpipe" Miss Quentin climbed down to make her escape from the Compson home (p. 214). In the original novel, however, the young girl, makes her descent from a pear tree—the same pear tree, in fact, her mother ascended years earlier to glimpse Damuddy's forbidden funeral. In light of such discrepancies, Faulkner's assertion that the pitchman/man with the red tie is a bigamist loses credibility. Considerable evidence from the 1929 novel offers the possibility that the man with the red tie may be gay and Jason, Miss Quentin and perhaps even Dilsey are aware of it. Faulkner's later attempt to change this character either through redress or misremembrance is just that, an attempt he made later.

John T. Matthews once wrote, "*The Sound and the Fury* is a novel that comes to yearn for an ending."[29] In addition to discussions of time and structure, countless essays over the past seventy years have attempted to understand the conclusion of Faulkner's text. Many critics have argued that the author's work in general and *The Sound and the Fury* in particular deny readers an ending. Walter Slatoff may have put it best when he said,

> Probably the most crucial indication of Faulkner's intention is the fact that the endings of all his novels not only fail to resolve many

> of the tensions and meanings provided in the novels but also seem carefully designed to prevent such resolution. Above all, they leave unresolved the question of the meaningfulness of the human efforts and suffering we have witnessed, whether the sound and the fury is part of some larger design or whether it has signified nothing in an essentially meaningless universe.[30]

Although it does not resolve every question raised in the novel, the possibility that the man with the red tie is homosexual does afford it (or, at least, allow it to approach) a conclusion. If the man with whom Miss Quentin escapes is gay, then negative readings of this young woman and her flight are called into question. The sexual orientation of the traveling showman would tell readers that the sufferings they have witnessed may not have been meaningless. Rather, they might have liberated one young woman from the oppressions of a doomed, dysfunctional family. Referencing Bakhtin's remarks on the transformative power of medieval carnivals once again, the man with the (gay) red tie could have helped Miss Quentin be "reborn for new, purely human relations" (p. 46). The money she "steals" from her uncle may free her from the despotism and exploitation that has characterized both her existence and her mother's. Thus, even though Miss Quentin's escape signals the end of the "old" Compson line, it may simultaneously mark the beginning of an entirely new order.

During one his many pursuits of Miss Quentin and the man with the red tie, Jason vows, "I'll make him think that dam red tie is the latch string to hell" (p. 151). If this character's tie does, in fact, announce his "inversion," then Miss Quentin's wise decision to enlist the help of a homosexual rather than a heterosexual man suggests otherwise. Making her dramatic exodus on Easter Sunday, the young girl could prove that the gay man's tie is not a latch string to the same hells occupied by her mother, but a rope leading to her own redemption.

Notes

1. Joan Williams. "In Defense of Caroline Compson." in *Critical Essays on William Faulkner: The Compson Family,* ed. Arthur F. Kinney (Boston: Hall, 1982), pp. 402–407.

2. Irving Howe, "The Passing of a World," in *Twentieth Century Interpretations of "The Sound and the Fury,"* ed. Michael Cowan (Englewood Cliffs, New Jersey: Prentice-Hall, 1968) p. 38.

3. Mikhail Bakhtin, "Rabelais and his World," in *Literary Theory: An Anthology,* ed. Julie Rivkin and Michael Ryan (Malden, Massachusetts: Blackwell, 1998), pp. 45–51.

4. Jonathan Ned Katz, ed. *Gay American History: Lesbian and Gay Men in the U.S.A.,* rev. ed. (New York: Penguin, 1992).

5. Havelock Ellis, *Studies in the Psychology of Sex, Volume II: Sexual Inversion,* 3rd ed. (Philadelphia: F.A. Davis, 1926), p. 351.

6. In the opening minutes of Andrea Weiss and Greta Schiller's film, *Before Stonewall: The Making of a Gay and Lesbian Community* (MPT, 1984), one of the founders of the Mattachine Society, Henry Hay, also comments on the way in which red ties were used as symbols for homosexuality. Discussing the methods by which gay men found each other in the 1920s, Hay remarks, "Sometimes, you would look into a person's eyes, he would look into your eyes and all of a sudden you'd know through the eyes. You knew each other by a red necktie. It was very daring to wear a hanky that matched the tie. The moment you saw that, no matter what the color was, you figured that you had, that there was a brother there. After you had cruised each other by chasing each other back and forth from looking in the same window at the same thing for quite a while you might ask the person, 'Do you have a match?' or 'Can you tell me the time?' These were the little things that we would be using in the '20s, and we were still using them in the '30s I might add."

7. (New York: Harper Collins, 1994), p. 3.

8. All information on circus history was graciously provided by the Director of the Robert L. Parkinson Library and Research Center, Mr. Fred Dahlinger, Jr., at Circus World Museum in Baraboo, Wisconsin. In a series of phone conversations conducted in May 1997 as well as through several exchanges of information through the mail, Dahlinger and his staff compared the type of show present in *The Sound and the Fury* with their archives on carnivals, circuses, two-car circuses, tent theater troupes, traveling minstrel shows, and dog and pony outfits in the 1920s. His findings were then cross-checked with the Ringling Museum in Sarasota, Florida, as well as with carnival historian Joe McKennon. My conclusions are drawn from the cumulative findings of these investigations.

9. Dahlinger did discover that many equestrian directors wore red or orange top coats during the 1920s. According to his photo archives, however, when they did so, they always wore black pants, a white shirt and a *white* bow tie.

10. As one might imagine, if circus historians are unable to identify the type of show that appears in *The Sound and the Fury,* critics are even more perplexed by it. In the past seventy years, the event has been called everything from a "traveling show" (Donald M. Kartiganer, *The Fragile Thread: The Meaning of Form in Faulkner's Novels* [Amherst, Massachusetts: University of Massachusetts Press, 1979], p. 32), "traveling circus show" (John T. Matthews, *"The Sound and the Fury": Faulkner and the Lost Cause* [Boston: Twayne, 1991]. p. 34), and "carnival show" (John Pilkington, *The Heart of Yoknapatawpha* (Jackson: University Press of Mississippi, 1981], p. 56) to a "tent show" (Perrin Lowrey, "Concepts of Time in *The Sound and the Fury,*" in *Twentieth Century Interpretations,* p. 59) and even minstrel show. In accordance with this confusion, identifying the role the man with the red tie plays is even more schizophrenic. This character has been described as a "tent show pitchman" (Pilkington, p. 77), a "young man from the carnival" (Lewis Leary, *William Faulkner of Yoknapatawpha County* [New York: Thomas Y. Crowell Company, 1973], p. 57), a "carnival man" (William N. Claxon, Jr., "Jason Compson: A Demoralized Wit," in *Faulkner and Humor: Faulkner and Yoknapatawpha, 1984,* ed. Doreen Fowler and Ann J. Abadie [Jackson: University Press of Mississippi, 1986] p. 32; also John L. Longley, Jr., "'Who Never Had a Sister': A Reading of *The Sound and the Fury,*" in *The Novels of William Faulkner,* ed. R.G. Collins and Kenneth McRobbie [Winnipeg, Canada: University of Manitoba, 1973], p. 50), a "carnival lover" and "a boy friend from the circus" (Peter Swiggart, *The Art*

of Faulkner's Novels [Austin, Texas: University of Texas Press, 1962], pp. 101, 103), a "pitchman" (Edmund L. Volpe, *A Reader's Guide to William Faulkner* [New York: Farrar, Straus, and Giroux, 1964] p. 121; and John Hunt, *William Faulkner: Art in Theological Tension,* [Syracuse, New York: Syracuse University Press, 1965], p. 98), a "circus man" (Howe, p. 165), a "showman" (Duncan Aswell, "The Recollection and the Blood: Jason's Role in *The Sound and the Fury,*" in *Critical Essays on William Faulkner: The Compson Family,* ed. Arthur F. Kinney [Boston, G.K. Hall Company, 1982], p. 209), a "circus hand" (Kinney, p. 315), and even a "circus vagabond" (Bernhard Radloff, "The Unity of Time in *The Sound and the Fury,*" *Faulkner Journal,* 1 [Spring 1986] 64). Some critics have avoided characterizing the man with the red tie professionally. They simply describe him as Caddy's "daughter's boyfriend" (David Dowling, *William Faulkner* [London: Macmillan, 1989], p. 45), Miss Quentin's "lover" (Radloff, p. 57), the young woman's "man friend" (Kartiganer, p. 16), and, by one very cautious writer, as simply "a man" (Cheryl Lester, "From Place to Place in *The Sound and the Fury*: The Syntax of Interrogation," *Modern Fiction Studies,* 34 [Summer 1988], 151).

11. William Faulkner, *The Sound and the Fury* (New York: Norton, 1994), p. 145.

12. Tom Bowden, "Functions of Leftness and 'Dam' in William Faulkner's *The Sound and the Fury.*" *Notes on Mississippi Writers,* 19 (1987), 82.

13. Interestingly, Jason also uses the expletive "dam" in relation to circus clowns. Soon after Jason begins his pursuit of his niece the day she plays truant from school, he notes how her face is "painted like a dam clown's" (p. 145). Gay and lesbian scholars as well as circus historians have noted that many male circus clowns were, in fact, homosexual in the 1920s. Fred Dahlinger of Circus World Museum remarked that for a male to say he was a circus clown was practically synonymous with saying he was a homosexual. Thus, what may seem like Jason's incidental use, of this revealing expletive may be further evidence of his (and thus Faulkner's) knowledge of the homosexual and circus community. Given the ambiguous role the man with the red tie holds in the show, he could have been one of the "dam" clowns.

14. Doreen Fowler, "'Little Sister Death': *The Sound and the Fury* and the Denied Unconscious," in *Faulkner and Psychology: Faulkner and Yoknapatawpha,* 1991, ed. Donald M. Kartiganer and Ann J. Abadie (Jackson: University Press of Mississippi, 1994) p. 10.

15. John N. Duvall, "Faulkner's Crying Game: Male Homosexual Panic," in *Faulkner and Gender: Faulkner and Yoknapatawpha, 1994,* ed. Donald M. Kartiganer and Ann J. Abadie (Jackson: University Press of Mississippi, 1996), p. 52.

16. Faulkner's association with and even curiosity about gay men should not be mistaken for a claim that he was a homosexual. The images the author included in his works, the people with whom he associated and even the postures he assumed (such as the "failed poet" and the "wounded war pilot") may raise suspicions, especially among gay and lesbian scholars. Nevertheless, evidence that allows one to call the author's sexual orientation into question and evidence that concludes he was a homosexual are very different matters. In this instance, only the former seems to be present. For more on this issue, see Duvall, pp. 48–51.

17. Minrose C. Gwin, "Does Ernest Like Gordon?: Faulkner's *Mosquitoes* and the Bite of 'Gender Trouble,'" in *Faulkner and Gender: Faulkner and Yoknapatawpha,* 1994, p. 124.

18. In the past ten years, a number of articles have been published which examine the homoerotic/homosexual elements in *Mosquitoes.* Of these, I found

Lewis P. Simpson's "Sex & History: Origins of Faulkner's Apocrypha," (in *The Maker and The Myth: Faulkner and Yoknapatawpha, 1977,* ed. Evans Herrington & Ann J. Abadie [Jackson: University Press of Mississippi, 1978], pp. 43–70); Meryl Altman's "The Bug That Dare Not Speak Its Name: Sex, Art, Faulkner's Worst Novel, and the Critics," (*Faulkner Journal,* 9 [Fall 1993/Spring 1994] 43–68); John Duvall's "Faulkner's Crying Game," and Minrose C. Gwin's "Does Ernest Like Gordon?" especially helpful. In addition, the topic of the 1994 Faulkner and Yoknapatawpha Conference was "Faulkner and Gender," Many of the papers presented touch upon this issue.

19. William Faulkner, *Mosquitoes* (New York: Boni and Liverlight, 1927), p. 251.

20. Although none of the gender-bending characters in Faulkner's *Mosquitoes* wear red ties, the widower Ernest Talliaferro (who, incidentally, is a commercial buyer of women's dresses) wears red bathing suits with matching red bathing caps. No historical evidence indicates that any type of men's swimwear carried the same symbolic significance as neckties, but Ellis did remark that the color red "'has become almost a synonym for sexual inversion, not only in the minds of inverts themselves, but in the popular mind'" (p. 52). In this way, rather than use the more specific referent of red ties, Faulkner may have been drawing on the more general symbol of the color red to announce homosexuality in his second novel.

21. Minrose, Gwin, "*Mosquitoes*' Missing Bite: the Four Deletions," *Faulkner Journal,* 9 (Fall 1993/Spring 1994), 31–41.

22. Karen Kaivola, "Becoming Woman: Identification and Desire in *The Sound and the Fury*" in *Essays in Reader Orientation Theory, Criticism and Pedagogy,* 17 (Spring 1987), 31.

23. Bing Shao, "Time, Death, and Gender: The Quentin Section in *The Sound and the Fury,*" in *Conference of College Teachers of English Studies* (Denton, Texas: Conference of College Teachers of English Press, 1994), p. 56.

24. Judith Butler, *Gender Trouble: Feminism and the Subversion of Identity* (New York: Routledge, 1990), p. 78.

25. John E. Bassett, *Vision and Revisions: Essays on Faulkner* (West Cornwall, Connecticut: Locust Hill Press, 1989), p. 70.

26. Miss Quentin's connection with the man with the red tie should not be confused with a claim that the young woman is herself a lesbian. As both straight and gay people are aware, there is a significant difference between associating with homosexuals and being one yourself. Although the young woman has clearly been "initiated" into the gay world, no evidence from the text indicates that Miss Quentin is herself "inverted." Details such as the discovery of the package of condoms, in fact, stand in contrast to this condition. Based on Faulkner's portrait, the young woman appears to be heterosexual.

27. Arthur Geffen, "Profane Time, Sacred Time, and Confederate Time in *The Sound and the Fury,*" in *Critical Essays on William Faulkner: The Compson Family,* ed. Arthur F. Kinney (Boston: G. K. Hall & Co., 1982), p. 240.

28. Susan V. Donaldson, "Faulkner and Sexuality," *Faulkner Journal,* 9 (Fall 1993/Spring 1994), 5.

29. John T. Matthews, *The Play of Faulkner's Language* (Ithaca, New York: Cornell University, 1982), p. 104.

30. Walter J. Slatloff, "Unresolved Tensions," in *Twentieth Century Interpretations of* The Sound and the Fury, p.94.

JEFFREY J. FOLKS

Crowd and Self: William Faulkner's Sources of Agency in The Sound and the Fury

William Faulkner's letters to his publisher Horace Liveright, his agent Ben Wasson, and others, several versions of an introduction composed in 1933, and the explanatory appendix (composed in the autumn of 1945) may be used to reconstruct the conditions under which *The Sound and the Fury* was written and shed light on the author's psychological state at the time. Letters that Faulkner wrote to Liveright between October 1927 and March 1928 demonstrate an initial sense of hope, even euphoria, in having completed his third novel *Sartoris.* In his 16 October 1927 letter to Liveright, Faulkner says, "I have written THE book, of which those other things were but foals" (208) and in the same letter encloses instructions for the printer and asserts control over the title and jacket, for which he has already painted a conception. His euphoria was followed by frustration and despair at having his hopes dashed upon his third novel's rejection by his trusted publisher, to which Faulkner responded 30 November 1927 in a hurt and resigned mood: "I still believe it is the book that will make my name for me as a writer" (209). Though he now speaks of continuing to write intermittently, it is the very different tone, particularly the stillness and solemnity of this letter, that is striking. It was within this mood of isolation and rejection—the victim of a "crowd" of New York publishers and critics—that Faulkner protested that he would never again publish.[1]

Southern Literary Journal, Volume 34, Number 2 (2002): pp. 30–44.

Within three months, in mid or late February 1928, Faulkner in utter disgust writes to Liveright: "I have a belly full of writing, now, since you folks in the publishing business claim that a book like that last one I sent you is blah" (209), suggesting that he may have quit writing altogether. When he later responds to Liveright in early March, Faulkner's description of his current writing is quite tentative, saying of a novel that he hopes to finish that spring, "Maybe it'll please you" (210). In a letter probably of spring 1928 to Mrs. Walter McLean, his beloved "Aunt Bama," Faulkner speaks of his weariness in revising the manuscript of *Flags in the Dust,* stating that "every day or so I burn some of it up and rewrite it, and at present it is almost incoherent" (211). On 18 February 1929, Faulkner writes to Alfred Harcourt concerning the manuscript of *The Sound and the Fury* that Harcourt has briskly rejected: "That is all right. I did not believe that anyone would publish it; I had no definite plan to submit it to anyone" (212).

If the rejection of *Sartoris* and his hopelessness concerning further publication were reason enough for despair, Faulkner's anxiety regarding his mounting family responsibilities and the inimical relation of these new responsibilities to his future as a writer were other sources of worry. The awareness that he had, permanently he believed, failed in his attempt to gain a national audience for his fiction struck Faulkner at precisely the worst moment—just as he had undertaken a financial and an emotional commitment to Estelle Oldham and her two children, and would soon assume the support (as he must already have been more than vaguely aware) of an extended family and growing household. Separated from her husband Cornell Franklin, Estelle had returned to Oxford in January 1927. During the next two and a half years, Faulkner resumed the role of the "romantic swain," with their relationship purportedly arriving at "some sort of crisis" (Blotner 212) during the spring of 1928 while Faulkner was working on *The Sound and the Fury.* Amid local gossip over their intimate attachment, Faulkner felt compelled to marry Estelle despite his inability to support a family. That support eventually involved more than a dozen persons other than himself.

Accompanying the immediate burden of his commitment to Estelle was a related stratum of family trauma that may have played an even greater part in Faulkner's bewilderment, as it must have aggravated his sense of injustice at his rapid transformation from bohemian independence to patriarchal obligation. Declining from the prominent family it had once been, the Falkners as represented by William's father Murry had sunk to the level of a minor salaried appointment at the local university, a position that in Murry's case was matched by his obvious inadequacy for either cultural or political life. Faulkner's resentment of his father was acute, but there was an even more troubling problem in his relation to his mother, in whose critical estimation

Faulkner's rejection as an artist, for the time being at least, must have seemed to mirror that of his scorned father.

Thus, intense and manifold anxieties accompanied and nourished the composition of *The Sound and the Fury*. The first "Introduction" to *The Sound and the Fury*, written in the early 1930s, indicates that in hindsight the author understood the novel as a projection of his deepest feelings of rejection—indeed, as a figuration of his own condition of imaginative "death." Faulkner recognizes the autobiographical motive for the theme of victimization in the novel as he hints at the process by which he transferred his own sense of mistreatment by his publishers and his increasing sense of family responsibility onto the text of his fiction. In the "Introduction," Faulkner stated that he created the character of Caddy Compson "to look in the window of his [i.e., Faulkner's] bedroom" and that he created the novel as "something to die with" (224). That is, he imagined a central character in the novel as an observer of his own imaginative death, a death that coincided with the very creation of this empathetic observer. This observer would also accompany and comfort him in death and therefore assuage the stings that he had absorbed from the pack of untrustworthy publishers, including Liveright, Harcourt, and others to whom his agent, Ben Wasson, was circulating his work. Even six years after the composition of the novel, Faulkner's rejection is an intensely painful issue, and his response is implicit in the terms of the "Introduction": creating Caddy as an observer of his funeral redresses his isolation, for in Elias Canetti's terms she represents the origin of a mourning pack, a source of support aligned with the sacrificial victim/author.

If Caddy was created to accompany and solace the dying author—as the intimate and faithful "Little Sister Death" that Faulkner invokes elsewhere—the character of Quentin Compson must also be seen as a figure emerging out of the stresses that Faulkner himself labored under. Many of Faulkner's critics (including Cleanth Brooks, Louis D. Rubin, Jr., Lewis P. Simpson, and John T. Irwin) have remarked on the similarities of Quentin Compson and his creator, yet the precise nature of this similarity has not been fully analyzed. In Canetti's terms, Quentin's condition of stasis and masochistic self-torture can be viewed as a schizophrenic reaction to the severe psychological pressures originating in tensions within his relationship to family, race, and region. In a discussion of "Negativism in Schizophrenia," Canetti describes the schizophrenic personality as one "burdened with commands." The response of such an individual is to attempt to evade the command, either by doing the opposite of what is commanded, by doing nothing, or by carrying out the command in the reflexive manner of an automaton. The "lack of contact" of the schizophrenic, an obstinacy resembling the petrifaction of statues, alternates with opposite phases of "suggestion-slavery" in which one carries out commands rapidly and perfectly. One may compare the schizophrenic to the soldier on duty—both are frozen, rigid, awaiting commands that are based ultimately on the threat of execution, the universal punishment for military insubordination or desertion. Canetti also demonstrates that, although the schizophrenic "in a state of extreme suggestibility behaves as a member of a crowd would" (*Crowds* 323), he remains at the same time literally alone. Indeed, the schizophrenic imagination is replete with crowds. The contradictory experiences of sensing oneself a member of a crowd while remaining physically and socially isolated help to explain the immobilizing condition of schizophrenia, in which one disburdens oneself of stings of command by "stepping out of everything" and joining with others in a crowd, but this joining is, in the case of schizophrenia, an illusion (*Crowds* 324). Canetti writes: "no-one is more in need of the crowd than the schizophrenic, who is crammed with stings and feels suffocated by them. He cannot find the crowd outside and so he surrenders to one within him" (*Crowds* 324).

In Faulkner's text, no character more feels himself burdened by "stings" and at the same time less able to "pass them on" than does Quentin Compson. What most readers sense as Quentin's passivity, what some diagnose as sexual impotence, may be seen as an unwillingness (explained on one level as notions of "southern honor" and the proper conduct of the "gentleman") to pass on the stings that he has accumulated throughout childhood and adolescence. The single exception to this psychological immobility seems to be Quentin's fantasizing of incest, yet in his imagined transgression of the incest taboo Quentin is still attempting to dislodge those stings and commands that have originated in the family. Quentin's perverse tendency, however, is to seek out new stings—to provoke Gerald Bland, for example, whom he knows to be an expert boxer (a tendency toward self-punishment that his roommate Shreve MacKenzie understands no more than Mr. Compson, who simply concludes that "it's nature hurting you").

Quentin "learns" from his father the idea that man is an "accumulation" of the burdens of his ancestors. The origin of his psychological burdens, however, may be located more immediately in his mother's seizing of command. Noel Polk, who has provided a detailed reading of the maternal figure in Faulkner's early fiction, concludes that Faulkner was obsessed with presenting a "Medusa-like" figure of the adult female who is "everywhere in Yoknapatawpha, the county's resident genius of guilt and repression, the root of all problem" (66). The need to rid himself of the stings of maternal command is evident in Quentin's interest in shadows, which in a striking image he speaks of as a crowd waiting for a drowned man to die (55). In this metaphor of pleasurable death, Quentin imaginatively blends the river-symbol that he associates with a return to the mothering Caddy (a re-assertion of incest intended to transgress the control of a repressive maternal figure) with his sense of being the dead individual at the bottom of a heap of more vital human beings as figured in the shadowy gray depths of the River Charles. Indeed, Gail L. Mortimer finds that Quentin's ambivalence toward "the feminine" is figured in this very attraction to shadows and in the way that the shadow-crowd is understood as an alternative to filial duty.

Many readers have traced the failure of the Compson children to the coldness and remoteness of Mrs. Compson, whom Lee Jenkins compares to "a malignant force that stifles life at its source, the very antithesis of mothering" (144). Jenkins writes: "One must look to the limitations of Mrs. Compson as the underlying cause of the distorted and arrested development of the Compson children. Cold, self-centered, unloving, and hypocritical, she uses all those around her to satisfy her hypochondriacal needs and paralyzes and corrupts normal family relations" (144). Yet, if Caroline Compson, like the figure of Mrs. Bland whom Quentin later meets in Boston, is, in Jenkins's phrase, a "travesty of true motherly solicitation," she is also, in Canetti's terms, one who practices "the domestication of the command" that controls all master-slave, human-animal, and mother-child relationships. In each of these relationships, "a creature which is subject to another habitually receives its food only from that other." As Canetti explains, "a close link grows up between commands and the giving of food. . . . Domesticating the command means linking it with a promise of food" (*Crowds* 307). Underlying this relationship is the "original penalty" of primitive existence—the withholding of food—and though "modified" in domestic civilization, "there are stated penalties for non-compliance and these can be very heavy" (*Crowds* 308). In Canetti's theory, the "paralyzing" control that Mrs. Compson exercises toward her children, even creating scapegoats of Benjy and Caddy, is to some degree normative in all maternal behavior rather than a "travesty" of it.

In Faulkner's case, his relationship to his mother, the estimable Maud Butler Falkner, was entwined with his ambitions to become a writer—ambitions that surfaced in early childhood, as we learn from his brother, Jack Falkner, and other sources (Blotner 23). Literary ambition was of course connected with his desire to emulate his great-grandfather and namesake, the "Old Colonel," William Clark Falkner, author of *The White Rose of Memphis* (1881) and other popular works. A more immediate and powerful influence, however, was his introduction to the reading of the classics ("Shakespeare and Balzac, Conrad, and other fiction writers of the day" [Blotner 16]) that Faulkner received from his mother. Blotner cites information that "all the Falkner boys were too close to their mother, and they were emotionally tied to her" (19), and he speculates that for William, the oldest of four boys, the arrival of three younger brothers (including two, Jack and Dean, who were sickly as infants) created a strong sense of rivalry: "If such a situation could produce anxiety or even perhaps some resentment, it could also produce a wish to earn love through different ways, both by conventional gifts and gifts of achievement" (19).

It is the highly ambivalent relation with his mother that is significant: rejection or affection alone would not have influenced Faulkner's ambitions in the intense way that his love-hate relationship did. As Blotner writes: "Billy's love for [his mother] would shine through the letters he would write from distant places" (40). At the same time, the intense filial relationship carried with it the intolerable burden of retaining the love of a reserved and proud parent with high expectations for her children. Faulkner's "death" as an artist was not only a defeat of his own plans but, perhaps more importantly, a failure of his mother's hopes. Such a failure would entail not only guilt and humiliation but also bitterness at the fact of his having been "assigned" such an impossible task in the first place. Like that of Quentin Compson, Faulkner's relation to his mother involved repressed anger as well as open protestations of love. As is clear from Blotner and other biographical accounts,[2] it was a relationship that clouded all of Faulkner's other relationships with women, particularly his marriage to Estelle Oldham. When Faulkner was later examined for psychiatric complaints, his reaction to a physician who "conjectured that his patient might not have received enough love from his mother" was "icy silence" (Blotner 19).

Quentin's relationship with Caddy and with women in general is the most painful and revealing aspect of his position as the object of command. In Quentin's imagination, Caddy's marriage trunks are "coffins" (58); her crowd of suitors torments him because it underlines the fact of his exclusion. Caddy's marriage also signals the foreclosure of the incest option as a means of escape from domestic authority. In a related episode, Julio, as an "alien" (a double of Quentin who understands the burdening and transferring of stings all too well), detects Quentin's unconscious transferal of his incestuous desire from Caddy to Julio's (and Quentin's imagined) "little sister." Following the "assault," the pack that gathers in pursuit actually delights and amuses Quentin because it swells to a crowd, one of his rare moments of actual contact with others. Gerald's mother, the ever respectable and ludicrous Mrs. Bland, and the Cambridge girls accompanying the party are scandalized at Quentin's transgressive behavior because it lacks the appearance of "respectability," a concept that has much to do with Quentin's schizophrenia since "respectability" intends the prohibition of contact across social boundaries as well as the censorship of "low" public displays of emotional release—those gestures of embrace, anger, celebration, or lament from which "respectable" families (such as the Compsons and the Blands) abstain.

In the composition of *The Sound and the Fury*, Faulkner was much occupied with the matter of his own artistic death, and his representation of Quentin and Caddy Compson transmuted his feelings of imaginative death into compelling narrative figures of stasis and solace, respectively. Another character who reflects Faulkner's sense of disempowerment is Benjamin Compson. From Canetti's perspective, the position of Benjy in the psychic economy of the Compson household is that of the scapegoat. His identification in that role by Dilsey Gibson and even by those who may not yet admit it, such as Mrs. Compson, suggests that he is indispensable to the continuation of the family's order of command. The sense of a ritual scapegoat is strongly connected with Benjy through a number of images. In the first pages of the novel, Luster says that the pigs must "feel bad because one of them got killed today" (3) (this day of sacrifice is also the Christ-like Benjy's thirty-third birthday). Like Adonis, a classical figure connected with vegetation myth and scapegoat symbolism, Benjy will spend his season in hell, in his case at the state mental asylum. For those around him, as Canetti notes of the scapegoat in general, "the dead man has died for the sake of the people who mourn him," and there is always the insistence, by those implicated in his death, that the scapegoat should not have died. During the Easter service, as Rev. Shegog summons the "memory" of the blood of the lamb, the highly emotional response of the congregation arises not because they renounce sacrificial violence but because of their own implication in it. At this point in the novel, Faulkner has carried his imaginative analysis of crowds and power, beginning with his own sense of exclusion and victimization as an artist, to its reasonable and inevitable conclusion: the implication of every member of society in the persecution of the scapegoat. In the bitter autumn months of 1927, following the rejection of *Sartoris,* Faulkner surely must have glimpsed in Horace Liveright his own personal Judas, and, in others in the book trade, a host of Pontius Pilates indifferent to the fate of an unappreciated provincial genius.

At this point in his career, rejected and silenced by the national literary culture, Faulkner discovered a powerful sense of agency in his own condition as the object of lament, but he must also have sought to express his own fantasized assertions of survival and control. One of Cambridge's most intriguing residents—and one positioned in a highly significant relation to Quentin (and Faulkner) —is the "Deacon," a mercenary and domineering "servant" to generations of Harvard students from the South. Certainly, as Thadious M. Davis writes, "Deacon has mastered adaptation as a method of survival" as he greets new arrivals from the South and inexorably transforms himself from servant into master during the course of their residency, all the while enjoying immunity from the stings of command that, emulating the trickster-figure of African American tradition, he shifts to others. The Deacon and his descendants are in the process of assimilating within the same hegemonic New England culture from which Quentin, as an impoverished "gentleman" from a pariah culture, and Faulkner himself, as an aspiring author from the same region, are excluded. Settled in Cambridge for decades, the Deacon has established a family with a married daughter, has entrenched his son-in-law in the city work force, and has himself joined as honorary member of every parade in Boston—the parade being the sort of ritual procession that in Canetti's typology connotes permanence and survival.

Quentin's interest in the Deacon, however, involves more than mere envy of his position within hegemonic northern culture. The fact that the Deacon has remained at Harvard through generations of southern students fascinates Quentin, for the Deacon is connected with the "grandfather" fish and other symbols of ancestry to which Quentin is himself bound but by which he is also severely burdened. In Davis's perceptive reading, the Deacon functions as Quentin's double in the novel, yet one in whom Faulkner portrayed "what is missing in Quentin's white world" (94). Quentin is fascinated by the Deacon's success as one who is both black and southern. As a trickster figure, he turns his own scapegoat legacy to his advantage, a maneuver that Faulkner in metafictional terms is attempting in the very novel in which the Deacon appears. Given his invulnerability as a master of self-transformation, the Deacon projects a fantasized omnipotence: as Quentin intuits, he is not really a servant but a mercenary and somewhat of a bully in his relations with the hapless "young massas" in Cambridge. By his shrewd grasp of cultural roles, the Deacon has managed to seize a secure and profitable position within the national economy, just the sort of adaptation that Faulkner, the failed provincial author, has been unable to accomplish.

In a similar way, the character of Dilsey, like the Deacon, embodies qualities of integrity and command that may have inspired envy and even fear in an author whose own condition was at the time less sanguine. Dilsey's psychological authority over Quentin is suggested, as Jenkins notes, by the fact that "the only time Quentin seems to experience guilt, with respect to his intention of committing suicide . . . occurs in connection with Dilsey" (159). In similar language, the autobiographical text of Faulkner's "Funeral Eulogy" to Caroline Barr, on whom the Dilsey figure is partially based, stressed her "authority" and her force as "moral precept." In his later comment at the University of Virginia, Faulkner stated that the fictional Dilsey "held the whole thing together and would continue to hold the whole thing together for no reward, that the will of man to prevail will even take the nether channel of the black man, black race, before it will relinquish, succumb, be defeated" (qtd in Jenkins 175).

Davis, who has analyzed the psychological relationships of blacks and whites in the novel, interprets Dilsey as an "absolutely venerable character," the opponent of "the erosion of morals, values, and meaning" (109). According to this view, Dilsey is "the embodiment of the blacks' alternative vision" to the nihilism of whites, and the communal experience of the black church service offers a positive resolution to the novel (Davis 108). Along with many other critics, Jenkins also interprets Dilsey as a moral exemplar: she is "life's servant . . . a selfless human servant, literally and figuratively, striving to reclaim for all a vision of responsibility and humanity" (162). So idealized is the figuration of Dilsey in this reading that she accepts her servitude and becomes "a victim who conspires in her own victimization" and who even recommends the virtue of subservience to her children and grandson (Jenkins 163, 168).

Davis's and Jenkins's "defense" of Dilsey is perhaps commendable if one reads her character as that of the selfless but resourceful African American woman who embraces a sort of fundamentalist morality as a necessary means of survival. This idealized view, however, seems to obviate the possibility of her development into something beyond "life's servant": in fact, just this sort of development is implied in the novel's emphasis on Dilsey's visionary insight following the Easter service, her repeated witness to the death of others, and her implicit admission of her own role as a sinful human being within the crucifixion story. The climax of the Dilsey section, in fact, involves her transformation as Canetti's survivor figure into a condition beyond self-preservation, toward a more analyzed self from which the limitations of a competitive survivalism are more clearly perceived. In order to dramatize this transformation, an essential change must take place in Dilsey's own experience: in other words, Dilsey must be read as a flawed and dramatic rather than an exemplary figure.

From the moment Dilsey peers out of her cabin into the gray Easter morning, Faulkner emphasizes her dominance and invulnerability—an imperial posture that seems, like that of the Deacon, at odds with the author's own condition of disempowerment. Wearing the "colors and materials of royalty" (Davis 103), Dilsey faces a mass of "minute and venomous particles" that "needled laterally into her flesh" (an example of environment sympathetically fashioned to match her mental state, the stubborn force of righteousness deflecting the trifling but bothersome crowd). As Davis notes, Dilsey makes her way to church separate from her family and community ("Dilsey has transcended many of the ordinary aspects of social interaction" [105]), yet it is precisely this "transcendence" that, in Canetti's view, suggests the paranoia of the "survivor," the person whose imagination centers on surviving others, indeed on surviving as a solitary and victorious witness beyond "de first en de last" to the end point in time. If Dilsey were figured as exemplary to begin with, what could explain her emotional response to Rev. Shegog's Easter sermon with its focus on mankind's universal guilt in the "blood of the Lamb"? Does one imagine that she is weeping over her sorrow at the decline of the Compson family? It appears more likely that she has understood Rev. Shegog's text in more immediate terms and that she has positioned her own life story within the narrative of the Easter passion. Retracing the central

Christian text, she has exposed her own guilt as a minor tyrant within a great order of human tyranny and found assuagement through ritual communion.

Indeed, in Canetti's terms the domestic conflict between Dilsey and Jason Compson IV is best explained in terms of their rivalry for authority within the same household. In this regard, Lewis P. Simpson's discussion of the significance of Dilsey's character may be usefully compared to Canetti's theory of "the end of the survivor," which comes about only when human beings "face command openly and boldly, and search for means to deprive it of its sting" (*Crowds* 470). It is precisely the revelation of the hidden mechanism of power that Simpson interprets as the underlying importance of Dilsey's emotional response to the Easter service, for it is Dilsey who most successfully negotiates the opposition of mythic and historical consciousness. As Simpson writes:

> According to Faulkner's metaphysic of endurance as exemplified in Dilsey, the survival of the mythic consciousness and the imperatives of the historical consciousness unite in the unending drama of the human heart in conflict with itself. In this drama Faulkner seeks a myth of modern man. This myth would center, not in the struggle of man to achieve historical selfhood, but in his universal capacity to endure his own nature as man, in enduring this to realize his goodness and his evil, and in this realization to prevail over his confinement in historical circumstance. (134)

This "capacity to endure his own nature" and this "realization to prevail" over historical "confinement" are inscribed in the symbolism of the Easter service and are the burden of Rev. Shegog's sermon. Dilsey arrives possessed of a willful ego the equal of any Compson. Only during the ritualized service and articulate sermon does Dilsey bring to consciousness her own role in the sacrificial order of events.

If Dilsey is a rival for command in the Compson household, certainly the most extreme example of the survivor figure is Jason Compson IV. The creation of Jason Compson as a fictional character reflects Faulkner's similar emotions of defeat and resentment, and it also hints at his repressed motives of rebellion and guilt in relation to the duty of authorship with which he has been burdened by his mother. A number of specific parallels connect Faulkner's autobiographical condition and this, his most extreme and repressed autobiographical persona: like Jason's denunciation of Wall Street "insiders," Faulkner expressed resentment at his treatment by his New York publishers; like Jason's burdensome defense of family honor, Faulkner performed a lifetime of complex subversions, rejections, and affirmations of Falkner social standing. In a perversely satisfying way, Faulkner may have taken a good deal of pleasure in the creation of Jason's black humor, much of it directed at his own rueful and helpless condition.

From a very early age, perhaps dating to the death of his beloved grandmother Damuddy, many of Jason's acts are symbolic or actual death threats intended to ensure his own psychological survival at the expense of others. One of the attributes of monarchy ironically connected with the less-than-kingly Jason is omnipotence: Jason views himself in relation to Herod, to generals, and to other historical figures who have exercised the power of life and death over their populations. Jason's highly exclusive sense of his American citizenship, suspiciously guarding the right of "being an American" from immigrants and Jews, reveals his imaginative awareness that there are "not many of us left" (116). Like Canetti's model of the paranoid survivor, Jason is attracted to the possibility of exterminating masses of victims, although, typically, his fantasies play out on a scale that deflates his self-importance. At one point, he suggests that the pigeons and sparrows that have been desecrating the Yoknapatawpha courthouse might simply be poisoned. Jason's symbolic killing extends to his attitude toward sex and the body. He literally approves the castration of Benjy, but figuratively Jason imposes castration on a much larger group, including Caddy and her daughter Quentin, who he feels would be better off "castrated." Jason instinctively seeks to insult or control weak or apparently weak persons—his dependent niece, his sister Caddy, his "girlfriend" Laverne, and old Job, whose name, both as biblical Job and modern laborer ("job"), suggests his position as one who accumulates the stings passed on by others. An underlying cause, perhaps the ultimate cause, of Jason's paranoia is his apocalyptic sense of time, the mortal anxiety that John Irwin positions at the center of the novel's repetition and revenge rituals. Jason's anxiety that he is about to "run out of time" or that he must "catch up" leads him finally to confront his own death, which he has raced simultaneously against and toward throughout the novel. Like the Oedipus figure he suggests, outwitting his fate and thereby sealing it, Jason savors the grotesque absurdity of death, issuing threats, and anticipating the end of the world for himself and for others (185). In this respect, Jason—once his "rule" has been overthrown—resembles his brother Quentin, who is equally alienated from others but imagines himself as *already* dead.

While Jason Compson has been described by numerous critics—and by the author himself—as perhaps the most repellent character in Faulkner's entire oeuvre, there is an intriguing similarity between Jason's predilection for control and Faulkner's proclivity to accept the role of "patron" in relation to various dependents. Throughout his life Faulkner progressively took on the support not only of his immediate family (his wife Estelle and her two children by a previous marriage, and his own child Jill), but also a host of others including his wife's parents, his sister-in-law, his brother's widow and her daughter, and several long-time family "servants," who in fact soon became elderly dependents. While he complained of the financial and emotional burden of the patronage role, Faulkner seemed to relish his relationship to dependents such as "Uncle Ned" Barnett, an elderly black servant who joined the household along with Caroline Barr when the Faulkners moved into the old Shegog house in 1930. As Blotner points out, Faulkner "was responsible for their food, shelter, clothing, health care, and pay when he could afford it. That he should do this was exactly what Mammy Callie and Uncle Ned expected" (262). Faulkner's relationship with his servants was not that of an "employer" in the conventional sense, however, for he readily accepted his responsibility to provide for them long after they were unable to work.

Faulkner's relation to dependents, and Jason's similar relation to his household, can be clarified by a consideration of Canetti's theory of "domestication," according to which the control of the means of survival—food, shelter, clothing—forms the basis for an imposing and potentially tyrannical ordering of society. Jason's insistence on the attendance of his niece Quentin at "regular meal times" involves the domestic ritual of parental allotment of food and a discipline of ordered seating, replete with its own symbolism and ritual of stasis, censorship, and "permission to leave" the table when finished. At the same time that he emulates Mrs. Compson's domestication of command, however, the extraordinary hostility that Jason exhibits toward the long-suffering Dilsey may be explained by his underlying resentment of his mother's ultimate control. Projecting his guilty rebellion onto Dilsey, the other "black" mother, Jason tries to rid himself of the "sting" of his actual mother's command.

The Sound and the Fury itself may be read as a disburdening, in Elias Canetti's sense, of the stings of command experienced by the individual in relation to more powerful members of society. William Faulkner wrote his great early novel in the context of a deepening understanding of the process of victimization and, in effect, to memorialize his own metaphorical descent into death. In the fictional characters of Quentin, Caddy, Benjy, and Jason Compson, and in those of the Deacon and Dilsey, Faulkner explored ways of analyzing the psychological conflicts that were entailed in his own demise as an author. A reading of the autobiographical aspects of the novel reveals much concerning Faulkner's conception of his own role as an artist isolated within a provincial culture and misunderstood by the national culture of publishers and critics. Faulkner turned his own imaginative death into a source of agency as he invested his sense of personal loss in each of the major characters of *The Sound and the Fury*. In the novel's complex figuration of death and survival, Faulkner transmuted his own desperate sense of failure into victory through his creation of a novel of great depth and understanding.

Notes

1. The terms that Faulkner employs in his letters and other documents suggest Elias Canetti's conception of crowd ritual and consciousness in regard to death and dying. I will rely heavily on Canetti's ideas from *Crowds and Power* in this paper, particularly his concept of "the survivor" as a consciousness that attempts to ensure its own continuation by means of the sacrifice (actual or symbolic) of crowds of others. Canetti points to the existence of destructive survivor rituals in many cultures, including Near Eastern religious cults that prefigured the Christian crucifixion mythology.

2. See, for example, Joel Williamson, *William Faulkner and Southern History* (New York and Oxford: Oxford University Press, 1993): 164; 251; 357. See also James G. Watson, ed., *Thinking of Home: William Faulkner's Letters to His Mother and Father, 1918–1925* (New York: Norton, 2000); Richard Gray, *The Life of William Faulkner: A Critical Biography* (London: Blackwell, 1996); and David L. Minter, *William Faulkner: His Life and Work*. Rpt. ed. (Baltimore: Johns Hopkins University Press, 1997).

Works Cited

Blotner, Joseph. *Faulkner: A Biography*. One-Volume Edition. New York: Random House, 1984.

Canetti, Elias. *Crowds and Power*. Trans. Carol Stewart. New York: Farrar Straus Giroux, 1984.

Davis, Thadious M. *Faulkner's "Negro": Art and the Southern Context*. Baton Rouge: Louisiana State University Press, 1983.

Faulkner, William. *The Sound and the Fury. An Authoritative Text, Backgrounds and Contexts, Criticism*. Ed. David Minter. New York: Norton, 1987.

Jenkins, Lee. *Faulkner and Black-White Relations: A Psychoanalytic Approach*. New York: Columbia University Press, 1981.

Mortimer, Gail L. *Faulkner's Rhetoric of Loss: A Study in Perception and Meaning*. Austin: University of Texas Press, 1988.

Polk, Noel. "'The Dungeon was Mother Herself': William Faulkner: 1927–1931." *New Directions in Faulkner Studies: Faulkner and Yoknapatawpha*, 1983. Eds. Doreen Fowler and Ann J. Abadie. Jackson: University Press of Mississippi, 1984.

Simpson, Lewis P. "Yoknapatawpha & Faulkner's Fable of Civilization." *The Maker and the Myth: Faulkner and Yoknapatawpha, 1977*. Eds. Evans Harrington and Ann J. Abadie. Jackson: University Press of Mississippi, 1977.

Chronology

1897	Born William Cuthbert Faulkner in New Albany, Mississippi on September 25; first child of Murry Faulkner and Maud Butler.
1898–99	Family moves to Ripley, Mississippi.
1899	Brother Murry C. (Jack) Faulkner Jr. born on June 26.
1901	Brother John Wesley Thompson Faulkner III born on September 24. William falls ill with scarlet fever.
1902	Family moves to Oxford, Mississippi.
1905	William enters the first grade at Oxford Graded School.
1906	William skips ahead to the third grade. Grandmother Sally Murry Faulkner dies, December 21.
1907	Grandmother Lelia Dean Swift Butler (Damuddy) dies June 1. Brother Dean Swift Faulkner is born August 15.
1908	It is speculated that Faulkner may have witnessed the Lynching of Nelse Patton.
1909	Begins work in father's livery stable.
1911	Enters the eighth grade, and is increasingly truant.
1914	Faulkner takes his poetry to lawyer Phil Stone, which marks the beginning of a long friendship between the two. Faulkner enters the eleventh grade at Oxford High School, and drops out in December.

1915 Returns to school to play football where he suffers a broken nose. Quits school. Goes bear hunting at "General" James Stone's camp.

1916 Holds a brief position as a clerk at his grandfather's First National Bank, and begins to frequent the University of Mississippi campus where he writes verse under the influence of Algernon Charles Swinburne and A. E. Housman.

1917 Begins supplying drawings for *Ole Miss.*

1918 After trying to enlist in the U.S. Army, he joins Phil Stone in New Haven, Connecticut, where he begins work as a ledger clerk for Winchester Repeating Arms Co. Enlists in the Canadian Royal Air Force. Discharged in December and returns to Oxford.

1919 Poem *"L'Après-midi d'un faune"* appears in *The New Republic.* Enters the University of Mississippi and begins publishing poems in *The Mississippian.*

1920 Commission arrives as honorable 2nd Lt., RAF. Withdraws from the university.

1921 Presents gift volume of poetry to Estelle Franklin. Visits New York and works as a bookstore clerk; revisits New Haven. Returns to Oxford to work as Postmaster at university post office.

1922 Grandfather J. W. T. Faulkner, "the Young Colonel," dies on March 13. Poem "Portrait" is published in *The Double Dealer.*

1924 Publishes *The Marble Faun.*

1925 Leaves Oxford for New Orleans where he spends time with Sherwood Anderson. Contributes to the *Times Picayune.* Sails for Europe with William Spratling.

1926 Moves to New Orleans and Publishes *Soldier's Pay.* Collaborates with Spratling on *Sherwood Anderson & Other Famous Creoles.*

1927 Publishes *Mosquitoes.*

1928 *Sartoris* (curtailed version of *Flags in the Dust*) accepted by Harcourt, Brace.

1929 Publishes *Sartoris.* Marries Estelle Franklin, and publishes *The Sound and the Fury.*

1930	Buys land and names it Rowan Oak. Publishes *As I Lay Dying.*
1931	Birth and death of daughter, Alabama. Publishes *Sanctuary,* and *These 13.*
1932	Begins writing for MGM as a screenwriter. Father Murry Cuthbert Falkner dies on August 7. Publishes *Light in August.*
1933	Publishes *A Green Bough,* daughter Jill Faulkner is born on June 24.
1934	Publishes *Doctor Martino and Other Stories.*
1935	Publishes *Pylon.* Brother Dean killed in plane crash on November 10. Meets Meta Dougherty Carpenter.
1936	Publishes *Absalom, Absalom!*
1938	*The Unvanquished* is published; screen rights sold to MGM.
1939	Elected to National Institute of Arts and Letters, publishes *The Wild Palms.*
1940	Mammy Caroline (Callie) Barr dies, publishes *The Hamlet.*
1942	*Go Down, Moses* published.
1946	Viking Press publishes *The Portable Faulkner*, edited by Malcom Cowley.
1948	Publishes *Intruder in the Dust* published, elected to American Academy of Arts and Letters.
1949	Meets Joan Williams, publishes *Knight's Gambit.*
1950	*Collected Stories of William Faulkner* published, wins Nobel Prize in literature.
1951	Publishes *Notes on a Horsethief,* receives National Book Award for Fiction for *Collected Stories. Requiem for a Nun* published; begins relationship with Joan Williams, undergoes electroshock therapy for depression and alcoholism.
1952–54	Travels throughout Europe, and works on *A Fable* and *Land of the Pharaohs.*
1954	Publishes *A Fable,* begins relationship with Jean Stein. Daughter Jill marries Paul D. Summers on August 21.

1955	Accepts National Book Award for *A Fable,* travels to Japan for the State Department. Publishes *Big Woods.*
1957	Travels to Athens for State Department, publishes *The Town.*
1959	Publishes *The Mansion.*
1960	Mother Maud (Butler) Falkner dies on October 16.
1962	Publishes *The Reivers.* Dies of heart attack on July 6 and is buried in St. Peter's Cemetery, Oxford, Mississippi.

Contributors

HAROLD BLOOM is Sterling Professor of the Humanities at Yale University. He is the author of 30 books, including *Shelley's Mythmaking* (1959), *The Visionary Company* (1961), *Blake's Apocalypse* (1963), *Yeats* (1970), *A Map of Misreading* (1975), *Kabbalah and Criticism* (1975), *Agon: Toward a Theory of Revisionism* (1982), *The American Religion* (1992), *The Western Canon* (1994), and *Omens of Millennium: The Gnosis of Angels, Dreams, and Resurrection* (1996). *The Anxiety of Influence* (1973) sets forth Professor Bloom's provocative theory of the literary relationships between the great writers and their predecessors. His most recent books include *Shakespeare: The Invention of the Human* (1998), a 1998 National Book Award finalist, *How to Read and Why* (2000), *Genius: A Mosaic of One Hundred Exemplary Creative Minds* (2002), *Hamlet: Poem Unlimited* (2003), *Where Shall Wisdom Be Found?* (2004), and *Jesus and Yahweh: The Names Divine* (2005). In 1999, Professor Bloom received the prestigious American Academy of Arts and Letters Gold Medal for Criticism. He has also received the International Prize of Catalonia, the Alfonso Reyes Prize of Mexico, and the Hans Christian Andersen Bicentennial Prize of Denmark.

GAIL M. MORRISON is director of the South Carolina Council on Higher Education. She has written extensively about Faulkner, beginning with her dissertation at the University of South Carolina: "William Faulkner's *The Sound and the Fury:* A Critical and Textual Study" (1981).

STEPHEN M. ROSS is director of the Office for Challenge Grants, National Endowment for the Humanities. He is author of *Fiction's Inexhaustible Voice:*

Speech and Writing in Faulkner (1989) and, with Noel Polk, *Reading Faulkner.* The Sound and the Fury: *Glossary and Commentary* (1996)

ANDRÉ BLEIKASTEN is professor of American literature at the University of Strasbourg. His books include *Faulkner's* As I Lay Dying (1973) and *The Ink of Melancholy: Faulkner's Novels from* The Sound and the Fury *to* Light in August (1990).

PHILIP WEINSTEIN is Alexander Griswold Cummins Professor of English at Swarthmore College. His books include *Faulkner's Subject: A Cosmos No One Owns* (1992), *What Else But Love? The Ordeal of Race in Faulkner and Morrison* (1996), and *Unknowing: The Work of Modernist Fiction* (2005).

DANIEL JOSEPH SINGAL is professor of history at Hobart and William Smith Colleges. He wrote *The War Within: From Victorian to Modernist Thought in the South, 1919–1945* (1982) and *William Faulkner: The Making of a Modernist* (1997). He edited *Modernist Culture in America* (1989).

GARY STORHOFF is associate professor of English at the University of Connecticut, Stamford. He wrote *Understanding Charles Johnson* (2004).

MARGARET D. BAUER holds the Rives Chair of Southern Literature at Eastern Carolina University. She wrote *William Faulkner's Legacy: "what shadow, what stain, what mark"* (2005) and *The Fiction of Ellen Gilchrist* (1999).

THOMAS L. MCHANEY is Kenneth M. England Professor of Southern Literature and director of graduate studies in English at Georgia State University. His books include *William Faulkner's* The Wild Palms: *A Study* (1975), *William Faulkner: A Reference Guide* (1976), and *William Faulkner* (2000). He is editor of *Faulkner Studies in Japan* and co-editor (with Joseph Blotner, Michael Millgate, and Noel Polk) of the twenty-five-volume *William Faulkner Manuscripts.*

MICHELLE ANN ABATE is assistant professor of English at Hollins University. She wrote *Tomboys: A Literary and Cultural History* (2008).

JEFFREY J. FOLKS is professor of literature at Doshisha University in Kyoto, Japan. His books include *Southern Writers and the Machine: Faulkner to Percy* (1993), *From Richard Wright to Toni Morrison: Ethics in Modern & Postmodern American Narrative* (2001), *A Time of Disorder: Form and Meaning in Southern Fiction from Poe to O'Connor* (2003), and *Damaged Lives: Southern & Caribbean Narrative from Faulkner to Naipaul* (2005)

Bibliography

Abate, Michelle Ann. "Reading Red: The Man with the (Gay) Red Tie in Faulkner's *The Sound and the Fury.*" *Mississippi Quarterly: The Journal of Southern Cultures,* 54:3 (Summer 2001): 294–312.

Abel, Marco. "One Goal Is Still Lacking: The Influence of Friedrich Nietzsche's Philosophy on William Faulkner's *The Sound and the Fury.*" *South Atlantic Review,* 60:4 (Nov 1995): 35–52.

Anderson, Deland. "Through Days of Easter: Time and Narrative in *The Sound and the Fury.*" *Literature & Theology: An International Journal of Theory, Criticism and Culture,* 4:3 (Nov 1990): 311–326.

Aschkenasy, Neḥama. "Yehoshua's 'Sound and Fury': A Late Divorce and Its Faulknerian Model." *Modern Language Studies,* 21:2 (Spring 1991): 92–104.

Bloom, Harold, editor. "Caddy Compson." *Major Literary Characters.* New York: Chelsea House, 1990.

Brown, Arthur A. "Benjy, the Reader and Death: At the Fence in *The Sound and the Fury.*" *Mississippi Quarterly: The Journal of Southern Culture,* 48:3 (Summer 1995): 407–420.

Burton, Stacy. "Rereading Faulkner: Authority, Criticism, and *The Sound and the Fury.*" *Modern Philology: A Journal Devoted to Research in Medieval and Modern Literature,* 98:4 (May 2001): 604–628.

Chappell, Charles. "The Other Lost Women of *The Sound and the Fury.*" *Publications of the Arkansas Philological Association,* 20:1 (Spring 1994): 1–18.

———. "Quentin Compson's Scouting Expedition on June 2, 1910." *Essays in Literature,* 22:1 (Spring 1995): 113–122.

Cohen, Philip; Fowler, Doreen. "Faulkner's Introduction to *The Sound and the Fury.*" *American Literature: A Journal of Literary History, Criticism, and Bibliography,* 62:2 (June 1990): 262–283.

Davis, Thadious M. "Reading Faulkner's Compson Appendix: Writing History from the Margins." Kartiganer, Donald M. and Ann J. Abadie, editors. *Faulkner and Ideology: Faulkner and Yoknapatawpha 1992.* Jackson: University Press of Mississippi, 1995, pp. 238–252.

Decker, Mark. "I Was Trying to Say: Listening to the Fragmented Human Center of William Faulkner's *The Sound and the Fury.*" *Kaleidoscope: Exploring the Experience of Disability Through Literature and the Fine Arts,* 47 (Summer–Fall 2003): 6–9.

Folks, Jeffrey J. "Crowd and Self: William Faulkner's Sources of Agency in *The Sound and the Fury.*" *Southern Literary Journal,* 34:2 (Spring 2002): 30–44.

Fowler, Doreen and Ann J. Abadie, editors. *Faulkner and Religion.* Jackson: University Press of Mississippi, 1991.

Griffiths, Jacqui. "Almost Human: Indeterminate Children and Dogs in *Flush* and *The Sound and the Fury.*" *Yearbook of English Studies,* 32 (2002): 163–176.

Gunn, Giles. "Faulkner's Heterodoxy: Faith and Family in *The Sound and the Fury.*" *Religion and Literature,* 22:2–3 (Summer–Autumn 1990): 155–172.

Hahn, Stephen; Kinney, Arthur F. *Approaches to Teaching Faulkner's* The Sound and the Fury. New York: Modern Language Association of America, 1996.

Harrington, Gary. "Faulkner's *The Sound and the Fury.*" *Explicator,* 65:2 (Winter 2007): 109–111.

Kartiganer, Donald M. and Ann J. Abadie, editors. *Faulkner and Psychology/ Faulkner and Yoknapatawpha, 1991.* Jackson: University Press of Mississippi, 1994.

Kim, Yongsoo. "'Like a Ghost in Broad Day': The Politics of the Death Drive and Sublimation in William Faulkner's *The Sound and the Fury.*" *Studies in Modern Fiction,* 8:2 (Winter 2001): 259–284.

Määttä, Simo K. "Dialect and Point of View: The Ideology of Translation in *The Sound and the Fury* in French." *Target: International Journal of Translation Studies,* 16:2 (2004): 319–339.

Madden, David. "Quentin, Listen!" in Polk, Noel and Ann J. Abadie, editors. *Faulkner and War: Faulkner and Yoknapatawpha, 2001.* Jackson: University Press of Mississippi, 2004, pp. 102–119.

Martin, Robert A. "The Words of *The Sound and the Fury.*" *Southern Literary Journal,* 32:1 (Fall 1999): 46–56.

McLaughlin, Sara. "Faulkner's Faux Pas: Referring to Benjamin Compson as an Idiot." *Literature and Psychology,* 33:2 (1987): 34–40.

Medoro, Dana. "'Between Two Moons Balanced': Menstruation and Narrative in *The Sound and the Fury.*" *Mosaic: A Journal for the Interdisciplinary Study of Literature,* 33:4 (Dec 2000): 91–114.

Mellard, James M. "Desire and Interpretation: Reading *The Sound and the Fury.*" *Mississippi Quarterly: The Journal of Southern Culture,* 47:3 (Summer 1994): 496–519.

Miller, Nathaniel A. "'Felt, Not Seen Not Heard': Quentin Compson, Modernist Suicide and Southern History." *Studies in the Novel,* 37:1 (Spring 2005): 37–49.

Moore, Kathleen. "Jason Compson and the Mother Complex." *Mississippi Quarterly: The Journal of Southern Cultures,* 53:4 (Fall 2000): 533–550.

O'Neill, Peter. "The Work Ethic in *The Sound and the Fury.*" *The Bulletin of the West Virginia Association of College English Teachers,* 13:1 (Fall 1991): 81–87.

Railey, Kevin. "Cavalier Ideology and History: The Significance of Quentin's Section in *The Sound and the Fury.*" *Arizona Quarterly: A Journal of American Literature, Culture, and Theory,* 48:3 (Autumn 1992): 77–94.

Roggenbuck, Ted. "'The Way He Looked Said Hush': Benjy's Mental Atrophy in *The Sound and the Fury.*" *Mississippi Quarterly: The Journal of Southern Cultures,* 58:3–4 (Summer–Fall 2005): 581–593.

Salmon, Webb. "On Quentin's Absence from Caddy's Tree-Climbing Scene." *The Faulkner Journal,* 3:2 (Spring 1988): 48–53.

Shinya, Matsuoka. "Historicized Narrations in Faulkner's Appendix to *The Sound and the Fury:* Creating a Whole from Fragments?" *Journal of the American Literature Society of Japan,* 2 (2003): 39–54.

Skirry, Justin. "Sartre on William Faulkner's Metaphysics of Time in *The Sound and the Fury.*" *Sartre Studies International: An Interdisciplinary Journal of Existentialism and Contemporary Culture,* 7:2 (2001): 15–43.

Tokizane, Sanae. "Anecdote of the Vase: The Introduction to *The Sound and Fury.*" *The Faulkner Studies,* 1:2 (September 1992): 53–70.

Truchan-Tataryn, Maria. "Textual Abuse: Faulkner's Benjy." *Journal of Medical Humanities,* 26:2-3 (Fall 2005): 159–172.

Wagner-Martin, Linda, editor, *William Faulkner: Six Decades of Criticism.* East Lansing: Michigan State University Press, 2002.

Wolff, Sally; Minter, David. "A 'Matchless Time': Faulkner and the Writing of *The Sound and the Fury.*" Barbour, James and Tom Quirk, editors. *Writing the American Classics.* Chapel Hill: University of North Carolina Press, 1990, pp. 156–176.

Acknowledgments

Gail M. Morrison, "The Composition of *The Sound and the Fury*"; *The Sound and the Fury: A Critical Casebook,* edited by André Bleikasten (New York: Garland, 1982): pp. 33–64. © 1982 Garland Publishing. Reprinted with permission.

Stephen M. Ross, "Rev. Shegog's Powerful Voice"; *Fiction's Inexhaustible Voice: Speech and Writing in Faulkner* (Athens: University of Georgia Press, 1989): pp. 36–45. © 1989 University of Georgia Press. Reprinted with permission.

André Bleikasten, "An Easter Without Resurrection?"; *The Ink of Melancholy: Faulkner's Novels from* The Sound and the Fury *to* Light in August (Bloomington: Indiana University Press, 1990): pp. 125–145. © 1990 Indiana University Press. Reprinted with permission..

Philip Weinstein, "'If I Could Say Mother': Construing the Unsayable About Faulknerian Maternity"; *Faulkner's Subject: A Cosmos No One Owns* (Cambridge: Cambridge University Press, 1992): pp. 29–39. © 1992 Cambridge University Press. Reprinted with permission.

Daniel Joseph Singal, "All Things Become Shadowy Paradoxical"; From *William Faulkner. The Making of a Modernist* by Daniel Joseph Singal. © 1997 by the University of North Carolina Press. Used by permission of the publsher. www.uncpress.unc.edu.

Gary Storhoff, "Caddy and the Infinite Loop: The Dynamics of Alcoholism in *The Sound and the Fury*"; From *The Faulkner Journal,* Volume 12, Number 2

(1997): pp. 3–22. © 1997 by the University of Akron. Reprinted by permission of the University of Central Florida.

Margaret D. Bauer, "'I Have Sinned in That I Have Betrayed the Innocent Blood': Quentin's Recognition of His Guilt"; *Southern Literary Journal,* Volume 32, Number 2 (2000): pp. 70–89. © 2000 Southern Literary Journal. Reprinted with permission.

Thomas L. McHaney, "Themes in *The Sound and the Fury*"; *Literary Masterpieces, Volume 6: The Sound and the Fury* (Framington Hills, M.I.: The Gale Group, 2000): pp. 61–100. © 2000 The Gale Group. Reprinted with permission.

Michelle Ann Abate, "Reading Red: The Man with the (Gay) Red Tie in Faulkner's *The Sound and the Fury*"; First printed in *The Mississippi Quarterly,* Volume 54 (2001): pp. 293–312. © 2001. Reprinted with permission.

Jeffrey J. Folks, "Crowd and Self: William Faulkner's Sources of Agency in *The Sound and the Fury*"; *Southern Literary Journal,* Volume 34, Number 2 (2002): pp. 30–44. © 2002 Southern Literary Journal. Reprinted with Permission.

Index